A Woodland Tale

To pat
God bless
signature

A Woodland Tale

Concerning How National Parks Came to Be

JOSEPH C. POSNER

RESOURCE *Publications* · Eugene, Oregon

A WOODLAND TALE
Concerning How National Parks Came to Be

Resource Publications
An Imprint of Wipf and Stock Publishers
199 W. 8th Ave., Suite 3
Eugene, OR 97401

www.wipfandstock.com

PAPERBACK ISBN: 978-1-6667-1902-4
HARDCOVER ISBN: 978-1-6667-1903-1
EBOOK ISBN: 978-1-6667-1904-8

10/11/21

To God, the Creative One
To my Mother, who taught me to read
To my Wife, who showed me the parks
To all Park Rangers, who have very important jobs

Contents

Introduction | ix

Woodland Walk | 1

Part One

1   The King's Mountain | 7

2   Procession of the Huckle Knights | 11

3   Troubles from Lands Afar | 26

4   A Tree Like No Other | 42

5   A Journey Begins | 58

6   The Wanderers' Home | 79

7   Bill's Great Flight | 110

8   Oxan's Edict | 126

9   The Heart of a Special Berry | 151

10   A Beast from the Great Outdoors | 170

Part Two

11   A Yawning Gap | 193

12   A Strong Seed | 201

13   A Sapling with Great Ambition | 223

14   The King's Advance | 234

15   A Woodland Duel | 241

16   Huckleberry Mountain | 263

17   A Ranger Goes Forth | 279

Epilogue | 285

A Park Visitor Guide (Glossary) | 289

Introduction

NATURE EXISTS AS A fine balance. It always has done, and it always will. As for us humans, we are constantly wondering how best to approach nature so that we may preserve it. Sure, there are some who couldn't care less; there are damaging companies, harmful pesticides, and some down-right ignorance, as well as terrible care of Earth's creatures. But on the whole, deep in our souls, humans wish to care for the natural world.

Because it exists in such a fine balance, the question becomes: how can we best demonstrate care? All around us are habitats, ecosystems, and wild creatures, and every day we interact with many living communities different from our own. Just think how many times we walk past ants or disturb birds. I think that the very first step toward true care of nature is realizing that it is often the smallest creatures, the ones that we ignore, that make such a big difference. Phytoplankton generate about half of the world's oxygen, for example.

Now, such an understanding is the starting point for my tale. It is important for us to consider the life and contribution of all creatures to nature's balance. It is also helpful for us to recognize that in order to truly care for something, we have to commit to the task every day of our lives. This doesn't mean we have to take action at every turn, but it does mean that we must begin to live in a way that reflects what we care for.

Caring for something cannot consist of single isolated acts. You cannot hug your child once and claim to care for them, just as you cannot paint one wall and claim to care for your house. In the same way, you cannot make one contribution to an endangered animal fund and claim to care wholly for nature. We have to invest our lives. This may sound like a lot of work, but actually, it's easy to care for something once you have fallen in love with it. If you fall in love with nature, it will not become burdensome to demonstrate care; it will become joyful.

Now, we fall in love through transformation. When we experience the natural world, we are transformed by its beauty and splendor. The sights transform us, so we fall deeper and deeper in love. To truly care for nature, you have to be transformed; you have to fall in love.

For many, visiting a national park is the first time that they will have fallen in love with the outdoors. Aside from the breathtaking beauty, I believe that this is because, deep down, national parks represent what we all wish nature to be: a harmonious and beautiful ecosystem where creatures coexist. Of course, not all is well within national parks; there are fires, floods, and the cycle of life means that many creatures live at the mercy of others, but overall, the parks are protected from those who do not care. This is because they were created by those who *do* care—by people who fell in love. Our care for nature should not be restricted to national parks, but the principles on which they were founded can teach us valuable lessons—lessons that stoke nurturing fires deep in our souls that may otherwise have lain dormant.

That is where this tale comes in. There is no better way to be transformed than through experience, and storytelling is often the perfect way to experience something; through another's eyes. It is my hope that the characters in my tale will inspire those who follow their adventure to fall in love with nature, just as they have done. Hopefully, we too can care for our world every day, wherever we are.

At the end of my tale is a park visitor guide (the contents of the guide are signified like this: white pines, *Pinus albicualis,* throughout the tale), which is like the one that is handed to you every time you enter a park. The guide will teach you about the park life, and include special places that are mentioned in the tale.

Woodland Walk

HAVE YOU EVER WALKED through a national park? They are the most magnificent places, full of magical adventures, lively creatures, and wild imagination. The sights, sounds, and smells are unlike any other place on Earth. If you were ever to go on such a walk, there's no telling what you may encounter, and I'm certain that you will not leave the same as you entered. At the very least, you will have made memories that will last forevermore.

Firstly, you would definitely see a lot of majestic, tall, and elegant trees towering high above dense woodlands. The most amazing thing about these trees is that they all seem to be connected. In some ways, we can see these connections, but in other ways, they are hidden from us. For example, did you know that the great redwood trees on the California coast connect their roots underground, so that they are like one immovable force? Fascinating. We are learning more and more about trees all the time, and it is now even thought that they "talk" to each other using a complicated system through their roots! Aside from those wondrous aspects, trees have been around for millions of years, far longer than you and I, hence they deserve our respect.

While trees are certainly some of the most striking families found in national parks, there are plenty more waiting on each and every trail. Nature thrives in these lands; they are overflowing with abundant fellowship. If you were to continue walking, you might see all types of wildlife; creatures small and large, fast and slow, airborne and terrestrial. You might see a graceful doe flicking out her pink tongue to lick the dew from the bright green morning leaves, or you might see a small critter scurrying across the woodland floor. If not a doe or a critter, you might see a large, majestic bison, an absolute marauder of these parks. These legendary beasts possess an incredible amount of power, but they rarely use it, and they don't really seem too bothered about it. The bison splash splendid color on the surrounding woodlands. They are either a light or a dark brown, depending on their seasonal coat, and they have amazing scruffy carpets of hair surrounding much of their shoulders and back. The color of these bison is not necessarily impressive because it is brown (after all, there are plenty of brown animals), but *their* shade is wild and daring, making you want to join the bison in their marauding!

Enough about animals for now, but you should know that there are plenty more creatures that you may come across on your walk if you are fortunate, and some animals, like eagles, bears, and wolves, patrol the parks like rare legends, so you will only encounter them at the most opportune moment. They'll know where you are, so they will remain hidden to you if they don't want to be seen!

As well as animals, national parks are home to some of the most dramatic scenery in the world. These are sights that will surely transform you forever, and you are bound to remember them for the rest of your days. Cascading waterfalls, icy glaciers, and majestic mountains. Soaring high cliffs, dense woodland, and the vastest, prettiest of plains. The scenery is one of the best parts of walking through a park. Most interestingly, you can encounter and fall in love with scenes that you may not have expected. There is something to see in every corner, crevice, and cavern.

Now, trees, animals, and stunning scenery play an important part in this tale, but there is one more fantastic family that needs to be introduced. It is a family of prime importance. No doubt you will see plenty of members of this family on any walk through a park. It is important that I introduce them individually, as they are often most unfairly overlooked. These small things are hidden but can be found almost everywhere, and they are also small but effective. Sometimes they are hard to see, but they are colored wonderful shades of rosy red, bluey black, vibrant pink, and ripe purple.

You can encounter the members of this family nestled among bushes, hanging from trees, or even stuffed in the mouths of other woodland creatures. Apparently, they are most delightful to eat, squash, and turn into juice or even pies! This species can travel thousands of miles attached to (or inside) another creature or spend their whole lives on the same bush upon which they were birthed. Now, most of the members of this family are inanimate, but in this tale, that isn't the case. At all.

If you haven't worked it out already, the species that I describe is the mighty berry. A berry is usually thought of as a stagnant thing, unimportant and insignificant. In this tale, however, a berry of great skill and strength turns that popular understanding inside out. I very much doubt that you will ever think of a juicy berry in quite the same way again . . .

Part One

1

The King's Mountain

MANY AGES AGO, THE creatures of the Realms lived according to the rules laid out in the Ancient Manuscripts. We now know these Realms as national parks, but our tale takes place before that purpose arose. The creatures had to listen to the masters of their Realms and only acted according to their commands or the rules of the Manuscripts. The adventure that this tale recounts, though, would change that forever . . .

Did you know that some berries only grow at certain elevations? That is true of the huckleberry, which is the peculiar berry I spoke of earlier. They mostly grow at majestic heights, between 3,500 feet and 7,200 feet. Atop tall mountains and amidst gusting winds, they grow. There are many different species within the huckleberry family, but in this story, we are focusing only on two. The first is the wild mountain huckleberry, *Vaccinium membranaceum*. This species is a vibrant, alluring purple, clearly visible among the green leaves from which it hangs. It is from this species of huckleberry that the great king comes, through whom all national parks were created.

The second species is the North American red huckleberry, *Vaccinium parvifolium*, which accounts for most of the king's subjects. Since we will be hearing about the huckleberries quite a lot, we will simply refer to them as "the Huckles," so that talk of them does not become wearisome. We should not tire when speaking of them, because they have done some of the most wondrous things.

Huckleberries mostly grow west of the incredible Rocky Mountains, in dense forests and mysterious green woodlands. Despite the berry itself being rather small (just under half an inch in diameter), the plant upon which it grows can reach a height of about four meters. This is very useful, because lookout Huckles need a good vantage point from which to survey the woodlands in and around Glacier.

The huckle plant is a deciduous shrub with yellow, white, and pink flowers. According to the Elders (who will appear later in our tale), the flowers and striking color of the Huckles is what led to their persecution in days gone by. They have been eaten and stomped on by bears, stolen by birds, brewed into tea, and generally bossed about by all manner of woodland creatures. Forest folk say that in the Elders' Manuscripts, there are ancient pages concerning the history of the Huckle clan and how they came to be. Supposedly, growing tired of being eaten, brewed, and stamped upon, they grew to incredible sizes to defend themselves, vowing never to let themselves be bullied again. The truth of such things we may never know. What we do know for certain, from both the Manuscripts and just about every creature in the national parks today, is that everything about the Huckles started in one place.

That place can be found on a map, but you will need several maps. In fact, it will be helpful for you to have some maps beside you for the entirety of this tale, because they will help you learn the land. First, you need a giant map of the United States. Now, bear in mind that the Huckle clan existed long before the country as we know it came to be, but it is in this vast place that they resided. Now, on this map, you will need to look northward, near the border with another giant land, Canada (actually another place where huckleberries grow). There you should see eleven different states that touch the border. You then need to travel westward along that border and you should find, in the far west, a state called Washington (some Huckles there). Directly east of Washington, you should see a small sliver of land that expands further south. This is the state of Idaho (a few Huckles there, although they have been overshadowed by a mysterious clan called the Potatomen). Notice that Idaho is sandwiched in between two big states, with Washington to the west and another to the east. The state to the east is where our tale begins. It is named Montana.

Nowadays, not many people speak of or even visit Montana. That is surprising, as it is a place of splendid beauty. If folk had any idea that this was where the king's Realm was during the reign of the Huckles, perhaps they would pay it a bit more respect. It is a land of lakes, streams, mountains, and nights crowded with stars. It is known, according to current folk, as the "Big Sky Country."

It might be helpful for you to possess a map of Montana, but you only need to take a quick glance, because we will mainly dwell in one part of it. That part, today, is called Glacier National Park, and it is the king's greatest legacy. If you do indeed have a map of Montana, you should look northwest. Near a city called Kalispell, you should see a large patch of green, which will probably read "Glacier NP." Now much like we will call the Huckleberries "the Huckles," we will henceforth call Glacier National Park "Glacier."

This is where our tale truly begins. This is where the Huckles once lived. For this place, you will most certainly need a map. If you have ever been blessed enough to visit Glacier as it is today, you should have been given one, but if not, be sure to obtain one somehow. Looking at the map, you should notice that this park has a large number of lakes. This is partly because glaciers, titanic blocks of ice, melt and feed the lakes below, forming beautiful silver streams on the mountainside.

In the winter, Glacier is a wonderland. Deep blankets of snow and frozen lakes emit crystals of light, and the gleaming lake surfaces are flanked by trees in every direction, tall and evergreen. In the summer, much of this snow and ice melts, and the glory underneath is unveiled. Crystal clear waters ripple in the sunlight, peeling back in the bright morning to reveal shimmering stones beneath. Anyhow, enough about lakes, because remember, Montana is a land of lakes, streams, and mountains, and it is a mountain that we must now find.

On your map, find Lake McDonald. It should be easy enough to find, because it is the largest of all the lakes in the park. Once you have found it, cast your gaze west, then look around carefully and you should notice some campgrounds. These campgrounds are not part of our tale, because they are modern creations and were not relevant in the Elders' age; we are just using them for reference (in fact, some of the forest folk nowadays often complain about how loud they are). You should see a campground called Fish Creek on the northern bank of the lake. Near Fish Creek, you should see the actual creek, which runs north. Follow this creek with your finger toward Canada, passing two tributaries, and eventually you should find McGae Creek. Follow this all the way westward (toward Idaho and the Potatomen), and there you should see it— the great mountain.

It sits in the westernmost part of the park and is the only mountain in the area. You should notice it. It may have a little triangle to show where it is. I sincerely hope you have found it. It is called Huckleberry Mountain, and it is the home of the king. Now, in the time of our tale, the mountain was menacingly tall, and it shone a dark shade of emerald green, but a purple mist clouded its summit at all times. Long after our tale, the king lay to slumber once and for all near the bottom, and supposedly the mountain shrunk to the smaller size it is today.

Now, this mountain is of the highest importance, not just for the Huckles but for you and me. It was atop this very mountain that the Elders of the Realms—who are the Elderberries, the Ancient Pines, and the legendary bird (we will meet them all later)—forged the settlement of the national parks. It was on this mountain that the national parks began. The leaders of the United States nowadays look after the parks through the Department of the Interior, but that was not where it all began. Huckleberry Mountain was where it all began.

Now, we have to understand that in nature, great things often arise through fierce struggle. Much like the Huckles struggled to overcome persistent bullying and malfeasance, they also struggled greatly to gather the Elders of the Ancient Realms and alter the Manuscripts forever. This tale will tell of their struggle and just how the wondrous parks came to be. You'll need to keep your maps handy, and you may need some new ones for the duration of the tale.

In fact, there is one you will most certainly need, which you may as well source immediately. You will need a map of California . . .

2

Procession of the Huckle Knights

"Arise!"

A Huckle Knight bellowed into the bright spring morning. The day was clear, blessed with sweet sunlight and a gentle breeze. It foretold a warm and enchanting summer beyond. "Alert!" he continued. All creatures present knew what to do. In one synchronized sweep, the Huckles and the guest creatures swiveled sharply inward toward one another, like a crowd greeting a bridal party. The two sides were organized so that a pathway between them led to the stage on which the knight stood.

The green meadow at the foot of the mountain was a perfect location for the ceremony; it was flat, spacious, and close enough to the mountain. Although some of the guests made ambient noise, such as the buzzing honeybees and the thumping of a hare's feet (which cannot be helped, apparently), there was a still, solemn silence in the air. It was as if all of Glacier had decided to set this day aside out of respect for the ceremony. Even the creek, gently bathing in the spring breeze, dared not lap its waters onto the banks closest to the meadow. Instead, it rippled gently, almost still, as if silently contemplating. It was a scene of blessed tranquility.

The knight spoke once more. "We are here today to observe the knighthood of eight of our finest soldiers." He spoke with such authority that even the bears in the audience were sitting erect (they had a turbulent history with the Huckles), but the Huckle fixed his gaze not on the bears, nor on any other in the audience. Instead, his gaze was transfixed straight ahead, past the crowd and into the heart of the forest.

The knight's name was Rubus. Rubus was a Huckle larger than most. He stood four feet tall, around a foot higher than the average. Like the rest of his kin, his torso was ovular and his head was completely circular (much like a berry). Due to their being berries, the Huckles had no shoulders or necks. It is a miracle, of course, that they even had limbs or could speak or could think, but they could.

Most Huckles were rose red, but due to his seniority, Rubus was closer to burgundy, almost halfway between red and purple. This was because the higher the Huckles rose in rank, the more like the king they appeared. On their torso they had four miraculous but basic limbs; two arms and two legs. These limbs measured about a foot and a half each and appeared as entangled groupings of sticks and branches wrapped in twine. The limbs were quite thick, somewhat thicker than the deciduous shrub branch on which the Huckles originally grew. They were also incredibly robust, and while they may have appeared in danger of snapping, they were actually efficient and useful for all of the Huckles' tasks.

As mentioned earlier, Rubus was as close in color to purple as he was to red, and his clothing complemented his hue. He bore upon him the Royal Standard of the Huckle Knights; a golden loop belt (mostly superfluous and for display) and a charcoal-gray tunic (like that of a Roman emperor) were his principal garments. The clothing was gathered from all parts of the Glacier Realm. The belt was gathered from the miner moles of the north, and the tunic was fashioned from the strongest spider's web. Although the Huckles did not rule unfairly or unjustly, all the creatures in the Realm served at their behest.

Tucked into a wooden carcass on Rubus's right hip was a staff. This staff, and all Huckle staffs like it, were forged in Huckle Village alone. The master Huckle craftsman crafted them all, and if they did not come from him, they were not battle-ready, nor were they worthy. After he created them, they were left to harden in the heart of the mountain, and each one was blessed by the Elderberries. Wolverines, creatures of quite unbelievable strength and ferociousness, were beckoned forth from present-day Canada to test the strength of the staffs. The Huckles would have loved to have the mighty wolverines fight alongside them, but wolverines are much too stubborn and solitary.

The last item of Rubus's outfit was a crown, again crafted from branch and twine. It was adorned with other, inanimate species of berry, like the blueberry, *Cyanococuss*, and the redcurrant, *Ribes rubum*. Aligning his crown, Rubus straightened himself (as much as berries can) and looked down at a sheet of gray parchment held firmly in his left hand. "These soldiers have given everything in service to Glacier!" Rubus offered little thanks to the crowd for their attendance; they had mostly attended out of reverence for the king anyway. He also spoke with little arrangement, as if the crowd already knew why they were there and knew exactly was going to happen. "Our soldiers will stand on this stage and be appointed by the king himself!"

As he mentioned the king, he gave an almighty thrust, like someone learning to play a heavy instrument for the first time, and afterward, he paused. In fact, the entire crowd was hushed, and a cloak of silence enveloped them all. A fluffle of bunnies were seen whispering in the rather large ears of their mother, and on the left-hand flank of the crowd, an extraordinarily old female turtle in the front row lifted her head from her half slumber. Whenever the king was mentioned in these lands, creatures great and small paid attention.

Rubus spoke once more. "Today we will witness and celebrate the promotion of these soldiers into knights as they seek to serve the king and our Realm! On the playing of the berryrumpet, the soldiers will march from the forest onto this stage and will then be knighted!"

Afterward, he looked to the opposite end of the stage, where a slightly smaller, far brighter, red berry was standing. She was around three feet tall and was dressed with little decoration, just a lighter tunic of smoky gray. "Goji, proceed!"

Goji lifted her berryrumpet (a Huckle's trumpet) to her mouth and drew a deep breath. Her head puffed as her black dotted eyes squinted. The berries had no cheeks, so the taking of a breath required swelling of the entire head. Huckles' mouths and eyes, by the way, were very basic; two simple black dots for eyes and a black line that looked like a lace of licorice for a mouth. This was true for Huckles but true for Goji as well, who was not a Huckle but still a wondrous berry. *Brrrrrrr!* The berryrumpet played no melody, just a monotone singular blast, plenty loud enough for all the creatures to hear. Afterward, Goji pulled the berryrumpet away from her mouth, looking rather pleased with herself. At three, she was one of the youngest musicians in all of Glacier. Now three is late teenage years for a berry, as their years are far shorter than ours, although they can achieve just as much.

"Remain standing," said Rubus bluntly to the crowd while briefly looking at his parchment for a reminder of the order of events. The crowd knew what to do. They turned toward the back of the meadow, where the forest beckoned. Out of an opening between two white pines, *Pinus albicualis*, and from behind some rocks, the soldiers that had been awaiting came forth. Rubus glared at Goji, who appeared shocked. She had forgotten the next stage of the procession and quickly fumbled to bring the berryrumpet to her mouth. *Brrrrrr!* She recovered her form and blew to announce the approach of the soldiers.

They marched starkly onward onto the stage without looking around. The soldiers were, as you may have guessed, of a somewhat hybrid appearance, between Goji and Rubus, but the main difference was in their clothing. The gallant soldiers wore navy-blue tunics and helmet crowns similar to Rubus's, although slightly less elaborate. They stood around three and a half feet tall and were a deeper shade of red than Goji, more like a crimson but still very much red. The soldiers proceeded toward the stage along the path created by the crowd. There were eight of them, male and female, and they marched in pairs. As they marched, there were excited mutterings and whisperings from the spectators.

A small hare child, a leveret, whispered into his mother's ears, "Momma, can I be a soldier one day?" The child was beaming with startled excitement, impatiently thumping his feet on the ground. The mother grunted something of a reply but didn't really answer; she was more focused on the brave Huckles walking toward the stage. Of course, as the child would have already known, the answer was no. Only Huckles could be soldiers or knights. It was the Huckles, after all, that miraculously grew to an incredible size to defend themselves and the Realm. After this, they had taken it upon themselves to protect the entire Realm of Glacier, and over the years, they had protected it from wolves in the north and rogue bears from the Great Outdoors. They had even bonded together to create a gelatinous wall, much like huckleberry jam, to protect Glacier from fires.

Goji played a bold fanfare on the berryrumpet as the soldiers marched to the stage, and their powerful wooden limbs swung back and forth as they advanced. The fanfare was somewhat of a juxtaposition: Goji was the sweetest berry you could imagine, but here she was blasting on the rumpet with all her might at the soldiers' procession. If she'd had her way, she would have been playing a flute or a piccolo by the riverside, entertaining the salmon and trout that paddled by. She had been playing music since she was nine months old and had started learning as soon as she had begun living among the Huckles.

Rubus looked over at her. In his heart was a sense of frustration but also a deep, swelling pride. A turmoil existed within him, and he didn't really know how to deal with his conflicting emotions. Rubus knew that Goji didn't *really* want to be here, but at the same time, he wouldn't let her talents go to waste. You see, the Huckles were creatures of juxtaposition, and that was because they were very much going above and beyond what they were ever meant to be. Because they had completely altered their destiny, they often struggled with complicated decisions and emotions. They were *meant* to be simple, but they were far, far from it; they had done the most wondrous things. As a result of this great alteration, they were, well, juxtaposed.

The soldiers reached the edge of the stage. Before walking onto it, they aligned in perfect uniformity. The furthest Huckle to the left was in front of the elder turtle in the crowd, and the furthest right was in front of a civilian Huckle. The civilian Huckles, by the way, were about the same height as Goji and wore basic white tunics. They were a bright rose red, the color of a regular huckleberry.

"Come forth!" Rubus declared.

The soldiers climbed onto the stage one by one from left to right like a cascading staircase. As they did so, the elder turtle fashioned a slow smile, as slow as you would expect from an ancient reptile. At the same time, Goji lowered the berryrumpet but remained in position. Her body language portrayed her desire; she would much rather be elsewhere.

Rubus looked down to read from his parchment. "On the reading of the declaration of the greatest berry proclamations, today you shall hereby be declared as Knights of the King under a berry ordainment. You have served our Realm with great bravery and honor, and today you shall receive the grandest of titles!"

The soldiers stood in perfect stillness.

"I, Rubus, and court musician Goji, declare witness to this grand event, and on the blowing of the rumpet, you will come face to face with the king himself. Will you proceed?"

The soldiers immediately raised their right arms in salute, ready for the moment. They were all of a similar size and posture. Although their deep navy uniforms shone brilliantly in the spring sun, their faces were battle hardened, and they bore scars and cuts from skirmishes, along with gashes in their berry exterior that revealed a deep red jelly-like substance beneath. Rubus briefly surveyed the soldiers, as if looking deep into their seeds. Every Huckle had a seed for a heart. "Very well," he calmly announced. "Goji, proceed!" Goji picked up the rumpet and, drawing a deep breath, played her loudest fanfare yet. This time, however, she turned toward the mountain. *Brrrrrr!*

The fanfare started loudly and vibrated the entire foot of the mountain, but it faded as it reached the summit. The soldiers lowered their arms. For the first time during the procession, they broke their stern, determined gaze. They seemed . . . nervous. The crowd, too, held a collective breath, and every creature from bear to fieldmouse was hushed. At this point, some river dwellers joined the procession, surveying from the edge of the river. They knew the rumpet call. From the turtle and the Huckle civilians at the front to the hares and deer in the middle to the bears at the rear, all of Glacier was hushed.

The same young hare from earlier, an eager little fellow, whispered into his mother's large ear again. "Mother, is he coming?" His feet thumped ever louder (much to the annoyance of a buck next to him).

"Shhh!" the mother snapped, motioning to her child to pay attention.

"But where is he?" he quietly whimpered.

"Michael! Will you be qui—"

"Look, there they are!" remarked an excited young turtle from the front row sitting near the elder turtle.

At once, the entire crowd, including the soldiers, looked sharply upward toward the peak of the mountain. Much like a blanket of silence had cloaked the crowd earlier on, a blanket of strict reverence descended upon the crowd now. The fish splashed, the Huckles gasped, and the bears shook their behinds. From the mountain's summit, that is, Huckleberry Mountain, an eerie purple mist wafted downward toward the meadow. The mist had a long way to travel, but it was eerie nonetheless. It circled daringly above the mountain's peak, darting through sunlight rays, and all of Glacier focused on the mountain, the Realm's beating heart. As the purple mist wafted downward from the summit, a distant but clear humming of voices began to sound. They were the quietest but clearest of tones.

"Who are they?" the young hare squealed. His ears were completely erect.

The distant voices drew ever nearer. As they sounded, musical notes formed around them; purple treble clefs and notes on a stave. They drifted onward as new notes formed.

"They are—" the mother began.

"The king's band." Rubus finished the sentence under his breath, such that none could hear. Indeed, the king's band had begun their descent of the mountain.

At first, two male Huckles appeared, about nine feet apart. They carried with them small drums forged from the thickest of leaves. The first two Huckles looked similar to civilians, although they were dressed slightly more flamboyantly, with gold belts and crowns similar to Rubus's. They passionately beat upon their drums with thick branches.

Dum, dum, dum, dum, dididdy, dum,

Next was a line of four Huckles. These were slimmer than the two in front, almost as if they were halfway to being squashed. As a result, they appeared extremely ripe. These Huckle musicians had small circles of metal like cymbals, gifted by the mole miners, and they crashed them together in a rhythmic pattern. They were colored a ruby red and wore navy-blue tunics similar to those of the soldiers. A beautiful plethora of color was beginning to emerge upon the mountain.

Crash . . . crash . . . crash . . . crash!

If you have ever heard a marching band, I'm sure you can envisage this scene. The difference between this and a marching band was that this band had singing and a purple mist from which emerged real musical notes. You'll remember me saying that the Huckle clan existed hundreds and thousands of years before humans. You'll also remember me saying that the Huckles have done many wondrous things. Well, this was the first of many. They were able to create real musical notes out of purple mist from the mountain, long before humans created music.

After the four slim, ruby-red Huckles, a wonderful sight emerged. The eerie but beautiful voices that the young hare had heard not long ago now echoed from the mountain and far yonder, into the Glacier woodland beyond. Clear singing voices shattered the silent tranquility of the spring afternoon, captivating the crowd below. The singing choir was a group of six female Huckles, who looked similar to Goji but slightly older. These choir Huckles were slightly wrinkled from their years, appearing prune like, as all older berries do. They wore charcoal-gray tunics like the drummers at the front, so the pattern went gray—blue—gray.

In addition to the tunics and belts, the choir Huckles wore crowns like Rubus, the first of the band to do so. Their crowns were made of a lighter shade of wood than his, a cypress wood. Lastly, they wore exuberant floral chains around their torsos. The chains of pink, purple, and blue had been masterfully constructed by the busiest bees in all of Glacier; they had been working on them for weeks. It was now quite a spectacle, as I'm sure you can imagine. All of the band marched in uniformity toward the meadow below, with the drummers now about halfway down. Purple notes floated between the musicians.

And then the song. By now, the once quiet, shrill voices were clear and harmonious. All of Glacier seemed to know the words. And indeed, they should: It was the king's song.

Dum dum dum, off with his head, the king
is purple, the king is not red!
Dum dum dum, he is the king! All those
in Glacier must bow to him.
Dum dum dum, oh do you know why, for one
single pie several children had to die!
Dum dum dum, off with his head, the king
is purple, the king is not red!

Now I told you that Glacier is a beautiful place. A place of vibrant color, peaceful streams and sounds, butterflies and buzzing bees. All of this is true, but I'm afraid that the king of Glacier had a more menacing side too. Everyone in Glacier gave him the utmost respect, and if they didn't, there were sure consequences. Any Huckle children who didn't listen to their parents or were just downright naughty and wrong, the king had them squashed and turned into huckleberry pies! Any who opposed him, the king squished, squashed, and stretched, including all types of creatures. As a result, the inhabitants of Glacier often quaked in fear when they heard the song.

Dum dum dum, off with his head, the king
is purple, the king is not red!

Like the choir Huckles sang, the king was a striking purple, not red like the rest of the Huckles. He belonged to the second species of huckleberry of which we spoke earlier, and only he was alive from that species. Down below in the meadow, many Huckles had begun to sing along, particularly younger ones who had aspirations of becoming soldiers and knights one day. The other creatures of Glacier simply stared, captivated by the increasingly loud musical notes, which were clouding the meadow in large wafts of purple mist.

As the band descended toward the meadow, a deep thud began to join the increasing plethora of sounds. It was incredibly deep, almost like a mini earthquake or eruption. The young hare was not so excited anymore. His wide-eyed marvel had turned into a deep fear, much like many of the creatures around him.

Thud, thud, dum, dum!

The deep drumming reverberated all around, dominating the hearts of the creatures below. The first drummers were now about three-quarters of the way down the mountain, with a considerable gap between them and the slim cymbal players and the same gap between the choir behind. It was now the turn of the two terrifying Royal Drummers. These drummers were some of the largest and most fearsome Huckles in all of Glacier. They were a dark, deep red, bordering on purple, much like mahogany, and they wore bright gold tunics that stretched from the tops of their torsos to their lower limbs. They also wore belts like other Royal Huckles, but their belts were not gold; they were thick, deep twines of oak, blended by the master Hucklesmith. The oak belts were decorated with colored rocks deep from the lakes of Glacier, some carved into bits, creating a mosaic-like pattern. They also had helmets like Rubus but much larger, and lastly, they had giant shoulder pads formed of thick pine tree bark covered in thorns.

It was a terrifying sight. It would have been understandable for Glacier folk—after all, bears and wolves could be pretty fearsome—but it was not understandable because of the giant drummers' unbelievable size. No berry should be fifty feet tall, but the Royal Drummers were. As a matter of fact, no creature should be that much larger than the rest of their species, but these Royal Drummer Huckles dwarfed the civilians with their gigantic proportions. They even seemed to dwarf the mountainside.

Thud, dum, thud, dum!

The deafening thudding completed the music of the royal band, now sounding throughout the whole of Glacier (perhaps even heard by the Potatomen in Idaho). The Royal Drummers were large, magnificently strong, and somewhat disfigured due to their unnatural growth. In another tale at another time in another land, they would perhaps best be described as trolls, so that is what we shall call them from here on forth.

On their torsos were attached huge drums made from Royal Bark hide, like those of the drummers at the back of a marching band. They also wielded huge clubs made from leftover bone, gifted to the Huckles by great creatures of the southern lands (who seek to preserve the materials of those who have joined the life cycle of their Realm). The trolls carried these gargantuan drums with effortless ease. They had to stay well clear of the rest of the band, lest they accidently smashed their kin.

The king's song went on:

Dum dum dum, off with his head!

At long last, the smaller drummers who had appeared first reached the foot of the mountain. The crowd gazed on. Almost immediately, they marched to their positions on the stage, splitting to stand on either side, and as the music grew louder and louder, the rest of the band arrived until there was a bountiful collection of Royal Huckles on the stage. Little Goji had almost become lost among the performers. The Royal Drummers, unthinkably large, stayed at the foot of the mountain, just before the stage. Of course, they were far too big and would have fallen straight through. Once the entire band was present, the music stopped suddenly. The Royal Drummers played their last four beats without the rest of the band before turning sharply to face one another.

A blanket of silence cloaked the air once more. Every creature's gaze was firmly fixed on the peak of the mountain, while the band stood aligned in military fashion. Only Goji, the sweetest of berries, seemed to crack a smile. At the peak of the mountain, the purple mist had now cleared, and the last treble clef wafted away into the open Glacier sky. In the meadow, budding leaves were sprouting from the trees behind, reaching for the mountain peak. All of Glacier, far more than those present at this procession, was aware of the imposing figure descending the mountain.

A gentle tumbling sound broke the silence. From somewhere near the middle of the mountainside, a loose rock trickled down and landed near the troll drummers. A few more rocks tumbled, and large chunks of stone bounced off into the deep woodland on either side of the mountain. Had the stage not been placed perfectly in the meadow to avoid this, the rocks may well have squished many of the folk below.

The deep rumbling gripped the spring afternoon. As the rocks tumbled downward, the lake rippled violently, its water greatly disturbed. Some of the younglings in the crowd glanced at one another. There were even some murmurs about leaving or escaping—of course, not an option. The royal band did not for a second break their intense gaze, and as a figure appeared at the summit, Michael gasped louder than any hare should be able to gasp.

"It's . . . it's . . . it's him!" His delicate ears quivered as he pointed at the mountain peak.

Looking toward the peak, the crowd let out a collective gasp. The mist had disappeared, and a humongous figure blotted out the spring sun, creating a dark, cool shadow on the meadow below. The crowd could not yet quite make out the full appearance of this figure, but they had no doubt as to whom the menacing shadow belonged.

"The king!" cried a young prickle of porcupines who had been sitting on the floor near the front.

Goji whimpered, while Rubus held his gaze, even though struggling to do so. Some buds nearby seemed to flower at an increased speed, and some simply fell off their branches. It was from the top of the mountain that the king began his descent. The king and protector of Glacier. The king of the mountain. The Huckleberry King.

Now, national parks are full of incredible and amazing sights and scenes. There are nights full of stars, canyons deep, and the most majestic of mountains. But in all of nature there has never been a spectacle like the king. I told you that the Huckles had done some of the most wondrous things. Well, the king had done the first of these things, as he was the first to grow to a magnificent, incredible, and unbelievable size.

No berry should have talked; no berry should have moved or fought or created staffs as weapons. No berry should have created Realms that they then defended. But they have. Certainly, no berry should grow to one hundred feet tall. But *he* did. The king was simply ginormous. He trampled small trees, tramped through lakes and rivers, and was often mistaken for a mountain or a hill. From a distance, birds of prey could be seen circling above, close to his head. Sometimes they just soared because they were gravitating to his greatness, but sometimes they perched upon his crown.

As he bounded through the glades and woods of Glacier, smaller songbirds could also be seen darting from the bushes below, and creatures small and large would speed away at a frantic pace, not wanting to be squished underneath. Unfortunately, many had indeed been squished over the ages. Luckily for the small creatures, he did not walk often, spending most of his time at the top of the mountain, but when he did, the whole of Glacier knew, because the entire band came with him, playing the king's song as they traveled forth.

> *Dum dum dum, off with his head!*
> *The king is purple, the king is not red!*

Purple. The great Huckleberry King was indeed purple. As we have seen, the Huckles transformed into different colors based on their royal rank. The same energy that seemed to have brought them to life also seemed to transform their color. The higher a Huckle rose, the closer they became in color to the king, whose shade was best described as a mulberry purple.

You see, the Elders had known of the king's potential since he was a young warrior berry, but they had not expected this. No one did. The king had grown to this stupendous size and had completely taken over the Realm, which he then saw as his duty to protect. In order to express his excellence and his lordship over the rest of the Huckles, the king wore a bright red tunic, much like the red of the common Huckle. This giant tunic had taken the strength of all the forest spiders in Glacier to create. He also had a belt like Rubus's, but his belt had interlocking loops of gold, silver, and bronze, the only one like it. The king's limbs alone were around forty feet long and resembled small trees. If you were ever to see him traversing the forest, you would have seen a trail of destruction in his wake; destruction that the much smaller worker Huckles and all the small woodland creatures would have to clean up afterward.

You would also see his crown.

The king's crown was perhaps the most remarkable spectacle other than his size. Despite his enormous berry head, it was a crown that even he struggled to wear (some say that he takes it off in his private quarters and has terrible marks; we may never know). You see, when the king was first conquering the Realm, forcing the animals into submission and squishing his enemies, he encountered a worthy adversary. The trees. As you may know, trees are incredibly strong and robust beings, and the king often struggled to contain them. Once he had, however, all of the trees in Glacier submitted to him. Thereafter they lived peacefully in these lands alongside one another, but only in these lands.

To display his power and conquering of the trees, some years ago the king had uprooted a western red cedar tree, *Thuja plicata*, and had decided to start wearing it on his head. It may sound ridiculous, but an uprooted tree is a marvelous sight. The long roots and damp earth are raw and untamed, so for the king to wear one upon his head was a severe warning to the rest of Glacier.

As well as being far greater, taller, and stronger than the other Huckles, the king was older. Much older. The Elderberries have attempted to work out the king's age, but it is very difficult to say when he became a living, moving, warrior Huckle and not just a berry for bears to feast upon. No one knows when that moment occurred. If the king were much of a conversationalist, he might admit that he did not know either. But he didn't talk much, so it remained a secret.

What he did remember, however, was his early days as a warrior. There were not many other Huckles around in those days, so the king had roamed Glacier on his own, making his name known. In the Huckle Halls, at the Royal Palace, there were countless books and scrolls describing the early days of the great Huckleberry King. His adventures included the taming of bears, the catching of giant fish, the squishing of wolves, and, of course, the uprooting of trees. The king had made the Realm his own. Nowadays, all the creatures knew him and his song. They knew where he lived and when he left the mountain. They all paid attention to his orders and edicts. It was his land, and he was the king.

As the remarkable berry began his descent of the mountain, the sun bared its face once more, unveiling the forgotten sky beyond. The sunlight slowly crept back into the meadow, where the terrified crowd could begin to make out the king's physical features. You could see the signs of his age in his thick berry skin, as some of his deep purple exterior sagged and created ripples in his torso.

His limbs were similar to the regular Huckles', branchlike, although his were complete trees. They used to be young western hemlock trees, *Tsuga heterophylla*, until the king came along and at some point in time attached them to himself. The aged limbs creaked as the king advanced, bearing the weight of his majesty. The last item that completed the king was his staff, which he carried everywhere. This was a huge western cedar, stretching from the ground to near the top of his torso, around seventy feet tall, and on top of this staff was a bushel of nonliving huckleberries, which the king carried around to remind him of his humble past.

In the meadow, those in the crowd marveled at the awesome scene.

"He's so big!" the porcupines squealed.

"Look at his crown!" a small bear cub yapped.

Some of the adult bears sat at the very back of the crowd, decidedly unimpressed.

Remember, the bears had a testy relationship with the Huckles because of a troubled past, especially with the king. He had sent many of them flying through the forest, great lumps of black and brown fur hurtling through perplexed trees. They dared not express their dislike then, so they just sat at the back of the crowd in silence. Michael the young hare said naught; his gaze was transfixed and his feet were thumping violently.

Goji and Rubus glanced at one another. They had been preparing for this moment for a long time. Rubus slowly turned toward the crowd.

"Behold your king!" he cried.

The king was now in full view, and he cast an ominous, masterful glare toward the congregants below.

"Here he comes!" The fish in the river squealed as one school.

The entire meadow quaked as he moved. Since the king was rather large, he made it down the mountain hastily. As he drew nigh, the Royal Band and the knights-to-be could be seen constantly shifting and moving around, vying for the perfect position. Clusters of rock trickled down the mountainside and gathered into piles at the bottom.

Goji, who was perhaps the least interested in the king, was more captivated by the floral patterns worn by the choir. She wondered how hard the bees must have worked to create them. She was so dazed, in fact, that she almost forgot to play her rumpet to announce the king's arrival. Rubus gave her a sharp glare, and Goji noticed him from the corner of her eye. She quickly fumbled to grab the rumpet and play. *Brrrrrrrrr!* It was her loudest blow yet, and it was heard just as the king arrived at the foot of the mountain.

He had arrived. No one made a sound; none uttered a word. Even the lake's waters remained perfectly still. The king towered high above the small crowd. He was so tall, and his torso so large, that he could only fit half of the crowd into his vision. We shouldn't forget, he could have squished them all instantly if he'd wished.

To announce his arrival, the king stamped his staff twice on the ground without speaking. Remember, he is not much of a conversationalist. As he stamped, the soldiers moved hastily forward, ready to become knights. They reached the very foot of the mountain, toward the back of the stage, and bowed at the foot of the king. He looked at them for what seemed to be an age, and then lifted his staff.

"You wish to be knights?" The king spoke slowly. His deep voice boomed through the meadow, seeping into the heart of every creature great and small, and the gentle wind carried his words onward and out to all the Realm. Distant songbirds fluttered as he spoke. The soldiers sharply shot up from their bowed position and immediately glared at the king's head. They then raised their hands in salute. He surveyed them and occasionally used his staff to poke at their torsos as if checking for sturdiness.

"Hmph!" said he.

The king said no more than this single sound. It almost seemed like a chuckle of discontent. He took much pride in his clan and deeply loved the Huckles, but in recent ages, his temperament had become somewhat removed. Something had happened to his seed heart, although the creatures of Glacier did not speak of it. He looked at Rubus and then at Goji, then he reached for his staff and took some berries from the bushel on top. One by one, he passed one to each of the soldiers, to be kept for the rest of their lives. The soldiers proudly placed them on their crown helmets.

With that, the king cast a glance at the crowd and stamped his staff two more times. It was like lightning striking a forest floor. Goji, this time prepared, lifted the rumpet to her mouth and blew. *Brrrrrrr!*

The king turned and ascended the mountain, and the entire crowd watched him as he went forth. Several golden hawks followed him, circling his crown and torso, and his strong legs creaked beneath. The younglings in the crowd were stunned; some of their jaws had dropped to the floor. The king's band, still gazing intently, followed him back up the mountain, moving in rehearsed uniform fashion. They resumed the king's song:

> *Dum dum dum, off with his head, the king*
> *is purple, the king is not red!*
> *Dum dum dum, he is the king! All those*
> *in Glacier must bow to him.*
> *Dum dum dum, oh do you know why, for one*
> *single pie several children had to die!*
> *Dum dum dum, off with his head, the king*
> *is purple, the king is not red!*

What a terrifying song. He was a terrifying but great king. He had come down the mountain to turn the soldiers into knights. As hawks circled above, the trees swayed, and the crowd quietly murmured, the great Huckleberry King, the protector of Glacier, the most magnificent of berries, ascended back to the peak of Huckleberry Mountain.

3

Troubles from Lands Afar

COLD WATER SLOWLY TRICKLED into Rubus's rock cup. It was made from limestone, *Carbonite sedimentary*. The Huckles only drank water, and they had cleverly found a way to carve hard rocks into cuplike shapes. As the water splashed and swirled, a concerned look was plastered onto Rubus's burgundy face. An anxious berry was he.

"Stop worrying," said a calm voice in a wavering tone. Another Huckle elongated his words as if to lecture Rubus. Rubus broke his transfixed gaze to look at the berry opposite, another senior Huckle Knight. This Huckle was tall, almost two feet taller than average, and he had a toned, athletic build (as much as any berry can be toned and athletic).

"If you were I, Vernus, you would realize that I have every right to be concerned." Rubus spoke in an authoritative but calm manner. He was a leader who always tried to keep his temper from fraying.

"Look, Rubus, you need to enjoy the night. The news can wait. It's probably not much to concern us anyhow." Vernus was a confident Huckle, a young male in his ripe prime. As he shrugged Rubus's concerns away, he finished the last of his water and slammed his rock cup down onto the wooden table defiantly. Quiet music sounded somewhere close to them. "Come, let's get back to the others. Tonight, is for celebration!"

Vernus motioned toward a large oak door behind them, beyond which was the main hall of festivities. Rubus glanced for a moment at his inferior, then slowly rose from his rock seat to follow him. Mainly, Rubus was tired and wanted to avoid quarreling. It had been a long tiresome day; the procession, the feast, and the hanging weight of the news from the past week, it was all a lot for a berry to take in. They are, after all, supposed to be simple beings. Vernus heaved the large door open, his muscular frame bulging as he did so, and a wave of sound crashed over them. The senior knights were greeted by joyful and triumphant scenes. In a large wooden hall, a great number of creatures and Huckles of Glacier had gathered to celebrate the knights' procession.

At one end of the hall, a diverse and colorful band played joyful music. It was not as dramatic or as daunting as the king's song, but it was striking nonetheless. On the stage were three Clark's nutcracker birds, *Nucifraga columbiana*. They sang alongside each other, hovering gleefully in the air as they produced beautiful notes. Now, there were no misty purple notes this time, as they were reserved for the king. Also on the stage was a northern hawk owl, a *Surnia ulula*. He was the main act. He sang deep crescendos that coasted through the hall and into the Glacier night beyond. He was perched near the front of the stage on a thick branch ornamented with shiny things, which had been placed there especially for him.

At the back of the stage was a deep wooden tub filled with water. Out of the water leapt colorful fish, who timed their leaps with the music, rhythmically splashing. The fish were colorful rainbow trout, *Oncorhyn-chus mykiss*. There were musical porcupines behind this vibrant group, playing berryrumpets and berrytars and banging berrydrums, but they seemed of little importance compared to the colorful main cast. It was a tremendous sight; the finest musicians from across Glacier had been gathered for the night's celebration.

Across the hall, Huckles and other woodland folk were dancing the night away. Huckle couples young and old spun in circles, throwing each other up and down. They danced together in fours and sixes. The guest creatures from Glacier in attendance were hares, beavers, elk, and a few (only a few) fuzzy black bears. Great hanging lanterns swung from the ceiling, dappling the dance floor beneath in circles of light. The hall itself was large and rectangular, made from bright pine wood.

Now at this point, something should be said about the use of wood in Glacier and all of the Ancient Realms. You know by now that the trees were the Huckles' most worthy adversaries, causing them all manner of grief and obstructing their plans. This had particularly occurred when the two had different ideas for the maintenance and wellbeing of the Realms. Despite their quarreling, much of Glacier and the Huckles' works were forged out of wood, from their shelters to their halls and the village and even the Royal Palace of the Huckleberry King. The reason behind this was quite simple and wondrous.

The forests of Glacier Realm, and all like it across the United States and the world, exist in cycles. Rocks form, plants die, creatures pass on, and new life emerges. That is the cycle of a forest. Much more could be said about this, but it would take a long time, and we must return to the festivities. But know that the wood therefore comes from ancient trees that have served their time in the cycle of forest life. The trees accept this; it is not an insult to them. After all, there are many more trees than most other species!

The jubilant wooden hall was decorated in typical Huckleberry fashion. It was long and rectangular, emblazoned with purple and red banners, with great swinging lanterns of bright warm fire dangling from the ceiling. Now, fire was not looked upon fondly in the forest, but the Realm needed it nonetheless, so they sought to control it as much as they could. At the sides of the hall, the banners stretched from floor to ceiling. They had been woven according to the Royal Commission by the scurrying spiders of the deep earth and hollows of Glacier. There were twelve bright red banners, six on one wall and six on the other.

These banners contained different scenes from the Huckle clan's history, so it was like a passing story of the Huckles' past as you looked around. There were stories of mighty battles and momentous occasions of saving the forests, acts of the great king, and also stories of kinship, warmness, and kindness with the other Glacier folk. Ancient tales of woodland past. On one banner, there was a mighty image of the Royal Huckle Knights chasing away a rogue wolf, *Canis lupus*, as it had strayed from its pack and attempted to decimate some Huckles. Rogue creatures sometimes came from outside any of the Realms, from the expanse known as the Great Outdoors. This particular scene was from a winter's day, and fierce weather raged as the Huckles forced the wolf away from Glacier with a mighty fury. On the banner, their staffs were raised toward the wolf, who bore terrible snarling teeth. The Huckles did not like to harm other creatures too much, even if they were belligerent, so they simply chased them away from Glacier when they could.

Of all the banners in the hall, one stood out the most. It was positioned behind the merry band at the far end, to the left of where Rubus and Vernus were standing. It was centered on the wall, and all of the other banners seemed to point toward it. The banner emitted a purple glow over the entire hall, like a radiant centerpiece that held all before it in a mastered trance. This was the king's banner. Despite its magnificent allure, this banner was simpler than the others. It was bright purple, with two darker purple stripes along the side, and at the top, in the center, was the Royal Huckle Crest. This was the crest that the Huckles wore emblazoned on their tunics and carried into battle with them at all times. It was simple, but to the point.

It was remarkable, really. Many kingdoms that we know of in our time and in times past bear images of savageness, violence, and destruction to intimidate and frighten their enemies. They include skulls, animals, and weapons on their crests. The Huckles, in contrast, have managed to claim the whole Realm of Glacier as their own with a simple berry as their crest. Well, it is actually two red huckleberries, hanging off a thin branch with two leaves. It reminds the Huckles of their past, and perhaps bids them to recall that they *belong* to the land as much as they have taken it for their own.

In the hall, aside from the banners, there were long wooden farmhouse tables adorned with water, nutrients, and fruits, which were all arranged in marvelous platters on shimmering shiny silver dishes. Now, it should be explained that the Huckles had a very simple diet. Water. They ate, drank, and lived on water. They managed to learn how to cultivate nutrients from some fruits, but water was their staple nonetheless. There were large vials and vases of water on the tables, shaped from clay and limestone, and the Huckles took great care of them. Let us not wonder how the king and his troll drummers grew to their size by drinking water, because there is much about Huckles that we will never understand.

There were shaggy brown rugs on the wooden floor, gifted by creatures of the south, and there were numerous doors leading to other rooms. Also, just about wherever they fitted, flowers of the most vibrant colors were dotted all around. Pink, purple, white, and deep blue flowers were squeezed in between vases, hanging from walls and lanterns, and worn by many of the creatures. The busy bees of Glacier had been working all of the day before and on the day of the feast, preparing the hall. The bees were great companions of the Huckles, and they had watched them grow in power and stature in the land with tremendous pride. Supposedly, the bees had had a hand in helping the Huckles spread in the earliest days. They should be considered respectfully in our tale, and in any mention of any Realm or forest anywhere, because, just like Huckles, they have done the most wondrous things. There are many types of bees, but the bees that had helped decorate this hall were golden northern bumblebees, *Bombus fervidus*.

At the other end of the hall, there was a large open doorway leading out into the starry spring night beyond. In the winter, this door was closed tightly, but for now, it was wide open. Above the doorway there was a wonderful array of berries in a wooden lattice structure, complete with thistles, branches, and holly leaves. This had been a joint project between the bees and the other creatures, who had been eager to decorate the hall for the grand procession.

All in all, it was a most jubilant scene. The Glacier folk had been eagerly awaiting the evening, and they now danced and conversed with great glee. The two long tables on each side of the hall had an assortment of fruits and leaves for the other creatures and large bowls of pollen for the wonderful bees. There was impenetrable harmony among the woodland folk; they respected the Huckle supremacy, and the Huckles made sure they were welcome. It was a night of celebration, respect, and joy; it was the Glacier Realm at its most harmonious.

In a corner of the hall, Goji was dancing gleefully with a young doe, twirling and bouncing with wild excitement. She was the sweetest of berries and always seemed to have a special spark. As the music floated into the still night beyond, from another corner Rubus surveyed the hall with deep concern. It comforted him to know that Glacier was in a state of glee, but the troubling news weighed wearily on his heart.

"I know what you are thinking," Vernus interrupted Rubus's thoughts, "but they do not need to know. Look how much fun they are having!"

Rubus turned to him. "Perhaps, but the Royal Knights must be prepared," he replied. Vernus let out a deep sigh. He knew that his commander would stop at nothing to keep the Realm safe and do the king's bidding.

"Very well," Vernus said. "I shall let the knights know, and you gather the rest of the Royal Court. Let us at least enjoy this ni—" Rubus ignored him, then bounced off toward Goji with fierce intent.

"Leave her be, Rubus!" Vernus gave a subdued shout, not wanting to interrupt the evening, but Rubus ignored him again. He made his way across the hall, darting past bears, deer, hares, and porcupines as he went. Goji slowly stopped twirling and bouncing as she saw Rubus approach, and her boundless smile slowly began to fade as she noticed Rubus's solemn demeanor. Slowly, she and the young doe stopped twirling.

"Hey, Rubus," she said sweetly.

"Come, Goji, we must talk."

"But me and Fawn are dancing," she said forlornly, already aware of Rubus's next response.

"Come, Goji!" Rubus did not shout but lightly tapped his foot, his request turning into more of an order.

Goji's smile disappeared. She sadly gazed upon Fawn, and they waved farewell to one another as they separated. Fawn drifted to the center of the hall and Goji followed Rubus outside, dragging her feet as she went. They exited the hall through the large doorway whilst the flowers and assortment of berries hung overhead. The joyful music played on behind them.

The two were alone in the cool spring evening. A gentle breeze was present and the distant silhouettes of the giant mountains were illuminated under the moonlit sky. Some woodland folk say they can sometimes see the king sitting out alone at night amidst the mountains—the truth of which we will never know. Outside the hall there were no other buildings; it was alone on the far side of the mountain. Blades of grass gracefully danced in the night. Rubus and Goji stood face to face, the lights of the festivities flickering behind them.

Rubus spoke first. "I am sorry to take you away from the celebration, Goji, but there is something we must discuss."

"It's okay," Goji replied slowly.

Of course, it wasn't, but she didn't want to disappoint Rubus. Goji's eyes glinted in the encompassing moonlight. As she looked up at Rubus, you could see deep within that she hoped she would not need to leave Glacier any time soon, as she was having such fun.

Rubus spoke again. "We have had grave news from the south. The great trees have not responded well to our message."

About three weeks had passed since three Huckle Knights had been sent south by a Royal Commission. Their assignment was to form a truce with the trees, and the entire court had expected the negotiations to go well, but they hadn't. The Huckles had been sent back without agreement, and according to whispers from the woods, they had been in grave danger of being squished by the trees.

"What does that have to do with us, Rubus? They are so far away. We should just leave them be," Goji whimpered, now almost in a desperate plea.

Rubus responded frankly. "No, Goji. You know the decrees of which the Manuscripts speak. There must be order across all forests and Realms in this entire land, or there is no order at all."

The Manuscripts outlined rules for the creatures of all Realms to follow. Their purpose was to avoid conflicts such as the one emerging between the Huckles and the trees. If you remember, the two had serious disagreements because they had different ideas about how to manage the Realms. In particular, the king believed that the Huckles were growing in power and that the trees, and the Manuscripts, should respect this.

Their disagreements had begun to affect the harmony of the Realms, becoming a grievance to the creatures within. Sometimes the trees argued, for example, that the bears should be able to eat wherever and whatever they wanted to, whereas the Huckles believed they should be limited and that certain parts of different Realms should be bear free. Also, the trees often dominated the forest growth. This was not always on purpose, but their majestic roots simply overwhelmed the undergrowth, something for which the Huckles harbored great disdain. If the Realms were to be run in an orderly manner, such disagreements simply could not go on. For now, the Huckles were only affected in Glacier, but as we learned earlier, they grew in other places and had plans to expand into other Realms. And then there was the king's great bereavement. This was a topic of constant conversation and hearsay among the creatures of Glacier. Many years ago, the king had lost someone very dear to him, and supposedly, the trees were somehow involved.

Goji began to tear up. She had no desire to depart Glacier, but she knew that this moment had been coming. Rubus interrupted her sorrowful thoughts. "Goji, the whole court must travel south to accompany the king."

"*I* don't need to go! All I do is play the berryrumpet!" she replied.

"Goji, you know the Royal Commission. When the king travels, the whole court must travel."

"The king does not need us to go with him! He will be fine."

"Watch your tongue!" Rubus snapped. The Huckles must be careful when mentioning the king.

At this point, Goji became vexed. Among all the Huckles, she could perhaps be said to think most critically. She was, after all, different. She did not always display the same reverence for the king as the rest of Glacier.

"Well, I shan't be going, Rubus. I belong here in Glacier. I have been enjoying sweet companionship with the bees, with the hares, and with the woodland deer."

"Goji, you are a member of the Royal Court. You have been all your life," he replied.

Goji's face was downcast. She loved Rubus and didn't want to let him down. "I just enjoy playing the rumpet," she said.

Rubus's gaze suddenly intensified. "Goji, you must join us. You are part of the king's court!"

Goji looked up at him. Her eyes were now full of tears, warmly trickling down her ripe red cheeks. "I . . . am a creature of Glacier . . . and I belong here!" Suddenly, the saddened berry turned away from Rubus and swept away into the night. Disappearing among the shadowy trees, she left a trail of sadness in her wake. Her weeping could still be heard by Rubus a few moments later, penetrating the silence of the cool darkness.

Rubus sighed deeply and gazed at the canopy of stars that blanketed Glacier, creating what looked like a barrier against the forces beyond. Rubus knew how difficult this would prove to be. He loved Goji, but his royal duty was to make sure that she obeyed her commands.

Disheveled, he walked toward the lake that snaked around the mountain and proceeded toward the old wooden bridge that crossed it. He was on his way to the royal quarters of Huckle Village, which was nestled away from the mountain and hall, deep in the beautiful, pristine Glacier woodland. The night shone on. Once he had reached his quarters, he fell into a sleep, and a deep dream enthralled him . . .

The knights hacked their way through the thick tangled forest. It was a stifling hot afternoon, and rich rays of sunlight burst through the crisp green trees. They tripped and bumbled their way onward, stumbling and struggling through the chunky branches and foliage. Many of the trees grumbled as the knights made their way through, but they were mostly used to such disturbances.

"It came from over this way," said Ripus.

Ripus was an immense Huckle. He was possibly the fittest and strongest of all the Huckle Knights, and his bright navy toga rested on his robust berry frame brilliantly. His helmet crown shone with numerous species of berry, which had been awarded as medals of valor.

"Lead the way, Ripus!" Lingon followed behind. He was an equally impressive Huckle, just slightly lower in rank than his superior. Both of these Huckles were in their physical ripe prime and were colored a deep maroon reddish-purple. They were two of the highest-ranking knights in the Royal Court. Behind these fearsome warriors, a young Rubus nervously trudged along. He was not yet a high-ranking knight, but the longer he followed in the steps of the two before him, the more he was destined to become one.

"The watchers told us that they had heard a great struggle somewhere in these woods. Sounds as if it may have been a wolf pack," Ripus declared. His voice was bold and deep.

Earlier in the day, some diligent watcher Huckles had scouted a major disturbance in the woods beyond, around three miles from Huckle Village. Because the forest growth was so bountifully thick, the watchers could not see the disturbance unfold, so they reported straight to the court that something had occurred.

"Wolves, bears, wolverines, eagles, no matter who they are or what they want, they'll know not to meddle with us Huckles!" Lingon exclaimed, ever the confident berry.

"What if they are still here?" Rubus humbly enquired.

"Then, young Rubus, if their motives are impure, they will meet our mighty Huckle staffs," Ripus declared. He was clearly the leader of the group. Lingon chuckled in agreement, sincerely enjoying the prospect of a tussle with some meddlesome beasts. The Huckles feared little, and it had been a long time since an infringement of any kind had taken place in these lands.

The summer sun blazed across the deep woodland. Bristling porcupines, gentle deer, and chirping birds inhabited the forest. The undying beauty of Glacier stretched as far as the eye could see. In the midst of this impenetrable beauty, the three Huckle Knights wafted through the greenery. As they ventured forth, the ever-confident Lingon churned out an audible whistle, piercing the ambient forest beyond. His whistle was a familiar tune:

> Dum dum dum, off with his head, the king
> is purple, the king is not red!

The other two did not join in with his melody, but they were very familiar with the music. Rubus, who was behind Lingon, noticed small purple notes forming and floating away. Whenever a Huckle recited the king's song, in any form, the mysterious purple notes appeared.

> Dum dum dum, he is the king! All those
> in Glacier must bow to him.

As the whistling continued, some nearby songbirds seemed somewhat taken aback at their natural niche in the forest being replaced.

Rubus wondered what lay before them. The knights continued through the forest for some time, and Lingon whistled all the way as they hacked and whacked their way onward.

Suddenly, Ripus spoke. "Lingon, stop whistling."

At first, Lingon did not hear his leader, as he was lost in a musical trance.

"Lingon! Stop whistling!" Ripus turned around abruptly and motioned for silence to both of those behind him. "I hear something."

Sure enough, a faint sound was emanating from the woods ahead.

"I hear it too," replied Rubus, wanting to contribute something to the venture.

The Huckles proceeded, working their way through the woodland, which was decreasing in thickness. The faint noise ahead grew gradually louder.

"It almost sounds like . . . crying," said a surprised Lingon.

Indeed, as the noise grew closer, the unmistakable sound of weeping was becoming clearly apparent.

Ripus had a confused look on his face. "Yes, crying it is," he said.

"It doesn't sound like there are many of them," Rubus added.

He was quite right; there were no sounds penetrating the forest other than the shrill crying.

"Maybe one was left behind?" enquired Lingon.

"Perhaps," Ripus replied. "Whatever it is, stay on guard. We are drawing closer."

The weeping was now the only audible sound in the ambient forest, and Lingon's emboldening whistling had long been forgotten. Some ten feet away from them, the knights noticed a thin ridge of bushes, from which the crying seemed to emerge.

"Get down, and ready your staffs," Ripus whispered with an expert quietness. He was clearly used to leading daring operations and quests. "Take cover behind those bushes!"

The puzzled Huckles stealthily moved toward the ridge of bushes. "Lingon, do you see anything?"

"Nothing," he replied.

The source of the crying made no indication that it was aware of the group's presence, and the group had no clue what the source of the crying was.

"Can you see it?" whispered Lingon.

"No," said Ripus as he peered through the forest.

"It can't be the wolves," Rubus interjected.

"Let's peek through these branches," Ripus decided.

Slowly, Ripus pried apart some of the thick branches that were in front of them, the only thing between them and the crying. Remarkably, he saw nothing of note. "There's nothing there."

"What!" The other two looked disbelieving, possibly for the first time gazing upon their mighty leader in doubt.

"I saw nothing that could pose a danger to us," Ripus said.

"Well, what shall we do?" The two were gravely confused, as much as a berry can be confused. Ripus looked puzzled, but only momentarily. If there were any sense of danger, the great Huckle Knight might have taken more than a second to decide his strategy, but to him, there was little to fear. "Raise your staffs. On my count, we will burst through these bushes."

Rubus and Lingon knew what to do. They had been in countless situations such as this before. They had hunted wolves, wolverines, and bears. They had once even taken on a marauding mountain lion from southern lands, whom they had encountered as the lion was traversing the continental divide.

If you could have seen both sides of this scene, perhaps from a bird's-eye view, or maybe even if a passing bird in the woodland canopy had caught a glimpse, it would have appeared most humorous. The three Huckles were in an offensive crouched stance with their staffs raised, ready to burst through the bushes and pounce on the mystery beast. They were completely uninformed as to what awaited them on the other side. "Ahhhhh!" Led by Ripus, the knights burst through the bushes with remarkable efficiency and skill. Their stance was true, and their mighty crowns were emblazoned upon them. That which they laid eyes upon left them completely aghast.

Huckles are not often surprised. They are the ones doing the surprising. Everywhere they go, the creatures and folk of all the Realms still find it hard to believe that there are giant berry warrior folk reigning over Glacier. I'm sure you were surprised to learn that there is a one-hundred-foot-tall berry known as the king tramping through woods and lakes, flinging bears aside and summoning all types of creatures to his behest.

Alas, this scene in the meadow surprised even these surprising folks. The Huckles had burst through the bushes into a small meadow, or rather, a gap in the trees, and in front of them, as clear as the sunlit day, lay a baby.

A very small baby.

To make matters even more surprising, it was a berry baby. Now, the Huckles do not create babies of their own. The king had been the first to come to life, and after that, his great power extended out to berries near him. It was his power that gave birth to the Huckles, and they simply emerged from branches when they were brought to life.

The mystery baby lay wrapped in a white sheet of some kind, so only her face was visible, obviously flooded with tears. The baby was a ripe red, much like the regular Huckle folk. The knights looked upon her, still shocked, but not just because it was a baby.

"What in all of Glacier . . . ?"

"That is not a Huckle baby," declared Ripus.

As was mentioned, the Huckles do not create babies, but they appear as babies when they first emerge from their branches. The Huckles had never seen a "living" berry outside of their own, so the three of them were completely flummoxed.

"How can this be?" enquired Lingon.

The baby cried on, but the knights were now too stunned to notice or even care. High above, a small family of songbirds darted between the trees from one end of the clearing to the other, perhaps laughing at the scene. "There are no other berries living than us!" Lingon went on, slightly annoyed.

Following Ripus's lead, the three dropped their staffs. They had clearly wildly overestimated the danger. Slowly, Ripus walked toward the crying babe, who took no notice of the advancing knight. As he moved closer, he noticed nothing drastic except the small differences between them. The baby was slightly thinner and had slightly more wrinkled skin. She was also a bright red, similar to the reddest Huckles but even brighter. Aside from this, more importantly, Ripus could *feel* the difference, as could Rubus and Lingon. This baby was a berry all right, but it was not a huckleberry.

"What do we do?" Lingon almost sounded panicked. He was completely out of his element.

Ripus stopped about three feet away, truly puzzled. He had seen many situations in his time as a knight, but this was the most surprising. He shuffled his crown while he thought, perhaps a sign of unsettledness, then uncertainly, he turned away from the mysterious berry baby and back toward the others. "This is not Huckle business," he announced in a matter-of-fact tone. "We were sent here to investigate a disturbance, and there is none. We shall report this back to the king, but no more." Although Ripus spoke affirmatively, he was clearly unsure.

The baby wailed louder, now rocking from side to side in the meadow grass.

"What? We can't just leave it here!" Rubus pleaded.

"Ripus is right. This is no business of ours." Lingon agreed with his leader.

"It's a baby! If we leave it here, some wolves may very well get to it. Or worse!"

"It is not a Huckle, so it is not for us to take care of!"

"I think we should bring this baby back to the king," Rubus decided.

"Rubus, the king has more pressing concerns than a lost baby," Ripus replied.

"But this is a berry of some kind. Surely the king will be interested?" Rubus was pleading his corner but fighting a losing battle. The baby's wailing grew ever louder, perhaps hastening Lingon's and Ripus's opinion of the whole matter.

"We should leave, Rubus," Ripus said.

"No! It's a baby."

"Rubus . . ."

"This is not right. It's here by itself. We need to—"

"Rubus!" Ripus, ever the commanding berry, put his authoritative foot down. Truth be told, Ripus was trying to lead, but this was a situation that required the utmost improvisation. He was doing what he knew best while making it up as he went along. "We are leaving now and returning to the village!" With that, Ripus stormed back to the gap in the bushes from whence they had emerged so defiantly. Rubus looked at Lingon and then at Ripus, and he knew he had been defeated. Lingon wore something of a smirk. He was interested only in the fiercest adventures; no time for babies had he. He followed immediately after Ripus, not even glancing at the berry baby as he left. Rubus stalled for as long as he could, gazing upon this helpless babe, seemingly abandoned and left in the woods alone. It was a heart-wrenching sight. He reluctantly broke his gaze and turned to follow the others.

As they stumbled through the woods on their return, none of them spoke a word. The only sound was that of crunching leaves beneath and the whacking of branches in front. It was not so much that the Huckles were angry at one another; it was more that they were still most per-plexed. What they had experienced was a revelation not only to them but also to the whole of Glacier if they ever found out.

A bit later on in the day, the beaming sun had given way to a cool afternoon. The crisp leaves swayed gently in a light breeze, and a careful wind swept through the woods, as if some dawning revelation had come upon the entire day. Lingon hacked at some branches. He was the least affected by this serendipitous turn of events. Rubus looked at his back, feeling annoyed. Rubus was still a young Huckle, and as such, his char-acter was still very much being formed, open to change. As he walked, the events wheeled round and round in his mind. He contemplated them deeply, as much, of course, as a berry could contemplate.

After a while, Rubus began observing the woodland surrounding him. The Glacier woodland was serene, tranquil, and untampered with. A female thrush, bright, bronze, and speckled with black, rode the wind through the pine branches, clutching a mouthful of grubs for her young. A prickly porcupine scurried out from some earthy hole, gently waddling into a patch of fresh leaves. It buried itself among them, almost as if it were bathing in the leaves. The forest was an endless cycle of life, beauty, and friendship. Even Huckles, simple, miraculous beings as they were, could contemplate beauty, and the more they saw, the more they under-stood it. Rubus knew of nowhere else he would rather be, and he couldn't imagine why anyone would want to be elsewhere either. He gazed at the mother thrush, delighted to be sharing a forest with her, and then a small raindrop plopped from a nearby leaf onto Rubus's head, rolling down toward his mouth. It had started to rain.

Suddenly, Rubus stopped. Stopped in his tracks. Now, in the com-mon tongue that you and I speak, when someone has an idea, we often say they are struck by lightning. We cannot speak of such things now, because we dare not envision the consequences of a four-foot berry being struck by lightning. Rubus was hit by a raindrop, not struck by lightning. He stared intently at the thrush mother, who seemed to notice his gaze, and she cast a twitching glance back at him. He glared at the thrush, then at the other two Huckles in front of him, then back at the thrush. Another raindrop hit him.

"I will take her!" Rubus bellowed for the whole forest to hear.

The rain slowly precipitated, and the two knights in front paused. Lingon cast a frustrated glance into the air, while Ripus was seemingly glued to the spot. "I will take the berry and watch over her."

Lingon snapped a stick and dashed it aside, turning around slowly. "Rubus, the king will never allow it." As he spoke, he looked toward the sky.

"Why not? We have no idea. Nothing such as this has occurred in Glacier before," Rubus responded.

Ripus interjected. "How do you know it is a 'she,' Rubus?" He was not completely sold, but he was more open to Rubus's suggestion than Lingon was.

"I do not know, but I believe I am meant to take her!"

Lingon sniggered.

"I mean it, Lingon! I will take her and raise her as my own. It is completely wrong to leave her abandoned here."

"And what if the king doesn't allow it?" Ripus asked.

"Then I will bear the full consequences."

Ripus stared at Rubus. He now knew that he was most serious, as no Huckle would bear the wrath of the king lightly. The three stood in a triumvirate in the still forest. The songbirds created an audience for the tense berries; they were perched with interest on nearby branches, awaiting the decision. A silent hush blanketed the forest.

"Fine," Ripus said solemnly.

"For goodness—" Lingon began.

"We will take her to the king, and if she is granted a Royal Charter, you can raise her."

Rubus brushed past Lingon and approached the leader, extending his hand in gratitude. "Thank you, Ripus."

Ripus nodded his head, and the two knights shared an endearing moment. The truth was that Ripus had been bewildered by the entire episode, hence why he was open to Rubus's idea. With that, the Huckles headed back toward the meadow, this time with Lingon behind.

Back in the meadow, Rubus approached the baby berry. She had fallen asleep, seemingly exhausted from crying. He gently stooped down and scooped up the heart-warming berry in his arms. A great fluttering filled his insides, and his seed heart became full. Gentle rain fell upon the knights as they stood in the shadow of the surrounding trees, and, aware of the commotion, several woodland creatures had now emerged to follow the proceedings. A porcupine family were present, as were two adult hares, and a mother thrush circled above. The woodland families wished to observe this serene moment. Rubus gently cradled the baby in his mighty limbs and looked down upon her, and from that point forth, his seed heart was never the same.

"You know, this little girl looks very similar to a goji berry."

In his earliest days as a knight, Rubus had pored over the great annals in the Royal Huckle Hall. Therein, one could find information on all types of berries, and goji berries, *Lycium barbarum*, had particularly interested him. Ripus nodded gently, agreeing with Rubus. Rubus pulled the baby closer to him, clutching her ever tighter in the cascading rain. "Then that is what you will be named. Your name will be Goji."

The forest was a witness; the creatures had seen it. Rubus had found Goji. He took her as his own.

4

A Tree Like No Other

GLACIER IS A WONDERFUL place, a magical, marvelous, mysterious place. But it is not the only place, nor is it the only Realm. In fact, there are many places around the world today just like it; there are lands with mighty forests, alpine heights, and tranquil summers. Glacier is only one such land, and it is only one such Realm. The country in which our tale is based, the United States, is home to many national parks that have their own unique characteristics, stories, and countless woodland folk, which, of course, are preceded by the mystical Realms in our tale. Whereas the Huckles were able to build their Realm in Glacier, the other Realms had their own special ecosystems, and there were hundreds and thousands of creatures who were not under the direct rule of the Huckles of Glacier. Our tale now requires us to meet some of them.

You should remember me saying, much earlier in our tale, that you would need some maps handy throughout, for navigation. If you still have them, you will need them now. Earlier, on the map of the United States, we found the state of Montana, home of the beautiful Glacier. This time, we are leaving the woodland haven and journeying to another state. It is one that you shouldn't have a problem finding, as it is rather large.

Starting from Montana, place your finger on the map and work westward toward the coast, further and further away from the Huckles' home. Eventually you should be in the state of Washington. After this, trace your finger down, all the way south, while hugging the coast, passing the state below Washington. If you have taken this journey in real life, you will have had quite the experience. You will have witnessed wild and beautiful coastland, serene sunsets, and dense woodland. The state of Oregon, which is the one below Washington, is a land of luscious lulling green.

South of Oregon, where your finger should now be, is quite possibly the most majestic of all lands. This is a state rich with woodlands, lakes, and mountains just like Glacier, but it is also home to swaying palm trees, glittering coastland, and barren deserts, open skies and vast prairie lands. At night, parades of stars litter the sky, all the way from the shimmering silver lakes of the south to the great Lake Tahoe near the center.

Fierce mountain lions and bobcats roam at twilight, unreserved in their predation, and in daylight, bald eagles freely roam the sky, while rummaging bears trudge their mighty paws through the woodland searching for food. There are many national parks here in this land, just as there were many Realms here in the Elders' age. As the state is so diverse and large, attempting to capture a glimpse of all the Realms would be futile, so you'll have to go and see them for yourself. Truth be told, there is not much in the whole United States—or should I say in the entire world—that doesn't also reside in this state. It is a very special place. This land is called California.

You may be wondering, if California is so inspiring, stunning, and majestic, why wasn't it explored earlier in our tale? Why didn't our adventure begin there? The thing is, when you are exploring, it matters not where you start or where you end, but what matters is the manner and quality of your exploration. Just like taking a walk in a national park, it is about how events unfold during the walk, rather than where you stop and start.

You should now seek out a specific map of this glorious land of California. Unfold it and you'll see for yourself that California is truly vast, stretching a somewhat regular distance from east to west but hundreds and hundreds of miles from north to south. It would be useless to try to find your way without adequate navigation.

In our tale, we will explore much of California, but we must now find our starting point. Due to its location, it should be, again, quite easy to find. Place your finger at the very northwestern point of California, and the nearest city should be Crescent City. Our location is close to here, so your finger won't have much further to travel. Move southward along the wild California coast and you should shortly see an intense patch of green, dense but small, named Redwood National and State Parks. This one-of-a-kind place is where our woodland tale continues.

෴

Living creatures, and life in all woodland, prairie, land, and sky, can only ever grow so large. Creatures are bound by the characteristics of their habitat, the food they eat, and the powerful forces of nature that keep things in balance. Now, there are some very big creatures in our world— majestic blue whales, giant elephants, and towering giraffes—and they all reach incredible sizes. But in general, creatures, and especially woodland folk, remain an acceptable size, as there is no need for them to grow excessively large.

There is one woodland family, however, that completely defies this arrangement. To be honest, I'm not sure if it's because they have been around for so long or because they are so numerous or simply because they do what they want, but I must tell you that trees have simply not followed the patterns of size in the natural order. Trees ignore the rest of the forest and grow to the most stupendous sizes. They tower above our world and life, and they are, by some way, the tallest living creatures in our world. Distant canopies appear as giant towers in the distance, rising like grand wise masters in forests new and old. According to the Ancient Manuscripts, due to their lofty heights, the trees were able to oversee all that happened in their Realms.

Now, there are trees, and then there were the Trees. In our tale, some trees are inanimate, like the regular huckleberries. But the Trees, well, they were all too alive, and they ruled over their Realms just as the Huckles did. These ancient beings were wise and knowledgeable beyond any creature, knowing the small movements of little critters and the larger movements of wild beasts, and, as you may remember, they were also very much connected. They communicated and coordinated in ways we will perhaps never fully understand.

Trees form great groups, and they communicate among one another. Because of where these groups are, they often look quite different in size, shape, and height. Some Trees were short enough to be conquered by the king, and some were so high that you would barely even be able to grasp their tremendous size from the bottom. In fact, if you stared at these giants for too long, you would begin to feel giddy, your head would begin to spin, and you would be altogether undone.

California, the glorious land where our tale now resumes, was (and is) home to a great many Trees. There were the Joshua trees of the south and the ancient bristlecone pines, Elders who will play an important part in our tale eventually. There was a group of towering Sequoia Trees too, and there were regular but wonderful oak and maple trees dotted all across the vast expanse. The Trees were bountiful. They grew and lived on the coast, flanked lakes, and congregated in thick forests. In California, there were so many Trees that there was an Annual High Legion of the Trees gathering, in which the leaders of all groups convened to discuss the affairs of the woodlands and forests across California. We will not venture into detail about that momentous event because it would distract us (just know that hundreds of Tree leaders trudging through California to congregate in Yosemite was a source of great entertainment to all the woodland folk). We will not dwell on such things in this tale, because we currently have some important folk to meet.

I hope that you are able to meet some of these Trees someday. I hope you are able to go from park to park, seeing and taking care of the ancient creatures. I hope you take your maps and the lessons you may learn from this tale and go to see the Trees in their forest home and respectfully admire the great things they have done. If you do, you should know that in the Elders' age, all of these Trees answered to one source.

That source is where your finger may still be, or may have been, or where you may have left a fingerprint. Redwood National Park is that source, and, just like Glacier, we will simply call it Redwood. Before it was a park, this happened to be a magnificent Realm, which a group of Trees reigned over, and still today, Redwood is one of the most ancient, wise, and important forests in the whole world. The mystique of the forest stretches far beyond the land of California, and any description of its populace very rarely does justice to it.

Redwood was a Realm equal in stature and wonder to Glacier. Its deep and thick forestry formed an impenetrable ambience of rustic woodland, and, much like Glacier, there were boundless scenes of beauty here. It was, and is, an ancient forest, the life of which dwelt palpably in the air. There were many similarities between Glacier and Redwood. Both were bristling in beauty and rich in life. There were, however, a few important differences. The main difference, which we must discuss in depth, was the Trees.

In Glacier, the Trees had been humbled. Great though they were, they very much submitted to the king, but here in Redwood, it was the Trees, not the Huckles or any bears or eagles or deer or other folk, that reigned supreme. The Trees were the guardians of the Realm, and the creatures here bowed to them. You should also know that whereas

Glacier was a diverse Realm of mountains, lakes, and plains, Redwood was mostly forest. There were a few streams trickling here and there, but it was the forest that abounded. The Trees had simply taken over due to their incredible size.

Now, all trees deserve our respect, as we learned earlier, and all the Trees in Redwood were indeed respected, but there was one that was revered above all others. That was the California coast redwood, *Sequoia sempervirens*. Quite simply, they were, and are, the tallest Trees anywhere in the whole world. As a matter of fact, they are by far the tallest living thing, and I very much doubt if anything will ever surpass or match them.

Nowadays, there are buildings everywhere, big and tall. Our tale takes place long before buildings emerged, but you should know that these Trees, who existed long before, are far, far taller than most buildings. They do, of course, still exist today, and they are just as tall now as they were then (some will even have grown). They scale the horizon with giddying heights, dwarfing the surrounding woodland. The average redwood is around 250 to 300 feet tall! For perspective, that's the same height as thirteen large adult giraffes stacked on top of each other.

These magnificent trees were the source of life in California during the Elders' Age. They oversaw all of the wonderful ecosystems throughout the land, and they judged and settled many disputes. The Redwoods did not use forged weapons as the Huckles did; instead they used their powerful branches and roots whenever combat was necessary. These mighty roots stretched from Redwood to the most southern deserts, through which they transmitted ideas and orders as well as calling other Trees and creatures to do their bidding. All the woodland folk of California knew of the Redwoods.

So, in this way, the Redwoods watched over all of California from their Redwood home. No one ever contested this, as the Trees were deemed perfectly capable. The Trees ruled by council; the group helped make decisions (this was most unlike the king, whose unruly temper would see him threaten any defectors with squishing). Every council, however, must have a head—a leader Redwood. There was such a Tree. There was certainly such a Tree. If you are ever to come across it in the present age, I would think that you will perhaps be changed forever . . .

It was an early forest morning. As the delicate morning dew soaked the undergrowth, a small mouse scurried from behind some leaves and into a nearby hollow. Up above, as the thin layers of dreary ocean fog began to dissipate, gentle spring sunlight crept in through the woodland gaps. This was the redwood coniferous forest, and the woodland creatures, those that lived for the day, were beginning to emerge. High, high above, a marbled murrelet, *Brachyramphus marmoratus*, glided among the forest towers. It was a fresh, crisp start to the day, and, as in Glacier many miles north, the weather promised a tempting summer beyond. Deep in the forest, past dew-soaked shrubs and groves, birds' nests, and earthy hollows, a forest clearing lay undisturbed. It was clearing of a vast size, perhaps fitting for some glorious midsummer concert of woodland folk. But alas, the clearing was reserved for the wise leaders of this Realm.

Huge mounds of earth had been prepared, which appeared as woodland thrones. They were formed by an inhabitant of these woods, the Townsend's mole, *Scapanus townsendii*. This was a fairly small brown mole with a long pink tail, and as it worked, it scurried underneath the dense redwood undergrowth, dodging the gigantic and momentous trunks. Due to his small size, it had taken the mole months to construct the earthy thrones, but he knew all too well the importance of the task. The busy mole emerged from an earthy hole on the very edge of the hollow and surveyed his work one final time before the council began. Contented, he nodded his head and scurried back underground. The clearing was prepared.

Thirteen earthy mounds lay in a circular pattern. One was slightly larger than the rest, with extra attention having been paid to its shape and structure. High above, the forest birds gently tugged at wantaway branches, no doubt seeking to use them for their nests that lay afar. Much like in Glacier, a still silence hung in the air, and a similar ambience pervaded. Redwood, though, had much more of a majestic feel to it. Whereas Glacier was most tranquil, there was a sense of greatness, giganticness, in the air here.

Once the morning had mostly passed, the time of the council drew nigh. The early dew droplets shook and trembled as a distant thumping could be heard, and the small songbirds darted away. Small twigs fell from their feet and beaks as they fled, while minuscule trickles of dirt broke off the earthen mounds, although they generally stood firm. *Thump, thump, thump!* The distant thumping drew closer and the sunlight intensified, preparing to greet the mystic congregants. *Thump, thump, thump!* Through the surrounding forest, a distant rustling occurred. The canopy of trees seemed to conceal some movement. *Thump! Thump! Thump!*

The sound echoed through the forest and beyond the clearing, while particles and clumps of dirt bounced off the forestfloor. Now that the sound was closer, it was clear that it was some type of walking. It was not walking as you and I know it, but more the movement of great figures, their steps aligned in rhythmic woodland harmony.

The walking was that of the majestic Redwoods, shifting past their cousins and friends in the rest of the Realm toward the clearing. As the thumping drew near the place of meeting, the first arrivals broke through the bank of Trees as gently as the sunlight coasting through the canopy's branches. The first Redwood soon stood in the clearing and looked around for her earthy hump. She was named Fir, and she was a senior member of the council. Fir was 300 feet tall and had been part of the council since its very beginning many, many ages ago.

The Redwoods had not changed much in their appearance. They were, after all, Trees. Whereas the Huckles had formed limbs and wore clothes and carried staffs, the Redwoods looked very much as you would expect. It was difficult to see their faces, as they were so high, but if a bird were fluttering high above, they would notice the Redwoods' faces; they were etched into the rippling trunks. According to the Manuscripts, they were formed over time as the Redwoods developed a deeper and deeper connection with the forest.

They also had two large hollow eyes, and their mouths were straight gashes across their trunks. This may seem very simple for a Tree so wise and ancient, but because of their stupendous size, their faces were incredibly large; around thirty feet from top to bottom. The branches and leaves of the towering Redwoods took the appearance of what you and I know as hair, but other than that, they looked very much like you might expect; like Trees. Unlike the Huckles, they had no need for adornment or decoration, as they were content with their rustic woodland attire.

Fir began to move toward her earthy hump, which was in the same position as it always was. As she moved, her magnificent trunk shifted from left to right as the roots beneath were revealed. These roots pulled Fir along; they were how she, and all Redwoods, moved. As they walked, they separated from the ground below, pulling large chunks of earth upward as they went. This, of course, was one of the sources of disagreement between the Huckles and the Redwoods. The Huckles often accused the Trees of unsettling the gentle balance of the undergrowth.

As Fir found her place, a deep thumping sounded as more Redwoods moved through the woods. Soon enough, behind Fir appeared

Balsam, a younger member of the group who had been a member of the council for about half as long as Fir. Balsam was roughly the same height as Fir and was a male about half her age. He was a strong and sturdy tree with much experience and wisdom.

Balsam's trunk was a light shade of chocolate brown, and he was in his fantastic prime. He looked at Fir and gently smiled, his gash mouth forming a giant chasm in his trunk. Fir had reached her mound and turned around, facing inward toward the rest of the circle. Noticing Balsam, she smiled back, and as she did, leaves fell slowly to the ground under the dynamic of movement.

Other creatures in California, Redwood, and Glacier usually bowed, curtsied, or even joined paws or beaks when they met; all were perfectly customary greetings among forest folk, but the Redwoods, however, did not have this freedom of movement. If they were to bow or spin or jump or shake, they would send shockwaves through the woods, catapulting mounds of earth, potentially destroying the homes of small creatures and altering the woodland landscape for the rest of time. Therefore they kept their movements to a minimum and simply greeted each other with endearing smiles.

Balsam made his way to the bottom of the clearing so that there was quite a distance between him and Fir. The Redwoods had developed a strategic pattern of entering the clearing so that they did not bump into each other as they made their way to their mounds. Behind Balsam entered ten more Trees, male and female.

There was Hickory, an older male with a fine head of leafy hair, whose twisted branches made him look like an ancient sage. Then there was Pine, a younger female who had a far slimmer trunk than the others. Next was Nutmeg, a stocky bullish male who was incredibly wide but somewhat shorter than the others (short is, of course a relative term, because it does not really apply to these folk). Behind these appeared Coulter, Gopher, Willow, Birch, Tamarack, Oak, and Sap. The towering Redwoods found their places in the clearing one by one and stationed themselves near their earthy humps.

Now, if this were a gathering of the Huckles or some other woodland clan, the congregants may very well have taken a seat on those earthy mounds or even stood on top of them, but these Trees did no such thing. Unable to sit or crouch or make any significant movement, they simply stood on top of the earthen humps and slowly sunk into them. The dirt enmeshed itself around the council's colossal trunks, and the Redwoods became rooted to the spot. They now formed a perfect circle, the same position that they had adopted during council meetings for hundreds of years. Ever-increasing sunlight beamed in from above as Sap, the last Tree to enter the circle, took his place, and twelve of the thirteen earthy mounds were filled.

You must remember that although the Redwoods had widespread influence and reach, they were somewhat limited in their movement. They could not run, leap, jump, or strike like the Huckles could. To make up for this, the Redwoods had learnt how to utilize their roots to tremendous effect. In the Manuscripts, it is written that these roots are capable of stretching all across California, passing messages far and beyond and even into the Great Outdoors. Therefore, each time the council met, they connected their roots to communicate. The strong roots passed through the loose forest undergrowth, casting rocks and earth aside like sand. Deep underneath, they tangled and merged like greeting hands, forming impenetrable connections.

Once Sap had been received by his earthy mound, a rumbling occurred as the Redwoods shot their roots from underneath them, and one could see the rippling and disruption of the forest floor from high above. At some points, the roots erupted from the surface like lava.

Once all the roots were connected in an intertwined, intermingled web, the Redwoods began to shake, and the ancient Trees began their ceremonial introduction, in which they rustled from side to side, swaying their towering trunks. To an eagle or hawk flying above, it would be quite the scene. They moved for several minutes, while loose leaves and branches fell to the floor. To the rest of Redwood, the shaking took the sound of a fierce rushing wind.

The shaking stopped. All of their eyes had been closed due to the ferocity of the movement, but they now began to slowly open them, and as they did, the outermost leaves on their branches began to glow a tinted gold, seemingly absorbing all of the surrounding sunlight. Once they had finished glowing, they floated off the Trees like wafting cotton spores and drifted slowly to the ground. As these golden leaves fell to the forest floor, they turned greener and greener, and by the time they had reached the ground, they had turned completely emerald. This was the way in which the Redwoods gathered.

"Greetings, O wise ones!"

Fir was the leader and speaker of the council. The Redwoods could speak audibly and had clear booming voices, but they also transmitted their messages via their roots (it was faster and helpful to older Trees who were hard of hearing). "We are here today to discuss the issue that has come upon us!" Fir was, of course, speaking of the Huckles of Glacier, who had recently sent ambassador berries to discuss their differences. Fir spoke with no particular urgency about this issue, as the Redwoods had encountered a wide number of occurrences in their time, and this was just another one of them. "We must address this issue now, as our great Realm may be affected by it."

The Trees glared at Fir with an ancient gaze. They all displayed similar emotion, not too concerned but equally engaged. They were very rarely fazed or flustered. Balsam, who had stood waiting, now interjected. He was the timekeeper of the council. "At this time, we must record our attendance. All who are present, make yourselves known."

One by one, clockwise from Balsam, the giant Redwoods lurched upward, and all of their branches and leaves shot toward the sky. As they returned to normal, hundreds of leaves and little branches fell gently to the floor of the clearing, which was now covered in leaves. All of those present performed this intriguing action until the cycle came back to Balsam. This was how the Redwoods recorded their attendance. "Very well," he declared. Balsam had no writing implement on which to record attendance, so he simply memorized those present. The Redwoods, like all Trees, had long memories, the likes of which could not be matched by any other creature.

The timekeeper was satisfied and cast a short glance at Fir. Of course, Balsam did not turn his entire trunk or even move any leaves; he simply moved his eyes as far to the side of his trunk as he possibly could. He also sent a message in root form, letting Fir know that the next stage of the council could proceed.

Fir spoke once more, both in root and out loud. The Redwoods spoke slowly, deeply, and clearly. When they spoke, it was as if they were beckoning all of Redwood to listen to their wisdom. "It has been many years since we have met together in this clearing. Since it has been so very long"—hundreds of years, actually—"let me remind you all that we shall not begin without the High One."

Now, they would not even have begun this section of the council if it were not for the fact that the High One of which Fir spoke took significantly longer to reach the clearing. This mysterious Redwood lived in a far more remote location, obscure and separate from the rest of the forest. Much like they restricted their movements, the Redwoods also had to consider carefully how they spent their time, as it often took a long time for them to get anywhere. They were in no rush, however; they had thousands of years to fulfil their purpose (unlike the Huckles, who often had under ten).

All twelve of the Trees waited contently, basking in the intensifying midmorning sun. Patiently they waited. To a passing thrush or starling, it must have seemed like an eternity, but the Redwoods would not be rushed. They stood assuredly tall in the clearing, titanic pillars of the forest. A marsh shrew, *Sorex bendirii*, scurried along the floor, zigzagging between unveiled trunks as he passed.

Silence.

The sunlight rays shone from above.

After some time, the faintest but most poignant of noises began to emerge. Far from the clearing, a scene of complete awe was unfolding. Like earlier, a deep thumping sounded through the forest, but this time it was far deeper, echoing into the very depths of the earth. The council themselves seemed to be struck by every thump, with their sturdy trunks being shaken to the core. Due to his position in the circle of the council, Oak had a good view of the eastern horizon, despite Coulter obstructing his view. He could begin to make out a faint image. "He is coming . . ."

As the image became clearer, the Redwoods on either side of Oak—Gopher and Willow—also saw the distant being emerge. The rest of the circle could not see, as they would not turn around. Now, it should be explained at this point that the Redwoods were not incapable beings; far from it. They simply had little reason for unnecessary movement. They much preferred to save their energy for the keeping of secrets, the harboring of wisdom, the growing of roots, and other such things.

The figure drew nigh. The thumping now reverberated throughout all the Realm, sending smaller creatures flying. *Thump, thump, thump!* The council sunk further into their earthy mounds to make sure they remained rooted as the thumping and shaking intensified. To the mice and shrews of the forest floor, it must have felt as though an earthquake were occurring. Fir, who was facing backward, began to form a smile, aware of the mighty figure drawing closer.

The approach was similar to that of the Huckleberry King. A difference, though, was the response of the creatures nearby. As this figure approached, a remarkable scene occurred. From the west, a wonderful palette of songbirds flew sharply toward the east, seemingly greeting the High One. Hundreds of speckled starlings, woodland thrushes, and acorn woodpeckers flooded the sky adorned in orange, yellow, and red. The birds formed a stunning rainbow of color as they shot through the spring air, and when they reached the moving figure, they began to fly around him in a perpetual circle, creating a barrier of sorts. As they flew and the High One grew closer, their beautiful voices chirped a melodious song.

Dum dididdy dum
He started as a stump
Dum dididdy dum
He walks with a thump!

It was the most splendid scene. Some of the songbirds chirped melodious sounds, while others sang words. The High One's song flowed throughout the Realm like a sweet forest stream.

Dum dididdy dum
He dwells so ever high
Dum dididdy dum
The High One is nigh!

The birds danced and chirped around the approaching Redwood, flying and darting in between one another. Back in the clearing, the remaining earthy mound had now begun to open up, making way for the king of the Trees. The council sent frantic root messages to each other, pulsating through the earth. They were eager to see him. As the thumping grew louder, more and more birds flew toward the High One.

Dum dididdy dum

By now, Oak, Gopher, and Willow could clearly make out the Tree coming toward the clearing.

He started as a stump

The Tree approaching was of incredible, otherworldly size. His trunk reached way beyond the canopy, brushing the clouds and seemingly disappearing up and over the horizon beyond.

Dum dididdy dum

The High One had an ancient appearance. His long face and branches were deeply set into his most audaciously sized frame, and he was the tallest thing that you could ever imagine. This Tree was almost twice as tall as the other members of the council, dwarfing other Tree species, and he would barely have been able to notice the Huckles. Anything other than a Tree positioned next to him would have appeared as an infinitesimal speck. It is hard to believe that such a sight was even real.

He walks with a thump!

The thumping finally stopped. Small woodland creatures littered the Realm, lying on their backs, upturned from the great commotion. The High One had reached the edge of the clearing. The choir of birds stopped circling and rested on his branches. The sunlight glared from behind him, and the magnificent Tree gazed down upon the council. The others, who had been eagerly awaiting him, fashioned jubilant smiles. He had arrived. It was the great Redwood, the High One. He was the tallest tree of all. As a matter of fact, he was by far the tallest thing ever to live upon our world. His name was Hyperion.

Hyperion was a Tree like no other. He is still very much alive today, although you will never find him. Once his purpose in this tale had been completed, he retreated into the distant heart of the Realm, hoping never to be seen again. If you were to see him, by some magical chance, you would struggle to even comprehend his mighty size.

The world of nature is daring, magical, and adventurous. Often, it disrupts our understanding and shatters our vision of what it should be, so that we are constantly surprised. This is the case with mysterious fish in the deep sea, wonderful land mammals of extreme speed, and now this simply stupendous Tree, the tallest living thing to have ever existed.

Hyperion stood at 380 feet tall—116 meters. The sheer magnitude of this size should not be understated. This is the size of almost twenty giraffes, who would be equally bewildered by the grand spectacle. Hyperion towered above everything. Some of the younger folk of the forest would swear that they had seen Hyperion's upper half breaking through the plane of our world and disappearing into the skies beyond.

Now that he had reached the clearing, the council looked up at him, wearing increasingly gallant smiles. Their branches and leaves shook with glee. By now it was midday, and the high sunlight kissed the radiant horizon from whence Hyperion had emerged.

"Greetings, old friends," he announced. His voice, like those of the others, was slow but sure, and as he spoke, it was as if the whole of nature spoke with him, merrily bouncing along to his every word. The birds chirped, the wind rushed, and the woodland earth below received his voice.

The birds who had formulated such a wondrous choir now gradually departed; their task had been done, and as they flew into the distance, some could still be heard chirping the mystic song of the High One:

Dum dididdy dum, he started as a stump

The melodic chirps dissipated into a distant trance as the birds flew further away.

Dum dididdy dum, he walks with a thump

Hyperion advanced, and with the council gleefully awaiting him, he made his way to the last remaining earthy hump, and his intense roots supplanted giant chunks of the ground as he moved. Even the sunlit rays seemed shocked by Hyperion's movement. As he crossed the clearing, they bounced and dodged his mighty figure as if making space for him.

Reaching the mound, the old Tree sank deep below, and an endless amount of dirt and earth crept up his trunk, rooting him in place. Afterward, a terrifying rumbling ripped through the spring silence, and Hyperion's immense roots collapsed the undergrowth, wrapping themselves around the rest of the council. Hyperion's roots were almost the size of all the others combined, and as such, he fed and received messages at the greatest speed.

With all members now present, Fir continued with proceedings. "All are now present, and the council may begin!"

Like a thunderbolt or a falling tree in a silent forest, a mighty sound ripped through the clearing. Hyperion had brought his foremost branches together in a booming clap. Shockwaves pulsated through the roots of all the Redwood Realm, and perhaps beyond to all of California. The council had begun. Now that he was here, Hyperion led. "Dear friends, this grievance has come upon us. We will attend to it with wisdom and valor, as we have done many times past." Hyperion's voice boomed through the clearing and beyond. So high was his mouth, he had the appearance of a king speaking from some great tower down to his subjects below. The council listened intently, as they knew that Hyperion's wisdom was like no other in the Realm.

"The Huckles of the north are noble creatures, but they must not be allowed to alter or change the Manuscripts."

The great old Tree had a solemnly gentle character. He was greatly concerned for all woodland life, but he was also strong of heart. "We, the Redwoods, must preserve our Realm and watch over the balance that the

Manuscripts bring to all life." Of course, the Trees could communicate only through their roots if they wished, but they chose to communicate verbally so that the rest of the Realm could also hear. Much like the Huckles, they wished to be at one with the forest. "The Manuscripts shall not be altered. If the Huckles wish to expand out of their Realm, they shall only do so under the guidance of the Ancient Writings."

The council ruffled their branches in agreement, forging a rush of wind in the clearing. The sun was now at its highest point, and the entire forest shone with emerald opacity. "These messengers sent from the north shall return to the Huckleberry King, and we will make clear that we will not cede to them." With this, the council could no longer contain their excitement. They twisted from side to side, shaking and dropping leaves from their branches.

"It shall be done!" Hyperion declared. His announcement meant that the council was mostly concluded. Formally, however, the Trees had one last act to perform.

One by one, each of them sent one of their thickest roots bursting through the ground. They emerged near the base of Hyperion, whereupon they created a type of barrier around his trunk, reaching about fifty feet high. One by one, the Trees sent their finest roots as an act of submission to the High One, and once the roots had all arrived, they bent over as if bowing to him.

High above, Hyperion was aware of their action, and intense pulses of energy coursed through his trunk, and he raised his two foremost branches high toward the clear blue sky, a magnificent scene of height and strength. The entire Realm bore witness, and the woods drew a collective breath before he lowered his giant branches, declaring, "It is done!"

A hawk soared high above the canopy over Redwood. Its piercing screech sounded for miles and miles. The Trees had spoken. The forest had heard. The council was concluded.

～

Now, the Redwoods are marvelous trees. They are tall, mighty, and elegant. But they are not the only tree. As we explored, there are wide Sequoia trees, mysterious Joshua trees, and beautiful Willow Trees. Deep in southern California, there are also the Ancient Pines. Like the Redwoods, they are still living today, and they also play a special part in our tale.

They were not tall and mighty like the Redwoods, but they were equally as important. The Redwoods were old. These were older. Hyperion was wise, but they were wiser. While Hyperion managed the affairs and ordered the creatures all across the Realms of California, the Pines often fed him crucial advice. They were the brains behind his great brawn. Perhaps they could have decided to manage the affairs of California alone, but they had chosen to hand all authority over to Hyperion, placing all things under his roots. Besides, the Pines had other desires. Being, as they were, Elders, they had seen plenty come to pass in their time. They desired to rest. Deep in a southern Californian forest, they were pretty much permanently resting in a deep slumber . . .

5

A Journey Begins

"Fire!"

A row of sharpened staffs streamed from behind the safety line. They wobbled as they sank into their targets; old forgotten tree trunks. "Ready . . ." Opposite the targets was a row of shining Huckle Knights. They were enamored with their royal tunics, and their Huckle crowns gleamed in the warm afternoon sun. It was now the very eve of summer, the month of May, and the knights were deep into their training.

"Raise . . ."

Standing behind the knights was Rubus, gazing intently. He had one hand raised, in line with his command, and he was totally focused on his task. Many of the knights were new and had not been to the Great Outdoors or another Realm before. They knew very little of lions, wolverines, fierce winds, and other perils. Rubus, of course, had made a career out of it. After the passing of the great Ripus, he had assumed command of the Royal Knighthood, and he was now the King's Commander. In his time in this position, two years now, he had been on numerous daring ventures to near and distant lands. He had fought off ferocious beasts, braved cold, icy winds and snows, and scaled eerie heights, greater than any Huckle should scale. The time was soon drawing near when he and the knights would be required to venture forth beyond Glacier, and this journey would perhaps be more perilous than all he had faced before.

"Fire!" Rubus shot his arm forward sharply and bellowed the command. The final slew of staffs soared through the air, demonstrating the grandeur and expertise of Huckle craftsmanship. The knights were training in a grassy plain in the middle of Glacier, where they were north of the mountain and of Huckle Village, and the nearest lake was Quartz Lake, a clear lake of sapphire blue. Here in the plains, scruffy, gruff mountain goats visited from the west, bears often ventured from the north, and eagles soared above. Rich, luscious grass blanketed the land. It was the perfect spot for some intense Huckle training.

Toward the edge of the plain, an old prune like berry looked on. He leaned on his oak staff, and his folding ripples of skin sagged like wrinkles. He was an old Huckle and a former member of the knighthood. Rubus walked toward him. "What say you, brother? Do you deem these soldiers worthy?" The older Huckle leaned on his staff, his old limbs creaking when he made any type of movement. He slowly turned his head toward Rubus, gently smiling all the time.

"I think that they will be fine, Rubus, so long as they are in your command."

This old Huckle was Lingon, one of the renowned knights of old. Lingon had served in many fierce struggles alongside Rubus, and although retired, he had come to support and survey this latest training. "You raised Goji as your own. I know that you can lead these knights onward for the king."

Now, Lingon and Rubus had had their differences. As a younger berry, Lingon was often described as brash and arrogant by his fellow knights. He had at first vehemently rejected Rubus's decision to raise Goji, and he was supposedly beside himself when the king gave his royal approval. The king had not taken to Goji as Rubus had hoped, but he had been allowed to raise her on account of him being a knight. In fact, the king had always seen Goji as something of an outsider.

"Rubus, you can lead these Huckles. They may be young, some of them new, but the Realm needs you all now more than ever."

Rubus knew his old friend was right. The news from the south had greatly troubled the Elderberries, and they saw only one solution. The king's court must travel south to the great Realm. From there, they would consult the Wanderers. Rubus nodded at Lingon, and they both turned toward the knights.

Finished with the training, they were now putting away their staffs, and a gentle lull of chatter emanated as they worked. There were no other woodland folk present in the plain, as the training was off limits and secret; they were alone with the distant mountains and the clear blue sky.

"Thank you, brother." Rubus took hold of Lingon's hand while gently moving forward to embrace him with a brotherly hug. He had to be careful due to the tenderness of the old berry.

"Of course, Rubus. Now go forth. Those knights need you."

Rubus stared at his former brother in arms for some time, deeply wishing that Lingon was younger and able to journey with him to the south. He and Lingon had ventured and conquered far and wide, perhaps more than any other Huckles had ever done or ever will. He wished Lingon could help him protect the knights, as he had feared for them for some time. Rubus had tossed and turned in his sleep for nights, for he felt the weight of the knights' lives upon his shoulders.

Rubus nodded at Lingon and slowly walked back across the plain toward the soldiers. Lingon watched his great brother. He had been amazed by how Rubus had taken Goji as his own, how he had loved her and raised her. He had developed a deep respect for his fellow Huckle, and seeing the whole process had changed his own life forever. For the rest of their time together as knights, Lingon could be found at Rubus's home, drinking water and singing songs, cackling, dancing, and merrily shouting, Rubus, Goji, and he. "You're a fine knight, Rubus, the finest of us all," he muttered under his breath. Lingon had no doubt that the knights would prevail.

Rubus reached the edge of the plain where the knights were gathered and immediately beckoned them toward him. "Come gather, King's Cluster."

The knights were collectively called a cluster, after a cluster of berries. They were the King's Cluster. "Our training is completed for the day." The cluster cheered. They were eager to join the birds, beasts, and fish in enjoying the splendid Glacier afternoon, but Rubus motioned for calm. "Just know, O knights, that out in the Great Outdoors, it is not so much about the skill you may possess, but more about when to apply it. Creatures in all Realms watch o'er us, my dear kin. They want to see that we can lead with wisdom, not just strength."

The knights hung onto the commander's words as he spoke.

"When we depart Glacier, we will be pressed with challenges like none before. It is in those times, fellow Huckles, that your ability will be put to the test." The knights looked at one another. Some nodded and agreed, while others simply took everything in. "Let us go forth now and enjoy Glacier today, for we know not how much longer we will dwell within it." The Huckles cheered again, as this was the moment they had been waiting for. They then broke out into merry song as they picked up their weaponry.

We are the Huckles,
Huckles are we!
We fight every battle, all in his name,
To protect our great land, our beautiful plain.

Rubus allowed himself a smile as the cluster dispersed. The knights' song fashioned a gleeful mood, which rose up to match the ambitious summer afternoon. Slowly walking toward the crowd, the old berry Lingon wore a beaming smile. He was enjoying the beginning of what would perhaps be his last summer in Glacier.

The jubilant spring colors danced along to the knights' rhythm, and bright yellow tiger lilies, *Lillium colombianum*, swayed from side to side nearby. They were an alluring drooping plant that had bright yellow petals that bent upward, with speckled dots all across their faces. Nature danced along with the Huckles. Rubus, wanting to return to the village, soon let out a piercing whistle that carried through the crisp Glacier air. The jubilant Huckles then turned toward the distant mountains, to where the whistle was targeted, and, responding to the call, a loud bleating flooded the plain, while furious hooves began to pound the mountain. Suddenly, a great number of strikingly elegant creatures broke through the line of trees alongside the open expanse.

The creatures raced toward the Huckles with wondrous speed, and the closer they came, the more their organized formation became apparent. At the head was the stag of the herd, named Morrow. Morrow was a mighty woodland elk, *Cervus canadensis*. Much like with the bees, the Huckles had struck an ancient partnership with the elk, and their importance in this tale should not be understated.

The elk are one of the largest land-dwelling folks in all of the land. They are a striking brown, dappled with white, and they run at a courageous pace. Herds of elk are to be seen across all of this mighty land. They are neither masters nor followers, but they are certainly not pushovers. The elk belong as much as any creature.

Morrow was an exceptionally large specimen. His great bulging hide was draped over his muscular frame, and his antlers adorned his head like mighty weapons. Reaching the cluster, Morrow screeched to a halt, and his herd stopped sharply behind. Like a victorious general, he let out a deep neighing snort as he approached Rubus. Morrow's deep breaths

punctuated the spring air, frightening the tiger lilies, who stopped swaying and dancing upon the arrival of the fearsome stag. A dark black patch
covered Morrow's mighty head, in contrast to his otherwise deep-brown
coat. Snorting loudly, he drew closer to Rubus, and damp sprays of saliva
steamed from his mouth and nose with every snort.

"Greetings, Huckle Knight," he said. His voice was gruff and sharp,
and he spoke with commanding authority. He had the utmost respect for
Rubus and the Huckles, but he did not consider himself subservient in
any way.

"Greetings, Morrow, and thank you for your swift arrival." Rubus
had to look up when he spoke to Morrow, who stood at around five and
a half feet at the shoulder.

"Where in Glacier are you traveling to today?" Morrow's deep
nostrils flared as he spoke. Behind him, the herd graciously awaited his
direction. All of them were a sleek and beautiful brown. Their slender
frames and delicate tails made them an enduringly pleasant sight upon
the Glacier plains.

Rubus responded. "Back to Huckle Village. Our training here is
complete."

"Very well." Morrow turned toward his herd. He towered above
them, and they all waited attentively for his command. With a powerful
lurch, Morrow bounced onto his hind limbs, the muscles of which were
some of the most powerful in all of Glacier. He hung in the air with his
vast back toward the Huckles and his furry underbelly toward his herd.
His front limbs swayed dangerously in midair as he let out another terrifying snort, and his incredible antlers spread almost as impressively as
the roots of the legendary southern Trees. I think that if the Huckles were
to have somehow become stuck onto one of his antlers, he might have
been able to carry three or four of them upon his head alone.

The herd knew what to do. Like the opening of a delicate silk
curtain, the cows (female elk) moved around on either side of the majestic Morrow. They trotted gracefully toward the cluster, each finding
a partner. Morrow then returned to his feet, slamming back onto the
floor, sinking into the delicate earth beneath as he did so. Once all of the
herd had found partners, Morrow bowed his mighty head, and the cows
crouched down beside their Huckle riders. The Huckles, smitten by the
entire process, gladly accepted this token of friendship and began to load
their equipment onto the back of the patient herd. The cows' ears flicked

as they waited, and gentle specks of white and brown covered their shiny summer coats.

One of them, named Alaska, flashed a gracious glance at her Huckle companion, who was also a female. "Greetings, Huckle." Her flowing eyelashes shone as she spoke.

"Greetings, elk."

The Huckle, whose name was Marsha, responded with glee, eager to ride upon the cow through the plains and rivers beyond. The Huckles and the elk had struck their ancient partnership long ago. The great Huckleberry King had realized that his kin would not be able to cover such large distances as he, as they had not, after all, managed to grow to his momentous size. To manage this, he had consulted the Elderberries, who had advised him to forge a partnership with some mobile creature in the Realm.

The king then searched far and wide, bouncing through all of Montana, not just Glacier. He inquired of bears, mountain lions, and even high eagles, but none were found to have the necessary numbers. The king needed a creature that traveled as a group, rather than alone. After many long years searching, the king came across Marrow in some Glacier woodland. Marrow was the grandfather of Morrow, a legend of the Glacier woods and an elk of great size. The Huckle King explained his plight to Marrow, who responded with his request that the king and any Huckle from then on must aid them in their endless quest for leaves. The king thought this odd, as Marrow was clearly a formidable creature, but the rest of the elk often struggled to reach the leaves at the very top of the branches in the deep woods, the ones they enjoyed the most. So the king agreed to his request.

Upon the peak of Huckleberry Mountain, the king, Marrow, and the Elderberries ratified the agreement, and from that point forth, any time a Huckle rode upon the back of an elk, the Huckles would help them reach the furthest leaves.

"Do you remember the terms of our agreement, Rubus?" Morrow asked.

"Of course, old friend."

Rubus was taken aback, but then he remembered that it had been some time since they had ridden upon the elk. This was because they had spent much time in Huckle Village recently, what with the procession and the celebration.

"Very well," Morrow declared.

By now, most of the Huckles had mounted their partners, whose stark beauty was not broken under the strain of bearing weight. They waited patiently, and their caramel ears graciously moved back and forth. Rubus mounted a cow himself, while Morrow trudged toward the front of the herd, ready to speed off across the plain. Rubus would ride upon a large cow behind Morrow, but Morrow himself would not be mounted. The herd assembled behind their great stag, with their Huckle Knight riders positioned carefully.

Morrow began to snort loudly, and he scraped his right forelimb against the ground below, rearing up as if preparing to charge into battle. "On my command!"

His deep voice resonated across the herd. Ahead of him could be seen the distant mountains from whence they had come. It was beyond those mountains that they were now heading. The sunlight rippled and gleamed upon the pristine brown coats of the woodland elk as they prepared to depart, and Morrow's snorting intensified as he bent down and forward toward the horizon. "Steady . . ."

Altogether, the herd prepared their slender frames by bending their heads forward, ready to embrace Glacier beyond. Some way at the back of the formation, an old berry maintained his beaming smile, thrilled to be alongside his friends and Glacier family. The Huckles and the elk were a partnership to be reckoned with. "Forward!"

Morrow leapt forward into an alarming sprint. All of his powerful limbs and muscles bulged as he powered across the plain, and his antlers pointed menacingly ahead of him. I dare say no force in Glacier or any Realm would have had the will to stop him.

Such was Morrow's prowess that he burst a considerable distance ahead of the herd, who gradually caught up and joined him in his advance. The beautiful elk pummeled forward with a rare combination of beauty and speed, bouncing into the warm sunlight before them. They advanced with devastating sharpness toward the mountains. Elk are not normally known for such speed, but their partnership with the Huckles had allowed them to discover and embrace certain magical qualities, perhaps owing to the Huckles' affinity for discovering inner powers not previously known.

They kept a steady pace as they crossed the plain, leaping over gentle streams and pounding the bare earth. The distant mountains shone in the golden sunlight, and their luscious peaks jabbed at the boundless sky as small frothy clouds hung in the still air. The Huckles looked at the mountains and the line of trees as they rode, embracing the serendipitous soul of Glacier that beckoned them. They were riding home.

On and on the Huckles rode. The bright sky dazzled high above as they traversed the Glacier plain. Not once did the herd break their formation, and their leader Morrow darted across the horizon like a raging bull, visible from miles away. They blazed a daring path, darting past trees, splashing through waters, and bounding over rocks. Eventually they reached the very head of Lake McDonald and began to ride alongside it; then the elegant herd was reflected in the still waters illuminated by the sunlight. On and on they rode . . .

The gate of Huckle Village was a tall wooden structure. Large oak pillars girded either side, with grafted branches of twine creating a strong support. Lofted high onto the pillars were two vibrant flags, hanging silently in the summer sun. They were flags adorned with the Huckle crest, on vivid display for all the Realm to see. Behind this robust gate and the flags was the bustling, thriving Huckle Village, home to the Huckles, where hundreds of them now lined the streets.

Huckle Village had a simple feel. The Huckles did not adorn their homes with valiant decoration, as they always felt that their true home was in the world beyond the gate, amidst the great Glacier forests. Due to this, there were a good number of trees and bushes here in the village. You should remember, the Huckles formed a truce with the Trees of Glacier, and since then, they have lived in harmony with one another here. The buildings that the Huckles lived in were simple wooden huts with circular doors. They varied in shape and size, but they all looked mostly similar. The huts were sporadically placed throughout the village, and bright swathes of greenery were dotted around the sides. Many of the bushes and trees had different types of berries growing on them, and the Huckles took great care to nurture and look after them.

On this particular day, the entire populace of the village was gathered around the gates, the village gates that led to Glacier beyond. A constant murmur and excitement emanated from the vibrant crowd, which was a colorful gradient of red. Watcher Huckles and younger folk darted in and out of the small gaps found between berries, bouncing off unsuspecting seniors. "Watch yourself!" they shouted.

Aside from these excited pesky younger Huckles, all the rest of the civilians were in a state of utmost alert, awaiting the fanfare announcement.

It was now late afternoon, and the early summer sun had begun to kiss the distant glacier mountains.

"Where are they?" an older Huckle inquired.

The great knights were not late, but the Huckles were in a constant state of worry about the most elite, no matter how punctual they were. The king's court was the Huckle clan's pride and joy; it gave them purpose, belief, and a way of making sense of their miraculous existence.

Some way behind the boisterous crowd, and out of earshot on a grassy knoll, a young Huckle in his adolescence stood behind a wooden stand, very similar to a lemonade stand except it was only water that was served.

"How much longer?" he asked. The young Huckle was named Yew. He was a rose red, the regular shade of Huckles. Yew had come from the furthest end of the village, the western side, where the village wall faced Huckleberry Mountain.

"Just be calm, young one." A prime Huckle leaned back onto the water stand, the wood creaking under his muscular weight. He raised a cup of water to his mouth and took a calm, deep sip.

"But Vernus, what if they are in some sort of trouble? It is getting late, after all."

Vernus finished his deep gulp, then he placed his cup down on the stand, sighed, and took a look toward the sunset sky. He slowly turned toward Yew, while the table creaked all the time. Yew was in awe of his great frame and wondered how any Huckle could ever grow so strong.

"Listen, Yew, I have been a knight for many years. You must learn that here in Glacier, we are untouchable!" Vernus gave a confident smile while lifting his hands in a jesting motion, as if daring Yew to doubt him. Yew uncertainly looked past Vernus to the gate, longing for the knights' return so that he could pack up his stand and return home.

"They will be here," Vernus said calmly. He had been stationed at the village, in charge of protecting it in the unlikely event of any marauding beast straying in from the Great Outdoors. Vernus, after all, did not require much further training, particularly the sort for novice knights.

The last attack on Huckle Village, by the way, had been years ago, when a hungry bear leapt the village wall and ravaged some bushes around some of the Huckles' homes. Needless to say, the rapacious bear was seen off just as quickly as it had entered, as the Huckles had assembled at lightning speed to dismiss the intruder. He never came back. It was a rare event, as folk in all of Glacier and beyond knew better than to disturb the village.

Vernus stood up straight as another came to join them.

"Hey there, Vernus; hey, Yew." A young female named Holly walked up to the stand. "Got any fresh water there?" Her voice was soft and sounded like a sweet lullaby. Holly was a garment maker in the village mill, producing tunics for knights, soldiers, watchers, and all civilian folk. She herself wore a vibrant pink tunic, making a delightful contrast with her bright red color. She was a most cheerful Huckle, and the sight of her lifted Yew.

"Sure do!" he replied. Yew poured Holly a cup of water before reaching over the stand and passing it to her.

"Thanks a bunch, Yew!" She looked at him with a beaming smile. "Say, you okay there? You seem a little edgy." Holly noticed Yew shuffling and looking at his feet while nervously moving from side to side. He slowly looked up, ready to explain, but Vernus interrupted.

"He's nervous." Vernus seemed to take humorous delight in the situation.

"What for, sweetseed? They'll be back any minute now!" The murmuring of the crowd continued, interspersed with the odd cackle of laughter or rapturous shout of joy.

"I'm fine." Yew shrugged, trying not to look Holly in the eye.

"Well, I don't believe that, now. I know a sad Huckle when I see one!"

"Look, I'm—"

"His older brother is a knight." Vernus sighed again and rolled across the front of the stand, leaning confidently in between the two.

"Well now, why didn't you say so, Yew? That's just wonderful!" she said.

"I guess."

"Oh, sweetseed, he's gonna be fine. Bet he'll make a great knight and all!"

Yew smiled at Holly. Behind them, the chatter from the crowd had begun to intensify, and a buzz of nervousness seemingly now matched Yew's tone. Above them, the valiant flags gently swayed in a late afternoon breeze, and the enduring sunlight blazed on, while soaring birds ascended around the distant mountains beyond. In Huckle Village, closer gracious songbirds could be heard chirping their early summer songs.

Vernus patiently tapped his feet while carefully surveying his surroundings. He had not an inch of fear in him. He was confident of the Huckle clan's purpose and direction. "Well, I'm sure they'll be here any minute now."

"I really hope so," Yew said.

"They'll be here, Yew," said Holly.

Brrrrrrrrrrrr!

The three turned sharply toward the watchtower near the gate, where a magnificent fanfare had suddenly sounded from a berryrumpet. It echoed through the village, loud enough to make every Huckle wobble on the spot, their wooden limbs rattling and shaking and their berry bellies jiggling. All at once, the civilians of Huckle Village looked up toward the watchtower, which was a wooden structure reinforced by light stone. High upon it, the court's rumpeteer had announced the arrival of the knights, who were now approaching the gate.

"Open the gate!"

Some soldier Huckles signaled to those operating the pulley system by the side of the great gate, and with all their berry might, they heaved and huffed while pulling a large wooden lever. The village gasped.

"They are here!"

"The knights are home!"

Excited whispers could be heard from the crowd. Yew's face brightened, and Holly gave him a reassuring smile. Vernus began to whistle gently, altogether undisturbed, and the mighty gate creaked and groaned as it gave too, unveiling the sumptuous Glacier outdoors. As it opened, it was as if a mystic aura floated inward, and the ambience of the Glacier woodland wafted through Huckle Village. At the end of the long, winding path that had been unveiled, majestic figures could be seen moving daringly closer.

The crowd sorted and sifted into two banks, creating a path past the gate and into the heart of Huckle Village. From where Yew, Holly, and Vernus stood, the crowd looked like a wonderful assortment of berries; different shapes, sizes, and shades of red. All of them had come to see their knights return home.

"Yep, here they are." Vernus spoke as though he had seen the scene one too many times before, like a restless warrior eager for greater adventure. The royal rumpeeter continued with the fanfare, ceaselessly playing as the knights drew closer. Behind the knights, the orange Glacier sun could be seen slowly sinking into the far-off mountains. The knights' work was done, and so was that of the sun. Banks of swaying trees bordered the path upon which the knights arrived, and as they moved forward, the trees showered them in leaves like the applause of a jubilant audience.

"Wow!" An excited Huckle child near the front gasped as the first figure drew to the fore. There was no Huckle, but a mighty beast emerged among the rainfall of leaves. It was Morrow. Morrow had taken the entire journey at full speed, not once looking back or slowing down. The Huckle folk looked at him aghast, in awe of his bulging muscles and vibrant shade. The crowd gazed on in suspenseful silence with a deep respect.

Yew leaned over the stand, whispering in Holly's direction. "Who is that?"

"That is Morrow, dear, the champion of the woodland elk."

"Those are huge antlers."

"Yes, dear. He is the mightiest elk in all of Glacier."

Some time passed as Morrow advanced, but he eventually went to wait in a grassy area just beyond the crowd. The trees along the path continued to rain down multitudes of leaves, so that the riders approaching were covered and unidentifiable until they had passed the gate. A second figure emerged from this shroud of leaves, and the crowd erupted into riotous applause.

"He is here!"

The next to appear was Rubus. The Royal Commander. The most renowned Huckle Knight. Many titles had he, but Rubus always carried himself as one who was more concerned for others. As his cow carried him closer, Rubus cast a quick look up at the watchtower, where Goji had been announcing his arrival. She did not look back down in his direction.

Rubus passed through the gate, waving at young Huckles as he advanced. He was one of the most-loved Huckles in all of Glacier, and he was a source of hope and inspiration to young and old. The commander passed through much serenading before joining Morrow in the greenery nearby. He then stepped down from his cow, patted her gently on the head, and thanked her for her service. In turn, she elegantly blinked at Rubus while nuzzling her head against his. The cows were affectionate and kind creatures. She then went and stood behind Morrow, who began to keep a mental count of arrivals.

Behind Rubus, other knights flowed in. The fanfare continued, the crowd never ceased applauding, and the gentle afternoon gusts continued to blow leaves into Huckle Village from the Glacier outdoors. Once all had arrived, Yew strained for a better view, searching for his elder brother among the knights. Before too long, he caught a glimpse of the young prime Huckle, who was busy unloading his gear from one of the cows.

"Do you see him, sweetseed?"

"Yes! There he is." He ran toward his brother, forgetting Holly, Vernus, and his stand. "Logan! Logan!"

The Huckles were busy leading the herd to a group of nearby trees. Once they reached them, the knights mounted the elk once more. They then reached into the trees to the furthest leaves, the ripest and most delicious. The Huckles plucked these leaves out of the trees in great bunches, and the herd gracefully chewed from their hands.

Back near the green, Morrow was engaged in conversation with Rubus. The two expressed thanks to one another after another harmonious meeting of one of Glacier's great partnerships. Morrow bowed his giant head before Rubus, so that it looked as if he could plow through the entire Huckle crowd, taking half of the small delicate wooden buildings in the village along with him. After they had finished munching on the leaves, the elk began to trot back out of the gate and toward the Glacier outdoors.

There was not so much applause, but rather there was deep respect for the passing elk from the civilian crowd, who watched on as they rode off into the evening. As they reached the threshold between Huckle Village and Glacier, Morrow let out a mighty cry. He leaned back onto his hind limbs as before and then darted off along the path. The gallant elk herd drifted off into the velvet Glacier evening, with the sun sinking into the distant horizon.

Back in the crowd, the knights were now greeting and embracing the civilians, and Rubus in particular was surrounded by adoring Huckles young and old. The knights towered a foot above than the rest of the crowd and were clearly identifiable by their gleaming helmets and close-to-purple shade. At the watchtower, a lonesome female berry could be seen descending the steps with her head down and her face glum. Some wondered what could possibly have upset her so in the midst of such jubilation.

Elsewhere, a prime knight finally found his younger brother.

"There you are, little brother."

"Logan!"

Logan had escaped the crowd and proceeded toward the water stand with his arms extended in a gesture of embrace. He held his mighty crown in one hand and what seemed to be a bunch of flowers in the other. The two brothers then embraced in a tight hug. Holly looked on endearingly, and even Vernus mustered a smile. He was, after all, a caring Huckle at heart.

"What's in your hand, Logan?"

"These, brother, are Glacier lilies, and they are my gift to you from the great plains."

Logan handed him a bunch of the bright yellow Glacier lilies, *Erythronium grandiflorum*. The flower was a wonderful striking yellow, with thin, courageous petals that curved back to reveal the sensuous flower. Yew took a deep sniff, and the fresh smell floated through his skin like osmosis, the scent alone taking him on his own journey through the plains. The Huckles appreciated all that grew around them and embraced the growth of Glacier wherever it was found.

"Thanks, Logan. Oh, I can't wait to hear about your time!"

"Indeed you will, Yew." He paused and looked toward Vernus and Holly. "But first tell me who these fine Huckles are."

Yew looked back at them. In his excitement, he had forgotten that they were even there. "Erm . . . this is Holly!"

"Hey, dear, great work out there!" Holly introduced herself with a beaming smile.

"And this is Vernus," Yew continued.

Logan chuckled loudly. "I know who Vernus is, Yew. He is the second-in-command, one of the greatest knights in all of Glacier!"

Yew stood stony-faced. He was not sure whether to look at Vernus and apologize or act like he already knew. Vernus simply smiled at them both.

"Not to worry, young one, we'll make a fine knight out of you someday," Vernus said as he endearingly put his hand on Yew's head. He then looked at Logan. "And you, well done, great knight!"

"Thank you, Vernus," Logan replied with a gentle bow.

"Anyhow, the hour is upon us. On your way, Huckles!" Vernus was quite right. The sun had mostly disappeared, and a slight chill wafted through the air. Twilight had come upon them, the time when the knights' night watch began.

Logan and Yew noted his command and began to walk toward their home.

"Thank you for watching over my brother, both of you," said Logan as they departed.

"Oh, he's a sweet seed."

Yew smiled and waved farewell to them both, vowing to remember who Vernus was next time. The brothers walked hand in hand back toward the heart of Huckle Village, surrounded by distant chatter and merry ado all around. Yew even forgot to pack up his stand and take it home. He would have to return tomorrow.

"I can't wait to hear all about it, Logan."

"You shall, brother; you shall."

In the Glacier night, Logan and Yew were immersed in deep sleep. They had spent the evening sharing merry tales, reminiscing about seasons past. Logan and Yew lived alone in a small hut far on the western side of Huckle Village. Logan had raised Yew as his own since their parents had been lost in a fierce winter storm.

Remember, the Huckles did not produce children as other creatures do; instead, they emerged from branches when the great life of the Realm that flowed through the king reached them. However, older berries bore responsibility for watching over the younger ones, and they took them on as children. They did also share affection and love for one another and thereby became parents together. In this way, Logan and Yew had been raised by their parents, whom they had loved and missed deeply.

High above their hut, the moon blazed upon Huckle Village and poignant stars shot darts of light. The leaves on the gentle trees shone silver in the moonlight as all the Huckles in the village slumbered in silence. Above the huts, a silent brown owl glided among the treetops.

It was an impressive bird, deep brown with speckles of white and a soft snowy underbelly. The owl had sharp talons and a beak almost like a hawk's. Although the creature relied on its hearing rather than its sight, it could make out the village below. It saw the great gate and watchtower at one end and the meeting hall at the other. In between, there were hundreds of simple structures, wooden huts in which the Huckles lived, and there were also trees and green spaces dotted all around. Not many other buildings existed, as not many others were needed. Much of the work the Huckles undertook, be it crafting, tailorship, or water-bearer, they did from their homes or elsewhere in the great Glacier Realm. The Huckles were still berries at heart and longed to exist with nature rather than above it.

The owl left the tree above Logan and Yew's hut and flew toward the meeting hall. This place was the only building with any kind of activity in this still night. With devastating sharpness, the owl silently swooped through the silver dark. He rested on a thick branch outside the hall, on a tree in the front yard. The hall was large and wooden, with two Huckle flags lifted high on some tree branches nearby. This was the only building in the village that had steps leading up to it. It was not the same as the hall of great festivities; that was on the other side of the mountain.

Inside, intense conversation could be heard. The owl possessed outstanding hearing and could hear the discussion from its perch on the branch.

"You must travel south immediately."

Deep inside the hall, there was a large circle of leafy humps, situated like chairs, and seated upon them were the most important leaders of the Huckle clan, leaders of great valor and acclaim. They were the leading knights and advisors; wondrous legends they could recount. Many of them wore special berries upon their chests—medals that they had been awarded.

On one of the leafy humps, the voice that had just spoken was sitting. Now, so far in our tale, we have encountered some curious sights, but this was perhaps the most interesting of them all.

They were the fabled Elderberries, *Sambucus.*

These were the most ancient, wise, and mysterious berries. They had traveled all across the lands, to different Realms and places, and they had attended important meetings, councils, and gatherings with the Elders from other Realms. It was they who had first come upon Glacier and named the Realm. It was they who, along with the other Elders, helped write the Manuscripts, the rules for all the Realms. All creatures from all lands knew of them, and here they were.

They were a cluster of berries placed upon a small tree, and there were around twenty of them. These berries were not an unnatural size, dressed, or weaponized; no, they were simply a cluster of berries. Theirs was a slim branch with rather a lot of berries on it, so that the branch was somewhat crowded. They were a deep shade of purple, deeper than even the king himself (some have said that the king began to turn this color because he took in so much of the Elderberries' great wisdom).

The Elderberries just were. No one, neither the Manuscripts nor the Ancient Pines nor the mystical Wanderers of the south, knew where they had come from. They were older than the Huckles and also older than most of Glacier. Supposedly, they were the very first thing to grow in the Realm. They had begun as a small bushel of berries on the banks of Lake McDonald, from where they had watched over Glacier in its earliest days, when it was still formless and without void.

These Elders had watched dense forests appear, fires rage, rivers overflow, and, most importantly, they had seen the rise of the great Huckleberry King. The Elders had always known how important he would be to Glacier, and ever since they had come across him, they had sought to advise him. The king had met them hanging from a branch on a summer day many ages ago, and ever since, they'd been just about the only creatures that could successfully advise him.

The Elderberries did not travel much in these latter years. They were mostly found in Glacier advising the knighthood or planted in the king's great palace high atop the mountain, where there was a permanent tree reserved just for them. That tree had no other leaves or branches, just a spot for the Elderberries, the first of the Elders.

Elsewhere in the circle, important Huckles listened intently to the Elders' words.

"Where is it that we should go, O wise Elders?"

Rubus was seated on a leafy hump closest to the Elderberries. He had some idea of where to travel to, but he was nowhere near as informed as they were.

"You must go to see the Wanderers."

Vernus, also present, then spoke. He sat opposite the Elders on the other side of the circle. "The Huckles have not been to the southern Realm for over forty years. What are we to do there? What are we to say?"

Vernus had become a vocal figure at these meetings. He harbored no disrespect toward the Elders, but he was always ready to speak his mind. Likewise, the Elders did not cultivate fear or expect reverence from the Huckles, but the knights had been around for long enough to know that their advice was the soundest that they could possibly hear.

"The Wanderers will be expecting you; they feel now the ripples of the land." When the Elders spoke, it was difficult to know what to expect. It was at times a chorus of voices, at other times only one berry, but at other times they could be heard debating points with each other before they spoke. Peculiar they were, but the legendary Elders were not to be made a spectacle of, for they were most remarkable. Their voice and advice had shaped the Realm more than any, foremost by guiding and counseling the king.

"The Elders are right." Lingon spoke from the circle, more slowly than the others due to his age. He had been around for long enough to know the wisdom of the Elders. "You must travel to the great south Realm. Only the Wanderers will be able to assist us."

"And who will go with us?" A female knight named Juniper spoke up. She was one of the leading knights in the king's court and had been around for almost as long as Rubus. She was of a similar shade except for sporting a deep black patch on her skin; a birthmark.

Rubus stood up. "The king's court must go. But the road will be treacherous, and many dangers will abound," he asserted.

At this point, the Elders remained silent. Their role was to provide oversight, not engage in meticulous details, although they did so occasionally, on personal request. Instead, it was Rubus's job to inspire his knights.

"And what of the king?" Juniper asked.

Whereas Rubus was the most vocal presence now, the king in his younger days had been much more hands-on. It was only recently, since his tragedy, that he had retreated from the rest of the clan. He was even absent now, from this most important of meetings.

"The king must travel with us; he is the only one to whom the Wanderers will listen," Vernus said, and Rubus and the rest of those present nodded in agreement.

The Elders, with their wise oversight, now saw the need to speak. "The Wanderers will need proof." This particular time, they all echoed as one voice, and all were in agreement. The rest of the circle remained silent. They knew of the Wanderers, of their keeping of the Manuscripts, but the Huckles knew not how to approach them. They were like distant legends.

"What can we show them that will prove the Manuscripts can be changed?" Vernus expressed an odd moment of uncertainty. Usually, he was the most confident of them all. The circle was silent, sharing his nervousness. The Huckles looked at Rubus for leadership, but Rubus, on this occasion, had none.

"May the road take us and the path enlighten us," he said. He looked around the circle, at the brothers and sisters whom he loved abundantly. He knew not what steps to take to secure their future and way of life in Glacier, but he knew that he would give his life to preserve it. Looking up at the ceiling and then sideways at the Elders, he abruptly stood from his leafy hump, expounding in a defiant tone, "With the king's great blessings, we will leave at sun's rising."

At his words, the Huckles rose as one. They embraced one another, then left the hall and passed into the night beyond. Before leaving, they each went over to the Elders and kissed the tree that they hung from. The Elders' words had guided them through many struggles, and the Huckles believed that they would do so once more. One by one, the Huckles left, leaving just Rubus and the Elders alone.

"Take us to the king. We will inform him and advise him of what is to come," they said.

Long gone were the days when the king would interact with all of the Huckles. The Elders, and to a lesser extent Rubus, were now the only bridge between the king and the others. Rubus would have to travel up the mountain on foot in the moonlight with the Elders in hand. He carefully plucked the Elders from the branch, then walked across the empty hall, delicately balancing the mysterious berries. He then left the hall and made his way down the steps into the warm night, onto the path leading to the rest of the Huckle Village. He did not walk toward the village, but instead he made his way to the back gate.

This gate was small and narrow, and only a few knew of it or went through it. It was on the other side of the village from the great gate. On the other side was a path that went straight up to the mountain and to the palace of the king. As Rubus walked through the night, he looked up at the sky and noticed the glaring stars, the shining moon, and also a brown owl in flight above . . .

Now, as you may be aware, owls have one of the keenest senses of hearing of any creature. The very owl that earlier had been perched outside the hall had heard everything that had been discussed within, and this careful owl now swept through the night, carrying the secrets it had heard. The bird passed over a great swathe of Huckle Village before cutting through the sky to perch on an open windowsill that was part of a lonesome hut surrounded by low bushes. The inside of this humble abode consisted of only two rooms: a room for sleeping and a room for living. Inside, an anxious berry sat perched upon her bed of leaves and earth. The berry motioned to the owl, and it shifted itself along the windowsill and onto a perch by the leafy bed. As silent as the still night outside, the owl gently whispered to her the secrets that it had heard.

Once the owl had finished, it turned and darted back through the open window, feathers falling behind it as it fled. The berry sat silently, deeply pondering what had just been revealed. With the moon as high in the sky as it could be, she fell back into her bed and flooded it with flowing tears. Goji would not sleep that night, as she knew the time had come.

❧

The crowd gathered once more before the gate. Morning dew hung from the tall wooden posts as if clutching on for dear life, while songbirds darted from tree to tree, the only jubilant creatures in sight. The Huckles were far more forlorn compared to the previous day, when they had met the knights with great celebration and triumph. Everyone had known, of course, that this day was coming. Rubus and other leaders had been updating the town for weeks, but it had fallen upon them so soon.

The knights were gathered by the gate. Beyond the gate, further down the path, Morrow and the herd would meet them. All around, families wept and said their goodbyes, some more prepared than others. The swift change of emotion from the previous afternoon to this morning was not surprising. The Huckles were simple creatures, and their emotions were easily bound to the tidings of time.

This, of course, was not true for Goji, who was not a Huckle. She was more complex than them. She cut a disheveled figure at the front of the group while clutching her rumpet tightly.

"You look exhausted, Goji." Rubus stood next to her. Both of them were at the front of the group, but Goji would not speak a word to him, nor look in his direction. The owl whom she had spoken to last night was perched nearby.

Loud shouting came from behind them. "Dear friends, brothers, sisters, you have known this day was to come!" It was not Rubus but Vernus who addressed the crowd. Rubus had been giving him more responsibility as of late, perhaps preparing him for the days ahead. "We go forth from you now, but only for you!" Vernus was standing on a stump in the middle of the group of knights, flanked on either side by the crowd, much like the previous afternoon. "We will fight for our Realm, and we will carry the great name of Huckle wherever we may be!"

The crowd was lifted by Vernus, with many offering shouts of approval. "Above all, above everything, above our lives, we will serve our Realm and our king!"

At this, the crowd erupted. Huckles young and old shook off their forlorn tone to cheer and applaud. Toward the front of the group, Rubus nudged a distracted Goji in her side. Goji jolted and then reluctantly drew the rumpet to her mouth, pursing her lips. Before she blew, she glanced at the owl perched nearby. The creature twitched its head, glanced back at her, and then flew away. *Brrrrrr!* The rumpet blew. The crowd let out a great roar, and the gate began to creak open. The lower Huckle soldiers, who were waiting to become knights, would manage all of Glacier while the knights were gone. The Elderberries would guide them if need be.

Behind the crowd, beyond the fence and high above, the king's distant song emerged and began to echo through the village. He had heard the rumpet, and so had his band. They had begun their descent of the mountain. The villagers pointed at them excitedly.

"Look!"

"The king!"

Whispers and murmurs could be heard all around. The king and his band would not be passing through the village. They would travel around the entire perimeter and meet the knights on a plain beyond. Not only did the king not want to interact with the Huckle civilians, he would also most likely have squished much of the village if he passed through.

The morning dew slowly dissipated. The Glacier sun began to illuminate the gray mountains beyond, and great swathes of light covered the plains that the knights would later traverse. "Friends, we depart you this day, but stronger we shall return. To the southern Realm we travel, as the Manuscripts must be altered!"

The crowd murmured in approval. They did not fully understand that of which Vernus spoke, but they agreed anyway. "To this land, to this Realm, to Glacier we belong!"

Goji played a booming fanfare as the crowd cheered on. The king's song sounded gently in the distance, a haunting melody echoing over the mountains. The gate was now fully ajar, and the great Glacier outdoors bore itself unto the village. The path beyond the gate was still flanked by trees in glorious bloom, and joyous songbirds leapt from their branches, beckoning the knights forth.

Vernus raised his staff, and the other knights raised theirs soon after, while the Huckle civilians raised their arms. The berries stood in solidarity in their Glacier home. Far behind them, the king increased in size as he descended. The great purple blob grew larger and larger every second. Goji paused the rumpet, and all of Huckle-kind looked at Vernus.

"For Glacier; for the king!"

The crowd erupted once more, and the knights then pushed forward. As they advanced, a knights' song began, joining in harmonic melody with the distant king's song beyond.

> *We are the Huckles*
> *Huckles are we*
> *We fight every battle, all in his name*
> *To protect our great land, our beautiful plain.*

A silent Goji and Rubus led, and one by one the knights passed through the great gate, motioned on by the crowd. The journey had begun.

6

The Wanderers' Home

Now, at this point in our tale, it would be fitting to reflect on the path that we have so far traveled. You should take a look at a map of the United States and take in the enormity of the land, as well as the parks and forests within that are teeming with adventure. Not only are these lands of luscious green and desert brown waiting to be explored, they are also always seeking to cooperate with the environment in which they belong in harmonious accord. For example, Glacier is home to chilling blocks of icy glaciers, high up in the snowy mountains. These glaciers only exist because of the temperature remaining at a certain level. Likewise, in Redwood, the trees only thrive because the soil that they call home is rich and nutritious. If the soil was altered, ruined, or changed, the trees may not be able to grow so majestically tall.

It is our job as adventurers and explorers to help maintain this harmonious balance. If you ever visit a national park, you should remember to follow the way of the land, rather than have the land do your bidding. The creatures, the woods, and the rocks want you to enjoy their home, but not at any cost. Their equilibrium is our responsibility, a duty we must willfully uphold.

Now, the very purpose of our tale is to tell how these parks came to be; exactly what it was that drove these forces of balance. The creatures—the Huckles, the Trees, Morrow, and the Elders—recognized the beauty of their homeland, the Realms of majestic mystery and beauty. Even before you or I were able to lay eyes on the daring peaks, the rolling plains, and the open skies of these lands, before they were known as parks, the creatures sought to protect and preserve them.

However, at this point, and where we will continue after this brief interlude, we will encounter an example of when that delicate harmony was at breaking point. The Huckles and the Trees had spent years bickering and arguing over discrepancies; they had debated the role of other animals in the Realms, debated the use of land, and debated which parts of the Great Outdoors should be considered Realms and which shouldn't. Their disagreements affected the creatures of all Realms because their influence was so widely felt. If the Redwoods stopped having their councils and stopped chairing the High Tree gathering at Yosemite, Trees everywhere would suffer. Similarly, if the Huckles felt ignored, Glacier would suffer. When one of the Realms suffered, they all did. That was the nature of the Realms then, and it is the nature of the parks now; they all have an important place and role to fill, and they rely on each other. The Ancient Pines and the Elderberries had attempted to bridge this increasing divide, but the Redwoods and Huckles kept straying from their guidance.

You may be wondering why such disagreements occurred between them, considering that their Realms were so far apart. Well, the Realms, and the parks now, are all interconnected in some way, even if they are completely different. Also, news travels fast in nature, and the migrating birds and beasts carried news to California of the Huckles' plans. Also, the Huckles' disagreements had begun with the Trees in Montana before they had escalated, and thereafter, the Huckles only saw one solution. They had to travel to the home of the Wanderers and edit the Manuscripts.

The Manuscripts had successfully kept all of the Realms in order for many years, but the problem was that no one could have foreseen the alarming size to which the Huckles would grow and how their influence would spread. To the Huckles and the king, the Manuscripts were outdated. They were too rigid; they needed to change, as nature had changed. Indeed, national parks change even now, and we must adapt and respect their growth. But the Trees believed the Huckles would overstep their boundary, altering the Manuscripts in a way that overly benefited them and Glacier. The Huckles, however, believed the Trees to be archaic in their traditions and thinking and that their old age mired new decisions that had to be made. They simply had to come to some sort of agreement, both for their sakes and for the sake of all the Realms.

Such an agreement would no doubt be difficult, considering the long, arduous history between them. In order to understand that long and important history, we must venture into the story of one of the foremost characters in our tale, whom we have not previously had enough time to truly meet. To understand the tumultuous struggles of the Realms in this age, we must take a deeper look into the life of that legendary berry, the Huckleberry King himself.

"Stop!" Vernus bellowed to the herd, who were pacing on at a terrific speed. The king's court, the cluster, and all of Morrow's herd were in the southern region of the state of Montana. Nowadays, there is a city near their location called Bozeman (for any wishing to track their journey on a map). Outside of Glacier, Montana was flat and fair. The dramatic peaks and dense woods were replaced by long, swaying prairies, and grass and golden grain were abundant. Although it was no longer Glacier, it was still a glorious land.

Up ahead, Vernus had noticed a blockade. The Huckles did not experience such difficulties in Glacier itself, as none would dare, but seemingly, some folk here wished to restrict their passage forth.

"Who do you think that may be?" A radiant Juniper pulled alongside Vernus. Both of them were perched on the edge of a small hill, looking down at the blockade below. Golden grains of barley danced in between them and the mischievous figures.

"I do not know, Juniper. But they do not seem to revere our presence."

Vernus was quite right. Back home in Glacier, the creatures would have either humbly bowed or rapidly dispersed at the sight of the Huckles. These figures, though, were unmoved.

"What's going on, brother?" Rubus joined the two. The triumvirate of knights were now majestically poised upon the hill.

"These folks do not bid us safe passing," said Vernus.

"Can you see who they are?"

"No, we are too far away, but they look rather large."

Indeed, the figures were bigger than usual folk, and they were certainly bigger than most woodland creatures.

"Let us go down," Rubus said.

Rubus signaled to the rest, motioning for them to hold position. The graceful cow upon which he was riding carefully selected her steps as she descended. Vernus and Juniper followed behind. As they drew closer, the figures ahead grew larger and larger. The knights began to see that they were creating a long line across the green plain, and on either side of them, the hillside was steep and difficult, meaning that the figures were blocking the only path onward.

The Huckles slowly approached while emerald leaves blew hastily across the plain.

"I think they are . . ."

"Trees." Juniper spoke in a foreboding manner. The Huckles then knew that this would not be a straightforward situation. The further they strayed from their Glacier home, which they had already begun to dearly miss, the more the Trees grew hostile.

"I'll handle this," said Rubus. He gently patted his cow, named Sika, and she responded by increasing her speed to a gentle gallop, her hooves effortlessly pounding the soft floor below. Rubus drew near the Trees.

"Greetings, fine Trees. May I ask your purpose here?"

The creatures of the Realms often asked each other about their purpose, as they knew this was the ordering of every Realm.

"Be gone, Huckle. We have orders not to let you pass." They responded as one voice, and a sweeping gust of leaves blew past as their raspy tone sounded across the plain.

"From whom do these orders come?"

"From the great Trees of the south and the High One, Hyperion."

Rubus listened intently. His desire was to keep peace between creatures as long as it could be kept. "We mean no harm to you or to Hyperion or to creatures in any Realm."

"It matters not what your intentions are, Huckle; you are not welcome to pass southward. Now be gone."

The Trees stood ominously firm. They were aspen trees, *Populus tremula*. They had long thin white trunks dotted with chunks of brown, with high green leaves. They were only around forty feet high, but that was much taller than Rubus.

"I can only reason with you for so long, dear creatures. There is one who journeys with me who will not bear it."

The Trees shook from side to side, seemingly an act of laughter. They would not be threatened by the small (to them) berries. Rubus looked back toward Vernus and Juniper, who were waiting anxiously atop the hill. Rubus did not have to say anything to communicate with them. Vernus had spent enough years with his commander to read him; they had a special connection between berries. Understanding the situation, Vernus signaled back toward the court, who had all been waiting, puzzled. He wanted them to wait a while longer while Rubus tried to reason, but he and Juniper knew that it was only a matter of time.

"Listen, Trees, our business is not with you. We wish to travel south, and we will harm none along the way."

"You are not in Glacier anymore, Huckle. Your words are meaningless here. You wish to dictate where we shall grow and how the Realms may exist! This shall not be. Now be gone!"

The Trees had had enough. They shook violently before twisting their thickest branches and launching a plume of leaves in Rubus's direction. The leaves shot past him like fierce hail, and some pounded his entire upper half. A mighty *whoosh* and a terrible wind swept the leaves into a tremendous cyclone. Had Rubus not had years of experience and tales to tell, he may very well have turned back. But he knew exactly what would happen next.

As the cyclone quietened, the leaves slowly drifted to the ground like gentle Glacier snow. Had it been any other situation, it may have appeared like a summer forest clearing, a woodland wedding, or a gentle celebration among Tree and woodland folk. But alas, the Trees had simply held back momentarily, awaiting Rubus's response.

It was not Rubus that moved, however. He remained perfectly still, gazing carefully at the unfriendly Trees. Behind the commander, a looming shadow emerged from the falling leaves, and the confidence of the aspens seemed to be sucked out of them. A deep thumping replaced the cyclone as the figure drew closer and closer, his shadow now engulfing them all. Rubus, still gazing at the trees, noticed a gentle purple mist waft past him and toward the Trees. The aspens, now seemingly shrunken, seemed to be searching for words, but any would have been cut short by the shrill song that began to emerge.

Dum dum dum, off with his head

The king had had quite enough of the delay. As you may have gathered by now, his patience was remarkably thin. Rubus stood perfectly still as the king made his way past Vernus and then, in a few strides, past him. The cows looked up at the king in amazement, wide-eyed and transfixed.

The king is purple, the king is not red

The Trees, who had initially shot their leaves violently toward Rubus, now seemed to be shedding leaves out of fear as the king's shadow blotted out the afternoon sun.

Dum dum dum, oh do you know why

The king's band stood just below the edge of the hill, some thirty feet away from Vernus and Juniper, and the troll drummers stayed back with the remaining knights for fear of squishing all around. Too many giant berries in one place simply wouldn't work. Once he had stopped and his shadow had been cast over the entire plain, the great king stood before the Trees. He towered above them, wielding his mighty staff in one hand while the other hung ominously by his side. The golden plain of grain was now eerily silent, and the Huckles on the hill became a hushed audience. If the Trees had had full capability of movement, they would have no doubt been looking at one another and flailing in a dire state of confusion. However, they could merely shake more leaves from their branches, attempting to look as strong as possible.

"Listen, Huckle King, the great Hyperion has ordered—" The Trees' desperate plea was cut violently short by the choir.

For one single pie, several children had to die!

With a thunderous crash on the final word, the king's left arm rose and clattered into the helpless Trees. Such was the force of the mighty blow that they were wiped out with a single stroke. The king may have appeared slow due to his awesome size, but he delivered the devastating stroke with incredible ferocity. The Trees were powerless to resist. They groaned and creaked as they fell sideways to the floor, all four of them falling at similar speeds. The roots that had anchored them to the ground so faithfully for years now gave way under the king's mighty arm. As they hit the ground, the last of their leaves were thrashed into the air. Those were the last leaves these aspens would ever produce.

The king said nothing. He simply gazed down at the felled creatures as if they had never been. The Huckles behind were also silent, and as the king turned to make his way back to the court, his song filled the air once more:

Dum dum dum, he is the king
All those in Glacier must bow to him.

He walked back in great strides and stopped briefly to look upon Rubus, who had watched the whole thing unfold. There was no conversation between the two, nor a Huckle's embrace. He glared down at Rubus like a disappointed father, aggrieved that he had had to intervene. The two had once shared a much closer bond, but since the king's tragedy, they had drifted apart.

Onward he then marched, past Vernus, Juniper, and the rest of the Huckle Knights. They were silently traumatized. Perhaps the only creature present who could stomach such tragedy idly was Morrow, who had a fierce resolve. Even he, however, would not engage in such merciless acts. He looked stonily at the plain, focusing on the path ahead. As the king reached the court, he resumed his position, surrounded on all sides by the troll drummers and some other knights carrying flags adorned with the Huckle crest. Before he gave the order to continue, he mustered three words in his mighty booming voice, the kind of voice that sinks deep into the soul. He looked at no one but gruffly declared, "Pick them up."

The king's troll drummers knew that the message was for them. Only they had the strength, after all, to lift and move the Trees out of their path. Once they had done so, Vernus, Juniper, and Rubus led the way forth, and they all continued in silence across the golden plain. The wind, grass, and swaying grain seemed to join this silence in awe of what had transpired. The Trees had been felled. The king had struck and forged their path onward.

❧

The Huckles rode on till sunset. It was almost three days since they had left Glacier, and they were growing weary. They had reached the very border of Montana, close to the state of Wyoming. Wyoming was a state of wondrous treasures and, most importantly, the place where the great Wanderers had made their home. The Huckles wanted to be at full strength before they met them.

Close to nightfall, the three leading knights scouted a small lake ahead. The Huckles felt at home near lakes, and they missed the lakes of Glacier dearly whenever they left. Rubus soon found an empty clearing by the lakeside, a good enough spot for the Huckles to rest for the night. He rode back through the cool afternoon and led the others to the campsite. Once they had all arrived at the campsite, some knights took Morrow and the herd to fetch some leaves in the forest nearby, and the Huckles then sat by the waterside, watching the sun fade into the western horizon as they shared tales and memories of Glacier summers past. They laughed the evening away, resting their weary feet and replenishing their seed hearts with the lake's cool whisper. The band played gentle melodies for the resting knights, the sounds wafting over the waters and creating small ripples.

Some way away from the merry chorus of Huckles, the king sat alone by the water. The troubled berry gazed into the deep lake, taking no notice of his kin. The king had struggled with his thoughts ever since the fateful day, and he could no longer process with others around. He had become more and more reclusive as time went by, no longer connecting with the nature surrounding him. Whereas before, he would have felt the lake upon which he gazed, it was now only empty water staring back at him. As the sun continued to fade, the king slowly fell into a lifeless trance, his great berry eyes lulling him aslumber until his thoughts transcended . . .

The king launched himself from branch to branch, a young berry of immense strength. He had the confidence of all the land, and there was much that he had yet to explore. It seemed that he would stop at nothing to pursue his desire and goal: liberating the Huckles from the persecutions of the past. On his travels, he had encountered beasts great and small, and he had conversed with many, listening to the stories and wisdom from ancient folk: bison, elk, and eagles. The king grew in knowledge with each passing year, growing in understanding of each Realm into which he ventured.

"Slow down!" A sweet voice beckoned from below.

The king looked below briefly and then laughed and launched himself with immense power onto the next branch. His strength seemed to know no bounds.

"You need to keep up, Bramble!"

The Huckle to whom he spoke was climbing far slower than he, a distant figure amidst the matrix of branches beneath.

"We can't all be super-berries, you know!"

"Ha! Perhaps I can grant you some of my power!"

Of course, he couldn't, but the king knew the weight of responsibility that his power brought. He knew that the rest of Huckle-kind relied on him in some way.

"Just slow down!"

The king quietly chuckled before settling down on a thick branch. He had to rest his feet on two branches on either side, as one alone would surely have snapped. Grinning contentedly, he leaned back against the trunk, looking toward the canopy above.

"I'm waiting . . ." He almost whistled the words, playfully mocking his distant follower. Slowly, the Huckle beneath clambered up the branches, carefully plotting her path to the king. She slipped a couple of times before eventually finding her way through the maze of branches, resting on a thick branch beneath him. "Out of breath, are you?" He was most amused. Indeed, Bramble was panting and taking deep breaths after the arduous climb. She was a beautiful rose shade of red but unique among Huckles in that she also glowed radiant shades of pink. Such was the blend of red and pink that she looked like a jubilant bouquet of flowers.

In Bramble, the king saw the loveliest of Huckles, and he had never seen a more beautiful creature than her. It had been a number of years now that they had spent in each other's company, and they had married last summer in a glorious woodland ceremony.

"I'll be okay. Just give me a minute."

The branches stood firm as they supported the Huckles, despite their awesome size. The king was now around fifty feet high, though clearly still growing, and the more he learnt about all things, the more he grew. Bramble herself was also quite large, around thirty feet high. Supposedly, she had grown just so she could match the king in height.

Love was not an emotion that the Huckles knew exactly what to do with. They focused mainly on living within Glacier and enjoying the land, but occasionally, the irresistible tide of love swept over them too. The king and Bramble had been swept like no other berries. In all of Glacier and all of the Huckle clan, there were no two berries fonder of each other than they. The king loved Bramble, and Bramble loved him.

"There's a great view up here," said the king.

"You're only a few branches higher than me!" she replied.

"Well, there's space for you," he said.

Bramble smirked at the king before making her way up some remaining branches and resting on a thick branch nearer him. The two berries were alone high in the woods. They had climbed the tree to share a view of Glacier from on high. It was a blustery September, so the green leaves were still present but biding their time. The berries looked at one another and laughed. Their laughter shook the frightened branches on which they stood, but they held firm.

"Well, we should get a bit higher, don't you think?" Bramble smiled, her searching eyes wandering into the king's deep mind. In all of his growing, learning, and strengthening, his greatest prize was his companionship with Bramble, and there was nothing he valued more. The flattered king puffed out his chest, then slightly crouched down, preparing to launch himself up once more.

"Onward for Glacier!" He lurched upward at a dramatic speed, leaving Bramble once more behind.

"Hey!" she called after him.

The king laughed loudly as he soared upward, sending leaves and small twigs flying beneath him.

"Get back here, your highness!"

Bramble was not one to fall for the king's tough veneer, as she knew the real berry within.

"Just a little further," the king muttered under his breath as he continued to climb. He wanted Bramble to have the best view possible. He finally rested on a thinner branch higher up, just strong enough to support his weight. Thoughtfully, he then cleared the branch nearest to him for her, and by the time he had finished, Bramble had caught up once more.

She cast him a daring glance before sitting on her prepared branch. Beyond them, the great Glacier horizon was the perfect setting, an image of tranquil harmony. Bold green trees and gentle lakes cut through the plush land, while occasional mountains of blue poked high into the hazy afternoon. The Realm was their playground, the perfect place for them both.

"Well, your highness, isn't this quite the picture?" she said.

"Indeed," he replied.

"Say, how high do you think we are?"

"Too high for you." He gave her a gentle nudge. Bramble giggled.

"Well, I guess I should thank you for leading me up here, your majesty," she said.

"Yes, that you should."

If berries could roll their eyes, that's precisely what Bramble would have done. She gave the king a sideways glance before playfully nudging him back, but the king absorbed her nudge like a thick rock. They sat for a while, losing themselves in the majestic horizon before them.

Bramble spoke, interrupting the silent evening. "Look, an eagle!"

"Where?" The king twisted his head sharply. He had a great fondness for eagles and desired to know them more deeply, but alas, the king was gazing into an empty sky. Bramble burst into laughter.

"Ha! The great king fooled! Two can play at your games."

The king remained silent, although he couldn't help but smile at Bramble's playful gesture. The two laughed at the situation before falling into silence once more.

"Hey . . . thanks," she said.

"For what?"

"Bringing me up here." She looked at him before extending her intertwined thin limbs toward his. As silver streams glistened far down below, the two berries twisted their limbs around one another, as trees wrapped their roots. They gazed into each other's eyes endearingly before turning back to the horizon beyond. There they would rest for hours, their limbs wrapped and intertwined.

"My pleasure," said the king.

For many hours, until the orange sun sank into the Glacier mountains, the berries rested in each other's embrace. The Tree felt them as they lay still upon it. At this time, before their unfortunate disagreements, the Trees were aware of the Huckles, and the Huckles knew that the Trees were important. But at this moment, all that mattered to the king was that the Tree supported him and Bramble, whom he loved very much. The berries occasionally turned and looked at one another, but mostly they stared at the wondrous Glacier land. They were content in each other's presence.

Night time came. Nocturnal owls could be heard hooting amidst the branches beneath, and at long last, the loving berries decided that it was time to leave.

"We should get going." Bramble sounded reluctant but looked forward to their next adventure together. He nodded, and slowly they unwrapped their tangled limbs.

"We should come up here again sometime," Bramble said sweetly. She was most grateful.

"Oh well, why not? Anywhere in Glacier, I can take you there," said the king.

Bramble rolled her eyes once more. "Let's get going, *O great one*."

She slowly began to descend, retracing her steps from earlier. The branches stood firm in the purple night.

"Careful now. There is not much light to be a lamp unto our path," the king warned.

Indeed, it was very dark now in the forest, and the moon was only a thin crescent, its power subdued.

"Well, my king, if you can lead me up with such speed, maybe I'll be the one to lead us down," Bramble said, smiling back at him. The king could not see his love, but he could feel her warm smile upon him.

"Down we go, then," he said.

The crescent moon hung high over the canopy, and distant stars reflected the meek light. The Huckles descended the Tree, retracing the steps they had taken upward. The occasional branch snapped, shattering the silent night.

"So, where shall we go next?" said Bramble. As she spoke, she looked up at her love longingly.

"Well, there's this mountain further north. I've always liked the look of it."

"And what would you do on this mountain?" She was intrigued.

"It's quite a large mountain. I thought I could build a home on it."

"A home? On a mountain? I don't want to live on a mountain!"

"Well, maybe you can wait at the bottom," he joked.

If it had not been so dark, perhaps Bramble would have thrown herself upon him in a playful tussle in reply to his humor.

"No, but I mean really, from up there on the mountain, I can see all of Glacier," the king continued.

"And?"

"I will be able to see to it that the rest of the Huckles are safe, of course."

"Well, yes, I suppose you would." She paused thoughtfully. "You know, you really do have a caring seed."

"It is my duty to protect and preserve our great Realm!" He puffed out his chest once more, adjusting his voice to sound deeper than it really was. Bramble chuckled as she felt down below with her feet for a steady branch.

"As I told you, dear king, you may be tough and strong before the whole kingdom, but kno—"

"Shh!" The king came to a sudden, abrupt stop. He grasped the very trunk of the tree, its bark collapsing due to his strength. Bramble stopped too, sensing his urgency.

"Do you hear that?" he asked.

"Hear what?"

"I think it's—"

"Wait a minute." Bramble began to sniff, and her nostrils twitched uncomfortably. "I think I can smell—"

"Fire," the king interrupted.

The king could hear it, and Bramble could smell it. A wildfire had started close by, and it was rapidly drawing closer to the Tree.

Bramble sounded panicked. "Maybe the wind has carried it from elsewhere. Perhaps we should just go down and head back."

"No." The king had spent many years among the dangers of the Great Outdoors and within the Realms. He had developed an acute awareness of the risks that the forest posed. Fire was no friend.

"Come, Bramble, we have to head back up."

"Back up? Why?"

"We will never make it down. The fire is closer than you think."

Bramble was the only berry that knew his friendly side, but she also knew him well enough to sense his urgency and realize when his advice should be taken.

"What . . . what will we do at the top?" She now began to tremble nervously, her speech intermittent. Her gentle eyes twinkled in the dark.

"I'll call out to the eagles. Now come, we must go." The king began his ascent of the Tree once more, but this time, he made sure Bramble passed him first. "Just keep going upward, Bramble."

Bramble stumbled as she ascended, as her feet were not as swift as his. Further upward, she gasped as a great *whoosh* flashed past them; a multitude of beating wings.

"What was that?" She sounded increasingly panicked.

"Just birds. They are escaping."

Indeed, the woodland had collapsed into a state of panic. Creatures on the forest floor scurried hurriedly across the leaves in a frantic state of confusion.

The berries soon reached the earlier plateau on which they had interlocked their limbs. Bramble stopped momentarily, pausing to catch her breath. "How much higher?"

"As high as we can go."

"The branches will not hold us for much longer." Bramble was right. The higher they climbed, the thinner the branches became. Taking note of her advice, the king looked around, into the woodland night.

"Eagles!" he belted at the top of his voice. He knew no special chant or call, but the forest knew him; they knew his voice. Someone would come. "If there is much smoke, it may take them some time to find us," he said, mainly trying to reassure Bramble. Bramble just continued to pant, still catching her breath. "Let us climb a bit higher. Perhaps it will be clearer for them," the king said.

The Huckles desperately scampered up the increasingly thin branches, but down below, a fierce roaring began to sound from the forest floor. Bramble looked down through the Tree. Sharp embers wafted through the crowded forest, and pinpricks of orange and fiery red floated invasively through the dark woodland. The fire had reached them. Bramble, not as athletic as the king, began to feel nauseous as the embers drifted by. "My head . . ." she complained.

"Come on, Bramble. Just a little higher."

Bramble lifted her arm to her brow, wiping beads of sweat off her troubled forehead. She took a few more precious steps before a branch violently snapped beneath her feet.

"Bramble!"

The branch crashed through the forest, colliding with others as it fell to its doom.

"Just a bit higher, Bramble!"

"I can't," she whimpered.

The fumes had encumbered her. The king looked up at her, then down to the forest floor. Violent tongues of flame were licking the helpless trunks. There was not a soul around in the forest; the normally vibrant community was desolate and long gone. The sickly crackling of fire could be heard seeping through the trees, all the while eating up branches and woodland foliage. The king knew that they had not much time left.

"Come on, I'll take you!" He took some frantic steps downward toward his beloved, who was now cowering in the heat. Courageously, the king wrapped his bulging arm around her shoulders and began to drag her toward the ever-distant canopy. "You'll have to take your steps, Bramble."

She nodded faintly. As the king used all his might to drag her upward, Bramble weakly lifted her legs toward the next branch, each step more painstaking than the last. The king proceeded upward with a mighty resolve, mustering every ounce of strength within him to rescue her. The Huckleberry King heaved and groaned as he ascended, and Bramble's head hung toward the forest floor. She had no hope without his help.

The fire raged fearlessly below. Violent flames danced higher and higher as luminescent sparks scattered through the dark. As they struggled on, a branch creaked beneath their feet. The king had to place both of them on one branch at times, and they threatened to give way.

"Eagles!" he anxiously screamed into the night. Very rarely had he known such desperation.

As the branches continued to creak, he knew that they could not go much higher. Bramble's eyes fluttered, closing momentarily. "Stay awake, my love!" His eyes had begun to tear up, and he felt a great deep ache in his innermost being. Far off in the night, the shrill cry of a gray wolf could be heard, a victim of the raging fire. The frantic king found a stable set of branches some way closer to the top of the canopy, and he knew that he had reached as high as they could go. His wild eyes searched the skies above for some source of salvation. Around them, smaller trees toppled over, capitulating to the blaze, and tall pillars of smoke began to cloud the horizon.

"I . . ." Bramble mustered all her strength to try to speak, her mouth quivering all the time.

"What is it, Bramble?" The king used his spare arm to cradle Bramble's head, lifting her up to speak.

"Water . . ."

"We will make it out of here. The eagles will be here any minute." The king began to sob gently. Great blobs of water rolled down his purple face, saturating Bramble's fair body below. He stroked her head with his other hand. For a moment, he forgot that they were surrounded by grave danger. All that mattered was that she was in his arms.

"My dear . . ."

"Yes?" The king wiped away his tears, trying to stay strong for her.

"The palace on the mountain . . ."

He stared at her, trying to make out her muffled words.

"It's a great idea."

The king nodded, treasuring every precious moment.

"You're a great king. I lov . . ."

The king's weeping grew. The painful swelling within him began to take hold, and he knew not how much longer he could bear to hold her in this state. "We're going to be okay."

A mighty screech pierced the suffocating night air. There are only a few screeches that can cut through rain, fire, or storm. One of those is the screech of the eagle, one of the mightiest creatures ever known. They are the champions of the skies. The king turned his head rapidly. The piercing screech had pulled a blanket of hope over his shattering heart. A bald eagle, *Haliaeetus leucocephalus*, was gliding toward the helpless berries.

The eagle knew no fear. He glided confidently through the night, his spectacular eyes scanning the scene before him. There were a few creatures in all Realms that the king knew his greatness could perhaps never surpass, only match. This eagle was very much his equal. Even now, in the most fearsome of nights, his lightning-yellow beak and talons and his stunning white head could be clearly seen.

"Eagle, over here!"

This eagle was named Pry, and he had heard the king's cry. He cut through the night toward the Tree on which they were perched and hovered effortlessly nearby. The king could make out his great size and plumage, even in the midst of the fire, and was deeply in awe of the wondrous creature.

"King Huckle, we have heard your cry." Pry spoke with a high pitch, but his voice was still most clear and striking. It defied the crackling fire. As he spoke, Pry's eyes flickered, reflecting the blazing fire.

"Thank you, great eagle. We need to get her out." The king nodded his head toward Bramble, who was drifting in and out of consciousness. Pry glared with his piercing eyes at the berries, his fantastic mind whirling and working. He then flew slightly back from the Tree and lifted his fearsome head toward the dim stars. The eagle let out an incredible screech that filled the air and drowned out the crackling fire. Had there been no fire, perhaps all of Glacier would have heard the cry; even the stars seemed within the mighty bird's reach.

The king cradled Bramble with his fierce arms as firmly as could be, then, deep in the night, the beating of wings could be heard. Through the black smoke, four more eagles joined Pry, hovering near him. Pry turned to the birds and issued clear commands. Such a gathering was rare for the legendary creatures; they mostly traveled the skies alone. Only Pry could beckon a group of them.

He then glided back toward the Tree, his puncturing eyes glistening ever brighter. "We will form a chain to carry you both out, but we must be quick." More branches snapped and fell below as he spoke. The fire was climbing higher and higher, swallowing the young Tree as it rose.

"My branch is firm and the Tree is young; it should hold us," the king said. The king was relying on the Tree's strength to hold him. The Tree itself felt great pain but did not express this to outsiders. Its roots quivered and shrunk from the welting heat.

Decisively, Pry raised one of his powerful wings and swept forward. The swoop of the eagle is one of the most unstoppable forces of any creature, and a rushing wind blew through his contour feathers as he sliced through the smoke. Pry drew close enough to grab the berries, but a virulent flame slapped the tree between them so that the fearless eagle was forced back. He let out a piercing screech once more.

The flames did not abate, and a scorching wall of fire blazed between them. The king looked down at Bramble, whose eyes were now fully closed. He wept greatly. "Oh, Bramble, we are nearly there." The branch beneath them began to creak. The king let out a sullen cry as he put one arm around the tree trunk. Using all of his knowledge and wisdom, the king spoke to the Tree, searching its innermost being, placing his faith in its strength. "Hold us, O Tree."

The branch creaked and groaned once more.

"Hold us!"

The branch could bear no more, and slowly it gave way. It snapped and buckled, tumbling down toward the blazing inferno. Bramble and the king sunk toward the fire. The king was knocked out cold as he crashed into a lower branch, which creaked as it received him but just about held firm.

Bramble, however, tumbled past the king and fell down below.

Her beautiful shade of pink and red glowed as it sunk through the forest, and her fair berry tone flashed through the night. The forest could sense the fall. The Tree's roots cried out. Deep inside him, even though he was out cold, the king's seed heart cracked down the middle, splintering and separating. Beyond the forest and in the night sky above, the solemn stars twinkled down.

Pry had heard the fall from the other side of the fire and knew he had no more time to waste. He signaled to the others, indicating to them to hold their formation. The courageous bird then shot forward at devastating speed, closing his eyes as he ruptured the wall of fire. He kept his eyes tightly shut as he passed but showed not an ounce of fear. As he reached the trunk on the other side, some of his great feathers were singed, and the sweltering heat began to ensnare even him.

He opened his eyes and looked around. Beneath him was the king, lying flat with his eyes shut. Pry dived toward him, his sharp beak piercing twigs and leaves. None other could have seen the forest floor at this time, as it was engulfed in flames and ash, but Pry's eyes sparkled as he locked his vision past the king and onto Bramble down below. No other creature would ever lay eyes on her again.

Swooping downward, he perched near the king, a great lump of a figure laid out on the long branch. Pry normally would not have attempted such a feat, but now he had little choice. The eagles' great minds are not clouded by many misjudgments, but often, it is their courage that leads them to untoward decisions. Pry summoned everything within him and shoved his head underneath the king's enormous torso, enough to prop it forward. With a magnificent thrust, he then burst underneath the king, his snowy white head appearing on the other side. The king was now laid upon the back of the awesome bird.

The fire crackled and continued to rage. Above the tree, Pry could make out the faint screeches of his companions. He did not want them to come in after him, so he knew what he had to do. The fantastic creature summoned everything within him to extend his powerful wings, and then strained and struggled as he became airborne. Pain and agony ached deep with every wingbeat. Not only was the incredible weight of the king weighing Pry down, the tremendous heat was sapping his strength.

He reached the wall of fire, and with a tremendous cry, he passed through as fast as his wings would carry him. He let out a searing screech of pain as he left the tree behind, his majestic head now covered in soot and ash. Some Trees who were blessed enough not to catch fire in the forest that day say they still remember the screech of the eagle as he mustered all that was within him.

Pry's companions shot toward him in a uniform sweep. Once he had passed the wall of fire, his strength left him. His eyes closed and his wings gave way. The king slid off Pry's tired back down through the night as the eagle fell above him. The creatures tore through the sky, legendary figures of the ancient Realms plummeting toward the fire. Such was the majesty of the falling creatures that even the raging inferno seemed to pause, paying respect to the awesome beings.

The other eagles watched, then separated with military precision and began to act. One swept toward Pry and clasped her talons tightly around his neck and legs before shooting back upward. Pry hung motionless in his companion's grasp, clumps of his plume feathers slowly drifting to the ground. The others gathered under the king, who was falling at a great speed. Two of the birds draped their wings over the third, so that they all connected, creating a bridge-like structure. They then assumed a perfect formation before catching the giant berry.

The impact initially pushed them downward, but eventually, they rose as one. Their strength and might was enough to carry the burden. The eagles met in the sky and then let out a final piercing screech, a victorious message to the night, to be heard by the moon and stars. The wondrous birds had executed a feat that no other creature could.

They left and began flying east, sharply focused on the way ahead, and as they disappeared into the black night, the Tree from which Pry had rescued the king fell slowly to the ground, crashing onto the forest floor. Bright sparks twizzled toward the sky and illuminated the night. There passed Bramble, the Huckle Queen.

༺ঌ

The eagles arrived at the village at the sun's first light, exhausted from the long flight. As they flew closer to the gate, the male Huckle in the watchtower blew the rumpet loudly. Huckles poured out of wooden huts, awoken from their slumber. It had been a worrisome night, since it was realized that the king and Bramble were not at home. A certain Huckle had paced around the entire night, his mind whirling and his heart aching.

The great birds circled above, scanning for a suitable landing place. As they spiraled closer and closer to a large grassy part of the village, every Huckle below could see that something was wrong. The female carrying Pry laid him down gently on the grass. He was as motionless as when she had caught him. The other birds landed with similar precision but arranged themselves so as to slide the king off their backs.

Gasps and cries echoed from the watching Huckles.

"The king!"

"He is hurt!"

The certain berry sprinted over to a companion eagle whose name was Soar.

"What happened?"

"A great calamity, dear berry. Our thoughts are with you."

The Huckle looked back and forth between the king and the eagle, confusion and anxiety pulsing through him. Aside from them, the other eagles were grooming and tending to Pry, who had started to come to, albeit clearly shaken. His sharp eyes appeared bewildered and deflated, and his radiant feathers were singed and scorched. Many Huckles around the scene had begun to cry.

"Where is Bramble?" the certain Huckle asked.

Soar looked at the ground, sinking her head in solemn silence. The Huckle's face contorted in great pain and anguish. Three times he struck his own head out of frustration, kicking at the grass below. "How?" The Huckle struck a delicate tone between anger and inquiry. Whatever had happened, he knew that it was not the eagles that were to be blamed.

"Rub . . ." The king quietly uttered broken syllables, his confident, booming voice subdued to a whisper. He painfully rolled onto his side, getting a better view of the most esteemed berry who had come to him. Rubus ran to his side.

"What . . . what has occurred, O great king? How is it that such misfortune has befallen you?" He spoke with disbelief and uncertainty. The king had barely ever been wrestled to the ground before, so the current circumstance was beyond recognition.

"The Tr . . ."

The Huckle leaned in closer to hear his king, who winced in pain after every utterance. "The Tree, Rubus; it let us fall." The king's eyes closed once more; his seed heart splintered and cracked.

The king shot up violently from his sleep. He had not encountered this darkest of nightmares for some time. Sleeping by the lake and being on the road brought back painful sights, sounds, and senses, particularly spurred by the encounter with the Trees earlier on. As he looked around, he saw that the whole lakeside was flanked by sleeping Huckles, and some way back, closer to the woods, the elks were curled up tight.

The lake was a still glass of black, the occasional ripples catching a sliver of silver glow from the moon's embrace. The king took a series of deep breaths before lying down once more. Inside his heart, he felt the aching pain of his split seed. It ached with a deep welling pain whenever this nightmare occurred. He then knew that sleep would evade him for the rest of the night. Until the sun's rising, he drifted in and out, with his mind and heart troubled beyond what any berry could have ever thought to endure.

The sun rose blissfully, and the lake was slowly warmed from its cold moonlit trance. The herd had been awake for some time, and their gentle hooves sifted through the morning dew in the near part of the woods as they gracefully foraged and sorted through any leaves that they could find. Morrow strutted back and forth alongside them, standing guard. Elsewhere, some Huckles were gradually rising, while some were still fast asleep.

Some way from the others, a lonely someone was sitting on a log, a distant figure of isolation. She was spotted by an early rising Huckle, Logan, who often woke early to physically train before the day. He wanted to be the best knight he could be. Wondering what troubled the lonesome berry, Logan walked in her direction, leaving the sleeping Huckles behind him. There was little arrangement to their sleeping situation. Some pointed up, some down, and some even appeared to be sleeping upside down. They do not suffer the same restraints during sleeping as you and I, and they make sure to take full advantage of it.

From her log, the grief-stricken berry noticed Logan's advance and quickly wiped her teary eyes clean.

"Hey, good morning." Logan opened the conversation in a troubled tone. He saw no reason why a berry could be so sad in such a beautiful setting. They all missed Glacier, but they had the utmost confidence that they would return, so the way Logan saw it, they should enjoy the Great Outdoors while they could.

"Hey," the berry replied in an exasperated manner. She had not expected to meet anyone this early, let alone engage in conversation. She had been embracing the time alone, and, like the king, she had not slept much. Logan approached cautiously.

While the lonesome berry was in a state of grief, she was not one to be dismissive or cold, and even now, she exuded the sweetest of auras. Sniffling and wiping away a few more tears, she shuffled along her log, inviting Logan to join her. He sat down slowly and then let out a long breath into the morning air. He looked out at the lake before turning to her.

"How's it going?"

"Erm, I'm just enjoying some alone time."

Logan paused. "You seem sad." He looked back at the lake and cleared his throat before continuing. "I'm Logan."

The berry forced a gentle smile. "Yes. The knights have spoken about you. They say you are quite the prodigy."

Logan chuckled, not sure how to direct the conversation further. She, however, was happy to direct the conversation away from her.

"And who are you?"

"I'm Goji."

Logan's eyes widened. He had no idea he had been speaking to an important musician.

"Wow, it's . . . it's great to finally meet you!"

Most of the knights had already met Goji, but Logan was early in his tenure and had not yet had the chance. Once again, she briefly smiled before speaking. "Yes, well, I'm sorry it's in this manner, Logan." She wiped her eyes once more, slightly embarrassed by the situation.

The two of them looked out at the lake. The sun continued its steady rise as the semi-sleeping Huckles tossed and turned back at the campsite.

"Well, isn't it beautiful out here!"

"It is."

"Then why is your soul downcast?"

Goji paused for a moment, wondering how much she wanted to divulge. The truth was, she didn't really know. She had only just met Logan, but she was naturally the most open and friendly of berries. She didn't know how to express her sadness because it was rare that she had known it. She swung her feet to and fro.

"I just miss fair Glacier, really."

Logan leaned toward her, looking as serious as he could. "Yes, I think we all do, but it's so grand in the Great Outdoors."

"I know, but I prefer it at home. I'm just different, I guess."

Logan looked at his feet. He wasn't much of an empathizer, but then again, none of the Huckles were. They weren't usually so sad or distressed. "Well, maybe you'll find something out here that you really like, and you'll take it back to Glacier with you."

Goji looked to one side away from Logan. She was still holding in her tears, and again, she didn't respond.

Logan sensed the awkwardness and tried to change the course of the conversation. "Say, do you know much about where we are headed? I have only heard stories."

"Yes, I do."

"What's it like? Who are the Wanderers?"

Logan's persistent questioning may have been irritating, but Goji was happy that the subject had changed.

"I haven't been, but I hear it's beautiful. Supposedly, the lakes are wider and deeper than Glacier, and the forests are . . . inconceivable."

"Wow. I can't imagine what it must be like if it's more beautiful than Glacier!"

"Creatures far and wide speak of it. Any that make passage through Glacier, they always mention it."

Logan paused to absorb her words. "And the Wanderers?" He now seemed to have forgotten all about why he had originally come to speak to her.

"The Wanderers are mythical beasts. They wandered for a long time in days past, searching for a Realm."

"And they found it in the great Realm of the south?"

"Yes . . . but it's a bit more complicated than that."

"How so?"

Goji could see that Logan was an enthusiastic knight, and she thought to herself that he should have her life instead. She, after all, had little interest in serving the king. "The Wanderers were led to their home by the Elderberries, the ancient Trees, and a legendary eagle named Pry."

Logan listened intently, like a mossy bank absorbing morning dew.

Goji continued. "They made a pact with the Elders that they could make the Realm their home so long as they kept guard of the Ancient Manuscripts."

Logan's eyes widened in disbelief. "How have I never heard any of this before?"

Goji chuckled slightly, finally at ease with conversing. It delighted her to see the knight learn and grow. "No reason, I guess." Goji was quite right. It wasn't that the Huckles did not value these tales, it was just that they were much too busy with ordeals in Glacier to concern themselves with them. Hence, they often became lost to more common folk, turning into woodland whispers. Also, the disappearance of the king did not help. He used to be the one to educate the Huckles, teaching and mentoring them. He no longer did.

"And why did the Wanderers need permission? Why couldn't they just stay there?"

Goji paused and searched her bank of knowledge deep within. "The Realm is beautiful but dangerous. The snow is fierce, and there are violent tremors."

"Violent tremors?" Logan looked down, puzzled, his lips imitating the sentence once more. "Like an earthquake?"

"Not quite. As the tales go, there is a mighty volcano in the heart of the Realm. The Elders considered it too unsafe to be a permanent home, but they were equally weary from carrying the Manuscripts from place to place."

"Ahhh, so they let the Wanderers live there as long as they looked after the Manuscripts." He paused. "That means they can't leave unless the Manuscripts do?"

"Right."

"Oh my, this is just so much to take in. I can't wait to get there!"

Goji smiled again, happy to have inspired him.

As she looked at him, she noticed beyond that more Huckles were waking from their slumber, stretching, and walking around. "Hey, we should get going. Everyone's waking up."

Logan turned around. He had forgotten where he was, so lost in his thoughts was he.

"Oh, yes!"

The two stood up and walked back toward the rest of the Huckles. Morrow and the herd were returning to join them, finished with feeding.

"Looks like we'll be leaving soon," said Goji.

"Yes. Thanks for telling me everything, Goji, and I'm sorry you're sad." Logan looked at her endearingly, wondering if there was anything he could do to console her.

"It's fine. I just miss Glacier. Nice to meet you, Logan."

"Onward for the king?" Logan attempted to lift her spirits.

"Onward for the king," Goji responded kindly, not wanting to let him down. Goji always did her best to make others happy, despite her current sadness. All her life, she had grown in ignorant bliss, playing and following Rubus out to the Glacier plains, gleefully learning the great skills of the berryrumpet. Now that she was older, questions kept circling in her mind like hawks high above. She knew that she was different, not a Huckle, but why? Rubus had always been truthful to her; he had even taken her exactly back to the spot where she had been found, but where was she really meant to be? If Goji were any other Huckle, she wouldn't have worried about such things; she would have simply got on with exploring and caring for Glacier, but Goji was different, and it was this inner sinking feeling that made her so sad to depart. She was worried that she never truly belonged in the first place.

As the two approached the campsite, Vernus could be seen counting and organizing the knights. The Huckles were getting ready to leave. There were murmurs among them, questions about where they were going and how they would get there. Rubus was also there, carefully patting his cow. He looked around and saw the two approaching. "Logan, Goji! Good morning!"

"Good morning, Rubus." Logan spoke in a beaming manner, illuminated by the magical tales he had just heard. "Goji has just been telling me all about the Wanderers, the Elders, and the Manuscripts." Rubus smiled at him like a wise father. He was a father to all the knights in a sense. "That's great, Logan. Now you should get going. We'll be leaving soon."

"Right." He saluted to Rubus. "Farewell, Goji."

Goji looked at Logan. "Farewell."

Logan bounced toward the rest of the Huckles with a spring in his step, looking forward to the days ahead. Rubus then turned to Goji, but she had already started drifting away, not wishing to speak with him.

"Goji . . ."

Goji briskly darted past him while concealing her reemerging tears. She followed after Logan, albeit some way behind him.

"Goji!" Rubus called after her with a crying plea. They had not spoken since they had left Glacier, and also not much in the days leading up to leaving. Goji would not open her heart or her thoughts to Rubus. Not only was she greatly troubled by her own mind, she was hurt by him. She felt that Rubus had been pushing immensely for her to serve the king, meaning attending the Elderberries' meetings and devoting her life to the king's affairs, and to make matters worse, Rubus had simply not listened to her concerns about leaving Glacier. She felt that he was being selfish, and that was not the berry who had raised her.

Rubus gazed on as Goji walked away. His mind had been weighed down by concern for the knights on the entire journey, and this strife with Goji only made things worse. It was worse for both of them. He made his way back, disheveled, and mounted his cow. Looking around, he could see that the others were mostly ready and excited. The Huckles would be making their way east, and they were now close to the Wanderers' home. A gentle, vibrant chatter sounded from the Huckles as they prepared to ride onward.

"Onward for the king!" Vernus spoke instead of Rubus.

"Onward for the king!" the chorus of Huckles responded with jubilant glee and lifted their staffs high. They began their march east, with the king and his band behind. As the herd trotted peacefully on, Rubus occasionally glanced at Goji, his heart heavy within.

Laughter flooded the room. Goji could hardly contain herself as Lingon and Rubus made their silly faces and noises. They were impersonating all types of animals they had encountered on their journeys as knights. Rubus, impersonating something, contorted his face so that it appeared thin and scrawny, then he made a great chomping motion with his mouth.

Goji paused for a moment as she pondered, trying to work out the creature. She was a very young berry and the sweetest of all creatures in the Realm. She was wide-eyed and warmhearted. Despite her different appearance, all of the Huckles in Glacier had taken to her because of the immense joy she brought.

"Beaver!"

Lingon smiled and clapped. "That's right, young Goji, and what do they do?"

"Swim in the water and build bridges." Goji's words were loosely formed, as she was still young, but her knowledge abounded. She had demonstrated tremendous abilities and understanding, confounding all of Glacier, even the Elderberries themselves. Only the king had not taken to her, as she was an outsider. Goji listened to all manner of folk and recited tales about all the Realms and the Great Outdoors, even far beyond Glacier's borders. She knew of creatures and their behaviors, what they could do and what they couldn't, and even where they liked to live. Goji was a special berry.

Rubus moved on to another animal. He stretched his arms out as wide as possible before gliding around the room and twitching his head sharply while looking at objects on the floor.

"Eagle, easy!"

"Haha, all right, Goji, no need to show off now! And what do the eagles do?"

"Fly and be epic!" Goji stood up and stretched her own arms out, gliding and crashing into Rubus. At her tender age, she was only half his size. They both laughed loudly as they tumbled to the floor, still in character. While down together, Rubus looked over at her.

"Well, young eagle, what have you learnt from your experience?"

Goji looked back at him, her wide eyes beaming excitedly.

"Erm . . . don't mess with an eagle!"

Rubus let out a great laugh as he held his stomach while looking toward the ceiling. Lingon, too, joined in the laughter. "Oh, Goji, you are some berry. You are a wild one, young one, but we love you."

Goji beamed as Lingon spoke the endearing words, then she rolled over to Rubus, bumping into his side. Together they lay on the floor, laughing and joking all the while. Goji was loved by Lingon, by Rubus, and by all the Huckles.

Morrow's deep nostrils flared. His momentous antlers turned toward the river along which they had all been traveling, and Rubus noticed his movement.

"What do you sense, Morrow?"

"Some creature in the river."

The river was long and wide. At some points, it trickled gently, but at others, it violently dropped into a ferocious stream. The gleaming waters were crowded with rocks and mossy banks throughout. They had been traveling alongside it for most of the day. Rubus looked toward the river, and sure enough, like Morrow sensed, streaming ripples were emerging on the river's surface. They seemed to be moving at the same pace as the traveling Huckles, as if keeping track of them. Rubus signaled to Vernus and then broke away from the group to inspect.

As he moved closer, a small brown head emerged from the water. To begin with, only the top appeared, but after that, the entire head shot up.

There in the water was a small brown face, squished, squat, and round. Its dotted eyes were similar to those of the Huckles, albeit far smaller, and the face had a most pleasing mouth, centered between thin silver whiskers. This creature was delightfully pleasant to look upon, a blessing for the soul that seemed to exude a vibrant comfort. It was a creature that encapsulated the little things of the Realm. Rubus had encountered a brown beaver, *Castor canadensis*.

The beaver's soft hair was soaked by the running water, and as she turned her head to look at Rubus, droplets were flung from her bark-brown coat. "Greetings, fair traveler. Welcome to the Wanderers' home!" Her voice was high and her speech fast, but she spoke with great enthusiasm, and her whiskers shifted furiously as she spoke. The furry creature gently split the stream as she moved silkily along. The beaver seemed perfectly content with her place in the water, and the water seemed perfectly content to carry her. The restful scene gave Rubus's troubled mind a welcome break.

"Hello there, fair creature. Who may you be?" As Rubus spoke, the rest of the Huckles looked on. On the other side of the river in which the jubilant beaver swam, there were a litany of trees, glorious in color and size. You might have thought the Huckles had had enough of trees, but here, they were inviting and serene.

The beaver spoke. "I am Cassie! And I am the welcomer for these most gracious of lands." As Cassie spoke, she occasionally hopped out of the water, skipping along with great joy. As she looked on, Goji smiled at the most serendipitous of scenes. Cassie's character was much like hers in former times.

"Well, Cassie, we come in humility and with good intentions. We wish to speak to the Wanderers," Rubus replied.

Cassie turned her head away from Rubus and looked forward. She then seemed to mischievously smile as she dipped back under the water only to return again seconds later.

"The Wanderers have been expecting you, Huckle. That's why they sent me to welcome you and check on you."

"Check on us?"

"Yes. The Wanderers are old friends of the Huckles, but they also know there is one amongst you in great pain." Cassie dipped under and back up again once more. "The unfortunate incident with the Trees just passed has reached their ears."

Rubus did not look back at the king, but he knew it was he that Cassie spoke of.

"And what are the Wanderers checking?"

"They believe this certain fellow to be unpredictable, and they wish not to sow disharmony in our great Realm."

In former times, Rubus would have defended the king with prideful honor, but now he knew that Cassie and the Wanderers were justified in their cautiousness. He subtly nodded at the little beaver.

She gleefully nodded back before continuing, "But also, I am here to lead you to your quarters."

"Our quarters?"

"Yes. You just need to follow us along this stream toward the grandest of rivers, and we will show you the way!"

"Very well, Cassie, we will follow. But what do you mean, 'us'? I see only one of you."

Cassie leapt out of the water once more, her gleeful little face now clear for all the Huckles to see, and as she dipped back under and forward, three even smaller brown faces popped out of the water simultaneously. Their minuscule heads were not much larger than an acorn or a clump of berries. Beaver children. Many of the Huckles swooned at the sight of them.

"How adorable!"

The Huckles did not usually express such emotion, but certain scenes in nature were simply too much to resist. Rubus fashioned a gentle smile. Yes, even the king looked in their direction. He did not smile, but he looked in their direction. If anything could distract a split seed heart, it was a group of beaver children.

The children cheerfully smiled with utmost enthusiasm, as if seeking to uplift the Huckles after their weary journey. They turned in perfect sync toward the Huckles and merrily squealed, "Follow us!" The delightful beaver family then dove under the water and wiggled onward, while the ripples from their movement paved the way for the Huckles to follow. Onward the court rode.

They were not quite in the Wanderers' home yet, but they were getting closer, and the landscape was changing. The path became more and more inviting and calm, and the rocks and trees seemed perfectly placed, forming a gentle landscape enamored with peace. Rubus, Vernus, and Goji remained mostly silent as they rode, as did Morrow, but the Huckles behind could not stop chattering about the beaver family. The group continued for many hours, most excited to experience the famed Wanderers' home.

After some time, at around midday, the Huckles came to a vast and wide part of the river. It had expanded greatly and snaked around across the Huckles' path so that there was no way onward for them. Vernus motioned to stop advancing, but ahead, Cassie and the children popped out of the water, in no way wearied from the journey.

"Just a moment, dear fellows." Cassie lifted both of her arms as she spoke, as if to announce some grand plan. She then turned around and shuffled her children along. They all suddenly dipped below the water, seemingly disappearing. The Huckles looked at one another, confused. The water was silent for a minute before the whole family suddenly burst from the river's surface, their small mouths and hands full of sticks and twigs. The Huckles applauded and gallantly smiled. Some of them even seemed to jump up and down for joy.

Next, the Huckles simply stood in amazement as they watched the beavers' great plan unfold. In a matter of minutes, the family worked like swarming bees, darting to and fro, diving under the water and back up. With precision and speed, they built a stick-like bridge across the stream, giving the Huckles a clear path to cross. The Huckles stood with their jaws dropped. Morrow, who had observed much of recent events, raised his head higher than normal with his eyes wide. He was most impressed.

After the bridge had been built, the beaver family stood before the Huckles like performers on a podium, and they wore beaming smiles as they displayed their fine work to the guests. "All done!" Cassie cried. Cassie's children leapt up and high-fived her outstretched paws.

"Yes, that is fascinating, Cassie. How did you assemble this so fast?" Rubus was genuinely shocked. He had witnessed many things over the years, but nature still sometimes took him by surprise.

"The Wanderers have blessed us, fellow Huckle. They wanted us to be able to build quickly in case of emergency or any guests, so they blessed us." She spoke with increased enthusiasm about the Wanderers.

"How so?"

"Not sure, really. We just spoke to them, told them we would watch the river, and we have been blessed ever since!"

"I see."

Spending time with the Wanderers indeed brought about some magical qualities. Supposedly, they enabled creatures to fulfill their great purpose and gave them potential to the fullest of their being. Cassie spoke on. "Well, anyhow, we're all done here, so we'll swim ahead. All you have to do is cross this bridge and keep following the stream."

"Right, well, thank you, and we'll see you soon," said Rubus.

"Bye now!" Cassie dived into the water energetically, clearly not tired from building the great structure. Her adorable children then popped in one after the other, each waving farewell as they disappeared. Needless to say, many of the Huckles were sad to see them go. Moving onward, they began walking across the bridge created for them. The king and his trolls would walk around, as they would have destroyed the structure and they were large enough to walk straight through the river. About half of the Huckles had crossed when suddenly, Cassie popped up once more on the other side of the bridge. She had a real sense of urgency this time.

"One last thing, Huckles!" She may have intended to speak to them all, but her little voice would only travel so far among the rushing waters. Only Rubus, Goji, and some others could hear her. "Once you travel about a mile that way, you are officially in the Wanderers' home!"

"As in the Realm?"

"Yes. Now remember, this is sacred ground, the ground of the Ancient Manuscripts. Be careful in our land, and make sure not to take anything. Try to leave everything as you found it!"

Cassie spoke passionately about her Realm. Rubus smiled, as he and the Huckles had every intention of treating the Realm just as they treated Glacier. It was, after all, the Wanderers' home.

"Farewell, Cassie."

"Bye!" She finally swam away, her brown tail wagging along with the stream.

The group marched the final mile before they reached the threshold of the Realm. The border was clear; not by sight, but by an atmospheric change. The Realm that they were entering generated a sense of awe and wonder among them. The Huckles drew a deep collective breath and crossed the border.

You will remember me reminding you that often in national parks, and in all adventures in life, it is not always about the beginning or the end. Sometimes you can experience something in between that is of incredible significance. So it is in national parks, and so it was for the Huckles here in this Realm.

So far, our tale has spoken of lands adorned with beauty and wonder on many occasions. This Realm and park, however, is truly the most wondrous of all. While the state of California is a diverse and great land and the parks there are wondrous, the Redwood Park cannot compare to this land's majesty. Likewise, while Glacier is an idyllic home of tranquility and calm, it does not compare to the Realm in which the Huckles now found themselves.

The rolling skies and fair meadows are only the beginning. Forests and rows of healthy trees are interspersed with great spectacles of color, and wild beasts, cheerful birds, and fair creatures joyfully roam, taking full advantage of the sheer beauty. Then there is the river of which Cassie spoke. It was and is perhaps the most tranquil river in any park. Many rivers cut through or even barricade the land, taking rocks and stray sticks with them as they flow. This river, however, carefully flows through the land, not disturbing the rocks to the left or the trees to the right. It opens up near fair meadows and respectfully narrows near banks of trees. It is a true work of art. Eagles dwell nearby and freshwater fish swim within, while the orange sunsets can best the world's finest paintings.

The sunsets. Sunsets here are like no others. The orange hue gently fades as the mystic blue night takes over, and at dawn, the hazy dust is peeled back by opaque light and the glorious sun illuminates the entire array of the land's colors: green trees, clear waters, and fair brown paths. Elsewhere, high passes overlook deep waterfalls that tumble gently like autumn leaves, and spectacular flora, flowers of pink, purple, green, and red, are dotted among creatures' abodes and commune in wondrous fields.

Creatures of all types dwell here. Eagles, beavers, great elk, wolves, and furry bears. There is no limit to the wondrous depths of this sacred land. This place happens to be the home of the Manuscripts, but in truth it is much more. This land is sacred because it is an encapsulation of all that makes the Realms and parks special. Most of the characteristics that can be found in other parks exist here; a part of Glacier, a part of Redwood, a part of Yosemite. A part of the soul of every Realm. You should be able to see it easily on your map, picking up from the Huckles' last location. Eastward from that place, in the northwest corner of Wyoming, you should see a large patch of deep green. It is called Yellowstone National Park. This was the Wanderers' home.

7

Bill's Great Flight

THE LITTLE BIRD'S WINGS beat rapidly as he raced through the forest. He would much rather be tucked into his cozy nest high above, but the message had to be delivered. Besides, he did not often have much to do, as he had no real purpose; he was quite a lonesome fellow. The black-throated gray warbler bird, *Setophaga nigrescens*, is a perfect blend of black and white, with long black streaks aligned on its soft snowy coat. It also has a small orange dash on its forehead, meaning that other birds are able to see it coming. There was no particular reason why this warbler bird had to deliver the message; he just happened to receive it first.

Hours earlier, he had been perched on a low branch on the very edge of the forest, looking out to the east, at the beginning of another mundane day for him, when another warbler bird had hurriedly flown toward his nest. They then spoke with great urgency, flapping and tweeting most animatedly, before the messenger spoke of the critical news that had to be delivered.

Onward now the second bird traveled with the news, through the thick forest, darting like a kingfisher over a lake's waters. He was reaching the branches of the higher Trees, much higher than he was used to. As the warbler reached a thick, high branch, he took a moment to catch his breath, and, panting violently, he glared at the heights that he still had to scale. Such was the arrangement of the Trees that the Redwoods could often resemble staircases, with long protruding branches passing over into the threshold of the Tree nearby. The Trees did not mind, as it actually made their communication easier. As a matter of fact, some Trees were so close and proximate that they grew into each other, creating couplets, with one Tree growing out of the base of another.

"What ya doing there, Mister?"

The warbler turned sharply, not expecting to meet someone this high up.

"Where ya goin? What's ya name?" the voice asked.

"Oh, erm, that's none of your business," said Bill. He spoke with a rather flat, businesslike tone. His black-and-white striped head twitched as he spoke, and he closed his eyes as he spoke some of the words.

"Say now, there's no need for that! I happen to know everywhere and everyone in this forest. And you, sir, look a little lost!"

Bill cast a sideways glance. He hadn't much tolerance for speaking with this creature, but he was indeed lost. "No, I am not."

"Yes, you are. A little birdie told me so." The creature slowly molded its face into a loose gelatinous smile, clearly pleased with the fine joke. Bill took a deep breath; he knew that this odd individual was his only way of finding the High One.

"Very well, how may I find him?"

"Him?" said the creature.

The bird twitched, his patience dwindling; the odd creature opposite him spoke rather slowly. "Yes, him. The great Tree, the High One."

"Ohhh, him! You mean him. Why didn't you say so? There are many 'hims' in this great forest, as there are many 'hers.'"

"Look, I really need to be going . . ."

"Hey now, time is only there to hold us back, little bird, and the more you try to save it, the more you will lose it."

Bill wore a look of disbelief as this untoward creature lectured it high in the forest. "And who exactly are you?"

"Why, I'm Maxine the Slug, don't you know?" Maxine was one of the most surprising, unusual, and colorful creatures in all of Redwood. She was a banana slug, *Ariolimax*. Banana slugs are rather large, slimy beings. They are mustard yellow with a black or brown head, and they have two slimy antennae with little yellow dots on the end. It was most odd. Perhaps these slimy beings wouldn't be so dramatic in appearance if it weren't for their notable size. Most slugs are perhaps the size of a large human finger, or double that at the most, but Maxine was the length of an entire hand.

"I have not heard of you before, Maxine. Well, my name is Bill."

"Bill the bird! Got ya. Well, I do be liking the colors on your coat, Bill, now what are ya?"

"I'm a bird."

"Yes, yes, but what kind of bird? I keep facts, ya know, about the forest and all things." Maxine's antennae twirled hypnotically as she spoke, as if probing Bill's inner mind.

"I see. Well, I'm a warbler bird."

"A wobbly bird. Got it." Maxine made a strange throbbing noise with her head, her mind seemingly taking in the information. She indeed had much knowledge about Redwood and all things within it.

"All right, Mr. Bill, wobbly bird, so you need to see the High Tree?" Maxine spoke slowly and disjointedly, almost as if sludgy bits of slime were blocking her as she spoke.

"Yes, that's right. I've an important message to deliver."

"Very well. You told me about yourself, so now I'm more the wiser, and for that, I'll tell you where to go." She squirmed and turned, leaving a great gloopy puddle of slime in her wake. Once she was facing west, she lifted the front part of herself and slowly moved her entire head, first in one direction and then in another. Unfortunately, her antennae were not useful for direction giving and the movement was sporadic.

"Ya gotta go that way, then that way."

Bill was stunned. Never before had he been spoken to so ineffectively. This giant yellow slug was clearly most knowledgeable but also most unhelpful.

"Erm . . ."

"Yep, that's what you gotta do." She pointed her head toward the west.

"Great, thanks, I gue—"

"And if you're ever in doubt, just follow the Trees!" she said enthusiastically.

Bill twitched his head. Maxine chuckled, sensing the little bird's frustration. "You'll see what I mean."

"Okay, well, that's most helpful, Maxine, but I really should be going now."

"All right then, Bill wobbly bird. Thanks for stopping by on my branch."

Bill nodded sharply, imitating a smile or gesture.

"Oh! One thing to remember. You're a songbird, so you don't fly long distances; you take more frequent trips between closer branches."

The bird winced with its little face, once again trying to process this strange set of circumstances. "I am perfectly aware, Maxine, thank you."

"Ahhh, but ya see, Bill, when ya get in the midst of the great Trees, sometimes ya mind goes a bit fuzzy wuzzy," Maxine raised her slow voice as much as she could and her slimy antennae went haywire, pointing to everything and anywhere. Bill cast her a sideways, suspicious glance. It was the most awkward of meetings high up in the Redwood forest.

"Right, then, well, I'll be leaving now."

Maxine lifted her slimy head up and down, her antennae bouncing in excitement. "Farewell, wobbly bird!"

Bill knew that however much longer his short life lasted; he would never forget this odd serendipitous meeting. It had already been a most interesting day for him. He puffed out his stripy chest before leaping up into the air and then proceeded precariously in the direction Maxine had suggested. Before venturing too far, he stopped and hovered in the air, much like a hummingbird. A revelatory thought crossed Bill's mind, and perhaps it would have occurred to him sooner had he not been so distracted. He swiveled sharply and faced Maxine, a gelatinous yellow gloop on the branch just below him. "Say, how did you even get up here? Shouldn't you be on the forest floor?"

"Ahhh, you're turning into me, wobbly bird, taking in facts and things! Ya see, the thing is, no matter how long it takes you, every tree can be climbed *eventually*." She looked delighted with herself.

"I see. Well, thank you, Maxine, and good to meet you."

"Farewell, wobbly bird. I'll be seeing ya now."

Bill turned and raced through the forest, bouncing from branch to branch much like Maxine had described. He wondered if he had already experienced this "fuzzy wuzziness" that Maxine spoke of and if what had just happened was actually real.

The forest surrounding him as he flew was a deep, alluring entanglement of emerald green and dark brown. Mossy branches were covered in clumps of growth, and layers of mist seeped through the towering Trees. Down below, scattered leaves lay undisturbed on the forest floor, and the occasional creature scuttled over the earth. Redwood was more humid and denser than anywhere else in our tale, and that was because the great Trees took in so much water. The morning dew droplets here appeared like large raindrops, dripping from the high leaves, and the morning ocean layer ghosted through the canopy like a sweeping cloud.

After traveling through the thick forest for some time, Bill had covered a large distance, and he began to feel concerned. He had not yet seen any sign of the High One or anyone else from the council. As the little bird began to feel nauseated, the Trees began to change, and instantly, Bill remembered Maxine's words.

"Follow the Trees."

Looking around wearily, he saw that the Trees had all begun to bend their branches in one direction, almost as if they were pointing or bowing down to something. Their thick trunks and branches smoothly curved and their leaves hung delicately. In their presence, Bill found renewed strength as he followed the way of the Trees. Onward he traveled, and the Trees became taller and taller. And taller.

The giddy heights began to sway the warbler bird, tossing him to and fro, and Bill's vision became increasingly hazy as he made his way through the mystic woodland. All around, he felt the weight of ancient minds and voices bearing down on him with ever-increasing intensity. Bill flew another forty yards, past some thin Redwoods, before he plummeted dramatically. He smashed against a branch some thirty feet down. All of a sudden, the words of Maxine the slug crossed his mind. A banana slug was the last thing he had expected to dwell on right now, but he now realized the wisdom of her words.

"You're a songbird."

Stunned, Bill managed to pull himself upright. His eyes gently twinkled as he made sense of his surroundings, and he saw that he was still rather high in the forest despite the fall, so he took a step back from the edge of the branch to regain his bearings. Once he was balanced, he looked back up to the spot where he had lost control.

It dawned on him that Maxine's prophecy had come true. Bill had flown a great distance without touching a branch, not something that songbirds normally do, and the mystique and aura of the Trees had overwhelmed him. Bill looked around. Towering above him were giant Trees with branches like thick staircases protruding from their great trunks. Bill knew enough to know that he was now in the presence of the council of the Redwood Realm. To his left he noticed a large stumpy female tree, whom he thought to be Fir, and to his right he saw a thinner, taller male tree, whom he knew to be Sap.

Bill knew what he had to do. If he could ascend to the top of just one of them, he would be able to see over the top of the canopy and find the High One. He took a deep, puffing breath. Such feats were extremely difficult for songbirds, as they usually lived closer to the forest floor, but alas, we have learned and seen that birds are often found engaging in daring, courageous feats that they really have no business engaging in.

Bill launched himself onto a nearby branch, slightly higher than the one on which he had started. Slowly, he worked his way up and around the great Trees, sometimes crossing over onto a more opportune branch. Each time he ascended three or so branches, he would mutter under his breath "I am a songbird," and then gently shake his head in disbelief as he realized he was taking Maxine the slug's advice so seriously.

After what seemed like forever to the bird, like me or you climbing some epic mountain, Bill found his way to the canopy, and above him, a strong blanket of Trees was all that separated him from the sky. Bill was now exhausted, but with one final surge, he pushed his way through the leaves and canopy, and the Realm of Redwood beyond opened to him in a way that would change his world forever. This was easily the most daring adventure in Bill's life, and perhaps that of any songbird, but it was easily worth it.

As Bill broke through the canopy, he was transported into the open Redwood sky, and a long mirage of Trees stretched as far as his small eyes could see. Such was the vastness of the forest and the giddiness of the horizon that Bill momentarily forgot that there was a forest floor far beneath him. A small songbird such as Bill would normally have been overwhelmed by pressure at such a daring height, but Bill seemed unmoved, perhaps spurred on by the mystical aura of his adventurous quest. All around him were looming clouds seeping slowly through the chilly air. Bill was on top of the world.

Lost as he was in this magnificent experience; the warbler suddenly remembered the reason for this magnificent expedition. A rush of cold air lashed him, snapping him back into focus. Had he not been gripping the Treetop for dear life; he surely would have plummeted far down below. He carefully began pivoting on his branch, delicately placing his feet as he spun around, looking in all directions. He gazed across the unending plateau of Trees to the east, to the south, and to the north until he saw it.

It was the most dramatic of sights. Here was Bill, on top of the world, overlooking the unending canopy, yet there was somehow still a sight higher than he. Far in the west was a simply unbelievable Tree, high above all earthly things. It protruded some seventy feet higher than the canopy, looking down upon all the Trees that immediately surrounded it. Bill had heard stories—all of the creatures in Redwood had—but never could he have imagined this. He took a deep breath, during which he realized his beak was gaping open, as he was flabbergasted at the sight on the distant horizon. The High One upon which he looked pierced the sky, making a gaping hole in the white, frothy clouds.

Much like he had done earlier after he fell, Bill renewed his composure and began to leap from treetop to treetop, bouncing across the canopy toward the awesome sight. While he did, he was muttering under his breath, continuously reminding himself, "I am a songbird." This time he was not reminding himself how to fly, but rather he was convincing himself that he really was in the canopy of Redwood on his way to deliver a message to the High One.

As with anyone who approached a tall Tree, the closer Bill drew, the taller Hyperion became, and Bill's giddiness returned as he bounced onward while looking up at the momentous spectacle before him. Giving his eyes and mind a slight rest, Bill looked down as he continued to advance. There below he could make out the Trees continuing to curve and bend toward the High One, and he recognized a few more council members. Bill kept his head down as he traveled, deciding that the dizziness may overcome him if he continued fixing his eyes on Hyperion. The branches and Trees blurred beneath his spindly feet, the colors merging into a vibrant blend of brown and green, and as he hopped from branch to branch, he occasionally skipped over a small tuft of cloud.

Onward Bill traveled, and the great Tree loomed closer. The quiet beating of his wings and gentle feet and a light passing breeze were the only sound in the high canopy. He traveled faster and faster until he suddenly smashed head first into Hyperion's girthy trunk. Shaken, he shook his wings and gathered himself yet again before looking up. The little bird's vision was completely encumbered by the vast pillar before him. He could not see around or above or over the trunk. All he could see was an unscalable chasm of branches. Once again, the giddiness returned, and the bird wobbled on the branch on which he was perched.

By this time, Bill was thoroughly exhausted. He had used all his energy to make it this far, so to ascend further now seemed impossible. His eyes became drowsy, and he felt the soft lull of slumber wash over him when all of a sudden, a rushing wind nearly knocked him off his branch. His eyes widened and he hopped on the spot, startled. Deep in the wind, he had heard a gentle whisper, an ancient voice.

"Come, little one."

Hyperion had spoken to him. His voice was deep and booming, and slow but sure. Every time he uttered a word, he seemed to pause before wisely contemplating the next one. What felt like a stone hit the little bird's stomach. It just struck him that he was now in the presence of the almighty High One of the Redwood Realm, the great Hyperion.

Before he had time to gather his thoughts, a deep rumbling sound came from nearby. Bill turned and saw a large creaking branch extending around the trunk of the Tree. It came toward him like some magical staircase, and when it reached Bill's feet, a single but stable leaf appeared. Shaking with reverence, Bill hopped on, and almost simultaneously, the entire branch began to shift back upward. Bill was carried high into the air, looking at the horizon from even greater heights than before.

He began to tremble. Not only was he reverently aware of whom he now faced, he was also rather cold. The branch had carried him to a tremendous height, so high that a layer of cloud now engulfed him. The canopy had faded and he was surrounded by a sea of white. Sensing his cold, a further leaf sprung from the branch and wrapped itself around the shivering bird like a cloak.

"You bring forth a message, little one," said the booming voice inquisitively.

"Y . . . y . . . yes." Bill could only whisper the words at such a giddy height.

"What is that you come to deliver?"

"S . . . some Tr—some Trees were attacked, my lord."

"Ooohhh?"

Loud creaking and a rushing wind pulsated in Bill's ears. The world seemed to turn upside down as Hyperion leaned back, his movement affecting the entire surrounding ecosystem. Bill clung on for dear life.

"And where did this malfeasance take place, little one?"

"F . . . f . . . far north, O High One, in distant lands."

"I see." The creaking Tree leaned forward, returning to his original position. "And what might this unfortunate attack have to do with Redwood?" Hyperion never spoke as if there was something that he did not know. The truth was, there was little that he didn't know or at least consider. His was asking the question because he was seeking an understanding from the bird's perspective.

"I . . . I . . . believe that the attack was carried out by him, O Lord."

"And who might that be?"

"The king of the north, O master. The one they call the Huckleberry King."

"Hmmm!" Hyperion's deep pondering surely caused an earthquake, and his whole trunk seemed to vibrate as he dwelt on the message. "Well now, what do you propose we do about it, little one?"

"I have no idea, High One." By this point, Bill had mustered up the courage to turn and face the Tree. Once he had, he could make out a giant gash of an eye, but the rest of his trunk face was too large for a little songbird to see.

"Well, little bird, *I* think we need to wait for them to come to us."

For the first time, Bill dared to think. He did not dare question the king, but he at least *thought* about the possibility of mentioning that he didn't understand. Once more, the king's shaking rumbled the entire woodland below. Bill was jerked back and forth, to and fro, high above the world. The king was laughing.

"Hahaha! I sense your thinking, little bird; it is good that you think."

The bird twitched his head, awaiting the king's next wise words.

"We cannot approach an angry king such as the Huckleberry. Only hostility and battle would come from such an effort."

Bill paused. Struck, enlightened, flummoxed, whatever the word may be, this little warbler songbird was amazed that the king had given such a simple but true response. Wisdom could be simple after all. That was the principle by which Hyperion and the council governed; they never overcomplicated things unless they needed to. "Yes, we must wait, little bird. Perhaps the northern king will have a change of heart somewhere along his path. After all, the paths we take, they lead us into . . . unexpected places."

It was as if Hyperion were speaking directly to him as well as referring to the northern king. Bill had thought he would be overwhelmed by meeting the High One, but it was instead his enticing wisdom that he would remember most. On his daring flight up to the canopy, he had indeed taken an unexpected path. He almost felt that this journey had been for him personally as much as it was to deliver the message.

"I say, little bird, it must have been quite the journey for you! You're quite a courageous one." Once again, the king's laughter filled the skies. Bill thought that it must surely have echoed through the entire world.

"Y . . . y . . . yes. I don't know how I'm going to get down," Bill stammered.

A loud creaking echoed from nearby and a great smile etched itself into Hyperion's large face, although he refrained from laughing this time. Perhaps he sensed the little bird's nervousness, and he had no intention of upsetting Bill. "I will get you down, little bird." A rumbling like thunder crashed through the skies. Beneath, closer to the regular-sized (if you could call them that) Trees, topmost branches reached toward the king, forming a staircase that led all the way down to the forest floor. Bill saw that small leaves were sprouting from them, much like the leaf he was standing on.

"H . . . how . . . did . . . ?"

"Do not wonder too much, little bird. Just be a part of the forest, and let the forest be a part of you."

Bill looked directly into the eye of the High One. His little heart was greatly moved. After all, any creature who came across this legendary Tree would be moved in some way.

"Thank you, Hyperion. I feel very glad to have delivered this message."

"Well, perhaps, Bill, it is I who have delivered a message to you."

"How do you know my n—?"

"Now, now, little bird, part of the forest." Bill nodded, realizing that the king was truly trying to speak to him. "Off you go now, and if ever you should come up this high again, remember that you are a songbird."

Bill looked deep into his eye. "I will."

Hyperion smiled once more, and an enlightened Bill hopped onto the first little branch step prepared for him. Branch by branch, he made his way down. He soon reached the canopy, then turned to take one last look at the mighty Tree and the heights that he had scaled. He could have dwelt in the High One's presence for much longer, but his task was now complete. Down Bill went until the High One's great face had disappeared, becoming covered in milky clouds and mist. Bill wondered if he would ever make it up this high again. He turned back around, took a deep, courageous breath, and hopped through the canopy, back into the ancient forest.

As he hopped down, leaf by leaf, he regained his composure and, slowly, his breath. It was now far later in the day, and the gentle sunlight warmed his damp feathers, which had been dripping with moisture from the clouds high above. Redwood greeted him like a warm home as he descended. Particles of forest floated through the air, illuminated by clear rays of sunlight. Bill was still rather high up, but after some time he could finally make out the mossy brown forest floor below. All around him were important Trees, no doubt gazing at him and watching over his journey. Bill was sure that he could feel their smiles upon him. Once he had descended to a manageable height, he turned around and looked up again. He was eagerly looking forward to telling this story to whoever he may come across for the rest of his days in the forest.

Bill reached the edge of a branch and was ready to fly off when a voice sounded from out of nowhere. Absolutely nowhere.

"Well there, Mister, back down, are ya?"

It couldn't be.

"I told ya, didn't I? All fuzzy wuzzy."

Bill turned toward her in disbelief. Maxine's antennae went haywire again, demonstrating the process of "fuzzy wuzzy."

"How did you get up here? We are nowhere near your branch!" Bill stammered.

"Ah, every branch is my branch because I am part of the forest," she replied.

"What?"

"Didn't you learn a darn thing up there?"

"You mean—" Bill glanced at Maxine, then twitched his head back up toward the canopy from whence he had come, and beyond toward Hyperion. "The High One sent you?"

"There you go, little wobbly bird."

"How? Why?"

"Well, wobbly bird, the great Tree makes sure that everyone in the forest knows their purpose."

Bill looked at Maxine more intently than he had done before, now noticing the slimy texture of her underbelly.

"The High One gave me a purpose . . ."

"That's right! If ya didn't have one before, ya do now!" Maxine squirmed rose toward the canopy, clearly very pleased with her work. Dollops of slime spurted from her as she shot upward.

"The High One knows about every creature in the forest, wobbly bird, and he makes sure we help each other out."

"But why did he send you to speak to me?"

Bill found himself speaking more and more slowly. He had, after all, spent all day in the company of extremely slow speakers.

"Because, little wobbly bird, if ya had met another bird, that wouldn't have made ya realize."

"Realize what?"

"That we're all connected in this forest, we are." She paused and pondered. "Oh! And I'm a *very* fast climber!" Maxine nodded her head as rapidly as she could, beside herself with laughter. It sounded somewhat like choking, as if she were attempting to empty herself of obstructive bits of slime.

Bill perched on the branch trying to take all of this in. It had been the most topsy-turvy day of his entire life; not what he'd expected when he'd first peeked out of his nest that morning. Around them, the Redwood air was silent and the sunlight cloaked the forest in its ambience. A dawning of peace and reverence wrapped itself around Bill, and he began to feel enlightened and useful. He felt more connected to the forest than ever before, and he was most pleased to serve a purpose in their Redwood home. The High One had given him a purpose; he was now a messenger. "Well, I think I should be going. I've a long way to fly back."

"That ya have."

Bill looked past the oddness of the creature and finally tapped into her good intentions. "Thank you, Maxine."

"You're more than welcome, little wobbly bird."

An odd squelching sound formed as Maxine manipulated her face, forging the slug equivalent of a smile, and in return, Bill nodded at her. After that moment of creaturely embrace, Bill looked around at the great Trees and then down to the forest floor, and a troubling thought crossed his mind. "Say, how are you going to get down?" he inquired.

"Same way I got up, little wobbly bird."

"It seems most unsafe. I can fly you down." Bill was unsure about offering this, but it had, after all, been the most empowering of days.

"Well . . . I am a very capable climber, I'll have ya know, but it's been a while since I gone through the skies, so if ya offering, I'll fly with ya, little bird!"

Bill twitched his head. He had had a great adventure today and was eager to expand on his newfound purpose. "Right, well, let's go then!" He enthusiastically hopped into the air, flapped his wings, and glided over to Maxine. He gently swooped down just above her and extended his spindly legs to grip the yellow slug, but when his little feet first gripped her, he immediately slipped and fell to the side. Maxine's slimy body was ungraspable.

"Say there, you're gonna drop me, little bird."

Bill panicked, fluttering from side to side, but he did not want to give up. Maxine sensed his agitation. "Just stay calm, will ya, Bill? Here in the forest, ya gotta find other ways around things sometimes."

"What shall we do? I'm going to drop you if I carry you like that." If Bill could have seen Maxine's face, he would have seen that she was smiling again. She lifted her slimy front half so that she was protruding into the air.

"Ya gotta pick me up."

Bill doubted himself. "I don't know. You may be too heavy!"

"Little wobbly bird, ya just been higher than anyone has ever been. Course ya can pick me up!"

Bill twitched his head and took another deep breath. Around them, Bill got the sense that the Trees were watching and cheering him on. He hovered above the slimy slug, who was waiting patiently and contentedly; he then spread his two little legs as wide as he possibly could and wrapped himself around her. It was a most uncomfortable experience for the bird, who felt like he was being bathed in gelatinous slime. Bill turned his head away momentarily in disgust before coming to terms with the situation. He had an idea.

"Ya got me nice and tight, Bill?" There was no sense of nervousness in Maxine's voice; she remained completely calm.

"Yes, I think so." Bill wrapped his legs tightly around her slimy body and pulled her upward. He then struggled and strained but could not get airborne. The bird took a deep breath once more and leant forward. Maxine wobbled, and her antennae swung to and fro as the two of them slid off the edge of the branch. Bill had used momentum (and slippery slime) to slide them off. They slid toward the edge, plummeted off, and fell through the forest air while the wind whistled fiercely past. Maxine's antennae pointed back toward Bill's squinting face as a trail of sludge lurched out behind them. "Wheee!"

Despite the precarious situation, Maxine was delighted. The lower the unlikely pair fell, the more forest creatures appeared, eager to observe the odd situation. Other songbirds, squirrels, and bugs ceased their daily duties to witness the alarming spectacle. A tremendous flash of yellow, black, and white rocketed by. The problem was, they were still going down. Fast.

"I'm going too fast!" Bill shouted over the roaring wind. "I can't fly!" Indeed, Bill's grip was slipping, and he struggled to pull Maxine into an upright position so that he could fly with her within his grasp. They were only falling, not flying.

"Ya can do it, Bill. Course ya can!" Maxine was perfectly relaxed, enjoying the miraculous flight. Bill had experienced some wondrous things today, and it had finally dawned on him that he truly had to listen to the slug, so he twitched his head and pulled with all his might. Bill strained, strived, and stretched until he began to bulge underneath. Nearby, a little pileated woodpecker, *Drycopus pileatus*, was watching the scene unfold with his mother. He stopped pecking on a trunk and turned around. "Woahhh."

The new friends continued to plummet through the air, falling closer and closer to the ground, while the fierce wind rushed past them. Suddenly, a thick branch appeared beneath them. It was so large that there was no chance of going around it, and they were heading straight for it.

"Come on, Bill. I don't wanna be turned into a puddle of sludge, ya know!"

Bill continued with all his might, pulling and pulling upward, but the branch drew nearer and they would soon crash straight into it. Bill's eyes widened as they approached; he had opened his mouth to let out a chirping scream when a clear, cloaking voice surrounded him.

"Let the forest be a part of you."

The deep clear voice of the High One, the great Tree Hyperion, pierced his very heart. Bill did not want to disappoint him. He refocused and pulled once more until his face was contorted and twisted as though in a fit of rage. The surrounding creatures gasped as the pair reached the branch, surely about to make impact, and then . . .

Whoosh!

Bill flew into the air with Maxine. Her slimy belly slid off the branch as he pulled upward. Bill finally opened his eyes, which had been closed tightly for some time. He was hovering in the air with Maxine firmly in his grasp. He felt on top of the world once more. It had been the most dramatic day of his life and perhaps that of any songbird. In this magical forest, truly anything could happen. As Bill hovered and floated with Maxine, who was squirming in delight, the forest creatures stood perched on nearby branches, jubilant in their applause.

"Look at that, Ma!" The young woodpecker tugged at his mother's wings in glee.

"Oooh!" A group of bright red ladybirds, a loveliness, swooned at the drama.

Bill looked around. Not only did he take great delight in the woodland folk being there, he felt at one with the group, the community, the Redwood family, his home. Below him, Maxine was still squirming and sliding in his tight grip.

"Bill, ya grippin too strong!"

Bill looked down. He had indeed been so encumbered with momentum that he had begun to grip Maxine too tightly. "Sorry!"

"Come on, ger' us down."

Bill drifted toward the ground as the surrounding creatures' clapping and cheering continued. He soon found a soft grassy spot and gently landed on the forest floor. It felt like a thousand years since he had been on solid ground. He carefully unfurled his legs from Maxine's slimy back and hovered in front of her, facing her once more. Immediately, she shot up into the air with great delight.

"Wahoo!" She was utterly jubilant. "That was fantastic, I tell ya! I ain't flown for years."

Bill twitched his head and looked at Maxine. It had never occurred to him that a simple flight could be so amazing.

"Thanks, little bird! I'll remember ya well."

A brief moment of sadness struck Bill, as it only now occurred to him that he would have to leave this part of the forest where the council and his new friend lived. "Well, you're always welcome to visit me."

"Ahhh, perhaps I shall, little bird, if ya needin' more adventure after all."

Bill smiled. "I think I shall."

"Well, that's wonderful, ya little fella."

"I'll tell you where I live, Maxine. You go eas—"

"Don't ya worry, little bird. I'll find ya."

"It's a mighty long way from here," he said.

"Well, it's a long way up to the High One too, but ya made it." Maxine's antennae pointed toward him as if congratulating him. In the excitement of his and Maxine's flight, he had almost forgotten about meeting Hyperion. Suddenly he began to feel incredibly tired.

"Well, I'm pretty exhausted, Maxine. I better get going."

"Farewell, little Bill."

Bill moved toward Maxine and nudged his little head toward hers. In return, Maxine extended her antennae, touching his head, and the new friends said goodbye. Bill leapt and hovered gently in the air. "Farewell, Maxine the slug."

"Farewell, little bird. Ya got a long way to go now. Remember, you're a songbird!"

"I'm a songbird."

Maxine rose and waved her antennae, and Bill responded with his beautifully patterned wings. He then turned east and flew away.

Bill made his way past mossy banks, high Trees, and sunlight rays. He had met the High One, he had met Maxine, and he would never be the same little bird again. He had been given purpose.

Deep pulses ran through the undergrowth, and buried earth trickled and crumbled due to the intensity of the traveling messages. Hyperion was sending them far and wide, deep under the forest floor. If his roots could have been seen, they would have been observed vibrating and shaking, almost threatening to burst forth into the forest evening.

The roots of the great Tree interlocked and wrapped around the roots of others, and the fierce pulses almost overwhelmed the roots into which the messages were passed. Down under the forest floor was the entanglement of powerful and mystical roots, spreading for miles around. They stretched to the edge of Redwood and from there into the rest of California. Hyperion was preparing the Trees for what lay ahead. The message from the king of the Trees was clear:

> *Be ready, my Trees. The king from the north and his*
> *cluster will come. Do not be afraid; instead stand firm.*
> *Be at ease and at one with the Realm always.*

8

Oxan's Edict

THE RIVER WAS FILLED with joyful Huckles. They were splashing, laughing, and diving all around. Morrow and the herd, meanwhile, were resting peacefully on the riverbank, occasionally getting up to lap some water from a bit further down the stream. On an isolated rock somewhere in the middle of the river, Cassie and her children were performing backflips into the water, much to the delight of the watching Huckles, who clapped and cheered.

It was the fourth day of their stay in Yellowstone, the most bountiful of lands, and the creatures were swimming in Yellowstone River. It was a river of sheer tranquility, a delightful array of colors and gentle sounds. Beyond them, fair meadows stretched for miles, their yellow haze seemingly boundless in length and width. It was a special Realm.

Last night and the nights before, they had slept comfortably in some woods nearby. Some actually had not slept, as they had been too excited to rest. A band of about twenty curious Huckles had woken late in the night and then crept carefully to a nearby hollow, where they met some boisterous raccoons, *Procyon lotor*. These raccoons told them all about Yellowstone, the sights to see, and the creatures far and wide. They also told them about the great volcanic underpass, the very heart of the Wanderers' home. After these Huckles had heard from the raccoons, they waited a few more hours till dawn's first light and then ran straight to the river. It was rare for Huckles to display such excitement away from home, but Yellowstone was enlightening, and the poignant pink and lightning-yellow sunrises created otherworldly hues that had gripped the Huckles' hearts.

The king had stayed in the forest, dwelling and reflecting on the journey so far, and the band had retired to a gentle clearing someplace in the woods to practice the king's song (despite having sung it countless times). They practiced for an hour or two, but their rumpet playing and cymbal crashing was drowned out by the distant joy of the playful Huckles. After some time, the band could no longer resist, and they dropped their instruments in the forest clearing, then ran through the woods and dived straight into the river. This made the sight all the more marvelous. The king's troll drummers were splashing wildly, tossing smaller Huckles high into the air. It was a splendid time, a moment of harmonious joy. A moment perhaps unique to this great Realm, where all of nature cooperates like a masterpiece, the layers of existence meshing with melodious ease. This was how all Realms should be.

Some of Yellowstone's other creatures had noticed the fun, and badgers, otters, and friendly ducks came to the river to join the Huckles. Fantastic eagles circled above. Despite all the jubilance, one berry had not joined in the fun.

"What are you doing sitting over there, Goji? The water is so fresh!"

Logan called out to Goji from his spot in the river. Just as he spoke, Juniper swam by and splashed him all over, causing rapturous laughter from the pair.

"Come on, sister, are you afraid of a little water?" said Juniper.

Goji cast her a sarcastic glance. "No, Juniper. I just don't feel like swimming."

"All right. Well, we'll be waiting!"

Goji shooed them away, very much appreciating her own space. Meanwhile, Juniper and Logan laughed some more, spraying splashes of water over one another as they disappeared among the jubilant Huckles. Goji watched. She would have liked to join them, but she was not one to fake having fun.

"Goji." A voice approached behind her.

Goji bothered neither to turn or reply, as she already knew from whom the voice had come.

"May I sit with you?" Rubus tentatively sat beside the lonesome berry after finding a smooth patch in the plush grass. He had just come from talking with the king, plotting for the rest of their time in Yellowstone.

"If you must," she said stonily.

"We should talk, Goji." Rubus glanced at her, but Goji was still watching Juniper and Logan.

"I don't want to talk, Rubus." She paused. "I can't."

"Why?"

"Because I don't know what to say!" Goji sharply turned and looked him dead in the eye. She had begun lightly tearing up, her tone a frustrated mixture of grief and anger.

"Whatever you need to say, I can receive it. I have always been here for you, Goji."

She turned away and buried her head in her arms, hiding her welling emotion. "I know," she replied. The muffled words of the sniffling berry meant the world to Rubus, as it had been more than he had heard for weeks. The life of berries is short. They do not wish to waste time in sadness and grief, especially toward their loved ones. Rubus slowly placed his arm on her shoulder.

"What is troubling you, sweet Goji?"

She slowly lifted her head from her arms, damp patches of tears appearing all around.

"I . . . I don't know how to fit anymore, Rubus."

"You will always fit with us. You have always brought joy and hap—"

"Happiness abounding." Goji had heard the words many times from different Huckles, especially Rubus. "I know, Rubus, but I need to be more than that now."

Rubus removed his hand. He was slightly hurt by her words, as he had always enjoyed telling Goji of the joy that she brought. "What do you mean, more?"

"I need to find where I fit, Rubus, and it would have been a whole lot easier if you hadn't pulled me out of the one place I truly belonged." She shot up and intended to leave, as she feared losing her cool. She did not want to argue with Rubus, so she promptly made her way to the woods behind them.

"Goji." Rubus called after her, "Goji!" a second time. "Goji berry! Come back here, for all the foresty goodness of Glacier!"

Goji stopped. Rarely did Rubus raise his voice toward her. She froze momentarily, while Rubus stared at her. Sensing his glare, she slowly turned and made her way back to the riverbank, gingerly planting herself down once more.

"You don't need to yell at me, Rubus." She plucked at blades of grass beneath her, awkwardly looking at him from the corner of her eye.

"Well, why didn't you come back?" Rubus looked straight at her. Goji paused, then lifted both of her hands and cupped her chin.

"I'll talk about things when I can. I just don't know how or when."

The two berries looked at the gleeful Huckles in the river. The distant banks far downstream were dotted with perfect coniferous Trees marvelously placed, as if they were surveying the riverside. The Trees here were most calm; they responded only to the Wanderers, who meant no harm to their guests (they were well aware by now that the Huckles were here).

After a lengthy pause, Rubus spoke. "Do you remember when we used to swim, Goji? We spent summer evenings at Quartz, diving until the sun set. We would even slide across Fish Creek in the deep winter."

Goji blushed slightly. "I remember."

Rubus chuckled. "I remember when I first taught you to swim. You know, you were a shy berry when you first came to us, but we always knew you were special. It was the sheer warmth of your heart."

Goji looked at the ground. She was used to kind remarks such as these, but being a humble berry, she sometimes forgot how to receive them.

"When I taught you to swim, you tried and tried and tried. You never gave up. It was the sweetest sight, Goji. A young berry, as small as could be, pushing with all her might in the great Lake McDonald."

Goji gave a slight grin and plucked at some nearby grass again. She hesitated before deciding it was time to speak. "Well, the best memory I have is when you helped me, Rubus. That time I nearly went under. You dived straight in like an otter and pulled me out of the water."

They laughed together, remembering the summer Glacier days. Afterward, there was a pause and a deep silence. Rubus looked intently again at her as she gazed once more at Yellowstone River. "And what about now, Goji? How can I help you now?"

Goji looked at her feet, her warm heart tingling inside. Deep down she wanted to burst out and tell Rubus everything, but she feared that doing so could cause an even wider rift between them. "I'm not sure, Rubus. I'm not sure."

The two berries sat in silence. High above them, puffy clouds hung in the clear blue sky. The river flowed on before them between the banks of perfect Trees and fair meadowland. The Yellowstone day lived on.

A small critter scurried across the explosive plain. She displayed remarkable agility in her scurrying due to years of practice. Her fleeting legs sped over the ground as she skipped around volatile hole after hole, executing sharp turn after sharp turn. She had to be careful. One wrong move in this most unpredictable of lands and she could trip and fall into the natural springs below; the fierce temperature was too much for any creature. These were the volcanic springs of Yellowstone.

It was a vast and barren stretch of bare black rock face. Giant circular holes descended to the springs below, stretching from one line of trees in the east to another in the west. To a red squirrel, *Sciurus vulgaris*, this was a most arduous journey to make. Her name was Izzy. She scurried to a nearby rock and clambered to the top, and small particles trickled down as she ascended. At the summit, she surveyed the land before her. She had to be quick, as it was almost twilight, but she was sure she was nearly there. Izzy's fair red coat was complemented by a snow-white underbelly, now slightly grayed by the journey. Her furry eyes were unkempt and scruffy, and her red hair stuck out in a multitude of directions, almost as if she had been electrocuted. The squirrel sprung headfirst off of the other side of the rock and bounced through the dark landscape toward her destination.

"Nearly there . . . nearly there," she muttered under her breath as she bounced along. Far below, at the bottom of the deep craters in the land, were boiling hot springs, welling deep from the core of the Earth. Such was the chemical contents of the water that dramatic colors were created in the craters: red, yellow, and luminescent green. Deep beneath Yellowstone, a fierce volcano rages that stirs hot waters. If it were ever to erupt, perhaps all Realms everywhere would be in dire trouble.

Izzy dashed on toward her destination, weaving skillfully in between the deadly craters. As she advanced, the occasional spring bubbled over and splashed into her path, singeing the already blackened rocks. For the most part, Izzy was unharmed, but from time to time, she had to make a dramatic roll or shimmy to evade the boiling waters.

After some time, Izzy could finally make out that which she sought. Ahead lay a dark cavern, a slight but tall opening in the bleak rock. Beyond the opening and up above was a bubbling snout. Now, the snout did not seem too threatening, but Izzy and all the other creatures in Yellowstone knew that it was mighty important. Way down inside the opening, Izzy could make out a distant glow, like a blinking fire illuminating the cave. Izzy quickened her pace, scuttling with increasing speed, and as she drew closer, the luminous craters grew in ferocity, bubbling and flowing over into the arid land.

"Good! They are home." Izzy spoke extremely fast, but her words were incredibly clear. As she spoke, her little teeth came to bear. Weaving past some more craters, she leapt over a large rock and made her way to the mouth of the cave. The Huckles had been in Yellowstone for a number of hours now, so the Wanderers had to know.

The mouth of the cave was wide and high, forged by some mythical beast. Above the mouth were three relics, seemingly fossilized into the rock; one was an eagle's feather, one a dark purple dried berry, and one a small wrinkled tree root, deeply embedded. These were the relics left here by the great Elders of the Realms. They were planted here in ages gone, to commemorate the Wanderers' pass.

Izzy stood up on her two hind legs and sniffed the air, her little nose twitching and rustling. There was a putrid smell of volcanic sulfur, the kind of smell that intoxicates and surrounds the senses. Izzy winced in disgust but knew that she had to carry on. She shook her fuzzy tail and scurried off into the cave, her eyes widening as she entered. As she progressed, a fearsome gust of wind brushed past her, and the ground shook with a violent tremor. Izzy had acute senses and awareness, as did many small creatures, so she knew that the violent rumbling was the deep volcano stirring beneath. This, after all, was the great volcanic underpass, the Wanderers' home.

Izzy scurried on through the dark passage, and as she turned a corner, the path was greatly illuminated. Roaring pillars blazed through gaps in the side of the cave, extending from plumes of fire forged by the volcanic activity beneath. At times, the flames ceased, but they were quickly replaced by others further down, so the cave was never fully dark. Izzy was not frightened, as she had delivered many messages before, but the cave still made her uneasy. Whenever a creature came through the underpass, it felt as though their very being was laid bare before the eyes of the Wanderers, their innermost thoughts and intentions exposed.

Deeper inside the cave, there were ancient markings on the walls, pictures of ancient scenes from the Realms. Some looked like vast plains with wild beasts of old, and some were simpler and depicted a single creature, like a picture of a great eagle high up on the left side. The pictures were brightly colored and striking, much like the luminescent pools of the hot springs. Elsewhere in the tunnel, caverns twisted and turned from the main path, with stalactites and stalagmites marking their openings. Izzy traveled on through the main tunnel until it began to open and enlarge. The fiery pillars continued to rage, occasionally emitting fierce swathes of heat and power.

Izzy soon found herself in a deep cavern, which was ominously engulfed in shadow. A bright flash of fire roared as the cave was illuminated, and Izzy caught a glimpse of a fearsome brown beast staring at her. Even though she had seen them many times before, the brief glimpse of the Wanderer made her jump back in fright.

Click, click. The Wanderer clicked her heels against the cavern floor. The sound echoed throughout the cave and into the tunnel from whence Izzy had come. The pillars of fire flashed and raged around them, dancing deep underground, responding to the Wanderer's summons. The cavern was now fully illuminated, and Izzy could clearly see the fearsome brown hide and coat of the mighty Wanderer. She stood silent opposite Izzy, whose bushy tail was standing erect.

"What news do you bring, Isobel?"

Izzy trembled. "They are here."

The Wanderer's eyes widened slightly. "Very well. I shall inform the chiefess."

Izzy stared as Xanya the Wanderer turned away, disappearing deeper into the cave. Izzy knew then that her task was complete. The great fires began to fade, and Izzy turned back to the tunnel and went out of the cave into the twilight. The white moon shone down upon Yellowstone, and milky stars collided with the inky blue night.

The king awoke with a sudden gasp. His nightmare had occurred once more, and a disturbing sound had awoken him. The Huckles had now been in Yellowstone for around a week, and after searching in vain for the Wanderers, they had not found them. He grabbed his staff (which he kept constantly by his side) and propped himself up. Looking around, he saw that the rest of his band was fast asleep. Whatever he had heard had only reached his ears and not those of the resting Huckles elsewhere on the silent forest floor.

The king noticed the rustling in the forest once more. Some large beast was approaching.

"Who is there?"

No answer came to the king, who was now awake and alert. As his eyes adjusted to the dark, he was able to survey the clearing, where the Huckles had earlier lain to slumber.

The rustling grew louder. Something was advancing through the Trees. As well as footsteps, the king could hear loud, deep breathing, like that of a strong wild beast. He tightened his grip on his staff. As the king walked over to his drummers, he noticed small gold and silver sparks floating above the other Huckles. Ignoring them at first, he shoved the troll drummers to awaken them, and such was the strength of his arm that he almost rolled the large berries over, but despite all of his might, the drummers did not respond.

"Wake up!"

No response came.

"Wake up, will you?" The king pounded his staff on the floor, demanding a response. The noise drew ever closer, now so close that the king was sure there were some figures present in the clearing with him. As he turned toward the sound, he caught a pungent whiff of the most intoxicating smell. Finally, the purpose of the floating sparks dawned upon him. Plants and Trees, of course at the Wanderers' behest, had released spores to bind the Huckles in an inescapable sleep; all of them save for the king. He glanced once more at the lifeless Huckles, completely impervious to the Yellowstone night around them.

"Darn Trees," the king muttered under his breath as he made out the shadow of his visitors. "Who are you?" he bellowed mightily into the clearing.

The beasts loomed large in the king's presence. Their dark, twinkling eyes could be made out around the moonlit clearing, penetrating the blackness.

"King of Glacier, Huckleberry of the northern lands, you must come with us."

"I said who are you?" the king bellowed even louder, and he swept his mighty staff across the clearing with a violent thrust.

"We shall not harm you, Huckle. We come on behalf of the chiefess."

"Why could she not come here herself?" The king held an aggressive stance, all the while clutching his staff firmly in his hands.

"You are a visitor in our lands, and you must meet the chiefess Wanderer at the place of her choosing."

Slowly, the king lowered his staff and relaxed his stance. He recognized the voice. He knew the shape of the great shadows on the clearing floor, and he realized that these were the Wanderers. "How did you find us?"

One of the Wanderers crept through the shadows, coming face to face with the king.

"As I said, northern king, you are a visitor to our lands. We know all that may come and all that may pass."

With reluctance, the king dropped his guard and reverted to his normal towering stance (which was still most imposing). He knew the Wanderers were there, but their appearance was still clouded in the Yellowstone night, so he could not yet make them out.

"And how are we to travel to see her?"

"We know you to be a king of great size, able to cover much ground. You can follow us through the plains."

"How far are we to venture?"

"It matters not, Huckle King. Just know that we will arrive before the coming of the morn."

The king was reluctant, but he had little choice. This was, after all, the reason he had come. "I see. Then we should make haste."

"Of course. Follow us."

The Wanderers turned and tore through the woods with alarming agility, and their giant heads obliterated and cleared any obstacle in their path. Now, the Wanderers were correct; the king was of magnificent size, and he was able to cover great distances. Often, he had kept pace with eagles, bears, and even mountain lions. The Huckle was able to move at a fearsome pace when necessary, and he demonstrated this now. While following the Wanderers, he began to sprint, occasionally leaping felled trees, boggy streams, and sharp boulders. One can only imagine the carnage and mayhem that could have been observed watching these mighty creatures plowing through the dark forest. Had the plants and Trees not released their intoxicating spores, surely the entire Realm would have awoken in a great fright.

It was a shocking but majestic scene as they bounded across the Yellowstone land under the watchful moon. The king hopped and bounced as they passed over grassy plains and cold streams, while the Wanderers charged ahead, leading the way at frightening speed. Their small tails flailed behind them as they sped. The summer stars, of which there were many, bore witness to these awesome beings traversing the fair land. The spores that had affected so many were dispersed by the traveling pack, and the king swatted away great clumps of them with his giant arms.

Nearby, some creatures from the Great Outdoors who had not been put to sleep by the spores came to observe the great noise that had lured them in the night. Wolves, high birds of prey, and large bears kept their distance on nearby mountainsides, watching keenly as the creatures ventured forth.

It was a liberating moment for the king. After many years as a recluse from his own kin, he was finally able to journey once more with creatures who matched his might and power. Onward he followed, and onward the Wanderers charged. Along the way, they came across some foul beasts; violent wolves from the Great Outdoors. The creatures hastily smote the wolves with alarming power. The king swung his staff and sent an alpha flying, while the Wanderers flicked a great many with their awesome heads. No more dared to confront them as they traveled onward through the night.

Sometime after traveling through Yellowstone, the Wanderer in front of the herd came to an abrupt stop, as he had noticed Xanya standing guard at the cave mouth (the Wanderers were agile creatures, able to stop and start at fantastic speeds). The king, too, sharply ceased his speedy pace. He used his staff as a brake, planting it firmly in the ground. The cave mouth ahead of them was dimly lit, a beacon of light amidst the inky darkness.

Now that we have approached the cave from different angles and via different creatures, you should now find it yourselves on a map. Yellowstone is a vast park, larger than Glacier. It is so large, in fact, and such is its position, that it stretches over three states. These states are Montana, Wyoming, and Idaho. It would be helpful if you had a map of Yellowstone with you now, so that we can pinpoint the precise location of these mysterious Wanderers.

Our first point of reference on the map is the entrance through which the Huckles arrived, where we met Cassie. This entrance is close to the place currently called West Yellowstone, which you should be able to see. The Huckles traveled a long way that day, following a tributary stream all the way east and passing modern-day settlements Madison and Morris until they arrived at the Yellowstone River. On their way, they passed Madison River, the great Caldera Edge, and the 'Roaring Mountain' to the north. On the banks of Yellowstone River, deep in the woods, was where the rest of the Huckles were when the king departed, all of them silently sleeping and surrounded by spores.

Having done that navigation, we are now able to chart the moonlit journey that the Wanderers and the king undertook. When you notice the distance that was traveled that night, you will come to realize the sheer speed that these creatures possessed. Back toward the west, not as far as West Yellowstone but stopping at Madison, you should notice a point called Firehole Falls, with a river nearby called Firehole River. Follow the river south, passing the Lower Geyser Basin, and we will finally arrive at our destination.

The place is famous now, and people from all over the world come and visit. Neither the Huckles, the Wanderers, nor the Elders would ever have known that it was to become quite so popular, even though they themselves held it in the highest regard. The place was the snout that Izzy had seen earlier as she approached the cave. It is a gateway to the volcanic activity beneath, and it erupts and spouts towering columns of water at mostly the same time every day.

The Wanderers had noticed it when they first settled in the land, and they then struck a partnership with beavers, moles, and other creatures to help them build a cave underneath it. The building was difficult work; the creatures became hot, bothered, and tired, but they knew the importance of the task. They knew that this was where the Manuscripts were to be held.

"We have arrived." The lead Wanderer looked back toward the king, nodding her head as she spoke. Xanya approached the herd, and tongues of vicious light billowed out of the cave behind her. Her enormous head swayed to and fro and her tail swung from side to side as she advanced toward them through the darkness.

"The chiefess awaits within." Her tone was sharp and brisk. Whereas most creatures that the king came across adjusted their tone when addressing him, the Wanderers did nothing of the sort and spoke to the king the same way they would speak to anyone else. The herd then split like a curtain, making a path by which the king could enter the cave. Five Wanderers flanked him on either side, following him with their eyes as he advanced. He walked toward the mouth of the cave and began to head inside.

"Your staff must be left out here, king of the north," Xanya ordered.

The king was taken aback. "I take my staff everywhere, Wanderer. There is no need for it to be left outside." He ducked his head and began to walk in, but as he advanced, a hefty hoof stamped down before him, kicking up a cloud of dust from the ground. His progress was halted.

"Your staff, Huckle. Out here." Xanya spoke firmly, her directions as clear as the Yellowstone moon.

"Listen, Wanderer, what concern is it to you where I carry my staff?"

"There are no weapons permitted in the presence of the chiefess."

"It is not a weapon."

"It was used to smite down Trees just weeks ago, correct?"

The king paused, glaring at Xanya with a stern gaze. Whenever he left Glacier, he had to remind himself that there were creatures in other Realms that simply would not bow to his demands or pay reverence as those in Glacier did.

"Very well," the mighty king conceded. He needed to speak to the chiefess more than anything else at that moment; it was his primary concern. "Where shall I place it so that it will remain safe?"

"Leave it out here with us, and we will guard the staff."

"You are going to wait in the moonlight until my return?"

"Yes, King Huckle. The chiefess and any inside the cave are guarded at all times, lest the entire herd is roaming Yellowstone."

"I see. Well, I implore you to guard it carefully."

"We will."

The sullen king took a final glance at the Wanderers around him, all of whom had watched his every move. He stared at Xanya once more, a look of sternness and grit on his great berry face. "Hmph," he muttered disgruntledly, then bent down and entered the cave. The moonlight shone down, and a wolf's cry pierced the Yellowstone night.

He passed through the cave far quicker than Izzy had. The flaming pillars of fire bothered him not; neither did the colorful inky markings that decorated the cave walls. There were, after all, very few things that unnerved him. Within a few minutes he had walked the entire length of the cave, and his booming footsteps almost matched the deep rumblings underneath. He soon arrived at the same cavern that Izzy had been in hours before. The cavern was dark again, and the luminescent glow from the spring pools on the surface were the only lights present.

The king did not even flinch at the pillars of fire raging around him. Soon afterward, approaching steps echoed throughout the cavern, and at the far end, a passageway was illuminated by a faint light; a passage into the deepest part of the cave. Closer the footsteps came, and slowly the king advanced toward them.

The pillars seemed to follow him as he walked, increasing in intensity as he passed, and the aqua springs on the cavern floor bubbled with increasing ferocity as the approaching steps grew louder. They were the sound of sturdy hooves clambering over the cave floor. The fire twinkled, as if eager to burst through the ground into the world above. The king stopped, and the ground began to rumble and shake. Volcanic activity beneath was causing violent tremors as the footsteps drew ever nearer; the springs bubbled, the fire simmered, and an unnerving rumbling shook the entire cave, then an intense flash illuminated the entire cavern. A roaring crack was heard as the fires erupted and the springs boiled over. From the passageway she emerged. The chiefess of the Wanderers.

You may have noticed that thus far, I have not specified the exact taxonomy of the Wanderers; exactly who they are. That is because, so far, we have only encountered them in our tale in the dark, but now that the chiefess was grandly illuminated by the flame-lit cave, the entirety of her being was visible, and so was the clear nature of these fascinating beasts.

They are some of the oldest and most renowned in any Realm and indeed in any park. They maraud the land with awesome power, although they seldom reveal it. These creatures are large and bulky and could lift most other creatures with a simple flick of the head. With their powerful and sturdy frame, these are some of the most frighteningly able beings. They possess tremendous speed, as well as the sturdiness to excel in different weathers. The Wanderers are covered in a great thick sheet of brown, with a rough carpet of scruffy hair around their enormous skulls, and lastly, the Wanderers have dramatic pointed curved horns, which they are able to use if necessary.

You should know that this creature is a beacon of hope and power to all national parks. It is a legendary creature, one of which past tales are told and many future ones will come to be. They are born and roam free. They are the great American buffalo, *Bison bison*.

The king looked down upon her. She was shorter than the king (most creatures were), but her enormous size meant that she equaled the king in mass and weight. She glared back at him with unnerving resolve. She was older than he, but the king matched her in experience of the Great Outdoors, the Realms, and the life of all creatures. Pillars of fire danced in the background, putting on a crackling show of light for the meeting of the two formidable beings.

"Oxan." The king lightly nodded his head, acknowledging the chiefess. Other creatures in Yellowstone normally bowed or lay down before her, much like they did for the king in Glacier. Oxan knew of the king's fierce temperament, however, and on this occasion, his simple acknowledgment would suffice.

The king began to introduce himself. "I am—"

"I know who you are, king of the north."

Oxan took a step closer to the king, and her mighty frame emerged from the dark shadows. As she nodded her thick shaggy head, her black eyes twinkled amidst the raging flame. Oxan was the chiefess of the Wanderers, and it was her word that they followed. The Wanderers did not run affairs like the Huckles did in Glacier, but their word was supreme, and all creatures in the Realm knew that Oxan's word was final.

Much like the Huckles were large, much larger than the average berry, the Wanderers were greater in size than the regular bison. They were not proportionally larger in the same way that the king was, or else they would have been the largest creatures in the world and would certainly have struggled to find enough food. But they were a formidable and great size, with enough strength to protect the Realm and certainly the Manuscripts.

"What is your purpose in Yellowstone, King Huckle?" Her voice was inquisitive and wise, almost as if she were subjecting the king to an interrogation. When she spoke, it was as if the entire immediate environment was focused on her.

"I have come to request that the Manuscripts are amended." The king stood erect, projecting his deep voice throughout the entire cavern. His trunk crown struck the roof of the cave, causing smaller rocks to trickle to the floor, and the ground beneath them shook once more as the fire raged on.

"I know of your quest, Huckle. But what is *your* purpose here?" Oxan took a step closer, emerging completely from the shadows. The fire now illuminated her fully. Her great shaggy hair was twisted and frayed, with three great locks protruding at the bottom, so long that they almost scraped the ground. On the left side of her face was a harsh gash stretching from her eye to the beginning of her torso. Supposedly, she had been attacked by a fierce cougar, who had attempted to steal the Manuscripts during their wandering in high summer. Oxan's eyes were deep and alluring. Inside, you could feel the weight of seasons, the ageless pouring of snow and thunder, the harshness of fierce hail, and the intensity of the blazing sun. The king looked upon her but did not answer her question.

"The Trees refuse to engage with us. Their acts have grown tiresome to me, as have they to all of Glacier."

With that, Oxan turned away, swinging her burly head as if motioning to the king to follow her.

"I know what it is that you desire, King Huckle." As she walked back toward the passage from which she had emerged, the king noticed three bounding golden rings on her tail; monuments to a great warrior. They shone in the firelight as she proceeded, glinting as her tail swung from side to side. Oxan and the king made their way to the dark passageway at the back of the cavern.

"You know of my quest, so you know that the Manuscripts must be altered."

The ground rumbled beneath them, and the king was beginning to grow somewhat restless. He barely fitted into the cave in which they stood, and, like any Huckle, he wished to be outdoors.

"Tell me, for whose benefit are they to be altered? Yours?" Oxan responded with a permeating calm. The king was not used to being spoken to in this way.

"Oxan, the Trees will not cooperate with us. As we have grown greater in number and might, they have only sought to limit and obstruct us."

"Ahhh." Oxan gave a revelatory gasp, as if she knew something that the king did not. They then approached the entrance of the passageway. It was narrow and dark; the king would only just be able to pass through. Oxan stopped before it and lifted herself onto her hind legs, much like Morrow of the great elk. She suddenly stomped down, and the earth cracked in two before her. The sheer might of her stomp forced the ground apart, and an earthquake of sorts created a fissure beneath them. The entire passage was illuminated by fires deep below, glaring through the fissure. Oxan didn't need to worry about the rupturing of the ground; volcanic movement would soon enmesh it back together.

She turned her muscular head back toward the king, who had grown increasingly uneasy about the cave. "Watch your step, Huckle." She sensed his uneasiness and that he did not want to progress. "You want to see the Manuscripts, do you not?"

She pointed her horns toward the end of the passage, as if to indicate the writing's whereabouts. The fire raged on and billowed below. Oxan now advanced down the passage, carefully distributing her weight across the rock. Her shaggy underbelly was illuminated by the soft glow of fire underneath, and the king watched her, then advanced slowly behind.

"I wish I had my staff," he muttered under his breath.

"Your staff would be no use here, king."

He was surprised at her interjection; it was almost as if she had read his thoughts.

"The Realm, the cave, the volcanic underpass, they respond to us."

The king did not respond. He knew exactly how this felt.

They progressed down the passageway, with the king three or four steps behind. His split seed heart wished to be reunited with the outdoors, though he knew he needed to be here now. As they pressed on, a faint attractive glow emerged from the end of the passage, like an alluring pollen flower to a buzzing bee.

"So, then, you wish the Manuscripts to be altered so that you may have dominion over the Trees?"

"No, Oxan. It is my wish that the Manuscripts reflect our importance to the Realms, as we have grown greatly."

"Ahh, great Huckle," she uttered with an air of disappointment, "what do you believe the purpose of the Manuscripts is?"

The king had had quite enough of her questioning. "I do not come for a lecture, Wanderer. There is urgency to my quest."

"I am aware of that, but the Manuscripts will not be changed just because of your urgency."

He cast a stern look at the back of her immense head.

The faint glow intensified at the end of the tunnel, and light filtered in through the passage, blending with the fierce flames beneath. The king was relieved to see that the passage was coming to an end.

"Here we are."

Oxan stepped out into another cavern, which was circular and eerily silent. It was most strange, because neither the rumblings of the underworld nor the raging of the fire could be heard. In the center of this cavern was a pair of thick oak branches intertwined and interlocked, creating a staff-like podium. There were a small number of buds protruding from the podium, which seemingly was rooted in the hard earth below. It could not have been fertile soil or natural earth sustaining the buds; instead, it was some mysterious force below.

High above the podium was a snoutlike gap in the hard rock, an open portal into the world above, and the white moon shone into the cavern, illuminating the podium in the center. There was, therefore, sufficient light, which was most surprising, as the flames were no longer present. The podium itself seemed to emit its own light, a natural glow that belonged to no other object.

"The Manuscripts." The king spoke victoriously, as if his goal had finally been achieved.

Indeed, upon the podium was a most alluring book. It was bound by rustic leather, and its pages were made from the thinnest sheets of tree bark. Luminous sparks of color hovered near them, as if celebrating the great age and wonder of the document.

Oxan made her way toward the podium. "Aren't they beautiful, king of Glacier?"

The pages, indeed, were the most intriguing sight in any Realm. Upon them were intricate markings, decipherable only by a few. They varied in shape and size, and some of the markings seem to have been formed by the claws of some creatures. For the most part, the writings and markings within the Manuscripts were inscribed by eagle feathers and cast by the Elders many ages ago.

Oxan broke the king's transfixed silence. "The Manuscripts are the rules for all Realms. Anyone who steps outside the guidance of these rules is to be cast out, with weeping and gnashing of teeth."

The king was well-versed in the Manuscripts, and he knew all about their writings, but he did not possess the same amount of knowledge as Oxan, whose purpose was to protect them.

"Well, the boundaries are being stretched, Oxan, and the Trees no longer respect them."

Oxan slowly turned and looked at the king. They had not met each other many times, but there had always been a deep respect between them. Oxan had seen the king when he was much younger, when the Wanderers underwent their great migration north during a bitter winter. During this migration, the Wanderers had crossed frozen lakes and at times had been completely covered in falling snow. Oxan had wondered herself if they would make it, but they did.

The king had also met Oxan some time ago when he had come to Yellowstone. The Wanderers had beckoned him south to look upon him, as his lore and acts had drawn their attention. Also, of course, they had heard about one another countless times from the Elderberries. The Elderberries had been here at Yellowstone when the Manuscripts were first given to the Wanderers for safeguarding, and they often spoke to the king of the mighty southern beasts.

"Did the Elderberries bid you to make this journey?" Oxan spoke in a most inquisitive manner. Though her voice was deep and strong, she was always curious to learn of others' behavior, such was the foundation of her great learning. She was very wise, almost matching in wisdom, perhaps, the Elder Pines and Hyperion himself.

"Yes. They sent us south to address this growing imbalance that has occurred, and we shall not leave until it has been done."

"But did they mention the Manuscripts, great Huckle, when they sent you south?"

The king paused. Since his day of great sorrow, his thinking had become narrow-minded and he had developed tunnel vision, so he only thought about what had to be done. He did not dwell too long on the Elderberries' intentions, as for him, they were not of the utmost importance. He shook his head and his crown ruffled above him as if he were shaking off the question from the chiefess. "Look, we are here. I and my kin have traveled a long way. Now we must proceed."

Oxan ignored him and pressed on to something else that her mind had revealed to her. "I sense a great pain in you, Huckle, and I foresee that your quest will reveal it." Oxan neither quivered nor shrunk as she spoke. Speaking to the king of personal matters could very well lead to a squishing in Glacier and a fierce response elsewhere. Indeed, his temper, only ever loosely held in check, now began to fray.

"That has nothing to do with this!" He straightened his mighty back to become as tall as possible, fitting as much of himself as he could into the cavern. In response, great tufts of smoke blew from Oxan's fierce black nostrils. She stood firm.

"And how do you suppose we edit the writings, Huckle? Will you be the one to bring about this great work?"

"No, you can do it, but we will agree on what is to be writ—"

"Without the Trees?" Oxan took a step forward, breath steaming from her nostrils, the moonlit night illuminating her dark deep eyes. The king clenched his fists. His body was tense and highly strung.

"The Trees are not here," he said. The two were now almost face to face, their eyes firmly locked.

Oxan spoke. "So they didn't tell you." She turned her head, breaking the stern gaze between them, leaving the king staring into empty space. She moved back toward the Manuscripts, seemingly reading from the page at which they were open.

The king, confused, spoke again, slightly calmer now. "What are you talking about, Wanderer? There is a simple task for us to complete."

Oxan's feet tapped the floor, and she circled around the Manuscripts while looking down upon them. Once she had completed a full circle, she flicked with her horns and the ancient pages shimmered as they turned. Gentle sparks flitted above the sacred book and ascended into the night. The book was now open on one of its last pages, and three mysterious symbols could be seen. The symbols were large and colorful, arranged in a triangle, with two below and one above. The king moved closer, veering around to get a clearer look.

"What are those?"

"If you don't know what these are, king of Glacier, you have no business altering the Manuscripts."

The king ignored her comment, bending down to get a clearer view. "This one here, the bottom right . . . it's a berry." The king was referring to a purple circle, which was one of the three symbols. It had been left by an Elderberry, and it was the imprint of a real berry upon the pages.

"Yes."

"And this one, a twig." He was most interested.

"Correct again."

The symbol to the left of the berry, at the bottom of the page, was the imprint of a twig; some of the brown bark was still stuck to the page.

"And . . . Pry." The king leaned back as if learning some magnificent secret. The final mark was a deep gash upon the page, left by an eagle's sharp talon. Had Pry not been able to restrain his strength, perhaps he would have torn through the entire document when he made his mark. The king gazed at the mark, deep in thought. It had been a long time since he had encountered something unknown to him.

Oxan interrupted his thoughts as if to speed him along. "Berry, Tree, and eagle . . . the Elders and founders of the Manuscripts."

"And these are their markings." He pointed at them.

"These are their markings," she confirmed.

Oxan circled back around the Manuscripts, once more coming face to face with the king, who was still transfixed in thought. As they stood, a gentle rumbling could be heard, strong enough to permeate even this part of the cave, breaking the tangible peace. The Manuscripts, however, did not wobble or shake. The king was in deep thought, but perhaps he did not want to show it.

"Do you know the meaning of this, Huckle?"

He was beginning to figure it out. The trunk crown on his head twitched from side to side as his brain worked. A gentle rumbling occurred once more from deep, deep underneath, then a gentle silence cloaked the cavern. The Manuscripts glowed ever more, and flicks and sparks emanated from them and floated up into the night. The king looked at the floor, somewhat in defeat and somewhat in anger. "The Manuscripts cannot be altered without all three founders." The markings confirmed this; they were the seal of each of the Elders. Oxan glared at him without saying a word. She walked over to the Manuscripts once more and shoved them closed with her horns.

"That's right, Huckle, and none of them are present."

The king lifted his head, and his tone began to turn desperate. "I can speak on behalf of the Elderberries; they have imparted their wisdom to me!"

"Perhaps, but what of Pry?"

"I have not seen him for many a year, but I know that he will fly here if I seek him out."

"Well, that may be possible, but what of the Trees?"

The king's eyes watered, his face contorted, and his fists clenched once more. "There are hundreds, thousands of Trees in this Realm! They could send a root message, and a reply would be here in due course."

"The Trees here are young, Huckle; they have never seen the wisest Trees. They do not have the authority to speak on their behalf."

"This cannot be!"

The king stamped his feet so strongly that splashes of berry juice splattered onto the cave walls, and a deep anger welled within him. Oxan simply stood sternly. "It is so, king of Glacier."

The king of Glacier was not so foolish as to attack Oxan—the success of such an attack would be debatable—but it was now clear why his staff had been removed from him. Right from the berries' entrance into the park, the Wanderers had sensed the anger in the great Huckle's heart. The sullen king now hung his head in silence, and a sloshing puddle of berry juice pooled on the floor beneath him.

"I know of your pain, Huckle, but this cannot be the reason that the Manuscripts are changed."

"Why did they send me?" The king's voice was now low and deflated, lower than it had been in some time. He was still looking at the floor, so his voice could barely be heard by Oxan. She took a step closer, and the king spoke again. "Why did they send me?"

"To whom do you refer?"

The king looked at Oxan, dishevelment etched on his face.

"Why did the Elderberries bless the journey south if they knew of these requirements?"

His tone and demeanor were broken, almost as much as on that fateful day many years ago. Oxan circled all around the Manuscripts again, positioning herself between them and the enraged king.

"That I do not know."

The king looked at her and then up at the sky through the snout in the cavern roof. His eyes twitched, and a determined resolve grew within him. The sunken berry slowly moved daringly toward the Manuscripts, believing that he would now have to change them by force. Oxan glared silently at him as he advanced.

"They must be changed. We must take our rightful place within the Realms." As he drew closer, golden sparks fizzled violently from the pages, shooting into the air.

"I wouldn't come any closer, Huckle."

He blatantly ignored her, stretching out a hand to grab the Manuscripts, but as he did so, sparks flew and scorched his arm. He let out a gasp of pain but continued to reach for them. As he got closer, with his hands almost touching the first page, a deep rumbling sound came from beneath.

"Step back, Huckle." Oxan spoke calmly and slowly moved away from the center of the cavern, leaving a large perimeter around the Manuscripts. As she did so, the ground around the Manuscripts began to open and the rock shifted and pulled aside. The king strained as he stretched out, the sparks still lashing his arm. The rumbling grew and grew. It sounded like a rampaging herd of Wanderers deep underground. The king was able to place one of his hands on the page of the Manuscripts, almost reaching them, when suddenly, violent steam hissed beneath, emitting from where the ground had opened. There was now a wide circle opening around the Manuscripts, and the rumbling and steam grew and grew so that the king could not get any closer to the ancient writings, as the heat was too fierce. He was straining with all his might to keep hold of one page of the Manuscripts, and his arms stretched and strained, but as the pressure overwhelmed him, the desperate king let out a bellowing roar, looking up the cavern snout and into the sky.

Whoosh! Suddenly, a tremendous pillar of water burst upward from underneath, surrounding the Manuscripts. The cavern rumbled and shook so powerfully that even the king was knocked off his feet, and he fell onto his back. He looked most perplexed. The opening that had been around the Manuscripts had opened so that the mighty waters could erupt. The awesome pillar burst through the cavern and out of the snout above. The wall of water was so great that the king could no longer make out the Manuscripts. They were completely concealed by the immense tower of water.

The pillar made a ferocious roaring sound as it bellowed up from the ground. The king was bewildered, and his crown was dashed to the far end of the cavern. Although his gaze was mostly fixed on the water, he could just about make out Oxan through the mighty pillar; she was seemingly glowing with energy. The king sensed that Oxan was not in the least surprised by the unfolding scene. The water gushed out of the snout for around a minute before slowly abating. As the torrential onslaught subsided, small droplets of water trickled back through the snout, showering the king and Oxan but somehow evading the Manuscripts.

The wall of water finally disappeared, and the shocked king saw Oxan and the Manuscripts before him. The room was steamy, and little beads of water still hung in the air. Slowly and gingerly, the king returned to his feet. His eyes were wide, and his mouth was an open gasp. Many things had he seen in his time in the Realms, but this eruption was extraordinary. It was not so much the force of the water, but more the fact that the Manuscripts lay untouched and completely dry.

The sparks continued to fizzle from the pages, and the writings rested in the middle of the podium as if nothing had happened. Slowly, Oxan moved toward the king, who was still on his back. As she did so, the gap in the earth that had formed around the Manuscripts began to close.

"The deep erupts at similar times every day, Huckle King. But if someone tries to disturb the writings, the waters rise instantly."

The king looked on, forlorn. He knew that there would now be no hope of retrieving the Manuscripts, let alone altering them. "What am I to do, then? How can we, the Huckles, exist peacefully alongside the Trees?" It was a rather odd scene; rarely did the king demonstrate such defeat, particularly in the presence of another creature.

Oxan slowly made her way closer to him. Her thick, shaggy hair was soaking and dripping with steaming water, but the eruption seemed to have had little effect on her. "You know what the Manuscripts say. All of the founding Elders must be present in order for them to be altered."

"And how am I to approach all of the Elders?"

Oxan paused, thinking intensely as she gazed at the king. She gave a mighty shake of her head, and hundreds of droplets of water were sent spraying all across the cavern.

"The Elderberries sent you on this quest. I am sure that they will be ready when the time comes. Pry once saved your life; he also will come to your aid." Oxan paused. She thought for a moment and then took one step closer to the king, now within close proximity.

"And?" the king inquired. His question hung suspended in the still-ness of the cavern, which was still thick with water and steam.

"You must venture on and see the Trees. Only they can guide your quest."

The last of the small water droplets trickled to the cavern floor, and the sky above was finally visible once again. The king looked up toward it, his face hard and concerned.

"How am I to face the Trees?"

"You must. If not for you, for Glacier and for all of Huckle-kind."

"It cannot be!"

The king stamped his foot on the cavern floor once more, and water and small droplets of berry juice sprayed onto Oxan. "How can the Elder-berries have bestowed this quest upon me, knowing my deep hatred for the Trees? How am I to stand before them?"

Oxan was still unnervingly calm. "It is not my quest, Huckle, so I cannot mold your heart. Perhaps this is the true aim of your journey." Oxan moved one of her front feet to her long shaggy hair, gently strok-ing it with her hoof. "Yes, there is much on this path for you to learn, northern king."

He picked up his soaked crown from the floor; the great Tree trunk bedazzled with berries. He placed it back upon his head as if reasserting his power.

"Well, so be it. The Trees in Glacier have listened to me before, and they will do so again. The Trees of the southern lands will be no different!"

Oxan smiled and chuckled lightly, her brown hair still dripping wet.

"I think you'll find that these Trees are not so easily persuaded. Tell me, do you even know where you must travel?"

"Yes, of course; to the land of the Redwoods, to the high Trees, north in the southern land."

"Ahhh, but that is not the case, my friend."

The king paused. Further frustration was etched on his face. It had been a long time since he had been proven wrong or outwitted on as many occasions as he had been on this night.

"Where must I travel, then? Who will grant this request?"

Oxan moved over to the Manuscripts, still dry and still sparkling. She used her curved horns to point to one of the symbols on the first page, the embedded branch.

"Do you know who it was that left this mark?"

The king leant over, more cautiously this time, to look at the Manuscripts and looked at the page quizzically. Shortly afterward, he recognized the nature of the mark from his years of experience.

"The Elder Pines? I must go to them? But it is the Redwoods that dictate; it is the Redwoods that direct the entire southern land."

Oxan turned toward him. She would not openly admit it, but she was somewhat disappointed in the king's approach. Perhaps she just oft forgot the greatness of her own wisdom and prowess. "Well, well, great northern king. It seems even you, after many years roaming and exploring, have much to learn. Do you not know that the wisest among us are not always the most obvious? Sometimes it is those hidden or those silent that have the most to say. Perhaps this is another lesson that you ought to learn on your journey."

The king glared at Oxan for a long moment. He had had quite enough of being outwitted by this brown beast, and he decided that it was time to leave. "Very well, chiefess. I'll be leaving now." He turned his back toward her and the Manuscripts, his upper body still dripping from the incredible eruption of water that had taken place.

"Just remember," Oxan called out to him one last time as he made his way back toward the narrow passageway, "you never really leave a place until you've learnt what it has to tell you. If you haven't learnt anything, you never truly arrived."

The king looked back at her. For a moment, his eyes widened and his stance relaxed. Earlier on, when he was a younger berry, he had been much more receptive to the advice and counsel of all creatures, as he had had faith like that of a child. It was only since Bramble's passing that he had struggled to take their words to heart, and his heart had become conceited and cold. Now, though, Oxan's words cut through like none had done in a while, although the king did his best not to show it. "Farewell, Wanderer."

As the king walked on toward the passageway, the flaming tongues of fire followed him. Behind, Oxan glared. As he left, she closed the Manuscripts with her horns before tapping her hooves on the cavern floor. An echo filled the cavern, audible out of the snout and beyond, and to any who may have been dwelling around the volcanic pass. Oxan passed around the Manuscripts and made her way to the passage leading out. She tapped her feet once more and the flaming tongues were extinguished. A gentle sizzle sounded as they subsided and retreated back to the deep.

Now, if you are reading this tale, you should know that the volcanic underpass where the Wanderers dwelt is still a magnificent place to this day. It is known the world over, and the deep waters still erupt, albeit not at Oxan's command. It is, in fact, one of the most recognizable parts of beautiful Yellowstone. It is in the exact spot that we found on the map when tracing the journey through the night. It is a legendary sight. Its name is Old Faithful.

9

The Heart of a Special Berry

THE KING WAS SITTING anxiously on the forest floor. The summer sun flickered through the Trees as it had done every morning, and the early dew encumbered all that dwelt around him; mossy branches, fallen leaves, and damp twigs. A gentle gust and a subtle chill dwelt in the morning air, for it was now late summer, the month of August. Although the king had much to reflect upon, he knew that the Huckles had to depart Yellowstone soon. There was, after all, little chance of them making it to the southern lands if they delayed till winter. By then, the way would be too tumultuous, and the land was fierce. High above him, a small songbird looked down upon the scene. She twitched and jerked her head sharply, often glancing at the king.

"Yes, bird, we are leaving soon."

There was an urgency and alertness about the king as he muttered under his breath. A deep spark had been awakened within him. It was the same spark that had driven his exploration of all the Realms so many years ago. He looked up at the songbird. The king knew that all in Yellowstone was under Oxan's command and that songbirds were no different; the bird had come to prompt him. Flustered, he grabbed his staff and planted it into the ground, using it to push himself up. Brown pines and other bits of forest fell from him as he stood, and such was his height that many of the leaves took a long time to drift to the floor.

Looking around, the king saw that many of the other Huckles were finally awakening, as the spores from last night had retreated. "Up!" The king went around prodding with his staff to speed up the process, starting with the giant drummer trolls who were stretched out on the floor. Slimy gushes of dribble and ooze streamed from their mouths as they awoke from their slumber. One by one, the Huckles awoke. They stretched wide, oblivious to the king's recent experience, and took in the morning sun.

"Ahh, look, the season's a' changing." One of the smaller members of the band was looking down and grabbing his skin. It had begun to sag and wrinkle slightly, and small folds were appearing. As it was still late summer, the wrinkling was not so dramatic, but come winter, the Huckles would look very different, with dramatic folds and creases all over. This was the life of all berries, and, as a matter of fact, all things in the Realms changed by season. The Huckles did not feel in the least inconvenienced by the change, because it helped them to keep a grasp of time.

The king spoke. "Yes, it is, so we must move on quickly."

The band simultaneously looked at the king, somewhat surprised. This was one of the fullest sentences he had produced in some time.

"To where are we headed?" It was one of the choir Huckles, with her beautiful garland of berries gleaming in the sunlight, that mustered the courage to respond to him. The king did not respond immediately but kept prodding sleeping Huckles, sometimes quite sharply, in the side.

After he had poked and prodded each slumbering Huckle at least three times, he looked toward the forest and responded, "South, to the land of the great Trees."

The lukewarm sunlight bore down upon them, and all of the Huckles gazed southward in the same direction as the king. He was looking through a gap in the Trees onto a woodland path that lay beyond. Some of the earliest autumnal leaves had begun to drift slowly toward the floor, landing gently below. It was this path that the king's band would take. Southward they would go.

Rubus lay peacefully asleep. It was the most peacefully he had slept in some time, because he knew that he and the rest of the Huckles could not be harmed here in Yellowstone. The knights had fallen asleep on the riverbank, on which they had spent most of their days in this wondrous Realm. Goji, who was sitting along from Rubus, was wide awake.

She was still struggling with her sleep, despite her and Rubus's conversation earlier on. While waiting for the other Huckles to awaken, she looked up to where a gentle tweeting sound was coming from a branch nearby. It was the same songbird that not so long ago had spoken to the Huckle King, although Goji did not know this. The bird twitched and tweeted, seemingly trying to communicate something to her. Had Goji not been so concerned with other things, perhaps she would have summoned the bird and been able to receive its message. Alas, the bird twitched and chirped until it knew its task was futile, then flew away.

Goji looked over some sleeping Huckles to find Rubus, who was still fast asleep. If he was asleep, it meant that the rest of the Huckles were as well, as it was always Rubus who arose first, Rubus who woke the other Huckles, and Rubus who started the day. This had always been one of the qualities of his that Goji admired greatly. Rubus put the other Huckles before himself, and rarely did he demonstrate selfishness. Goji knew, after all, that it was this very selflessness that had taken her in. She often wondered what her life would have been like if Rubus had not come to her.

She loved Rubus, and deep down she wanted to make him proud above all things. Rubus had taught her how to talk, how to hear, how to play music, and he had taught her the most amazing things, including the deepest secrets of Glacier. All manner of plants, fruits, and creatures, Goji only knew what they were because Rubus had shown her. Often, in days past, they would go on woodland walks and Rubus would lift Goji up onto his back or hold her hand as they strolled along. He would tell her of all the things that they encountered; their names, what they did, and what their purpose was. Without walks like those, Goji would not have become the berry she was today.

Perhaps most importantly, Rubus had taught her how to play. It took many months and seasons, but, patiently, Rubus taught his beloved Goji to play the berryrumpet. He taught her to blow, to use her breath, to be patient, until eventually sweet melodies could be heard all around Huckle Village, gently drifting from the window of Goji and Rubus's little hut. Goji would never forget the great sacrifices that Rubus had made to guide her and love her. They had developed a bond that not many in all of Glacier ever had. It was all the more painful to her, then, that the relationship between them was strained. Goji simply could not understand why Rubus kept pushing her to further devote herself to the king and why she had to leave Glacier and accompany them on this journey. She did not, of course, think too highly of the king himself, particularly of his dismissive tone toward Rubus. Goji saw Rubus's great efforts for the Huckles, and Goji quietly thought to herself that the king did not appreciate them. To add to this, Goji knew that the king had always rejected her on account of her being an outsider. It made less sense, then, that Rubus was pushing her to serve him more. She pondered where the two of them would go from here.

As Goji stared at Rubus, her seed heart a delicate balance of joy and anxiety, a small scurrying could be heard nearby. Goji's hearing was excellent, and she could hear the sound from a long way away. It sounded to her like a small woodland creature, and its hurried scuttling suggested that it was drawing closer with urgent intent. After a moment, sure enough, a small creature burst out of the nearby trees behind the riverbank, weaving in and out of the sleeping Huckles on its way to Goji. Near the same group of trees, the songbird from earlier could be seen perching on a branch nearby. She was out of breath and panting hard, as if she had just returned from a tiresome journey delivering a message. The bird had indeed earlier delivered its message to the scurrying woodland creature who was now hurrying to pass it on to Goji.

As the scuttling grew louder, Goji could see that it was a fluffy, plump red squirrel. Her bushy tail shot sharply into the air, and her soft white undercoat was exposed as she leapt across the floor. Sprinting at full speed, the squirrel collided with some Huckles on the way, and disgruntled groans could be heard as the sleeping berries were disturbed. Izzy skidded to a dramatic halt as she reached Goji, spraying blades of grass and debris onto her. Goji could not help but be slightly taken aback.

"Greetings, north-comer. I am Izzy the red squirrel. I come with a message from the Wanderers." Izzy blurted out the words at full speed, catching her breath quickly in between words.

Goji had to pause to take in the situation before she responded. "Hi, Izzy, nice to meet you. How exactly did you find us?"

Izzy responded instantly, as if the message she had to deliver was bursting within her. "The Wanderers have known all along where you are, and now it is time for you to depart."

"Oh." Goji paused thoughtfully. "They have known where we are? Why have we not seen them?"

"The Wanderers appear when they wish, but they are aware of all that happens in Yellowstone, even if they may not be found."

"I see." Goji looked around at the other Huckles, who were still fast asleep. Izzy's high-pitched voice was too quiet to wake them up. "Well, Izzy, I'm afraid we cannot leave instantly. Our king, for whom we came, is not present with us."

Izzy nodded rapidly. "The king of the Huckles has already been made aware of Oxan's edict, and he is due to meet you at the southern pass on the way to the great mountains."

Goji raised her eyebrows. Although not surprised, she was most irritated with the king, who had not bothered to come back and retrieve the rest of them. "Oh, has he now?"

"Yes, and now you must do the same." As Izzy spoke, she continually gestured southward with her tiny fingers.

"Why must we leave so suddenly?"

"The blustery autumn draws nigh, and the path before you must be journeyed before the bleak winter."

Goji looked out at the river. As much as she wanted this quest to be over, she would be sad to leave Yellowstone, such was its allure and irresistible beauty. No creature that ever comes across Yellowstone leaves untouched. She turned to the squirrel, half wishing that they could switch roles. "Very well," Goji said reluctantly. "You stay here while I wake the others, so that they can hear the message from you."

Izzy gave a sharp nod, then scurried back toward the Trees, where she climbed to a high vantage point. "Gather them over here."

Goji watched as the little creature scurried away, her bushy tail still pointing to the sky. Goji then moved along the riverbank, waking the Huckles one by one. Unlike the king, Goji was gentle and shifted the sleeping berries from side to side, talking softly in their ears. One by one, they awoke from their slumber. Such was Goji's care that she even went to the river and fetched cold, fresh water for the parched berries and soaked some nearby leaves for them to suckle on.

"What is the hour?" Juniper woke up somewhat gracefully compared to the others, slowly wiping the dew from her eyes.

"Good morning, Juniper. It's early morn. I have received an important message from one of the creatures of Yellowstone," Goji explained as she handed her some soaked leaves.

All around, the Huckles woke, some peacefully and some with obtuse stretching and yawning. A plump, awkward Huckle named Rasp lost his balance as he stretched, then tripped on a nearby rock and rolled down the riverbank into the cold water. The laughter that ensued was enough to fully wake the docile Huckles. Through the now jubilant crowd, Goji could see Rubus walking toward her. He seemed concerned, as if he had forsaken his duty by not being the first awake. "What has happened, Goji?"

Goji responded with her eyes on the floor, still uncertain about how to interact with him. "I received an important message from one of the creatures of Yellowstone. She is over there."

Rubus looked at the Tree that Goji was pointing out. High on top, he could make out the small brown creature frantically waving her arms, trying to get the attention of the berries below. Rubus and the other Huckles looked at the tree, puzzled, trying to make some sense of this early morning. Slowly, the Huckles made their way across the ground that they had been sleeping on, past the dark patches that they had made in the grass. Goji shifted to the back of the crowd, not wanting to explain any more of the situation to Rubus, and behind them, Rasp climbed up the riverbank, dripping wet.

With Rubus in front, the Huckles reached the bottom of the Tree. Above them, Izzy was waving frantically, displaying vigorous emotion on her small face as she tried to communicate with the Glacier folk. Her hair and tail were completely fuzzy; it was as if she had been spun round and round. Despite all her mighty efforts, Izzy could not speak loud enough for the berries to hear, and the Huckles stood confused, some still half asleep, some scratching their heads, and all looking increasingly puzzled at the tiny creature in the Tree above.

"Greetings, creature of Yellowstone. What news do you bear?" Rubus stepped forward out of the crowd, projecting his voice loudly up to Izzy above. He tried to be respectful, despite not being able to hear a word she was saying. In response, Izzy kicked and stamped on the small branch on which she stood, still straining with all her might.

"What is your name?" Rubus asked. Izzy shouted with her mouth wide open, bellowing so loudly that she seemed in a fit of rage. She shot her arms out like shooting stars, but she still could not be heard. Rubus looked around at his fellow Huckles, who simply shrugged. Some of the Huckles began to chuckle softly at the bizarre scenario. The perplexed Huckle commander looked up at the Tree once more, where Izzy kicked and screamed again before giving in. She crossed her little arms and legs and sat down upon the branch, wholly fed up and bothered.

"I cannot hear you, little creature!"

Goji pushed through the crowd of berries, much like Izzy had skipped past them when they were sleeping earlier. "Let me speak to her."

"Goji, I cannot—"

"Just let me speak to her," Goji said sharply. She was frustrated that they had been put in this position in the first place. The king had not bothered to deliver the message himself, and now this little squirrel was embarrassed and fed up high above. Goji tapped lightly on the Tree, and Izzy peered over the edge of her branch as if looking down from an unscalable cliff. "I can definitely hear you, Izzy the squirrel." Moments like these were common for Goji. Back home, she was always trying to make the creatures of Glacier feel included. Izzy took a nervous glance at the other Huckles in the crowd. She seemed embarrassed to start talking again. Her tail had unfluffed, and she no longer appeared puffy and shocked, more deflated and sunk. Slowly, she glared down at Goji, who was gazing up at her lovingly.

"I'm trying to deliver the message to all of them," Izzy said.

As you may remember, Goji had exceptional hearing on account of her being a special type of berry, so she could make out Izzy's words as well as she could make out Rubus's and anyone else's. "I know." She tried to be as reassuring as she could to Izzy. "And if you tell me what to say, I will deliver the message to them."

"Why is it that you can hear me but they can't?"

"I'm just a bit different from them."

Izzy was skeptical but also grateful that someone could hear her at last. "Very well. Tell them that the great chief—"

"Wait!"

Goji politely interrupted the squirrel, waving her hands toward her as she spoke. She turned to Rubus and the others and then back toward the Tree. Afterward, slowly but carefully, Goji began to climb the Tree, reaching high for branches above.

"Goji, what are you doing?" Juniper exclaimed from the middle of the crowd.

Rubus was not surprised, as he knew the intentions of Goji's heart, and he had seen actions such as these many times before. During their times in Glacier together, Goji had scaled trees, dived into lakes, and even crawled into little burrows to speak to creatures. The way she saw it, she did not want woodland folk to have to leave their habitat or their home to communicate with the Huckles. Whereas creatures far and wide came to deliver messages to the king, Goji would always go to them. She wanted all to fulfill their purpose.

Now she was bravely climbing the Tree so that the squirrel could remain where it belonged. Ever since Goji had lived among the Huckles, she'd felt that this was a value that they had slowly begun to lose; respect for other creatures' natural habitats.

"Careful up there!" Rasp shouted from the back of the crowd, still shivering from the cold of the morning lake. Goji looked down at the berries with a look of contentment, and on her face Rubus could sense more joy than had been seen in her for some time. The Huckles looked on as she scaled the Tree, and once she reached the top, Izzy scooted back, making space for her on her branch. The valued squirrel sharply stood aloft and perched as if meeting royalty.

"Greetings, northern traveler. That was great climbing." Izzy's little nose twitched as she spoke.

"Thank you, Izzy, and thank you for making space on your branch. Now, let's be on with this message!"

Izzy nodded. As Goji bent down to her level, the squirrel put her hand to her own mouth as if she were telling some mysterious secret. Bit by bit, the squirrel passed her message on to Goji, who projected it loudly to those below.

"Huckles of the northern land!"

Goji spread her arms wide as she talked but was careful not to stand in the way of Izzy, so that the Huckles below could still see her.

"You have been welcome guests in our Realm, but now your path must continue onward. You must journey south, past the mighty mountains, past the yawning gap, and on to the barren, scorched lands."

Rubus stepped closer to the Tree; he was now at the base of it. It was much like when he and Goji had played when she was little. She used to climb high up a Tree and pretend to be the king speaking to the creatures of the forest. "Where is the king? Why has he not passed this message on to us?" Rubus asked.

"The king has advanced onward and will meet you at the southern pass, past the lake deep and wide."

Rubus still appeared puzzled, so Goji bent down to Izzy, asking her for more information, and Izzy was happy to explain.

"The king has met with our mighty chiefess, Oxan, and received an edict. Here in Yellowstone, all of the Realm flows as one. There was no need for him to come back for you, as Oxan's creatures have passed on everything you need to know."

Izzy's words were only partially true. Unbeknownst to her, the king did not realize that Oxan would have the message passed on to the rest of the Huckles, so he really should have come back to meet them. Dramatic urgency had descended upon the king, and he had developed tunnel vision in terms of the quest. Rejoining the Huckles had not been the first thing on his mind. Selfish ambition had he. "Very well." Rubus did not question the king's actions in the same way that Goji did, as he was most loyal. "So how do we proceed to this southern pass?"

"There is a wooded path that will lead you southward. Should you become lost, Oxan will be aware."

The Huckles looked at one another. They had known of the Wanderers' great influence and reach, but they hadn't realized that it was this strong.

"And when will we get to meet the chiefess?" It was Logan who spoke from the back. Indeed, many of the Huckles had been excited to meet the Wanderers after hearing tales of them for many years. To leave Yellowstone without meeting her would be a great disappointment. Izzy tried to temper their expectation.

"If the chiefess wishes to make herself known, she will reveal herself to you."

The Huckles murmured among one another, some confused, some disappointed. Such was the magnetic allure of Yellowstone that the disappointment of leaving was starting to dawn upon them.

"Can we not stay for a few more sunsets?" an unseen Huckle enquired from the crowd.

"I'm afraid not, for your quest is of great magnitude. The life of all Realms, and the harmony therein, is dependent upon it."

A quiet moan echoed from the crowd. Rubus spoke, wanting to raise the morale of the cluster. "Very well, creature of Yellowstone, we bid you thanks for our time in your Realm." He lightly touched the bottom of the Tree as he bid goodbye.

Izzy closed, "Our Realm will always be open, and those who seek its beauty will find it." With that, she scurried down the Tree and off into the woods behind. The red squirrel did not look back at the Huckles, as she was still somewhat embarrassed by the previous episode. Afterward, Goji slowly made her way down the tree, confident and sure-footed, and the Huckles watched her. When she reached the bottom, the Huckles were waiting with their eyes wide in amazement. Some were aware of Goji's special abilities, but many were not.

"Well, to the southern pass we go, then." Goji spoke to the crowd.

After looking at Goji with pride, Rubus turned and began to organize the cluster. They picked up their belongings and took final forlorn glances at the beautiful river where they had spent most of their time. Rubus whistled loudly into the air, and the familiar thump of Morrow and the herd sounded soon afterward. It was time to venture forth.

They had some way to go meet the king and his band at the southern pass. As they journeyed, they witnessed sights, smells, and sounds that made them all sadder to depart. The heart of the Huckle desires nature, after all, and the life of the Realms. Nowhere in the whole of the United States is this life found in greater abundance than at Yellowstone. They passed golden meadows, silver streams, lush dancing Trees, and high waterfalls, all of which reminded them of home. Some way along their journey, they noticed a large rain cloud in the east. A little further along, the cloud subsided and a glorious rainbow emerged, arching high and wide over a broad plain of grass. The colors of the rainbow defeated the gray behind it, creating a beautiful palette of color in the broad sky, and beneath the rainbow a number of elk could be seen grazing peacefully. Had they not been transporting the Huckles, Morrow and the herd would surely have gone to share fellowship with them.

It took the group two days to pass through Yellowstone to the southern pass, and they spent one night camped on a high ledge overlooking a waterfall. Gentle snores could be heard amidst the falling water, and as the Huckles slept peacefully through the night, crystal splashes of water bounced off the smooth rocks below. All the while, small songbirds and little woodland critters followed the Huckles unseen, making sure for Oxan that they were on the right path.

The next day, they traveled through woodland until a large blue lake began to emerge, the very lake that Izzy had mentioned.

"There it is," said Vernus.

"Yes, we must surely be close now," replied Rubus.

"I wonder if the king is already waiting for us."

"I should think so."

The Huckles took a break by the lakeside. Morrow and the herd went off in search of plump leaves, and the Huckles took in one of the last sights of Yellowstone that they would encounter. The lake was wide and deep, with a lone island way off in the distance.

"I'm really going to miss this place." Logan moved alongside Goji, who was looking out over the water. It was a rare notion for a Huckle to miss anywhere outside of Glacier.

"Yes, it's beautiful. Such wonderful creatures. They all seem to belong so perfectly," she replied softly.

Logan picked up an ovular stone and threw it far into the lake. "Say, are you feeling any better?"

"Huh?"

"You know, before we came into Yellowstone we were talking about your life, missing Glacier and all. I wondered if Yellowstone has impacted you."

"Oh. Thanks, Logan. Erm, I'm not sure, really. I just want to enjoy it while we're here as much as we can."

Goji was, of course, not revealing all that was within her. She was still confused and distressed. One thing that she knew now for certain, however, was that the rest of the group needed her for the remainder of their journey. She was certain that there would be more episodes like what had transpired with Izzy, and she couldn't bear to think about what may have taken place had she not been there. She had to bury whatever was within her for now, for the good of the Huckles, for the good of Rubus, for Vernus, Juniper, Logan, and all. She sighed deeply and picked up a stone near where Logan had just picked up his. She then looked at the solitary island, alone but visible. It seemed to be so central to the lake, as if it would not be complete without it. She arched her arm far back and threw the rock toward it.

Later in the day, the group reached the southern pass. The late summer sun had already begun to depart, and the path upon which the Huckles had traveled all day widened dramatically as if expanding to the world beyond. In the middle of it now, facing the south with his back turned, was the Huckleberry King. His band surrounded him, and while they waited, they were practicing melodies and producing clear, strong purple mist notes. As we have learnt, the king had very little patience, but music did not seem to be something that bothered him. Perhaps it reminded him of the melodic rhythm of life found in all Realms, the rhythm that had grown him into the berry that he was. The king sensed the approaching group and turned to face them before they could reach him. "Where have you been?"

Rubus was somewhat surprised, much as the band had been the day before. Not only had the king asked a question, he had also initiated the conversation. "We left as soon as we received a message from Oxan, my king."

The king cared little for Rubus's explanation. To him, the cluster should have searched for the king and found him, presumably by communicating with the creatures of Yellowstone. The king, perhaps, forgot that this Realm was not his own. "Well, we must be leaving now. Bid farewell to this place."

Some way behind Rubus, Goji looked at the king with contempt, deeply unsatisfied with his approach to the situation. Rubus, however, glanced at the king wonderingly. He sensed a change in his attitude; in his face and in his heart. Only Rubus could read the king in this way; only he had spent long enough in his presence.

The king turned back and faced the southern road, and Rubus turned back toward the Huckles. They were tired and despondent. It had been an emotional experience for them in Yellowstone, and the thought of leaving weighed heavily on them, particularly (as they had heard) as the road ahead was hard. The season was changing, and their quest was a long way from being over. Many of them would have happily remained in Yellowstone for some time longer and then returned home. For the first time, Rubus was not sure how he would motivate his knights. Luckily for him, it would not be his words that would lift them.

Out of a bush nearby, Izzy came crashing through some branches. She braked at full speed beneath Goji, knowing not to repeat her attempts to speak to the whole crowd. Goji stroked her head gently before leaning down to listen to her. She then began projecting her words to the group.

"The Wanderers are nigh!"

The announcement drew gasps and excited exclamations from the crowd. Rubus looked at the king, but his gaze was fixed on the southern road. From nearby, deep drumbeats could be heard. No words like the song of the king or that of Hyperion sounded, just deep drumbeats, and soon, from Trees on each side of the path, the first thick brown heads emerged. They passed through the woods with grace and strength, a combination rarely found but present in these legendary beasts.

The Huckles stood rooted to the spot. Many of them had grown up with tales or heard passing rumors, and now the mighty Wanderers were before them. They began to line both sides of the path while the drums continued to sound. There came three waves of the Wanderers, so that the lines on the path stretched long and wide.

"What are they doing?" Logan whispered to Goji.

"I think they are seeing us away."

Indeed, she was quite right. The Wanderers had come to see the Huckles off to the southern lands as well as bless their journey. After the line of Wanderers stretched as far as the Huckle eye could see, the drumming stopped and the Wanderers faced inward. No creature that came forth carried a drum; the deep sounds were a mystery of the forest summoned for the Wanderers alone. An eerie silence hung in the air as the

Huckles stood amazed. They could hear the snorting of the Wanderers and the occasional swiping of their hooves upon the ground.

"What now?"

"I don't know, Logan. I've not met them before." Before Goji had time to bend down to Izzy and ask, a deep drumming sounded from the forest once more. This time the sound was deeper and louder, so deep that it shook the seed hearts of some. All around, woodland creatures could be seen scurrying this way and that. Some of them raced deeper into the woods from where they had come, but some of them came to the path and stood alongside the Wanderers. The drums went on and on until the path was completely lined with creatures big and small: The family of Yellowstone. The king was unmoved; he had had enough of the Wanderers for the time being.

The drumming stopped, and on the left side of the path, a loud creaking sound could be heard, like trees in a violent storm. The rest of Yellowstone, even the blowing winds, seemed to stop at the approach of Oxan through the woods. The Huckles looked nervously toward the creaking sound. The Trees on that side of the path had bent down and in-ward, as if bowing, and in the same way, the creatures that lined the path had stooped low in respect. The Wanderers fell to one knee while other creatures, wolves, elk, and strong birds, knelt in their own way. Cassie and her children had made the long swim down from the river; they were bundled into cute little balls of fur, paying homage.

Oxan advanced through the woods with a powerful presence. As she passed the Trees, it seemed as though they were trying to bend lower. In the day, and not in the dark of the cave, she could be seen more clearly. Her scruffy coat was a courageous shade of brown, and her giant hooves sunk into the earth as she walked, leaving behind gaping footprints, while her horns glistened a menacing white. Despite the awesome presence that Oxan mustered, one could still sense her age and wisdom. Her black eyes were deep and wide, and every Huckle that glanced at her felt as though they were opening up to a new world. Their home of Glacier was no lon-ger the only place they knew. To come here, to see Yellowstone, to see the Wanderers and now the chiefess Oxan; the Huckle Knights would never be the same.

Oxan stepped onto the path where the Huckles and the king stood, then tapped her hooves loudly on the ground. The creatures of Yellow-stone rose as one, and the Huckles remained silent. Oxan trotted around them as if checking they were ready for battle. She looked them up and down, sometimes even prodding gently with her horns. Many of the Huckles were petrified, and great beads of berry juice sweat dripped to the floor. Once she had fully circled them, she came close to Rubus, who stood between the knights and the king. "Well now, you must be Rubus."

"Yes, I am—" Rubus yelped as he felt a sharp pain in his heel. Looking down, he saw a furious Izzy motioning to him that he should bow. She tossed her arms into the air as if Rubus had committed some unspeakable crime. Rubus took a quick glance at the king, whom he felt he was betraying, before gingerly bowing. But when he was halfway down, Oxan used her horns to prop him up, stopping him from bowing lower.

"That will be quite enough, Huckle of the north." Rubus stood upright, an awkward look etched upon his face. "Thank you, Izzy. That will be all now," Oxan said to the squirrel.

Izzy stood on her hind legs sharply, then nodded quickly and scurried off at a frantic speed, joining the line of creatures on the left-hand side.

"You are the leader of the Huckle Knights, correct?"

"Yes. I am Rubus, first servant to the king and lead commander of the Huckle Knights."

Rubus tried not to make eye contact with Oxan, but the pull of her weighty eyes was too great, like the force of a strong river current.

"Well now, Rubus, I am here to see you off, onto this next grand stage of your journey."

Rubus looked back toward the king, but he was still facing away from the others, seemingly unmoved by the whole scenario. "The king is the one with whom you should converse." Rubus was trying to remain as loyal as he could.

"I have spoken to him enough, commander. He knows what he must do. It is you to whom I now speak."

Rubus now looked deep into Oxan's eyes. He had the feeling that Oxan knew more about himself than he did; more about him, more about the king, more about all of the Realms. She spoke again before he could. "Tell me, commander, what do you know of the Ancient Pines?"

"They are the Elder Pine Trees of the southern land."

"Indeed, and do you know of their purpose?"

"Not too much, chiefess, but I believe they had a role in the forming of the Manuscripts."

"That is correct indeed, and it is for that reason that you go now to them."

Rubus nodded. He did not understand why this was their path, but it did not matter much to him. Of greater concern was the welfare of his knights and the king. The Huckles could and would go on. "What if we lose our way?"

"The way is clear, commander; it is only your judgment that could make it cloudy. You keep your thoughts pure and you will find it every time."

He nodded once more. "And what of the king?" It was a most odd scenario for Rubus to be asking another creature to give him wisdom concerning the king, but clearly, she had gotten through to him in some way.

"He must find his own way." She paused and gazed at him intently. "Just know, commander, for your quest to succeed, the king must realize that he needs you all as much as you need him." She cast her gaze across the entire Huckle crowd while speaking. Rubus was encouraged by her words. Seeing that she had reached his heart, she began to trot off, but then she paused and glanced at Goji beside him.

"Well now, you are a special berry."

"My name is Goji," she replied.

"Yes, I have heard the tales." Oxan looked her up and down, spending more time analyzing her than she had done any other creature. She squinted her eyes as if sensing something within her. "You did not want to take part in this quest."

Rubus stood stone-faced next to her, and the words hit Goji like falling branches.

"I—"

"You do not need to explain yourself to me, Goji berry. It is your own self that you must convince."

Goji was also pulled into her eyes.

"You cannot run from your purpose, berry; that is not the life of the Realms. The more you run, the more you will be directed back to your path."

"Where . . . is that path?"

It was an astonishing scene. Here were two of the most renowned berries in all of Glacier, and in the middle of the woods they were taking advice from a creature whom they had never met. "One may plan their steps, but it is the Creative One who plots our course." With that, the great chiefess walked away, and the gold rings on her tail swung to and fro. She walked back toward the bent trees from where she had come but stopped on the edge of the woods before she went in. Turning around, she uttered some last words to them both.

"Berries, in your quest, you must work together. Remember also that there are other creatures whose burden you must bear." Rubus nodded, but at that point, her words were unclear to him.

He and Goji stood silent, and Vernus, Juniper, and Logan looked on. The drums sounded once more, and the creatures lining each side of the path turned and went back into the woods. The Wanderers departed one by one along the same path down which Oxan had disappeared, while the Huckles looked on in awe.

Once all of those from Yellowstone were gone, the late summer sun bore down with a fading light. The journey had to commence.

"Let's go." The deep booming voice of the king interrupted the serene forest ambience, and the court moved forward. The Huckles mounted the herd and moved as one, with Rubus in the lead. Slowly, they filed around the king and his band until the normal formation was resumed. The journey south had begun.

The Redwood Council stood gallantly in the clearing. The High One was a number of minutes late, but it mattered not. Trees are never rushed. Some of the leaves of the great Redwoods had begun to fall, meaning that the top halves of the Trees, which resembled heads of hair, were now showing many gaps. It mattered not to the Trees that the seasons were changing. Trees are never worried.

"The berries are on their way here." It was Sap who spoke first. His voice was loud and strong, and the wind carried it far beyond the council. In this way, many of the woodland creatures nearby knew about the goings-on of the Realm and affairs beyond. You might have thought that the Trees would want to keep their council meetings a secret, but it was not of concern to them that the forest might hear.

"Yes, that is why the council has been summoned. We must prepare the forest accordingly." Fir spoke with an authoritative tone. Once she had finished speaking, some leaves fell from her, as she was an older Tree. The council had indeed been summoned to discuss the matter at hand. All of them, minus the High One, were present.

"What preparations are we to make?" Oak had an incredibly thick trunk. Some woodland folk say that somewhere deep in his lineage, he shared ancestry with an oak Tree.

"For that, we await the High One's advice." Fir was perhaps the wisest of them all. Her trunk was etched with memories. Many songbirds had carved words and beautiful songs of praise into the trunk; messages of thanks and adoration. Oak bent forward ever so slightly, as if gesturing that he agreed with her.

The Trees waited silently in the clearing. The occasional passing of a songbird and the soft falling of leaves were the only sounds to be heard. Unlike in Glacier and Yellowstone, the change of season was not felt as harshly in Redwood. The forest is well equipped for all seasons. Adding to all the wonderful aspects of the Redwood Trees, there is this; in times of fierce wind and storm, they bind their strong roots together underground. The Trees create a dynamic and unshakeable network of roots, and when they band together in this way, they simply cannot be uprooted. The Huckleberry King in all his might could not even hope to lift a single root off the ground. Such a wonderful feat demonstrates the Trees' preparedness for the harshest of climates. It is why they grew to such giddy heights and why they reigned over Redwood and all of California.

Before long, a deep thumping could be heard from afar. Over the horizon emerged the Tree named Hyperion. The songbirds, many in color, rushed to meet him as he approached, and they began to circle around him while chirping their melodic tune:

> *Dum dididdy dum*
> *He started as a stump!*
> *Dum dididdy dum,*
> *He walks with a thump!*

Onward Hyperion advanced.

> *Dum dididdy dum*
> *He dwells so ever high*
> *Dum dididdy dum*
> *The High One is nigh!*

He reached the edge of the clearing, towering above everything before him and behind him. The birds who had accompanied him flew in every direction, skipping from branch to branch, then away through the forest.

"Greetings, council." Once he had reached the clearing, the king moved rather quickly, then planted himself into his earthy throne. The council bowed gently, and many leaves fell to the ground.

"You will all be aware of why we are gathered here."

"Yes. The berries from the north come this way. They wish to battle with us!" Oak was not too fond of the Huckles and found it incredible that they would dare come to Redwood to challenge the Trees.

"No, Oak. It is no longer us that the berries seek."

The Trees were confused. Some twisted their trunks to look at their neighbors and some lifted their highest branches toward the sky. Even some songbirds who were perched around looked bewildered, as they had heard rumors that the Huckles had begun to traverse the southern pass.

"Who, then, is it that they seek, O High One?" Fir inquired.

Hyperion paused. "They are traveling to the Ancient Pines," he replied.

"The Ancient Pines? What business have the berries in the southern forest?"

"I do not know exactly how this journey may unfold, but I believe the Wanderers may have directed them forth."

The Trees, even Hyperion, sometimes took a while to learn things from Realms afar. They could pick up on the happenings in Redwood in an instant, but from a distant land such as Yellowstone, the messages took some time to reach them.

"Ah, so what will become of us? What must we do?" Oak asked.

"The Pines must be told; they have been in a deep slumber for many years. We must awaken them and tell them," the High One replied.

"Do you believe that they are in danger?" Fir responded.

"I believe that all is in danger if we do not act as one."

"Very well. We shall give word to all we can. We shall tell the cougars, the eagles, and the bears. They will travel fast to the southern lands to awaken the Pines," Oak said confidently.

Now, you may be wondering why the Trees could not simply pass a root message to the Pines there and then, but the truth was, these Ancient Pines were most reclusive and did not wish to be disturbed often. Somehow or other, though, they always managed to uncover the whisperings of the Realms. Hyperion's trunk creaked and groaned as a smile was etched across the entire width of it. "Yes, Oak, some creature will deliver the message, but you should know, dear friend, that size is not everything, especially in the forest."

"But who will go? We must alert them."

"I think we have done just enough," he said calmly. "Come, council, let us bind together our roots, and let us stand firm in the midst of this great trial, for all Trees and for all Redwood."

The undergrowth rumbled as the thick roots burrowed through. All members of the council wrapped their roots around one another, creating a bond as strong as anything could be. The ground throbbed as the roots pulsated. Far and wide, the Trees sent the pulses, and the messages went forth at lightning speed. Through the entire forest and beyond, the word traveled.

☙

Some way away from the council, on the edge of the forest, a small black-and-white bird was perched delicately on a thin branch. A light rain had begun to fall, and the passerine trembled as the air grew cold. Birds are much smaller and frailer than other creatures, so they must be careful of their temperature.

He swooped down onto the branch below and rested next to a large leaf that had been soaked by rain, then used his beak to gently sip the water and nutrients from the leaf. As he drank, the veins of the leaf pulsated. The bird was making sure that it had got the message correct. He trembled once more as a cold wind swept past.

"Awaken the Pines of the southern forest," the bird muttered to himself. The thought of journeying most of the length of California frightened him, but a creature far greater than he had shown him that he could overcome mighty heights. Sometimes all it takes to conquer our journeys is a little bit of belief. The bird puffed his chest and spread his wings as wide as he could. When he used to make long journeys, he used to imagine himself as an eagle or a hawk, some awesome bird capable of legendary journeys, but now Hyperion had revealed to the bird that he had an important purpose just as he was. He did not need to pretend to be another. Bill thought to himself that he could do all things through Hyperion, who strengthened him. He took one more look to either side, then caught a passing south wind and started his journey. To the southern forest he ventured forth. It was Bill who would deliver the message to the Ancient Pines.

10

A Beast from the Great Outdoors

RAIN FELL AS THE Huckles journeyed on through the southern pass of Yellowstone. Their hearts were heavy as they departed the land, and many of them feared the road ahead. The pain of missing Glacier and now leaving the wonder of Yellowstone . . . it was all beginning to weigh on them. None was more afflicted than Rubus. Perhaps only he and the king knew that this journey was nowhere near complete. If they were swift, they could reach the southern land before snowfall, but if not, the path would consume them.

"Who exactly is it that we are visiting, brother?" For all of his brimming strength and potential, Vernus was mostly in the dark about the quest. His knowledge of Glacier excelled, but he knew little about the ancient secrets of the Realms. To his credit, the young leader wanted to learn.

"We are going to see the Ancient Pines of the southern land. Some say that they are the oldest Trees of all."

"Wow, I bet they are more wrinkled than even us!" Vernus looked down at his torso and at the wrinkles forming due to the change of season. The second-in-command was attempting to be humorous, light-hearted, but Rubus's mood could not be lightened.

"They are very old, Vernus, yes."

The rain fell heavily, but through it, the Huckles could still see the beauty of Yellowstone. The seasons made the Realm no less wondrous; its allure simply adapted. Lining the fields of the path on which they traveled were striking harebell flowers, *Campanula rotundifolia*. These were a lilac purple, and their petals were shaped like a cup or a bell. The enticing color of these flowers gave the Huckles hope, and the purple shone elegantly through the falling rain. Wherever one may be in nature, there is always a touch of life nearby, ready to breathe into a weary soul.

"And what are we going to these Trees for?"

"They are important to the nature of the Manuscripts."

"Ahhh, but for what?"

"Vernus, I must insist that you cease with these ques—"

Vernus suddenly gasped and yelled. The cow underneath Rubus had buckled and fallen. Her delicate brown legs crumpled beneath her as she tumbled, and Rubus was tossed violently from her back. He slammed hard onto the ground and rolled through the rain into the fields, crushing harebells beneath him. Vernus raised his fist for the group and band to stop, and the Huckles in formation screeched into those in front of them. But none of them had suffered a fall as hard as that of Rubus, who lay wincing in pain, with the rain still cascading upon them all.

Immediately, Vernus left his cow and went over to his commander, and he saw that Rubus had suffered bad cuts and grazes. Behind Vernus, Goji too rushed to Rubus's side. His eyes widened when he saw her. Rubus loved her deeply.

"Are you well, commander?" said Vernus.

"Yes, I think—"

"Oh my, I think your arm is snapped."

Rubus rolled slightly so that his left arm was no longer underneath him. Indeed, some of the strong branches and twigs that held a Huckle arm together were in terrible shape. Rubus's arm was shriveled and weakened. Interrupting their thoughts, behind them a sudden and terrible snarling sounded, as if danger was imminent. It was a fierce and ragged bobcat, *Lynx rufus*, from the Great Outdoors. Behind them, the cow that had tumbled was crying out in pain. Goji rushed over to protect her while Vernus faced up to the creature.

They dared one another to advance. The bobcat was small but ferocious, and its soft spotted coat was matted by the falling rain, so it appeared deranged and untamable. Piercing yellow eyes struck fear into the Huckles, while Vernus and the creature circled and circled, staring intently at one another.

"Come, foul beast," Rubus roared.

As if accepting his challenge, the cat leapt forward with its sharp claws extended. The cluster gasped, but the outsider was no match for Vernus. He rolled calmly underneath the foe, evading its sharp swipe, and once on the other side, he grabbed the creature's tail and spun it around, his fierce arms bulging with power. The creature swiped at him once more, but Vernus shimmied backward before drawing his staff back, then, with a sure and steady blow, he landed his weapon powerfully on the creature's head. The bobcat was stunned and retreated immediately. Vernus was poised, ready for its next advance, and sure enough, the cat bounded along the ground toward him, snarling all the time. This time it landed a paw on Vernus, who yelped as he was cut. The cluster gasped again, but Vernus showed fierce resolve, and he drew back his staff once more, then struck firm and true into the underbelly of the beast. This was a blow too many, and the enemy winced, exuding an aura of retreat. Vernus let out a great roar, but the creature had already sensed defeat. It looked around before whimpering as it darted away. The bobcat had been bested by the second-in-command. The cluster looked on at the mighty Vernus, and they applauded him with adoring praise.

Behind this scene of victory, Juniper was tending to Rubus and Goji was tending to the fallen cow, who was in a worse state than him. Her legs were cut and bruised, and her eyes were dark and dreary. "No, no, no!" Goji's eyes began to well up with tears thicker than the raindrops. She glanced at Logan, then at Morrow, who had approached them hastily. "These creatures are exhausted!" she cried.

The cows were indeed very fatigued. They would never show it to the Huckles, nor would Morrow even notice, as they were the most noble and integral of creatures. They would never give up on their task, and they would certainly not be the ones to compromise the quest.

"We must find shelter for the night." It was Vernus who spoke, returning with his staff held triumphantly in his hand. In Rubus's absence, it was he who was the commander. Others nodded in agreement, so Vernus rode gallantly back to inform the king. The Huckles and the herd found some nearby woods and took shelter for the night.

Deep in the night, rainfall pattered against the forest floor and a continuous woodland rhythm sounded against the leaves. Like she had been most nights, Goji was wide awake, and this time she had climbed a Tree. Her head was in her hands as she pondered the outcome of their quest; would it continue so perilously? As she reflected, light approaching footsteps could be heard through the falling rain.

"Goji, what are you doing up there?"

Goji could not quite see the figure in the dark, but her sharp hearing meant that she could recognize the voice. It was Juniper. "I can't sleep, Juniper. I'm fine, though, honestly. You can go back to sleep." Although the rain was a nuisance to them while traveling, it did not affect the Huckles' sleep much. Indeed, back in Glacier, the Huckles would often sleep outside, away from their little huts, and the knights on their training exercises would be made to camp out in the rain. It was very much a part of berry life.

"Now, something tells me you're not fine," Juniper said.

Goji sighed, as she knew that Juniper was not going to leave so easily. "All right, I'm coming down." She slid down the tree, landing with a light thump at the bottom. She could now make out Juniper's face. Juniper was a fair berry; her mahogany tone was complemented by wide, bright eyes and plump cheeks. There was an aura of elegance surrounding her. "I had not expected to meet anyone out this late. How did you know I was here?" said Goji.

The two were some two hundred yards from the campsite, where the Huckles and the herd were resting together. Some of the Huckles had snuggled together with the cows, and some of the cows had taken shelter with the larger Huckles. Often in nature, when troubled times strike, creatures must band together.

"Heard you leave the campsite earlier," said Juniper. She stood with her arms folded.

"Oh. Well, what's up, Juniper?"

Juniper glared at her. She had a motherly instinct and knew that there were likely to be many things troubling the sweet berry. "If you're worrying about Rubus, he's fine. He's resting well on a comfortable leaf bed."

"I know, Juniper, but what about tomorrow, and the next day, and the next day?" Goji had real concerns. Much of the road lay before them, and Rubus seemed in no condition to travel after his fall.

"Well, I don't know exactly, but I do know it's time for the rest of us to step up."

"But we cannot lead like Rubus could. How are we going to organize the cluster? Maybe you can, maybe Vernus, but whatever will I be able to do?" Goji's anxiety was a mixture of concern for Rubus and the realization that she needed his guidance more than ever. It had dawned upon her that it was only with him around that she was ever able to find her way.

"Listen, Goji, you're the smartest, sharpest, and kindest berry of us all. If there's anyone we need, it's going to be you."

Goji burst into tears. She made a low whimper as she cried, barely audible through the pouring rain, then she thrust her head into Juniper while wrapping her arms around her. Juniper was shocked but responded kindly by embracing Goji, putting one arm around her torso and the other around her head. "I don't know what to do!" Goji's voice was muffled by the low crying. Tears rolled off her face and joined the falling rain. "I am trying my hardest to help, but with Rubus hurt and the herd tired and the king . . . well, the king, I don't know what I can do."

Juniper put her arms on the crying berry's shoulders and stood her up straight, then looked deep into her eyes and spoke as true as any Huckle could. "Listen to me, Goji. You are the greatest thing to have ever happened to the Huckles of Glacier." Goji wiped her eyes and looked at the floor, not sure how to receive such a compliment. "You carry more greatness than us all, and without you, our quest will surely fail."

Wiping away more tears, Goji whimpered some words. "But I just don't know what to do."

"I think . . ."

Juniper used her arms to gently lift Goji, whose shoulders were slumped toward the forest floor. "I think that you should be you. Be the incredible berry that you are, and your path will unfold."

Juniper's words sounded somewhat like Oxan's, although they now touched Goji's heart with greater reach. The motherly berry put her arms around Goji once more and embraced her in the falling rain. With that, she turned and left.

Goji stood alone in the falling rain, like the lonesome island in Yellowstone Lake. Little beads of moisture dripped from her head onto the floor as she pondered Juniper's words. Close to her, she noticed a songbird struggling to find its feet, slipping and sliding on the forest floor. Goji reached over to the bird, cupped it in her two hands, and lifted it high onto a branch just above her. The bird chirped cheerfully, thanking Goji, and flew upward to a higher branch. As Goji was drawing her arms back to her side, the words of the chiefess from days before echoed in her mind.

In your quest, you must work together. Remember that
there are other creatures whose burden you must bear.

The rain fell as the dawning realization came to the special berry. She turned and fled back to the campsite where the other Huckles slept. She knew what she had to do.

⁂

The next morning, Vernus woke to see Goji pacing up and down. Like she had on previous mornings, Goji was waiting for the other Huckles to wake. The rain had ceased, but the ground was very wet, and many of the Huckles were splashed with mud and damp leaves, so some of them had woken up and immediately searched for somewhere to bathe.

"Wait!" Goji yelled at these departing Huckles, who turned around, confused and tired. Vernus, now fully awake, walked over to her. "What is it, Goji?"

"There is something we must do," she replied with urgently.

The rest of the Huckles were now waking as well, but they were per-plexed at the scene that awaited them; it was not the way a berry was used to waking up. Rubus was lying down in the center of the campsite, resting carefully on a thick, gentle bed of leaves, and the king and his band were nowhere to be found. Much like back in Yellowstone, they had camped in a separate part of the woods.

"What do we need to do?"

"We need to speak to the herd. They . . . they need to know we ap-preciate them," she stammered.

A puzzled look was etched on Vernus's face. The words that Goji spoke, the care that she demonstrated, it was unique to her. It was not that the Huckles were unkind in comparison, it was just that Goji had a special heart, and it often took them a while to understand her actions. "Appreciate them?"

"Yes. We have been riding them for weeks, months now, and they are tired. We need to thank them."

"I see."

Goji was right. The cows were affectionate creatures, and they hoped to strike strong relationships with whoever they met, and as a result of this, they hoped to feel appreciated. "Where is Morrow?" she asked.

"I believe he is patrolling."

Often, late at night, Morrow would patrol the grounds on which the cows were camped. He would puff out his chest and lift his antlers high into the air; an awesome and powerful figure patrolling through the dark. It was something of a mystery when he slept. His shift was not yet finished that day, as the herd were only just awakening.

"We have to find him."

"But—" Vernus looked back toward the Huckles. There was supposed to be a leading knight around at all times, and with Rubus resting, that was him.

"They'll be fine." She swatted away his concern with fierce determination, then darted off toward the path by the woods in search of Morrow. She looked back at Vernus, but he was rooted to the spot. "Come on. They'll be fine!"

Vernus hesitantly followed.

Morrow was indeed patrolling the path, with his mighty antlers protruding high into the sky and his hind legs bursting with strength. After spending some time searching, Goji and Vernus approached the mighty creature. Goji was most confident, whereas Vernus was more cautious. "Mighty Morrow, we must speak with you."

Morrow turned toward them. His antlers swung and almost knocked the Huckles off their feet. "What do you require?"

"We need to speak to all of the herd." Goji spoke like one preparing for a great battle. Vernus was confused. Goji had not yet even explained to him what this was all about.

"What is there to speak of, little berry? We are completing what you ask of us, and all we ask for is the finest leaves in return."

"Well, I just have a bit more to say."

Morrow turned away from her. He had little room for sentiment, and he was focused on the task, as always. He started to trot down the path away from them, still patrolling the lands for danger.

"Please, Morrow!" Goji was not one to raise her voice or yell. Her tone here was more pleading, but Morrow did not budge.

Vernus awkwardly stepped forward. It dawned on him that Goji had expected him to speak at some point. "Morrow, Glacier calls upon you. If we do not act now, much will be lost. Do you not miss the green plains, the rolling hills, and the plush grass? Glacier is our home, and we must preserve it."

Goji looked at Vernus. She was delighted that he had intervened. Morrow stopped suddenly, and his hefty head hung in the air like some giant monument. "What is it that may become of Glacier?" The elk were not aware of the motivation behind the quest. Morrow made it his business not to intervene in the Huckles' details.

"We do not know, Morrow, but we know that we must reach the Trees."

"And what is it that you need from us?"

Goji stepped forward. "I need to speak to the herd."

"What do they have to do with this?"

"I just need to speak with them."

Morrow looked at her and then back at Vernus.

"I do not pretend to understand your request, berry, but if you wish to speak with the herd, so be it. I shall continue to watch over them, a strong tower which they may run toward to be saved." Morrow turned toward the woods and proceeded back to where the herd was camped. "Follow me."

"No, I need you and the herd to follow me," said Goji.

Morrow turned around as if struck by an enemy. He was not used to being given such orders. His large size seemed at that moment intimidating to the berries, even if they were long-time acquaintances. They warily took a step back.

"I mean . . . if you would be so obliged, great Morrow, I request that you gather the herd and come with us."

Morrow snorted violently into the air before continuing into the woods. "I will gather the herd and meet you at the camp when the sun is at mid sky."

"But Morrow, none of you have yet seen where we are cam—"

"I know where you are." Morrow marched on through the woods, and sticks and leaves crumpled beneath his mighty weight. Vernus and Goji stood on the path. They looked at one another, and without saying a word, they walked on through the crisp morning back to the rest of their kin.

It was midday, and most of the Huckles were now freshly bathed. They had found a small waterfall that had formed due to the heavy rain. Now they sat around the camp sharing stories and memories of their journey so far, while Rubus was still resting in his bed of leaves. Vernus informed Juniper of what Goji planned to do; Goji had told Vernus all about it on the way back to the camp. She was now pacing up and down the camp once more, going through her words. Rubus watched her, wondering what she was doing, but did not beckon her over. He did not want to disturb her.

After some time, a multitude of feet could be heard pattering in the forest. The Huckles turned as one to face the woods, from where the sound came. Morrow appeared first, with his deep nostrils flaring and his antlers pointed high. He strolled in and found a spot, standing confidently. After him, all of the cows piled into the Huckle campsite, taking their places behind Morrow. Refreshed as the Huckles were from their sleep and the restful morning, many of them still looked tired and down. Some of them bore stark cuts and bruises.

The Huckles looked at one another, confused. They all banded together so that the herd was opposite them. As soon all the herd had come into the campsite, Goji rushed to a nearby tree and climbed it at a determined pace. Vernus and Juniper looked on. Rubus, too, was following the situation from his leafy bed. He could not stand, but he could still observe his surroundings. Much like when she had passed on Izzy's message back at Yellowstone, Goji found a good position on a strong branch before projecting her voice loudly for all to hear. "Friends! There is something I must tell you all, from the depths of my heart." The Huckles were greatly puzzled. They were only used to grand announcements from either Vernus or Rubus, although the eldest among them also remembered announcements from the king.

"You all know that I am not a Huckle and that I am a different breed of berry." Rubus could see that Goji was speaking with as much passion as she had ever had. So passionate was she that her color darkened as she spoke. "In all my years in Glacier, there is one thing that I have learnt that is more important than everything else." She paused to catch her breath. "I was an outsider, but I was taken in, and now I live and breathe amongst you." She looked intently at the Huckles as she continued. "The deep lakes, the swaying trees, the fair plains, and the setting sun of Glacier—I have experienced all of these things because of you, the Huckles, and now that we have set out on this quest, there are moments when you have needed me."

A gentle murmur came from the Huckle side of the campsite. They all seemed to agree with the impassioned Goji, and some were nodding their heads. The radiant berry on the tree continued speaking to their hearts. "Now, just think about our quest and where we would be without other creatures!" She then stopped momentarily. Partly she was giving the Huckles time to think, and partly she was catching her breath. The Huckles' nodding intensified as their minds were roused. Their minds flashed back to Cassie, to Izzy, and to some other small creatures they had met along the way. "Don't you see?" she continued. She spread her arms wide, as if she was trying to embrace them all. "We are the creatures of the Realms, whatever our land and wherever our home. A soaring eagle high in the great skies above or a wriggling earthworm in the undergrowth below; we all have purpose, and we all must work together!" By now the cluster and the herd were both looking up at Goji, intrigued. Some of them began to respond with light cheers, and, as they have done so often in our tale, jubilant songbirds came and joined the occasion,perching on the branch below Goji.

"Now listen, Huckles, there is something important I need to say to our friends, and you must bear it in your seeds for the rest of our journey." Goji pivoted on the branch so that she was facing the herd. "You, dearest herd, you have carried us with loving care throughout our quest."

Their ears pricked up.

"We still have a long road ahead, and only you can get us there! Whenever you carry us, we help you with the highest leaves. This is the ancient agreement, but today, we must go beyond that agreement! Our journey should be based on friendship. We in the Realms should not work for one another as a burden, nor should we take each other's places. We work together!"

Some of the Huckles seemed surprised that Goji was suggesting forsaking the ancient agreement. The Huckles were, after all, creatures of agreement and simple principle. Despite their hesitancy, she continued and said one last thing to the herd. "In the past we have called you servants, but let it be this way no longer, for you will now call us friends. For does a servant know their master's business?" The herd's eyes widened, and Goji turned back to face the cluster. "My fellow berries, you have been riding these elk for weeks and months. They are tired and exhausted from the heavy burden!" The Huckles looked at the herd opposite them. Indeed, for the first time, they noticed genuine exhaustion, which they had not noticed before that day. The Huckles were simple beings, and they only picked up on a few emotions at any given time. "If the herd is to continue carrying us all the way to the southern lands, we must be alongside them and must not lord it over them. You, Huckles, you must appreciate them and their work, seeing them as equals and partners in our Realm."

The Huckles were in a deep state of reflection. Such was their simplicity, however, that it did not take too long for them to reflect on what Goji had said. They could only process so many emotions at the same time. It was not that they were incapable or stupid; instead, it was more that they just focused on what they needed to think about. "Goji is right!" Logan shouted from the crowd. "The herd has been good to us. We should care for them, for they belong to Glacier as much as we do!"

"Aye!" A rising chorus of Huckles were agreeing with Goji, and they were looking at the herd in an entirely new light. Such was and is the nature of the parks; a small creature like Goji can bring about significant change. Morrow moved to the back, overseeing the entire situation. A smile slowly formed on Goji's face as she sensed that her plan was working. "You belong to Glacier, and Glacier and all the Realms must work together. We can no longer bend other creatures to our will to fulfill our commands!"

Juniper looked up, smiling.

"The Realms are for sharing, for friendship and preservation of our way of life!" Loud cheering came from the Huckles, and a stomping of feet sounded from the herd. Goji knew that now was the time. "So, my fellow berries, and you, lovely herd, embrace your fellow creatures, for they are your partners in this wondrous way of life. We are the creatures of the Realms!"

Goji lifted her hands high to the sky. The songbirds below leaped and chirped with joy. With a shout and a cheer, the Huckles jumped up and down, and the herd lifted onto their hind legs in approval. Once the rapturous applause had subsided, they began to move toward one another. They were nervous at first, but eventually the old partners fully embraced. The brown coats and red and purple skin became an intermingled sea of creatures, boundless in love toward one another. The Huckles hugged and kissed the cows, while the cows rubbed their heads affectionately against the berries. Many were laughing, and some were in tears. Goji looked upon the scene with great delight as she stood upon the Tree, just as the king had stood upon his mountain and made his own proclamations many years ago.

Eager to join in the festivities, Goji made her way down the Tree. At the bottom, she was greeted by joyful creatures who hugged and embraced her. Vernus burst through the crowd toward her. "Out of the way!" He took a brief look at her and then used his burgeoning strength to lift her onto his shoulders. Rubus used to do the same when she was just a child, and Goji laughed sweetly as Vernus heaved her into the air. Through the sea of creatures Vernus carried Goji, while all of them cheered and shouted for joy. The Huckles beat their staffs against the ground.

"Well done, Goji, you were great!" A smiling Juniper beamed up at her.

After passing through the rapturous crowd, Vernus stopped toward the back, where Morrow stood tall. "A fine speech, berry. Now I hope that we can carry forth this vision together."

Goji broke into a boundless smile, tears of joy welling in her eyes. "Morrow!" She leaned from Vernus's arms to hug the great beast, wrapping her arms around his thick neck. When she broke her embrace, a figure approached, and the crowd fell silent.

Behind Morrow, Rubus approached. He hobbled toward them, his arm still in terrible shape, causing great discomfort. He had watched the entire scene and listened to Goji's speech from his tree bed. All of the cluster and herd watched as Goji, on top of Vernus, stood opposite Rubus. She hopped down, and the two berries looked at one another for what seemed like an eternity. When he could hold it in no longer, Rubus burst into tears. He leaped forward and embraced her. Goji too could not hide her emotion. The two berries were wrapped in each other's arms.

"I love you, dear sweet Goji. You are a special berry."

"I love you, Rubus."

The crowd erupted. For the rest of the creatures' lives, they would remember this day, and at that very moment, all across the land, legendary creatures felt the rumblings of greatness, tremors of change.

Deep inside a volcanic pass, a mighty bison smiled.

From the branch of a tree in a palace, a cluster of berries vibrated with joy.

High above, on an eerie cliff, a mysterious figure with a deep scar on his face looked over the edge of his wide nest home. He sensed movement in the land below.

Bill rested on a thin branch. It was early September now, and the cold air had started to drift in from the eastern mountains. It had been a mighty journey, but rather than being tired, the bird actually felt rather refreshed. On his way he had passed through beautiful, breathtaking lands while meeting and making new friends. Sequoia, Kings Canyon, and Yosemite were some of the grandest stops that he had taken. Among everything else that he had to do, the Trees at Yosemite had told him that he must inform the Redwoods not to forget the arrangements for the High Legion Tree Gathering in early spring. They were patiently waiting for the details.

If you look again at the map of California, you will notice how remarkable Bill's journey was. Down below Redwood and to the east, you
will see the bountiful land of Yosemite. This place is too marvelous for us
to explore in detail here, but hopefully another time will arise. Beneath
Yosemite and slightly to the east is a smaller patch of green called Inyo
National Forest. Around here, in continuance of our tale, you should
search until you find a small town called Bishop, which is the closest
place to our destination. You should see, slightly north of Bishop and to
the east, another small patch of green. It is the Ancient Bristlecone Pine
Forest.

We have met many fabled creatures on our journey, but the Ancient
Pines are the oldest and wisest of them all. The oldest among them was
Methuselah, whose wisdom easily surpassed that of Hyperion, Oxan,
Pry, the Elderberries, and the king (who had much to learn). Methuse-
lah's deep wisdom matched her many years, for she was and is the world's
oldest Tree. In fact, she is the world's oldest creature.

In the forest were other Pines like her. They had tangled, spiraling
branches, with trunks twisting in many directions, and their bark was a
light shade of brown. Although those in Redwood directed California,
these Pines were the brains behind it all. It was they who had signed the
Manuscripts along with the others and they who directed and advised
Hyperion. It was as if the Redwoods were the Word that the Pines had
sent forth into the world.

The Ancient Pines at the edge of the forest where Bill was perched
were perfectly still, as if frozen in time. The forest could only be described
as ancient and mysterious, and the deeper Bill flew, the more he felt as
if he were being transported into another world. The air reeked with
age. So old were the Trees that they appeared dead. They were not, of
course; instead, they had learnt to grow in the way that best suited their
environment.

The Ancient Forest was at a high altitude and hence was not a
thick wooded forest like Redwood. The Trees here were dotted among
the sparse backdrop like ancient relics, and old rocks, plants, and bushes
sporadically littered the forest floor. Occasionally, a large mountain hare,
Lepus timidus, leapt from behind a rock and dashed to another. Everything was rather silent, and everything was rather old. Bill felt slightly
uneasy, as the eerie silence of the forest was not like the bustling of Redwood back home. On top of that, he was now somewhat lost, and he did

not anticipate the fortune of coming across a wise banana slug here. He took a quick break on a taller Pine.

The branches of this Pine were twisted and turned, and they shot off toward the sky in a multitude of directions. Bill thought that it was unlike any Tree he had ever seen. The thick trunk protruded from the ground, and the random direction of the branches made the Tree look like a violent explosion of lava from underneath that had been frozen in midair. Bill drew a deep breath upon the branch on which he was perched.

"Excuse me? You are an Ancient Pine, yes?" Bill waited for a good moment, but no reply came. "Excuse me?" He looked at the trunk, where the Redwoods' faces were, hoping to see one on the Pine. Bill flew all around the trunk and back to his branch, then looked up and down and around. No reply came, so he flew onward, away from the Tree.

"Come back here, little bird!"

The little warbler bird came to a screeching halt in midair. Such was the force of his stop that some of his plumage was ejected off him and his eyes widened in a state of shock. The Tree's voice was deep and slow, so that, even more than with Hyperion, Bill felt as though the Tree were talking into his very soul. Slowly he turned around and hesitantly made his way back to the branch. "What is your name, bird that hath disturbed my slumber?" Indeed, the Tree had been fast asleep, but the life energy of Bill had awoken it.

"Apologies! My name is Bill. I'm a warbler bird, and I have an important message for you, the Pines."

"A wobbly bird, eh. Well, I've never seen one of you in our forest."

"No, I'm a warbler bird."

Such was the age of the great Tree that his eyes and mouth could not open while he spoke. Bill saw where his face was, but only crusted flakes and etchings of bark fell as he uttered his words.

"Well, mister wobbly bird, what have you come to tell us that we don't already know?"

Bill was somewhat taken aback. "I come from Hyperion. He asks that you prepare for the coming of the northern king."

"Hyperion? Northern king?" The Tree paused for a moment. "Doesn't sound like a strong enough reason to be awake, wobbly bird. You'd better take this to Methuselah."

Bill gave the tree a sideways glance, confounded by his lack of enthusiasm. "Very well, and where may I find her?"

"That way."

The Tree lifted a branch and pointed to the west. There was an ancient creaking and groaning as it did so, and bits of old bark fell to the floor. "Well, thank you." Bill flew off, confused. From all he had heard of the Pines, they were supposedly most wise and powerful, but this Tree had seemed incredibly laid-back.

Bill flew on through the forest until he saw Methuselah. He had not been given any more directions, but it was easy enough to spot her. Methuselah was darker than the other Pines, and she had a wide girth and countless twisting branches. Such was her shape that she looked like she could be a comfortable home to some creatures all on her own. Bill landed softly on an upward-shooting branch. He had barely landed when an ancient voice came from the Tree.

"Hello, little bird. Bill, isn't it?" Methuselah had either been awoken from her slumber, was already awake, or had been aware of Bill during her sleep; it was unclear which.

"Yes. How do you know my—?"

"News from Hyperion you bring, isn't that right?"

Bill was stunned. "Yes. How could you possibly have known that?" He now realized that she was most definitely awake.

"Oh, I know a lot of things, little bird. You see, when you are my age, there isn't much to be doing but knowing things!"

"Right." Bill tried to understand.

The Tree smiled. "So, tell me, Bill, how was your journey? A mighty long way you have come."

"It was great, thanks. I met many on my way."

"Mmm, and how are preparations for the High Legion coming along?"

"Well, I think."

"You hear that, old Pines! The legion is going to be quite something this year!"

Around Methuselah were six or seven other Trees. They were similar, but she was larger than them all. She was also clearly much older and had more branches. Her companions murmured with tempered excitement as Methuselah mentioned the gathering. The Pines were, of course, special guests at the gathering, and they always had a clearing reserved just for them. "So, little Bill, let me tell you what to take back to Hyperion."

Bill's beak dropped in amazement and frustration. "No, I brought a message from him!" The flustered bird jumped and down, flapping his wings. "The mighty northern king is on his way, and there are whispers in the woodlands that Pry, the Elderberries, and Oxan know of stirrings in the Realms and that you are the last to know!"

Methuselah paused. She had been ever so slightly waving her branches as she spoke, but now she stood completely silent in the forest. She then turned slightly in order to address her companions. "You hear that, Pines? All of the Realms knew something before us. We are late to the party!"

The Trees erupted with laughter. Bill did not think that Trees could laugh so hard. They creaked and groaned while lifting their roots up and down and slamming them into the ground. The little bird looked around, confused. Their fantastical laughter echoed from the forest and into the distant mountains beyond.

"I don't understand." Poor Bill was perplexed.

"You know, Bill," Methuselah had to compose herself as she spoke, stopping herself from breaking out into further fits of laughter, "I really thought the Realms would have learnt their lesson by now."

Bill spoke again. "But you are the last to know! Hyperion sent me here because your roots are isolated. They cannot message you, and you are cut off from the Realms!"

This was true. The Ancient Pines were lonesome dwellers in the forest. Their home was not directly in a Realm, and they did not live nearby or talk to anyone nearby. As a result, the great Trees of Redwood could not always communicate with them directly. The Pines, though, rather enjoyed this existence, as it was most conducive to their sleeping pattern.

"And what difference does that make?"

"You are amongst the last to hear the messages!"

Methuselah slapped her thickest root down onto the ground, and the entire forest shook as the Trees erupted in laughter once more. "Bill, we are the Ancient Pines. We have been here for many, many years, and there is nothing that escapes our attention."

Bill paused. "You mean you already knew?"

"Knew about what? About the king? About the quest? About the Manuscripts?"

"What Manuscripts?" Bill questioned.

"Exactly!" The Pines laughed again. "We know all things before all creatures, Bill. Perhaps Hyperion has forgotten this, or perhaps . . ." she paused, maybe for dramatic suspense, "perhaps he is getting dizzy up there!"

The Trees were beside themselves. One of the Pines actually fell onto the ground, uprooting himself, such were his fierce hysterics. He would have to be picked up by some bears and replanted later on.

"So, I made this whole journey for nothing?"

"Well, you have Hyperion to thank for that. Now, while you are on the way back, tell the Trees in Yosemite that we will be late to the gathering this spring. The problem is . . . we keep getting messages late!"

Laughter erupted once again. By now, many of the Trees' roots were fully exposed on account of their continual lifting from the floor. Slightly disheveled, Bill now took the hint. He flapped his wings and took off, heading back north. A long journey awaited him. Before he went, however, he had an inquiry for the Trees. "Say, how do you know what's going on everywhere if you are sleeping all the time?" He had heard of their constant slumber and noticed it upon his arrival.

"Ahh, well, little bird, sometimes the best thing to do is sleep, and wake up when there are important things to do."

Bill shook his head and turned to the north. As he left the Ancient Forest behind, he could hear sniggers of laughter coming from below. It was a cool afternoon. Bill knew to avoid the great mountains, where deep snow had begun to fall, which would only increase, what with winter nigh. He made his way back, stopping at Yosemite on the way, of course . . .

⁂

The cluster and the herd had spent a number of days at the campsite. They were resting, recuperating, and bonding. They shared epic tales with one another, traded memories from Glacier, and went on occasional rides together. They were forming friendships like never before, and it was the start of something great. Goji knew, and so did the other berries.

"Well, I think this is going to be fabulous," said Vernus.

"Quite right, and all thanks to Goji," replied Juniper.

Goji smiled. "Say, I expect we'll be on our way soon. Any news from the king?"

No one had heard from him for some time.

"Perhaps he is reflecting," said Vernus.

"Perhaps," said Juniper.

"I hope he likes our partnership." Goji was still not fond of the king, but at the very least, she hoped he would see the bonds they had formed.

After all, she had heard of his communion with many creatures in his earlier days.

Later that night, before they lay down to rest, the Huckles and the herd were sitting around a small fire (it was very tightly controlled). Morrow was speaking to them of ancient journeys he had made across snowy passes and mountainsides. All were listening intently, deeply engrossed in his tales. After some time, as Morrow was speaking of crossing a fearsome river, deep, troubled footsteps could be heard approaching. The crowd turned toward the woods and saw the great figure of the Huckleberry King. He did not look too pleased, and he was gripping his staff firmly in his hand.

"What is the meaning of this?" his soul-striking voice boomed, almost extinguishing the fire. He moved closer in to the crowd and stood ominously over a Huckle who was lying peacefully on top of a cow.

"Look, great king, the herd have become partners with us! Goji has spoken to all of our hearts about the meaning of working together." It was Vernus who spoke.

The king snarled and looked at Goji. "Outsider," he said coldly. Suddenly, he grabbed the head of the Huckle beneath him, lifting him with ease, and dramatically flung him aside. The crowd gasped, and the fire died. Almost as quickly, he kicked at the cow with his burly feet, and she too was brushed away. The campsite was now dark and quiet. "Get to sleep! Tomorrow we depart for the southern lands." Morrow rose fiercely, and his nostrils flared as he confronted the king for harming a cow. He skidded across the ground and kicked his hind legs with fearsome strength, but despite his greatness, the king was far larger than he. The king puffed out his chest and lifted his staff as the elk approached. Morrow was no match for the king, and he knew it. Looking around at the rest of the herd, he slowly backed down.

"Do your job, elk."

Goji was furious. She jerked toward the king but was held back by Juniper, who whispered sharply in her ear, "No, Goji. You will only make things worse!"

The king looked upon them all. He was very tempted to squish them there and then, but then his quest would not be complete. He turned back into the night, swiping and taking down some Trees as he left. The camp was stunned. Shocked and silent, they went to sleep that evening under the stars. There was still much that needed to be resolved in this tale.

❧

The next day, the Huckles left at the crack of dawn. Despite the events of last night, they were rejuvenated (they were somewhat used to the king's mighty grumpiness by now anyway). There was gentle chatter and good morale as they began their journey south. The cluster rode ahead, while the king and his band were distant behind (the king wanted them to be further back than normal, for he was still in a great grump).

As the Huckles made their way out of Yellowstone and south, they came across a spectacular, once-in-a-lifetime sight, which spurred them on for the rest of the journey. "Wow!" Juniper expressed her delight, and many of the other Huckles gasped as well. As the morning haze disappeared and the daylight strengthened, a spellbinding mountain range came into view. These peaks rose so dramatically from the ground, and to such a bewildering height, that the sharp white slopes cut into the sky as if they had been torn and dragged up from the earth. Three main peaks were clustered together with other smaller peaks, soaring above the horizon like a watchtower for the whole world. The trees on the foothills looked hopeless compared to the majesty of the mountains.

"Those are incredible!" Goji spoke. She was riding alongside Rubus lest he should fall again. Rubus could ride well, but he had to take occasional breaks to rest his arm. "I've never seen anything like it." Indeed, the special range was the largest and grandest spectacle the Huckles had ever witnessed, dwarfing Huckleberry Mountain. As the sun changed its hue, so did the magnificent sight reflect a wondrous change in color. The mountains became steeped in purple, so that they shone like a royal throne. It was as if they were reminding all creatures, Tree, Huckle, and eagle, that they could not be conquered or tamed. The most awesome thing about them was that they stood alone, and there was no other mountain range or pass nearby. They were lonesome titans on a flat plain. Such was their solitary existence that it almost looked as though they had been placed there by a giant or the Creative One.

The Huckles stopped completely to take in the view. The pressure and weariness of their journey slowly eased as the majestic mountains pierced every seed heart. The berries were reminded of how small they were and how great their journey was. Just like in Yellowstone, they fell in love with the grandeur of the mighty peaks. Their world was opened, and their hearts and minds were renewed. Goji and Rubus had taken a moment to sit down on the path, and by now, the king and his band had caught up with the group. Although the king insisted that they move on, the band was too enthralled. Some were moved to tears.

"So, this is what's out there." Logan looked on in wonder.

The Huckles gazed upon the grand spectacle for the rest of the sun's light and then camped out under the stars and the shadow of the mountains. The next day, they set off south again, but no matter what became of the rest of their journey, they would not forget what they had witnessed that day.

You can look south of Yellowstone on your map to find this majestic place yourself and join the Huckles in their experience. They are a truly wondrous sight. They are the Grand Tetons.

Part Two

11

A Yawning Gap

AT THIS JUNCTURE, YOU should know that our tale is in its last stage. You may find this odd, considering where the Huckles were and how far they had yet to venture. If you look at the Grand Tetons on a map, you will see that California is some way away. In fact, the Huckles still had more ground to cover than they had already crossed. Despite this, you should have understood by now that the length of a journey matters not, nor is any one part of it more important than another.

On a journey, you can learn more at the start, or at the end, or in between the two. Such is the way when you explore a national park and take a walk on a trail. The main part of your experience could be at any point, and you may spend the rest of your walk contemplating it. This is most important, because it teaches us to value all parts of our journey, not just the final destination.

The Huckles and the king still had an important task to achieve, one that would change the Realms forever, but regardless of how the rest of their tale transpired, they had learnt so much already. The hearts and minds of the Huckles had been opened in ways that they did not expect, and they would never be the same again. They had plenty to dwell on, and this kept them occupied for much of the long road.

Take a look at a map and see the path they took. They kept going south away from the Tetons, through southwest Idaho, and straight on through Utah (supposedly the Potatomen watched the Huckles with great curiosity as they passed, but we will never know, as they were never seen). The journey was long, and the weather was taking a turn for the worse, but the Huckles' hearts were full of joy and deep memories, the kind that caused wonderful stirrings deep inside. If you need help tracking their journey, you should know that the path they took was similar to the present-day Highway 15, although this was, of course, nowhere to be seen at the time. They crossed sprawling flat lands, crystal lakes, rivers, and grand prairies. They camped out under the stars, singing and dancing with the herd (the king retreated far away in the evenings to escape the joy), and they took shelter from the rain in mighty clefts of rock. Sometimes they stopped for days at a time, building robust dens out of wood. All the while, they grew increasingly close to the herd, forming bonds that would last forever.

For the most part, they advanced at a steady pace, without stopping for too long, but one day in early November, they came across a land they simply could not ignore. A coyote, *Canis latrans*, was journeying from his home in the Arches Realm when he came across the northerners. He bid the Huckles well on their quest and told them that they were now in the land of the Yawning Gap. The Huckles recognized the name, as Izzy had mentioned it (through Goji) in her important speech upon the tree, back in Yellowstone. The Huckles deeply treasured the memories they had made during their journey, but they were also hoping for more. They were about to make an unforgettable one . . .

Morrow panted as he drew near the campsite. The air was cold and shrill, and his breath blew out of his nostrils like steam. He had been patrolling the land at night like he always did. It really was a mystery when the mighty creature rested. He was a legendary elk, advanced in years, and, as he had told the Huckles in his campfire tales, he had made a lifetime of unforgettable journeys. Although he would never show it, this particular quest was beginning to take its toll on him, and his coat had begun to age slightly. Although it was turning toward its usual dark brown winter shade, it was lighter than usual, and his antlers were showing signs of wearing down. On certain edges they were blunted, no longer pointing with bold ferocity. Despite this, Morrow would soldier on, of course. He would not let the herd down, nor would he give up on the quest.

As he approached the camp's perimeter, he could hear the sound of snoozing Huckles and see the gentle breathing of the cows. More and more, they had begun to rest side by side. Sometimes the Huckles would fall asleep with their heads on the cows, weary from a long day of walking, and the cows would nestle their heads affectionately into the squishy berries. They all grew tired from the lengthy walks.

And walked they had. The group had covered a tremendous amount of ground in the fall months, and they had traveled so far that they had had little time to do what they loved the most, which was to spend time with nature. They were not able to jump in the crisp brown leaves or bathe in the lakes before they turned to ice. Such was their weariness that even the king finally agreed to a week-long rest.

So, they had been camping now for three days. They had been sleeping for most of the time, but the cluster and the herd were intrigued by their new environment, as it was unlike anywhere they had ever been before. They were camped by a roaring river, which they had followed from further upstream. Although they were high on a ridge, the river was clearly visible to them, and they would have loved to go down and play in it as they had done at Yellowstone. This was the Colorado River, one of the most important rivers in all the land, and this was the state of Arizona. Now, much of Arizona is stark and lifeless, but there are parts of it that defy description. Great wide desert. Plains of bronze sand and vast expanses stretching far and wide, while stars crowd the sky above as if fighting for space. It was warm here in the day, especially for November, but the nights were bone-chillingly cold. Only Morrow with his thick coat could bear it. The Huckles slept through the night to escape the plight, huddling close in groups, and sometimes they asked the cows to lie on top of them (as uncomfortable as that may have been!).

As Morrow trotted through the open Arizona desert, approaching the campsite, he noticed a lone figure awake on the edge, gazing up toward the stars. It was Goji. Although she was in better spirits, sleep still eluded her. These days, it was more deep excitement in her heart that kept her awake rather than struggle and strife. With her superior hearing, Goji could make out Morrow's approach from a long way away, particularly considering the emptiness of the desert. "Where have you come from, Morrow?" Her voice was skippy and excited, as it had been for months now. Goji often caught him returning at night, wherever they had been camped.

"Patrolling, of course, young berry. You should really sleep more."

"Well, I could say the same about you!" She smiled and looked at the stars again.

Morrow looked concerned but did not dwell on it too deeply. She had, after all, proven to be a most capable berry. "There is a tremendous rift in the ground that way, where the river cuts through. I expect it is a fine place to see the sunrise." Morrow pointed his mighty antlers to the north, where there was a path fairly straight ahead. It led up and up, scaling barren brown rock and dirt. With that, he walked off silently, perhaps to sleep . . .

Goji didn't pay much attention to Morrow's suggestion at first, but then she realized that it had been a while since she had seen a really beautiful sunrise. They had witnessed some on the plains of Utah over the last months, but the ground there was low and the sky cloudy. Perhaps here, where the sky was clearer and warmer, she would witness the majestic yellow once more.

She got up from the rock on which she was sitting and walked in the direction Morrow had pointed out. It was a long and arduous path, but Goji had plenty of energy, as it was still early in the day, and her spirits were high. She hopped and skipped northward for some time, kicking and flicking rocks and dirt on the way. The land was still dark, but as there were few obstructions, she was able to keep a straight path. The air grew purer as she ascended, so she took several, deep enjoyable breaths, then, after some time and much climbing, Goji reached what she felt was sure the point of which Morrow had spoken. She could instinctively tell that there was a deep drop beneath her, so she did not proceed any further. She took several steps back and found a smooth rock upon which to sit. There she waited patiently for the sun, which had just started its slow ascent over the horizon, although for now, it was hidden from view.

After some time, most unexpectedly, she heard footsteps behind her. Goji was surprised; she was usually alone in her early morning ventures. "Hello?" she called out into the shrill desert. Her voice bounced and echoed over the vast expanse.

"It is I, Goji." It was the sure voice of Rubus.

"Rubus, what are you—? How did you know to find me here?"

"I heard you and Morrow conversing."

"But your arm! Are you well?"

Rubus's arm would never be the same. It had lost much of its twine and wood, so that it now appeared like the roots of a thin tree. He could still move, but he had to be careful of falling, tripping, and scraping his arm, lest he worsened it. "I will be fine."

Rubus had followed Goji's path at a good distance. Goji could have heard him, of course, but she had been too eager and excited to notice.

She spoke to him. "Morrow tells me of a great rift in the land here, says it is a good place to watch the sunrise."

"Ah yes, well, we haven't observed a good sunrise since Yellowstone." Rubus was missing the sunrise too. The Huckles always missed the aspects of nature that appeared in Glacier, and they held them dear in their hearts.

"Well, I guess we'll find out!" Goji said.

"That we shall."

Dawn was drawing ever nearer. The chill had begun to lift from the air, evaporating like a blanket, and the warm, stifling heat of the desert began to settle.

"Have you enjoyed your journey, Goji?"

Goji looked at him. It seemed odd to her that he was asking such a question, considering her elated mood. "Yes, of course. Can't you tell?

Rubus moved forward and took his place on the rock by Goji, sitting next to her. Before he sat, he rested the staff that he had been carrying to support himself when he walked. The king had been gracious to Rubus and had snapped a tiny splinter from his own staff to give to him. Even the king remembered Rubus's stubborn loyalty deep down in his broken seed heart.

"It was nice of the king to give you a staff." Goji looked at it observantly.

"Yes, yes." He paused to adjust himself. "You know, Goji, the king was once like you and I, a berry whose chief desire was to partake in nature and know its overflowing depths."

"Hmm . . ." Goji gave an unconvinced murmur.

Wanting to justify himself, Rubus continued. "The trouble is, he knew not what to do with his great power. His early days in the woodlands of Glacier were a delicate balance. He was trying to interact with the Realm but at the same time mark a place for the Huckles."

"Well, I don't see why he needs to push anyone around to do that." Goji folded her arms as she spoke.

"Perhaps, but you see, nature does not always operate in the way we hope it will. There comes a time when we must accept that the balance may not shift in our favor. That is the life of the Realms."

"And the king is trying to shift this balance in favor of the Huckles, is he?"

"Yes. That has always been his idea." He looked at her. "Before his fateful day, he accepted much more of a balance, but now, he will do whatever it takes."

Goji peered out toward the cliff edge. A dim hue had begun to settle, and the thick darkness was penetrated. The faintest of glows softened the edges of the sharp rocks. "Well, I think we have to work together and just accept that things won't always be perfect. Sometimes things will go our way in the Realms, sometimes they won't. But if we try and change too much, well, our whole way of life will be ruined."

Rubus peered into the distance. He had often shared Goji's thoughts, but he had little way to make them known. He was bound in loyalty to the king. "You know, I know that you didn't want to leave Glacier, and I know that you don't want to move up in the court, but I still think you can, Goji." Rubus wanted Goji to have a high position in the king's court, because he believed in her contribution and believed that her sweet, warm heart could bring wisdom and happiness to Glacier. Goji did not answer him, but instead continued peering into the distance. The faint glow had grown lighter, and the soft edges of the rock now shone an enticing bronze. The last of the stars high above were beginning to retreat.

"I think that you have an important part to play in this quest, Goji. Perhaps you will be more important than us all."

Goji looked at her feet before replying. "I just want us to work together with others to preserve Realm life. We've seen it in Yellowstone, so why not in Glacier?"

Rubus nodded in agreement. "I'm glad that this journey has been a blessing to you. For I see that you have learnt lessons that you will carry for the rest of your days, even beyond my time."

Goji looked at him sharply. "What do you mean?"

"I have always been trying to prepare you, Goji, for such a time as when I shall be no longer."

"Rubus! That's a long way from now! Let's enjoy the rest of this journey and then think about the future."

Rubus smiled. By now, there was enough light for Goji to make out his tone, a mahogany shade of red. He was wearing his Huckle crown and his bright tunic, both of which had been worn down by the long journey. Goji shifted closer to him and rested her head on his shoulder. The two sat silently for some time as dawn began to unveil its mighty splendor. The rocks and the ground were just about visible, but now the world began to truly unfold before them.

Ahead, the first glimmerings of a miraculous sight were soon revealed. "Oh my, look!" Goji gave an excited squeal as she surveyed the sights that were being unveiled. It was a grand, fresh experience for them both. Remember, the Huckles were well acquainted with the woodland environment. On their journey, they had come across much beauty, but the desert was new to them. There were dramatic valleys and falls in Glacier, but they were unlike the harsh, stark allure of the desert.

The rock began to glow golden brown and red around them as the sun ascended. Bouncing off the obtuse formations was a golden reflection, as if the world and the Realm they found themselves in were enshrined and cloaked in wondrous glory. The two berries rose and walked slowly to the edge of the rock face in amazement.

The sight before them was unlike any they had seen before or would see again. They proceeded carefully, trying to maintain their balance. The land that unfolded threatened to dizzy them or lull them into a trance, such was its splendor and giddy height. The light of day now abounded, and the brownish-red surface glowed and glistened as if no creature had ever set foot in this Realm. Goji and Rubus eventually reached the very edge of the rock face, and stretched out before them was an inexplicable vast expanse. The opposite side of the tremendous rift was just about visible to Rubus and Goji, and there they could faintly see the shapes of trees and other rocks.

They stood speechless.

Once they had regained their composure, they were able to look down beneath them, where the rock was harsh, steep, and jagged but still seemed somewhat elegantly placed. Nooks and crevices protruded all the way down like some divine puzzle, and far beneath, the sparkling river was streaming along. It could be heard ever so faintly crashing against smooth rocks, and it flowed through the base of the great rift like a skillful serpent. The clear water glistened and swept over rocks, gently making its way yonder. The other side of the rift was so far in the distance that Goji and Rubus wondered if it was still a part of the same Realm.

The berries basked in the growing sunlight as they peered out. The vast expanse was incredible. At times, they grew slightly nauseated, as they were not used to such open spaces with little tree cover. "Look, Rubus, this place is incredible," Goji exclaimed. Rubus looked at her and smiled. As much as he was enjoying the view, his heart was more pleased for her. He thought to himself that she had now seen a great number of sights and places, and that warmed his heart. She would have stories to tell forevermore.

Goji stumbled slightly. A few rocks flew from beneath her, tumbling into the great depths below. Rubus held out his staff to steady her and she grabbed it sharply, regaining her footing. The two berries were too enamored to worry or be cautious, so they both laughed at the stumble. The rock trickled down the cliff face and fell below. Such was the depth of the drop that they did not even see it touch the water.

"I'll never forget this place. We have to bring the others here later," Goji said.

The two dumbstruck berries stood on the rock face until midday, gazing across the magical rift. They wondered and marveled, occasionally discussing the future with one another, but mostly they sat in silence together.

Goji, Rubus, and later the rest of the Huckles had enjoyed an unforgettable time experiencing the Grand Canyon, and for the rest of their days, they would not forget it.

12

A Strong Seed

THE HUCKLES VENTURED ON through the vast land of Arizona. The nights were cold, and the days were warm. Despite the weather, they made it through the land at a hasty pace, as there was little to obstruct their path. They rode over bare plains and desert land while glaring stars watched over them at night and pointed cacti, *Cactecaeae*, showed the way through the day. The Huckles spoke to some of these fauna along their journey and found out that the Cacti had been expecting them. The Cacti were distant relatives of the Trees, so they were familiar with the important events that were unfolding. They had no bone of contention with the Huckles, as they were very much outsiders to most of Realm life and swore no allegiance to anyone in particular. One Cactus that they met, named Pointifiucs, was from the Saguaro Realm and had journeyed north to visit some companions.

It was a good job that there was little woodland between the Grand Canyon and California, as the Huckles may have encountered serious hostility if there was. Rumors circulated among the Trees that the Huckles were drawing closer, and as the days grew shorter and winter grew nearer, they strengthened their roots even more in anticipation of an arduous battle to come. The Trees knew that there were very few creatures who could trouble them, but they also knew about the might of the Huckle King, who could uproot a Tree with a single thrust.

If you look on your map, you will again see that the Huckles had traveled an awfully long way. If they had made this journey on foot, they surely would never have made it, and crucially, if they had not formed loving bonds with the herd, perhaps they would have forsaken the quest, for it was the cows that had borne much of the heavy load. Fortunately for the cluster, they were passing through a stretch of Arizona that was relatively green and small in distance. It was the thin northern part to the west of the Yawning Gap. Before leaving that area, they stocked up with a bountiful number of leaves for the herd, and then did the same when they reached the forested lands that lie in a curve of the sparkling river. If you follow Colorado with your finger, you can trace their path. Of course, the Huckles loved the water, and they stuck as close to it as they could.

Eventually, the brave Huckles passed through the state of Nevada, in which they did not stop for long. By now, the desert nights had become increasingly cold, and they longed for woodland cover. Onward they pressed, and if you look at Nevada on the map, you should follow its border with California, and you will see along here a present-day settlement on the site where the Huckles then rested, called Amargosa Valley. Of course, there were no buildings or towns or people there at this time, but it was this point that the Huckles had now reached. They were close now, so very close, to the land of California, the land of mighty Trees.

"Will you calm down, Rubus?"

Rubus was pacing up and down, as he often did. The Huckles had stopped for a short time, as the sun had been beating down unceasingly upon them. Vernus, unlike Rubus, was sitting with his head reclined almost as if he were sunbathing.

"We will soon be entering the land of the trees, Vernus, and many dangers await us. If you hadn't noticed, we aren't the closest of companions to them right now," Rubus declared anxiously.

"Correct you are!" Vernus lifted his hand slowly, as if pretending to be concerned. Rubus looked at him in slight disbelief, but Vernus continued, "And what exactly is it that concerns you?" Rubus stopped pacing. He knew not how to answer that question entirely or if he even had an answer at all. The toll of the quest grew ever weightier upon him as it drew toward its final stage. Now that his arm was not as strong, he often struggled in his thoughts, wondering how he could best defend his knights. "I suggest that you relax, Rubus, and let your yoke be easy and your burden be light." With that, Vernus rolled over onto his side and prepared to take a gentle nap in the glaring sun.

Some of the Huckles (such as Vernus, clearly) had somewhat forgotten about the tumultuous tribulations that they had faced on their journey thus far, and their anxiety had been calmed by the serendipitous memories they had formed. Because they now had such close communion with the herd, the journey was made to seem easy. When they needed help, the cows were there, and when the cows were tired or faint, the Huckles would aid them. Rubus looked at Vernus briefly before darting off. There was much on his Huckle mind, and he feared the worst; such was his nature.

Some way away from the rest was the king, sitting daringly on a hill close to the border. He had been sitting there for a number of days, preparing himself for what was to come. There was a deep temptation within him to depart now without the cluster and fulfill this quest on his own. Things would be much easier, he thought, without them slowing him down. Deep down, though, he was concerned that some of the Huckles may face fierce confrontation in the land before them. He had heard many tales and rumors of the southern land but had not yet visited it himself. He knew that the Trees here were some of the most renowned in all the Realms and that the Huckles faced a fierce battle if they attempted to overpower them.

Deep in the Redwood forest , the ancient council was meeting once more. They sensed now that the Huckles were close, so they stayed in the sacred clearing at all times, as they did in times of trial and danger. There were now, therefore, noticeable gaps in the forest where the council members normally stood. Hyperion had been continuously pacing up and down through Redwood in deep thought. It was a mystical sight, seeing the giant in motion above the canopy. Small woodland creatures gasped and young ones drew closer to their parents, while fuzzy bears and elk were transfixed by the moving titan. A wonderful choir of birds followed the king wherever he went. Occasionally, some would switch and make space for others so that there was an equal number of passerines at all times. All of the songbirds in the forest wanted a turn to dance and sing around Hyperion.

Far south of Redwood, the Ancient Pines slept undisturbed. A gentle wind blew and rattled their mystic branches, and a few gray squirrels darted across the aged floor while large tumbleweeds weaved through the forest. The Elders had survived many ages, and they wouldn't be shaken or concerned by recent murmurings in the Realms. They knew all too well that this time would pass. The time beyond it, the result of this, our woodland tale, they did not know, but they were not worried in the slightest. Who were they to worry about tomorrow? They had seen and heard forests die, fires devastate, and witnessed ages come and go. When the land was renewed, they knew that they would be there still.

The next day, Goji, Logan, and Juniper were grooming some of the cows. They had been washing behind their ears and underneath their hooves, and the cows greatly appreciated it. The herd was most excited to visit the great land of California. Not only was it a land that they had heard much about, they also knew that deep bountiful forests awaited them, with leaves abundant. "California! The mighty southern land. I have heard so many tales," said Logan as he gently brushed his partner. "I hear that the great Trees are taller than anyone can imagine."

"Well, I hear that there are lands green and brown, mountains high, valleys low, and nights full of stars!" Juniper spoke as if reciting some legendary tale.

"How could one land be home to all of that?" asked Logan.

The three of them were conversing back and forth, and soon Goji stepped in, eager to share her deep knowledge. "Well, it is an ancient land, and the creatures work together in beautiful harmony, like we saw in Yellowstone." Goji, of course, had the most knowledge of the three. Though she had not been to the southern land herself, she had spent ample time as a young berry in the king's palace hearing passing tales. Also, Goji had made companions of any number of northward-flying birds that visited Glacier but lived in the south, and they would often tell her of California.

"I hear that the Trees have a High Gathering once a year," Juniper continued.

"Yes! I heard as much from Straw," said Logan. Straw was Logan's neighbor back in Huckle Village. She was a plump little red Huckle (some say that she always wished she were a berry of another kind).

"And how would Straw know?"

"I don't know, Juniper. Perhaps she has distant relatives from California."

Juniper looked at Logan as if he were being ridiculous, but he ignored her and continued speaking. "Say, I hear that the Trees are mighty and the beasts wild. I hear that the lands are watched by the Elder Trees, and that majestic birds circle above." He paused, and a troubled look grew on his face. "What are we to do if we must battle?" Goji stopped scrubbing the coat of her cow and looked at him.

"Well, we aren't going there to fight with anyone, Logan."

"Well, yes, that is the plan, but what if it does not go according to plan? What if the king gets to squishing and uprooting?" Goji started scrubbing again anxiously and harder.

"I'm sure he'll do no such thing."

"I sure hope not."

Goji paused momentarily. What if Logan was right? She hadn't considered that with the king's great grumpiness, he may make it difficult for them and the Trees to come to some form of agreement. She turned back to her cow and kept brushing its coat. The cows had heard the entire conversation, but they never interrupted or intervened, such was their elegant nature. The autumn sun shone, bronze, from above. Tomorrow the Huckles would set forth.

The spindly feet skipped across the slippery sand. As the lizard paced across the rocks, tiny fragments of shrapnel bounced from underneath him, spraying forward. From afar, this landscape took the appearance of high sand dunes, rather than rock. The peaks and the mountainsides were most unlike the snow-capped mountains of the north or the Grand Tetons near Yellowstone. These were the Funeral Mountains, and only the hardiest of creatures could hope to scale them. Not only were they slippery, steep, and menacing, they dwelt in the most extreme temperatures. In the summer, they were impossible to scale, and in the fall and the winter, the sun bore its face in the day, but the night cold would frighten the heart and soul of any creature. This weather, this climate, and this level of difficulty were typical of the land in which the Funeral Mountains stood. This was the Death Valley Realm.

It is the land that borders California and Nevada, and it was the land through which the Huckles soon had to pass. The foreboding name of this land is, and was, no mistake. Not much is able to grow in this vast, desolate expanse, for it is the hottest and driest place on Earth. The Huckles did not know this, of course; they did not even know what the Earth was.

Death Valley is a stark and desolate place. Barren stretches are bordered by baked peaks, and hot sands cover the surface, hued with a rusty brown and red tinge. Tumbleweeds blow through the open land undisturbed, and scorching swathes of sand cover the plains in brazen waves. Such is the heat and the dry climate that sandstorms are whipped up sporadically, and they rampage through the land, buffeting the steaming rocks in their wake. As well as sandstorms, tornadoes of wind arise, sending rocks and debris flying.

Despite the harsh climate, there was indeed wildlife in this volatile place. Death Valley is, after all, the largest national park in all of mainland

United States, and it was, in the time of our tale, the largest Realm. Well, this was true when the Huckles roamed the land. Now, they had heard rumors of larger, frozen Realms in the far north, past Glacier and out in the ocean past Canada, but that was beyond them.

Because of its tremendous size, it was not too much of a surprise, therefore, to find creatures abiding in Death Valley. Nature's creatures can thrive and develop in many circumstances, and it is often more necessary for them to work with their habitat than to find a new one. This is an important fact for me and you, and one that we must respect.

So there were animals across this vast Realm, much like there were in Glacier, Yellowstone, and all the other Realms that the Huckles had visited or heard of. The difference was, however, that here the creatures simply had to work with each other because of the desperately fierce environment. When they spoke and congregated, they managed their time efficiently, and they made extra efforts to look after one another.

The spindly feet of the lizard came to a screeching halt. He was a chuckwalla, *Sauromaulus*. They were large lizards with oily green coats much like olives, and their long tails swished to and fro when they paced through the desert, whipping up miry spectacles of dust and rock.

"Where is he, where is he . . . ?" The lizard, named Skim, had arranged to meet another at this exact spot. The folk of Death Valley had to make very precise plans. If they were too late or too early, the blazing sun or the mighty wind became overbearing, and they would be forced to abandon their plans completely. Almost as soon as he spoke, another lizard came flying through the brush. His feet skipped alternately off the ground, so it looked as if he was flying or gliding rather than running. In fact, the ground is so warm in Death Valley that reptiles, being cold-blooded, are required to stay off the ground when they can, lest they warm up too quickly.

"Sorry!" said the newcomer.

The lizards spoke quickly and softly. Their thin tongues whipped out of their mouths like slithering serpents. They spoke with sibilance at all times, the "s" sound rolling off their lolling tongues. Despite their slippery sound and appearance, they were actually noble creatures, and it should be known that there were far worse individuals than the lizards in those parts.

"Five seconds late you are!" said Skim.

A look of guilt was etched across Skid's face.

"I could have baked out here in the sun, Skid!" Skim raised his right arm toward the sun. It was partially to make his point to Skim and partially to raise that part of his body off the ground.

"Yes, yes, I know. I'm sorry. Let's just get this over with."

They both pushed themselves down toward the ground and then back up again. It was their way of agreeing with one another. They both wanted to get on with the message and get back to their cool rocks nearer the base of the funeral mountains, and besides, there were often terrible birds circling high above, looking for prey.

"Right, well, I have news for you to bring to the Great Horns. The Huckles are coming this way, and they are making their way to Hyperion," said Skim.

"Hyperion? I thought they were going to see the Elder Pines."

Messages from the woodland took longer to reach these lands in their entirety. Often, they were mired and hazy, such was the lack of Trees.

"Well, whatever it may be, they are heading through the valley," Skim continued.

"Right." Skid did a push-up off the floor. It was quickly becoming too warm for them. "And what is that to us?"

"We have to inform the Great Horns; they will want to know," said Skim.

The Great Horns were the guardians of the Realm. Much like the Huckles in Glacier, like Oxan in Yellowstone, and like the Redwoods, the Great Horns watched over all that came in and out of Death Valley.

"Right. I will let them know!" Skid said.

By now, the lizards were pretty much jumping up and down, such was the heat. The surface of Death Valley bakes like scalding charcoal, even in the fall. The summer was unbearable, a cauldron of fiery heat and humidity.

"Great!"

They nodded at one another. The lizards were enjoying each other's company, grateful to have fellowship in the harsh land, but as they jumped up and down, nodding and skipping to stay cool, suddenly a large shadow was cast over them. Both of them gasped in fright. They clambered and turned sharply, hiding behind some rocks close by. Once hidden, they could still see each other, and each noticed that the other was shaking violently.

"Is it them?" Skid's voice was shaky and scared. He looked up slowly to the skies as he spoke, where the naked sun let out all-encompassing rays of light that stretched over the entire Realm.

"I . . . I . . . think so." Skim's voice was equally frightened. The looming shadow had now engulfed their meeting spot. High above were three dreadful unfriendly birds swaying menacingly in foreboding circles. They flew above for what seemed like an eternity to the lizards, until the shadows grew larger and larger. The deadly birds were drawing closer to the ground. Skim looked over at Skid, and a look of great horror was etched on his face. His small teeth were chattering and his eyes were bulging. The lizards were terrified.

It seemed like one of the ferocious whirlwinds of the desert when the birds flew down. Their wings beat hard and strong, even though they looked ghostly and skeletal, and the limbs and bones of the birds were clear to see; they looked like ominous figures of death. Greater and greater the shadows grew until they reached the baking floor, covering the mountaintop on which Skim and Skid had met.

Skid looked over, but Skim was nowhere to be seen. He had hidden himself completely behind his rock. Skid peered over the edge of his, glancing at the terrifying scene before him. The birds were large and black; a black like a never-ending pit, like tar or coal. They had ghastly long feathers upon their wings with small, dirty pink beaks, and their eyes were minuscule, two little dots engulfed in a sea of darkness. They were a terribly large size, so when they stretched out their wings, they blotted out the sun from above, so that all could be seen was inky blackness.

These birds circled the skies of Death Valley, scouring the ground beneath for sorry stragglers. Mostly, they fed on the rotting carcasses of animals that had passed on to the great cycle, but sometimes they picked up small living animals too, and any pieces of fruit or vegetable that they may come across. These were turkey vultures, *Cathartes aura*. These ghastly birds were the great enemy of many in the Realms and skies in the Elders' age. This particular group, the one that had descended onto the mountain, were very nasty, and they bullied and picked on the smallest animals in Death Valley. The lizards in particular they pushed around with most malice.

One of the birds, who happened to be the leader of this group, landed with his talons in the dirt. His feet were scaly, slimy, and most unpleasant to look upon. After him, two more male birds landed, slightly smaller than the first. They landed ungracefully and unkindly, and their wings dropped sharply as they dug into the earth beneath them.

"Hissss." The head bird, named Snork, let out a voracious hissing sound. It was the most frightful noise to the lizards. It rattled and shook in the air like trapped steam escaping from a volcanic vent in the ground. The hissing crept up the lizards' backs and into their eyes, and all the little scales and horns on their bodies stood up sharply. Vultures lack the spellbinding awe of the eagle's screech or the awesome call of the hawk. All they can do is hiss.

Snork spoke first. "Say, brothers, what do you hear of these travelers from the north?" When they spoke, it was not much different to their hissing; both should rather not be heard.

"Easy pickings!" It was one of the other vultures, Slim, who had responded.

"Mwahahaha." The vultures laughed at Slim's words. It was a revolting laugh, as if the vultures had sharp bits of glass stuck in their throats. The lizards were already most uncomfortable, but now even the little bits of shrubbery and the rocks nearby seemed to dislike the birds. The brown tufts of grass leant away from the ugly group as their sickly laughter rattled around the mountaintop.

"Perhaps they will be protected by the Great Horns." The final bird, named Spike, was hopping around and mocking the creatures of which they spoke, using his black wings to imitate horns upon his head, and the vile creatures hissed in laughter again. Behind the rocks, Skim realized that he had stayed in one place for too long. He tried to stay calm, but he could not bear the scorching heat, and he let out an alarmed yelp as the burning ground scorched his underbelly. Realizing what he had done, he put his arm over his mouth as if to silence himself. Skid looked at him in terror, and the vultures ceased their sickly laughter.

"Did you hear that?" hissed Snork. "We have visitors." With a terrifying leap, the deadly bird hopped onto a nearby rock, his ugly black wings lifting him high, and some smaller rocks fell to the ground as he jumped. Skid looked at Skim. Momentarily, he jerked as if ready to leap to his rescue, but Skim motioned him back, as he knew there was little hope now. Though lizards aren't able to retain much water, there was enough for a little tear to roll down Skim's face. Skid, too, realized the fate that awaited his friend. Snork peered behind the rock where Skim was. His little body shook and trembled as he felt the terrible bird's presence above. "There you are!" The vulture dived down with an awful lurch and grabbed Skim with his ugly beak. Skim gripped his claws onto the rock with all his might, but Snork prized him off, and his little claws left sharp incisions on the rock face as he was pulled away. Skid dared not move. The ground underneath him was also scorching hot, but he would have to bear it.

Snork clasped Skim firmly in his mouth and flew into the arid Death Valley sky. The other vultures followed him closely, laughing horribly as they went. Skim's long tail dangled helplessly in the air as he was carried away, and Skid looked on. He knew that he would never see his friend again.

It was Goji herself who said that life within the Realms often does not transpire as one would hope. Indeed, despite the endless beauty, boundless life, and magical energy that exists in national parks, there is also a fiercer side. In all of nature, not just the parks, some creatures are predators and some are prey. This can often seem unfair, but it is not for us to try to save every creature, as much as our sentiment may encourage us to.

Like the Huckles were, it is more important for us to undergo transformations of love and wonder in our heart as we experience nature and national parks. This way, we can understand how to care for nature properly rather than mold it to our expectations. This is how we can care for our world; we must fall in love, we must nurture, and we must become guardians of the parks and nature as a whole. It is, after all, on this very principle that the national parks were established, as we shall soon observe. No part of nature exists by working completely alone, as there is always an element of harmony. Until another age, though, perhaps in a new creation long after our time, that harmony will never be fully complete, and that is a reality that we must understand. Often this reality is harsher than we wish. The Huckles, too, would soon come to understand this even more than they already did.

The knights were aligned in a military formation. They looked most determined and focused while the sun glared down and bounced off their wooden crowns, illuminating the path before them. It was a bright morning, and they were preparing to enter the final stage of their quest. As always, the king was at the back of the crowd. His troll drummers stood beside him, so that from him to the Huckles in front, it was a descending order of size. It must have looked very intimidating for any who saw the cluster advancing.

Rubus and Vernus rode side by side at the front, although they often fell back and inspected the Huckles, checked their staffs, and looked into their eyes.

"Today is the day!" Although Vernus had been speaking more of late, it was Rubus who delivered the speech that morning. "We have covered ground that no berry has known before! We have seen Realms and lands that those back home at Glacier can only dream of!" The Huckles murmured a low cheer. "Now is the time for us to fulfill this great journey. This day, we will set foot in the southern lands!" Rubus pointed toward the land beyond. It was the borderland, the start of California. Such was the desert that right now the biome looked very much the same, but they knew that this was the start of the fabled southern land.

Cacti all across the desert had guided their way and informed them of when California would appear. "So long as we stick together, we ride together, and, if necessary, we fight together, we shall have nothing to fear!" The Huckles cheered loudly. "We will venture forth for the king and for Glacier, to take our place and write our name where it belongs. We are the Huckles, and we ride for Glacier and the king!" The Huckles jumped up and down with excitement, and their berry stomachs wobbled while Rubus and Vernus rode along the front edge of the cluster, clattering their staffs against those of the others. "Forward!" Rubus yelled.

They let out a triumphant roar as they set forth, and since they were entering California, the band sang loudly. The king wanted the creatures of the land to know of his grand arrival.

> *Dum dum dum, off with his head, the king*
> *is purple, the king is not red!*
> *Dum dum dum, he is the king! All those*
> *in Glacier must bow to him*
> *Dum dum dum, oh do you know why, for one*
> *single pie several children had to die!*
> *Dum dum dum, off with his head, the king*
> *is purple, the king is not red!*

The song echoed through the empty desert. Onward they marched toward the border, and at long, long last, the Huckles had finally reached California. After some time, they slowed their march, the king's song subsided, and the last of the misty purple notes faded into the humid expanse. They could not afford to keep up their march for too long, because the heat dragged on and sapped their energy. Their water reserves were already low, so they had to make every bit last.

As they approached the border, two figures could be seen looming before them like a miry mirage in the desert heat. They were two palm trees, *Arecaceae*. They stood tall, and their green leaves hung like floppy hair on top. It seemed odd that they were present, as there were no other Trees around, so they stood completely alone. It was almost if they had been placed there by someone else.

"Huckles from the north!" The Tree on the left spoke. His voice was raspy, as though many bits of sand had become stuck in his throat over the years of desert life. "This is the border of California, and from the moment you step forth, you are in the land of the great Trees."

This time, Rubus did not even have a chance to speak. The moment the tall swaying Tree uttered those words, the fiery king plowed through the cluster toward them, flinging some of the knights aside as he forged his way through. "What say you, Trees? Do you wish to obstruct us?" The crowd was hushed and silent. They had not expected such affirmative action from the king.

"Not at all," the Tree on the right replied. "We are simply here to welcome all that may come into our land."

The king was most suspicious and had little time to interrogate the Trees. He lifted his staff high and menacingly, and some Huckles behind him gasped. "You Trees are never up to anything good." He said no more but swung his mighty staff through the stifling air. Such was the force of his blow that he whipped up a stream of dust behind him. His staff clobbered into the left Palm Tree, and it bent under the pressure from the blow, staying low and remaining silent. The king looked back toward the cluster, which had watched in fright. "Onward!" the king bellowed at them; he was in no mood for time-wasting. He marched on past the standing Palm, and the Huckles followed after. Interestingly, the king now took the lead, the knights in the middle and the band behind. The king wanted them all to travel as fast as they could through the barren land, so he had gone to the front.

Away from the Trees the Huckles rode, as the unforgiving layers of rock and sand glistened on the horizon. As they set forth, the Palm Tree left standing uttered to himself, "So it is true. The northern king does come bearing malice." Immediately, a brown speckled bird approached the Tree. It was a greater roadrunner, *Geococcyx californianus*. It had a brown spot on its head and a small black hanging feather. Its wings were gray and stained with the brown desert shade. The bird waddled toward the Tree.

"What happened?" The roadrunner looked back and forth as it spoke. It was not the clearest tone, as the roadrunner did not have the best speaking ability.

"Take this back to the west," replied the Tree. "The Huckles came forth into our land, and the king hath lifted his staff and struck my brother."

"Very well, then." The roadrunner pivoted on the spot and darted off at a tremendous speed, its little behind wobbling and swaying as it sprinted through the desert. The roadrunner himself would not deliver the message all the way to Redwood, but it would find its way eventually. After the bird had gone, the Palm looked down upon his brother (they had grown from seeds birthed from the same tree).

"They have departed, brother."

The other Tree slowly strained and straightened. It creaked quietly, but eventually returned upright. You see, palm trees are used to violent forces, winds, and buffeting storms, so the strike from the king had not uprooted the Tree. In fact, the two had planned it all along in order to judge the intentions of the king and feed the information back to the west.

"So, it is true; the northern one comes bearing malice," said the one recently straightened.

"Yes, it is so."

The Trees watched as the berries faded into the distant desert, while miry waves of heat stretched across the horizon.

The Huckles labored on through the vast empty land. Of all the stages of their journey, this was easily their least desired, and only the king was motivated to plow on. The harsh sun bore down on Huckle and cow alike, and they dreamed once more of grassland and fertile mountain plains. It was the thought of Glacier and the memories they had made thus far that pushed them onward. Some way at the back of the cluster, Goji rode close to Juniper. She had one eye cast disdainfully on the figure of the king way ahead.

"Why is his heart so cruel?" Goji had watched the clobbering of the Palm Tree in disgust. She made sure to speak the words quietly, so that no other Huckle could hear. She and Juniper had developed a strong bond in recent times, and Goji knew she could trust her.

"He was not always this way," Juniper replied.

Goji had, of course, heard this before, but it made little sense to her that the seed of a berry could change so dramatically. "Well, what happened?"

"Do you not know? His only love, Bramble the berry queen, she was lost."

The fateful day had been before Goji's time. She knew of it, but not the details.

"Lost? How?"

Juniper looked at the ground in dismay. "We do not speak of it, Goji, but the king has not been the same ever since. What is more, his seed was split down the middle."

"Split?" Goji looked shocked.

"Yes. The king's heart was split and fractured down the middle; some say beyond repair. He does not feel; he does not think or act in the same way as he did before."

Goji looked at the back of the king thoughtfully. He was a looming distant figure. "What could mend the seed?"

Juniper looked at her friend and smiled a warm smile.

"Ahh, Goji, only you could think of such a thing." She sighed. "Many have attempted to reach the king's heart, fabled creatures from all Realms, but none have succeeded. Rubus, the poor soul, has spent countless hours at his side, trying to simply get a word out of him."

Goji took some time to absorb the words. She had always seen the king as ruthless and cold, but she had not really considered why. "And why does he hate the Trees so?"

"He will not say."

Goji looked thoughtfully at the king once more. It had never bothered her much that the king thought of her as an outsider; instead, it was more pressing to her that the king was unkind to others.

After their conversation, she leaned over and gave Juniper a brief hug, bidding her farewell.

For hours afterward, the Huckles rode through the desolate plains of Death Valley. They stopped more often than usual so that they could catch their breath and rest. They were reaching the very last of their water, and they had a fine line to balance between taking their time through the desert and hastily reaching the bountiful heartland of California. Some of the leaves they had soaked in water for hours before departing the last of the forest, and these they fed to the herd. However, these too were running low, meaning the elegant cows wagged their tongues in thirst as they rode on through the desert.

Two nights passed.

The Huckles slept under the stars and departed again in the early morn. Never before had they experienced such extremes of temperature. They froze at night and wrinkled up in the day, but despite the heat, many of them had morphed into their most wintry skin. They had developed an internal memory of seasons past that reminded them of the climate back home. Therefore, they still reflected deep winter in their appearance. The Huckles carried Glacier with them wherever they went. Onward through the sun and the cold, the Huckles pressed on. They knew their quest was nearing completion, and besides, the king was moving forward at a pace not seen for many a year (as for him, he would very much like to have traveled even faster). They strode on.

It was their third day in the stark Realm. The golden-brown landscape had now become a familiar shade to the Huckles, and they felt that they had been passing through the sand for an endless age. Rubus and Vernus had been riding alongside the group, delivering uplifting speeches about the importance of their quest. They spoke of Glacier, of the king, and of the important contributions to the Realms that the Huckles still had to make.

Goji watched Rubus as he rode. Despite the fearless strength that he displayed for the Huckles, she could see past, look deep, and see his weariness. His berry skin sagged beneath his clothing, and his eyes were tired. Through all of this, he fought on. Faintness he showed not, for he would rather perish than be shown to be weak before his knights.

Goji loved him deeply. They had moved a long way on from their rift, and she thought to herself of the great times that lay before them. Rubus had raised her, stayed by her, and taught her much of what she knew. He was her friend, supporter, and father. She rode to the front of the cluster to speak with him, and she smiled as she thought of them riding together through the woodland of California, of which she had heard many tales. But when she was around halfway toward him, an ominous shadow was cast over the cluster.

It was the king who stopped first. Although he was disinterested at times, he was still a mighty warrior, and the Huckles knew they could trust him in times of danger. He turned sharply toward the sky and suddenly grasped his staff with a fierce tightness. An eerie purple mist drifted from him, as if he were preparing himself.

The Huckles were confused and frightened. They murmured to one another, "What is it?"

As Goji looked around, she saw that some of the Huckles were breaking formation in panic, scattering to the left and to the right. The shadow grew larger and larger before a black darkness descended upon them all. Goji looked upward, and high above were dreadful creatures, gliding in circles and blotting out the sun with their terrible wings. Slowly, they were descending closer to the cluster.

"Goji!" Rubus shouted at her anxiously, and she snapped her focus back before her.

"What is it?" She was very worried, more so than she had been at any point on their quest so far.

"These foul creatures are foes to us, Goji!"

An ugly hissing began to sound from above.

"What shall I do?"

"Take cover, Goji!"

The hissing intensified, and some of the Huckles began to shout.

"Rubus!"

She shouted after him, but it was too late. Rubus had departed from her and was readying the knights. He spoke courageous words and commanded them to stand firm. The Huckles were mostly fearsome, but they had only heard dark tales of the black birds, and above them now, the horrible hissing and cackling laughter filled the barren desert. The knights panicked, and some dropped their staffs.

"Do not retreat!" Vernus bellowed to the knights.

Goji looked on. Suddenly, one of the vultures swooped down and grabbed a berry with its ugly beak. He took it some way into the sky before Rubus leapt from his cow and launched himself hastily at the bird, skillfully smacking it with his staff. Such was the force that the sound could be heard far below. Uplifted by their commander, the Huckles bore their staffs toward the dreadful vultures, but they were not used to fighting such a foe. Back home in Glacier, they would have had their catapults at the ready for any airborne enemy.

The vultures continued to hiss and cackle above, and Goji looked on in fear. There was screaming and disarray as some of the cows darted from underneath the Huckles, while the vultures swooped down and knocked many off their feet. Occasionally, the knights would connect with their staffs fair and true, knocking the birds aside, but the vultures just rose again on their black wings. Rubus, Vernus, and Juniper stood in front of the group, battling with all their might. The sun bore down as the birds wreaked havoc upon the scattered Huckles.

After a while, it seemed as though the Huckles had turned the tide of battle against the horrible enemy, and the birds circled higher and higher, seemingly unable to penetrate the cluster. But Rubus turned around to rile the knights, lifting his staff victoriously, when it happened.

Snork the terrible swooped down toward him, his disgusting pink beak cutting awkwardly through the desert heat. He bore down upon Rubus and grasped him with his ugly talons. Rubus struck out with his staff, but it was too late. The bird had snatched the commander.

"Rubus!" Goji let out a desperate cry.

Vernus threw his staff toward the foul beast like a soaring spear, but it was to no avail. High above, Rubus jerked around in the clasp of the talons, trying to break free. Tears flowed down Goji's face, and she ran directly underneath the bird, gazing up at Rubus's struggle. Snork ascended higher and higher. He was escaping with the Huckle of renown.

When it seemed as though he were gone and that Rubus had been taken, a fearsome sound came from nearby. The entire cluster shook and trembled before turning around, and there before them in radiant purple was their warrior king. Such anger was written upon his face that the Huckles thought he had become some wild beast from the Great Outdoors. As the enraged Huckle prepared to thrust himself toward Snork, he crouched toward the ground and a powerful purple glow surrounded him, some mystical berry power. The Huckleberry King leapt toward Snork with all his might, and his powerful frame soared boldly up toward the bird.

Effortlessly, he reached the vile creature and grabbed its scrawny neck. With a wrathful force, he headbutted the villain, who had no hope against one so powerful. Overwhelmed, the foe dove toward the ground before releasing Rubus, then scuffled and scurried away. The vultures were gone. The king landed before the cluster, and as he did so, the ground beneath shook, and he forged a mighty crater. The Huckles stood aghast. Not for many years had they witnessed the king's power in this way.

"Thank you, king." It was Vernus who spoke, bowing before him. The Huckles applauded the might of their ruler, but from elsewhere, groans of anguish could be heard.

Goji and Juniper rushed over to Rubus first and saw that he was writhing in pain, while berry juice leaked from his wounds. His fall had been cushioned by some Huckles who had bonded together, but the fierce grip of the awful bird had begun to cut him in two.

"Rubus . . ." Goji could barely stand straight. She knelt before his side while tears like the streams of Glacier flowed from her. Rubus's heavy eyes lolled open and closed as he mustered enough strength to look down at his side, where berry juice was gushing from the gaping wounds. Slowly he looked at her. Juniper and Vernus now stood some way back, comforting one another, and at a slight distance stood the king, and although he would not show it, he was most distressed.

"Goji . . ." Rubus slowly spoke to her.

She cupped his head with her hand, and an aching lump formed deep within her seed. Her insides felt as though they were knotted and tied. "You're . . . you're going to be okay, Rubus. We're going to get you out of here."

"Goji . . ."

"We're gonna get you out!" She looked around frantically. "Help!" Goji turned and screamed with all her strength into the empty desert, but there was no one to hear her. Her sorrowful words bounced back from the unforgiving desert rock as the Huckles looked painfully on.

"Rubus . . ." Goji wept and wept. She burrowed her head into his torso, wrapping her arms around him.

Rubus winced with pain. "Goji . . ."

"Yes, Rubus?" Her voice was choked with tears.

He reached his hand toward her, and she gripped it tight. "I love you, Goji." He muttered the words as best he could. Watching the scene in untold distress, some Huckles came to give him aid, but he waved them away.

"I love you, Rubus. You are the noblest berry in all of Glacier. Your heart is strong and kind. I . . . I . . ." Her weeping encumbered her, and she could only speak if she gripped his hand tightly. Now there was mournful bellowing amidst her weeping, and her words were awash with pain and agony. Despite this, they were still sweet to Rubus.

"I want us to explore more, Rubus. I want us to swim in Lake Mc-Donald and climb the fair mountains. I want us to glide through the

Glacier plains with the elk, the goat, and the bear. I want you to stay, Rubus." She burrowed her head into him once more, pounding her fist on the ground. The gaping wound in Rubus's side grew larger, and he struggled to keep his eyes open.

"Goji . . ." With every ounce of strength, Rubus lifted himself so that he could look at her. "I have done everything I can for you. You are my greatest love. Neither the mountains of Glacier nor the fields of Yellowstone mean more to me. There is one last thing, I must beseech you."

Goji looked into his eyes. "Yes?"

"Goji, your seed must be strong. You are kind, compassionate, and caring. The Realms need you—Glacier needs you. Let your seed be strong."

Those were his final words. Rubus's eyes rolled closed and he drifted out of Goji's arms onto the floor. There in the desert, in the southern land, passed the mighty commander of the Huckle Knights. Rubus was gone.

Goji wept and wept. To this day, woodland legends still speak of the streams of sorrow that poured forth from her. Her head remained buried in his torso, and behind her, all of the Huckles wept as well. The king looked on in distress. There in the empty desert they remained for many hours, during all of which Goji wept. After some time, Juniper came to her. At first, she shrugged her away, but eventually she fell into her arms, and the two wept loudly. The cows created a circle around them, but they did not weep, as they did not want to create more sorrow.

An entire night passed.

As the other Huckles slept roughly, Goji stayed weeping by Rubus's side.

The next morning, she heard footsteps behind her. She looked back and saw that it was the king. She wiped her eyes before speaking gruffly to him. "What do you want?"

The king said nothing.

Goji looked back toward Rubus's still body before a deep rage welled up within her. She snapped upright and stormed over to him. Shoving one of his legs, she shouted, "This is your fault!" Goji then stormed off into the desert, her tears still falling, as the king silently watched. Such was her loud cry that Vernus and Juniper were awoken. They first noticed the king, who stood forlorn, then a fierce desert wind began to fester, and Juniper and Vernus quickly realized what had come to pass. "Goji!"

Juniper called after her, but there was no answer. Vernus looked at the king, who nodded his head as if granting them blessing to follow.

"Meet us in the northern forest," he said.

Vernus nodded. He knew not how he would find them later on, but he knew what he had to do now.

Vernus and Juniper left the others and plowed through the storm, where eventually they caught up with Goji. The storm raged on.

"Goji!" Juniper called.

Goji quickened as she noticed the two, but eventually Juniper reached her and held her tight, then Goji broke into flowing tears once more. "He's gone. He's gone, Juniper!" She thumped her fists against her.

"Goji." Juniper wept with her, holding her in both arms as Vernus looked on.

"We are here. We are all here. And he loved you, Goji. He always will be within you, so long as your seed is strong."

Deep inside her, Goji's seed began to crack, but as she dwelt in Juniper's arms, the voice of Rubus passed through her mind:

Let your seed be strong.

With all that was within her, Goji put her arms around Juniper. Still weeping, she searched deep within. She remembered the summer days spent with Rubus in the great Glacier woods. She remembered the wintry nights nestled together and the clear springs in warm lakes. There in the blustering sand, Goji remembered. She held Juniper tight as her tears flowed.

Her seed had cracked, but unlike the king's many years ago, hers would not split. Goji held on, and her seed was strong.

Back at the scene of Rubus's passing, fresh footsteps could be heard through the storm. The king looked upon the weary cluster and the herd. He knew that with Rubus and Vernus both gone, he must rise up and lead them. The footsteps drew closer, and some powerful creatures appeared through the hazy sand. They were desert bighorn sheep, *Ovis canadensis nelson*. The sheep shone a clear white with mighty curling horns, and upon the leader's head a lizard rode, much like the Huckles rode the cows.

"Greetings, northerners. We are the Great Horns, and we have heard of your plight." The leader's name was Grail, and his voice sounded like half speaking, half bleating. The king looked at them. Whereas he had been closed off to the creatures of other Realms before, his mood had begun to shift, perhaps out of necessity but also perhaps due to a change of course deep within. "Greetings," the distressed king replied.

"We have heard of your loss, Huckle King. The wind carries the news." The wind was indeed still ferocious, and millions of sand particles blew between them. As the storm raged on, some of the Horns rubbed heads with the cows, as they were common folk. The cows were grateful to meet them, as it was refreshment for their journey; weary had they grown.

The king nodded, not wishing to discuss Rubus anymore. "We will not find our way amidst the storm," he said.

"We will guide you out. Where is it that you seek?"

"We travel to the land north of here, but three have left us, and they will not make it." The king pointed west, where the three had departed.

"Very well."

Grail nodded to three Horns behind, and with their heads down, they dashed off toward Vernus, Juniper, and Goji, who by now would be far across the desert.

"Follow us, Huckle King, and we will guide you to the northern border."

The king looked at the cluster and motioned to them to follow, then he turned back to the Horns. "I have one more request of you."

Grail looked at him.

"One of our fiercest and noblest warriors, he has joined the great cycle. It is from Glacier that we come, and to Glacier he must return," the king said mournfully.

The leader of the Horns nodded at another of his companions, and they trotted over to the felled body of Rubus. Slowly, he gently scooped him up using his horns. The Huckles behind wept as they saw it.

"We will carry him with us to where we are now headed. From there, the rivers of the north, the Colorado, and other waters beyond will guide him yonder." With that, Grail led them away. The Huckles pressed on with deep pain in their hearts, as they knew not when they would see Rubus's body again. The king could not yet bring himself to motivate their seeds with words, but he constantly looked behind to check on their wellbeing.

Some way to the west, the three Horns paced through the storm. Finally, they caught up with the berries, who had been completely lost. The weary wanderers noticed their approach through the storm.

"Who are you?" Vernus's voice could barely be heard amidst the raging sand.

"We are the guardians of this land, and we come to lead you westward, into the heartland," a Horn named Grunt replied.

The berries looked at one another. Although they were in no mood to trust the creatures of this Realm, they knew that they now had little choice. Also, the appearance and voice of the creature was fair and true.

"Very well," said Vernus.

"Mount us," said Grunt. The berries mounted the Horns, and, much like they had with the cows, they traveled on through the desert land.

As Goji rode, she clutched tightly at her chest, and a deep pain coursed through her, aching in her seed. Summer days and winter nights flashed through her mind as she remembered Rubus. Despite her overwhelming sadness, she was determined to see to it that the quest was finished, to honor him.

Meanwhile, the king and the cluster rode north. The storm raged on, but the king positioned himself between the wind and the berries so that he became a mighty barrier. His seed was already cracked, so he could feel no deeper pain, but Rubus's passing had saddened him as well. Onward the cluster struggled until they reached the northern borderland of the desert. Rubus was gone.

13

A Sapling with Great Ambition

SOARING PAIN HUNG OVER the hearts and minds of the Huckles. The Great Horns had left them on the border's edge. As they trotted away, they butted heads with Morrow; not out of competition, but as a sign of mutual respect between the two. The cluster was now alone with the king, who had to lead them once more. Despite the cluster's weariness, the king was only more determined; the quest had to be finished, and they needed to continue sooner rather than later. The Huckles did not belong here. They had to get back to Glacier and the grasslands, lest they perish from sorrow.

They pressed on through the land just north of the desert. On your map you will see it; the land directly above Death Valley is mountainous, with patches of green. The weary creatures pushed on past Tin Mountain and Dry Mountain. Although the desert continued, there were more patches of grass than in arid Death Valley, so they stopped and drank all that they could, as they were greatly parched from being in the harsh desert. All the while, not a word was spoken, such was their deep sorrow. Onward they pushed. They were heading north toward the White Mountains, to the land of the Ancient Pines.

They seldom stopped, for they were no longer in the desert, and here the air blew chilly and cold. High atop distant peaks, the Huckles could see blankets of snow, and they knew they had to keep moving. Their skin now sagged in its winter form, and the cows' coats had turned a dark shade of brown. After two cold nights, they reached the Ancient Forest, and before them was a high rocky slope. The king began to climb but noticed that no one ascended alongside him. He looked down behind him and saw the forlorn faces of the cluster and the herd. He beckoned them up with his mighty arm, but they would not follow. "Come on!" he yelled at them, and raging impatience welled within. The Huckles could not ascend. The weight of their journey had grown too much for them to bear.

Morrow spoke for them. "They cannot climb." His tone was rather gruff, as he had not forgotten the king's grievous action against the cow months earlier.

The king pounded his fist onto the rock face, but he soon saw the unshakable despair in the faces below. The creatures were encumbered by exhaustion, and the king's eyes widened as he remembered their plight. His mind raced back to a certain summer evening many years ago, and images flashed into his mind of the passing of Bramble. She too could not climb any higher. "Very well. Wait here. I will return soon." The determined king then paced up the slope with frightening speed, and his powerful arms launched him from nook to nook. The cluster watched him ascend higher and higher until he reached the top and faded away.

At the top of the slope was an eerie mist. Snow was piled high on the ground, and there was little sign of life on the forest floor. The king plowed through, leaving gulflike berry footprints in his wake. He passed a thick Pine covered in snow, and once it was behind him, the Tree moved and slowly shook the snow from its branches; it fell to the ground in white clumps. The king looked back, wondering if the Tree was awake, but there was no voice.

Onward he walked. The mist grew deeper and eerier as he progressed. The Pine Forest had a strange aura; it felt as though nothing were alive, but at the same time, the ancient age of the forest permeated all around, and it felt as though the life of all things was present. Lingering creaks sounded as he walked on, and he thought to himself that he could hear small sniggers of laughter, but he paid little attention.

Beneath him, the ground rumbled as ancient roots pulsated, passing messages through the undergrowth. The king gripped his staff tightly. By now the snow reached his knees, and the bitter chill gripped even him so that he moved ever faster just to stay warm. After some time walking through the Ancient Forest, the king came to a small hill. In the summer, it appeared as a rocky cleft, but now that the snow had fallen, it looked like an unscalable mound. The king bent his shivering knees and launched himself onto the top. There, the mist was so thick that he struggled to see.

He moved forward, as there was no other direction in which to travel. The creaks and groans grew louder, and a songbird dashed past his face. He attempted to swat it away with his staff. The laughter from the Trees, now clear to him, filled the air. It was not, at least, malicious laughter like that of the vultures, which still haunted him. The king grew frustrated, eager to find her whom he sought. He knew of the Elder Pine, but he knew not where to find her. The bitter cold grew and grew, and the king grunted in desperation. Even he could not withstand such bitterness for too long. Summer days in Glacier flashed through his mind. All Huckles thought of home in the midst of dire circumstances. He opened his mouth to let out a roar of frustration, but a serene voice bellowed through the thick mist, interrupting him.

"Welcome, king of the north!"

The king snapped his gaze northward, from whence the voice had come, and small rays of light struck through the cloudy mist. The king moved closer and saw the faint outline of an ancient Tree. "We have been waiting ever so patiently." A Tree to one side sniggered at Methuselah's words. The Trees had not been waiting at all; instead, they had been sleeping very contentedly. The king plowed on through the blanket of snow until he could clearly see her. Through the mist, her silhouette appeared as a spirally raking figure, and her branches and trunk twisted and turned like violent sparks shooting from the floor.

"You are Methuselah?" The king moved as close as he felt comfortable; he did not yet know the intentions of the Pines.

"Yes. It is I that you seek. Tell me, northern king, how are the dear Elderberries?"

The king gave no reply; he had not forgiven the Elderberries for their misguidance. "You know why I come, don't you, Tree?"

Methuselah turned her thick trunk as if she had decided to face him. "I know why you have come, Huckle King, but it appears that you still do not."

The king stamped his staff onto the ground. Such was the height of the snow that it reached halfway up the ancient wood. "There is little time to waste, Tree. I have spoken to Oxan and seen the Manuscripts. They must be amended."

Methuselah's silhouette stood still. As she stood before the impatient king, large flakes of snow began to descend from the chilly heights. In the midst of permeative creaking and groaning, she leaned forward ever so slightly so that she was closer to him. "Tell me, berry, do you think you know better than I? It was I, Pry, and the Elderberries who marked the scripts, and you would tell me that they need changing?"

"You are old, Tree, and the Realms have changed."

Methuselah leaned back. "It is not they that must change, but you," she said calmly.

The king firmed his grip. "We Huckles have grown in Glacier for many years. It is our Realm and our home. As well, we seek to expand onward, just as other creatures have done."

Methuselah twisted her branches after the king had ceased, as if his words were irrelevant. "Do you not know, king? For the Realms to serve their purpose, the role of every creature must not lord over the others. It is you who must learn to serve Glacier."

"Glacier would have perished if it were not for me!" The king grew vexed.

"From what? By the hands of foul beasts? From fire? These are challenges that all Realms must face. They are overcome by following the guidance."

"Do not lecture me, Tree. You have not suffered the trials that I have overcome."

Methuselah could see into the king's heart, and he could not disguise from her the inner meaning that his words hid. "Yes, the berry queen's passing was a great tragedy," said Methuselah.

The king was slightly shocked at her knowledge, but it only angered him all the more. "Do not speak her name!"

Methuselah stayed calm. "Do you not see, king? It was not the fault of other creatures, the passing of your great queen." It was not Methuselah's intention to taunt the king, but she always spoke the words that needed to be spoken.

The king took a step forward and reared his great legs as if ready to launch toward her. "Your words must cease!"

Methuselah was still relaxed. "If only you had learnt by now, perhaps others would not have suffered a similar fate."

The king sensed that Methuselah was referring to Rubus. With that, he was greatly angered, and deep fury encumbered him. He launched toward Methuselah, swiping his heavy staff through the falling snow, but almost as quickly as he moved, an ancient but powerful root launched upward from the ground. Methuselah's limb ripped through the undergrowth, wrapping itself firmly around the king's plump body. He was trapped by her powerful grasp. She leaned in closer to him. The ancient one was normally an approachable Tree, blessed with humor and good accord, but now her tone grew markedly stronger. "You should know better than to attack me, berry." Seeing that the king had realized the futility of his attack, she loosened him and let him fall to the ground. Defeated, the king picked up his staff from the deep snow.

"Now, do you wish to move forward with this quest, or will the rest of your cluster suffer from your ignorance also?"

"The Manuscripts must be altered." The king's mind would not be swayed.

"They shall not be."

The king gripped his staff tighter than ever before. Such was his grasp that he almost snapped it in two. Despite the burning desire that raged within him, even he could see that his efforts would come to naught. Even he, yes, he, lacked the strength to challenge the oldest Tree. He had to take a moment to recollect himself. So rarely had the king backed down in battle, but here, he was forced to swallow his fearsome pride. "Well then, ancient Tree. What would you have me do, in all your wisdom?" He spoke with a light sarcasm.

Methuselah's raking figure bore down on him imposingly as she responded, "When you departed on this quest, whom was it that you sought?"

"Hyperion of the north is whom I sought. It is he that governs the affairs of the Trees, whilst you are his overseer, is that not correct?"

"Indeed." She paused and looked at the Pines around her. "Although we sometimes question if his decisions are down to earth."

The Pines sniggered. It was a peculiar moment amidst the tense standoff, but after all, the Elder Pines had watched Hyperion grow since he was but a young sapling, and they seldom missed an opportunity to tease him. Despite this, they loved him dearly. The king's tone was unmoved; there had been little room in his heart for humor for some time. "Well then, it is with him that I will take up my cause. And what if he would have the Manuscripts amended, for the great good of us all?"

"Well then, perhaps, northern king, we shall have it considered."

"Very well." The king turned to make his way back. The snow was falling heavily now, and the footprints that the king left were filled instantly. Methuselah had some final words.

"You should know something, Huckle King."

He stopped without turning, and clear white flakes of snow rested upon him as he stood.

"If the journey does not make you, then you have not partaken in the journey."

The king heard the Tree's words, but he did not dwell on them too hard. After Oxan, he had become somewhat weary of cryptic speech.

"Oh, and one more thing . . ."

The king stopped once more.

"If you are searching for your friends, you will find them in the high forest, westward from here. I hear that the sapling with great potential has encountered them."

The king's eyes widened. Not only had he momentarily forgotten about Vernus, Juniper, and Goji, it had also been a long time since he had heard any Huckle mentioned as a friend. He stood still in the falling snow before departing the Ancient Forest and heading back toward the cluster waiting below. Methuselah watched as he went forth.

"A sapling with great potential . . ." he muttered.

Goji lay wide awake. She had not slept since the passing of Rubus, and it felt as though a piece of her own seed had been ripped from her. She used to take joyful delight in the colors around her, and she used to be able to spot and hear little critters on the woodland floor from a high point. As she lay now on the high branch, she could only see gray, and her surroundings mattered not. It was as if she had been torn away from everything she loved.

As she sobbed quietly on the high branch, Vernus and Juniper slept a couple branches lower. They too were stricken with grief, but not so much that they were unable to sleep. The three had been dropped at the border of the desert by the Great Horns. Westward they had then ventured until they encountered a mysterious forest region. Had they been of sound mind, they would have been delighted at this dense woodland, which was similar in appearance to their Glacier home. Thick snow blanketed the ground, but they could still clearly make out the wondrous Trees and bountiful fauna. They had gone undisturbed through the impressive forest until they came across a most interesting-looking Tree. It was fantastically wide at the trunk, with heavy, thick branches protruding up and down. The Tree emitted an odd aura, as if it were bursting with greatness but not sure what to do with it. That night, they had climbed the Tree in the silence of the snow-covered forest. The only sound to be heard was the occasional clump of snow falling onto the blanketed ground below. It was now late December, and most woodland creatures had long disappeared.

It was on this great Tree that Goji now lay, with her heart aching deep within her. The painful swollen lump in her chest had not regressed. She kept going back over her life with Rubus, retelling his stories and reminding herself of his words. She thought to herself of the strife early on in their journey; had she not been so stubborn, perhaps they would have made more loving memories on the way. This she regretted deeply. She knew not if she would ever be the same. As she quietly sobbed into the night, the thick branch on which she lay shifted beneath her. The Tree had been still throughout the night until it was seemingly disturbed. Goji swept her tears away, not wanting to be caught crying.

"Hey! Who are you upon my branch?" The voice of a young Tree spoke to her. It was a clear but shaky voice, almost as if the Tree was nervous to speak.

"I'm sorry." Goji stuttered as she spoke, muttering through her tears.

"Who are you? What are you doing here?"

"My . . . my name is Goji, and I am a berry from the far north."

"Well, berry from the far north, what are you doing up here on my branch?"

Goji propped herself up in a sitting position. "We came through the forest late at night, and we had nowhere else to rest."

"So, thought you could sleep on me, huh?"

"I'm sorry. I'll get down."

"Ahh, what good will that do? You're already up here. Just quit sobbing, will ya."

Goji was momentarily infuriated. Who was this Tree to tell her to cease her crying?

"Well, I'll make sure not to disturb you for the rest of the night." She folded her arms and slumped back against the trunk, irritated, but as she sat in silence, the Tree shrugged the branch on which she sat, as if vying for her attention.

"Hey, look, I'm sorry. I don't do the best with strangers." The Tree paused and twisted slightly. "Well, to be honest, I don't do the best with anyone, really."

"So, your answer is to be cruel?" Goji was still not impressed.

"Look, I said I'm sorry. You just kinda shocked me is all."

Goji could see where the Tree was coming from. It must be odd, having a crying stranger upon your branches on a random winter night. "Fine."

After an awkward silence, the Tree creaked as it moved another branch.

"So, what's your name?"

"I'm Goji. From the northern Realm of Glacier."

"Wow! I've heard about you folks. Can't believe I'm finally meeting one!"

"Well, here I am. There are two others with me, down below."

"Really? Can't feel them on any of my branches. They must have gone off for a walk."

Goji paid no concern to the whereabouts of Juniper and Vernus for now; she just assumed that they must have switched Trees. "Well, what's your name?"

"My name's Sherman. I'm a Sequoia Tree, and one day I plan to be the largest Tree in all the land!"

For the first time in many days, Goji expressed some emotion other than deep pain. She sniggered at the Tree's grand introduction. "You? You're just a sapling, and you don't seem like a very tall Tree."

Sherman, at this stage in his development, was indeed an odd-looking tree. His branches shot off in sporadic directions, and his trunk was awkwardly wide. He almost looked like a mistake. "Not the tallest, the largest!" He sounded offended, and with that, Sherman's branches lowered as if he were slumping his shoulders. Goji sensed that she had saddened the Tree in some way, such was her connection to all things natural.

"Hey, I'm sorry. I didn't mean to be cruel." She reached for Sherman's trunk.

"It's okay. Guess ya got me back. It's just that folk often make fun of me like that."

"What do you mean?"

Sherman sighed. "Well, since I'm still a sapling, I go to this Tree nursery, right, but all the other saplings make fun of me because I'm so much bigger than them. They say that I'm too big for the forest." Goji stopped and pondered briefly. She had never come across a situation like this. As she always did, she tried to understand the creature's situation more fully so that she could help in the best way.

"What's the name of the nursery?"

"Well, it's the Sequoia Tree nursery, of course."

"How was I to know that?"

"Errr . . . because this is Sequoia Realm . . ." Sherman spoke in a matter-of-fact tone.

Sequoia is a little west of Death Valley, if you wish to find it on your map. It is a dense woodland, and the main inhabitants are great tall Trees, although not quite as tall as the Redwoods. According to the Manuscripts, these are the close cousins of the Redwoods, and they had been birthed after the council left some seeds during one of the High Tree Gatherings (Yosemite was not far away from Sequoia).

"I see," said Goji. She wished that Rubus were here to encounter this new Realm with her.

"Well, erm, yeah, but anyway, the other Trees in the nursery often make fun of me. They say I'm too big and that I'm awkward."

This was true. Sherman was a socially awkward Tree. He lived very much in isolation from the rest of the forest.

"Well, can't you take it up with someone else in the Realm?"

"There are no guardians in this Realm, if that's what you mean."

"What?" Goji was bemused. Of all the Realms in which they had been, there were guardians or watchers present in most of them; there were the Huckles that guarded Glacier, the Wanderers in Yellowstone, and the Great Horns in Death Valley. While not every Realm had such a creature, Goji would expect a dense woodland such as this to have some-one watching over it.

"Yeah, we just kind of fend for ourselves, you know," said Sherman.

Goji lay back on her branch and pondered Sherman's words while twisting a little twig in between her fingers. She was grateful that her mind had been distracted. "Well . . ." An image of tranquility had formed in her mind. Not only was Goji a nurturer for all of nature, she could begin to envision a place for creatures, knowing where they best fit. "Why don't you become the guardian?"

Sherman twisted his trunk sharply. If it had not been so dark, Goji would have seen that he was doing his best to look up at her. "What!?" He was so surprised that he nearly woke the entire Realm from hibernation.

"Well, you're going to be the largest Tree, aren't you? That means you'll be able to see all that goes on. I see no better fit than you, Sherman!"

"But . . . I'm just a small Tree right now. The others will surely never listen to me. What about Grant? He is a big mean bully, and he won't allow it."

"Listen, Sherman, do you know about Glacier?"

"Well, I hear whispers from the songbirds . . . but what about it?"

Slowly, Goji stood up on the branch. "You know that berries are very small?"

"Yes, of course."

"Well, I'll tell you, just like the berries now guard Glacier, you can guard this place!"

Sherman was now listening intently, and he created a small leafy platform for her to stand on.

"I must tell you of the journey on which we have been, Sherman."

"Go on."

"We berries began small, but the life of the Realm made us grow. The Huckle King grew so large that he was the most important creature in all the forest. Those from the Great Outdoors have tried to attack us and end our way of life, and so have fires, floods, and storms, but we have found a way to endure."

Sherman leaned in with great interest.

"We made a home in the Glacier Realm, but since then, things have become unbalanced, so we started this journey so that we may seek balance anew. We have crossed mountains and rivers, seen spectacular canyons and plains, been hot, cold, thirsty, and hungry." Goji began to tear up. "We have lost friends . . ." Sherman wrapped a small leaf around her. "But we have pressed on because we have found a way. Though the king and I have different ideas, we do both want balance, just in different ways; now all of Glacier looks to us because we belong!"

Distant footsteps sounded . . .

"The point is, you can grow too, Sherman. You can find your purpose, as we all can, and you can be the leader of this Realm!"

Some of Sherman's twigs shot up in excitement. "Wow, I never thought I'd hear such a tale!"

"There are many more like it!"

Suddenly, with a sharp crack, dark, ominous figures appeared in the woods, and Goji turned swiftly toward them. They were two daunting fully grown Sequoias, and at the bottom of their trunks, they had captured Vernus and Juniper and imprisoned them within their roots. The Huckles were wriggling and squirming in their tight grip. Goji gasped.

"You are coming with us, berry."

"What? No! She is a visitor here, and she's with me."

"Quiet, Sherman!"

Sherman shrunk down, and his leaves quivered. He did not have the courage to fight back.

Goji paced down Sherman's trunk toward Juniper and Vernus, not frightened by the colossal Trees. The imprisoned Huckles mumbled to Goji through the roots that smothered their mouths, but they could not be heard.

"What is the meaning of this?" Goji demanded.

"You come here to bring violence and battle to our land, berry, so we have come to bring you to the High One so that your advance will cease!"

"No, we come to seek agreement with the Trees! There were many of us, but the others were left behind. If we find them, we can—"

"We know of the king, and if we find him, we will bring him to the High One too." With that, one of the Trees shot some thin roots at Goji, trying to ensnare her.

"Wait!" Goji would not be taken prisoner. The Tree slowly retracted its roots, and Goji began to climb the trunk of her own accord, allowing herself to be taken. She thought that if she could reason with the High One, perhaps she could finish the quest alone.

"Well, I see that you are the wise one amongst you," said the Tree. Vernus and Juniper had not been so diplomatic and had initially put up a mighty battle, slashing and thrashing at the Tree's roots. "To the High One we now go forth!" The Trees began their march into the night. It would be some time before they made it to Redwood, so they made haste immediately.

"Oh . . ." The Tree carrying Goji stopped and turned around before it left. "Sherman, next time you think to defy us, remember that you are just an odd little sapling."

The other Tree laughed nastily, and Sherman shrunk further down, painting a sad, disheveled picture, but Goji looked back at him and waved. She hoped to see him again.

14

The King's Advance

THE KING HACKED HIS way through the Sequoia woodland. Behind him, the herd and the cluster labored on. The morale of the creatures had sunk to a desperate low, one that they had not experienced before. It was the pain of losing Rubus, the bitter chill, and the looming endlessness of their quest. Many of them wondered if the quest was still worth fulfilling. They had made many wondrous memories on their journey, but they had now reached their limit.

You see, this is often what it is like on a walk through a national park. The roads are sometimes long and arduous. You may grow hungry and weary, and you may run low on supplies, but it is at these points, however, that you must search deep within to find the meaning of the expedition. We walk through parks to experience the beauty that they hold, and if this beauty does not transform us from the inside, then we have not truly walked. It is only in this way that we will truly understand the magnificence on which the lives of all parks thrive. Only when we have grown to love them will we care for them, and for nature, with all our being.

It was such an understanding that dragged the Huckles on. They still wished to see the quest come to completion. They had fallen in love with lands other than Glacier, and they wished to see more. They now hoped that the lives of all Realms could thrive forever, so that they may live among them. In fact, many of the Huckles had decided that after the quest was complete, they would no longer stay in Glacier. They longed to explore, and they longed to continue being transformed from within. The beauty of all Realms had allured them. Such a change had occurred because they could see that other Realms were very similar to Glacier; they just looked slightly different from home.

That was much the case with where they were now. The Huckles had traveled westward from the Ancient Forest to Sequoia, with the king leading the way, and after traversing through the deep snow for a day or so, they came across Sherman, who had been most disheveled since Goji had departed. The king sensed that this Tree may be able to lead them onward.

"You, Tree, what is your name?" He spoke most demandingly; such was his urgency.

The sapling replied in a forlorn manner, as if all the sap had been sucked from within him. "M'name's Sherman."

"Have you come across some Huckles that passed through here? They would have been three in number."

Sherman straightened himself. "You know of the northern berries?"

The king gazed at him. "Of course. That is why I asked you."

There was a brief silence, and some Huckles behind sniggered slightly at the Tree's insolence.

"Oh, right . . . yes." Sherman shrunk slightly once more, embarrassed. "Say, you don't appear as they did. They were small, and you are mighty."

"Yes. I am the Huckleberry King."

"Oh!" Sherman creaked and groaned as he bowed down before the king. Such was his youth, he was flexible enough to bend low without creaking too much, but the king covered his face with his palm in impatience as more Huckles sniggered behind.

"Stand up, Tree," he barked.

Sherman snapped straight again.

"We need to know which way the Huckles went, right now," the king continued.

"Ohh, err, sure. They were taken by some taller Trees. They took them to the High One."

There was little sense of urgency in Sherman's tone, as he did not realize the gravity of the situation.

"What?!" The king lurched forward and grabbed him. Such was the force of his action that many of Sherman's brittle branches fell to the ground.

"Hey! I didn't have anything to do with it! I was here minding my own, making companionship with the one that is a striking red!"

The king shook Sherman from side to side like a mountain lion playing with a reed of grass. His anger boiled fiercely, and he began to lift the Tree upward, so that some of his roots became exposed. Slowly, the awkward Tree was being ripped from the earth. The cluster and the herd winced as they witnessed the mighty fury of the king.

"Wait! I'll take you!" said the rattled Tree.

The king paused. Sherman was suspended half in the earth and half out.

"I'll take you to the High One. I know the way!" Sherman was taking a great risk. By bringing the king and the cluster to Redwood, he risked incurring the wrath of the others in Sequoia.

The king stopped shaking but still gripped him tightly. "Why were they taken?"

"The High One and his council, they are readying for battle! There are rumors in the woodlands; they say you have come to wipe out the Trees and claim all Realms as your own!"

"And where will my kin be taken?" With every word, the king strengthened his mighty grip.

Sherman spoke like one being strangled. "To . . . the High One . . . where they will hold them until you have been subdued."

The king looked into the face of the young Tree, then paused for a moment before letting out a mighty shout that echoed through the forest, shaking every branch and leaf in Sequoia. Little droplets of dew and snow leapt from the rocks onto the floor. The mighty berry's rage was bedeviled with frustration, anger, and fury. To this day, the woodland folk of Sequoia can recount the furious anger of the Huckleberry King. Supposedly, little critters still shudder in fright thinking of it.

The king let down the frightened sapling. Sherman gasped as if re-capturing his breath, but before he could set all his branches straight, the king bore down on him once more. "Lead the way, Tree, and do not think that I shall forget your part in all of this."

Sherman glanced at him nervously before marching onward.

That very hour, all of them ventured northward. Sherman was in front, then the king, then the cluster and the herd. The journey would take many days, weeks even, but the king would not allow them to slow their pace. On toward Redwood they traveled.

༄

Goji, Juniper, and Vernus stood in the middle of the clearing. The Sequoias had brought them to the Redwood Forest around a week earlier, and since then, they had waited in the forest. Although the berries were not imprisoned, they were not permitted to move. They were restrained to a single branch low on a Tree near the clearing in which they now stood. If they did move, they would be surrounded by the creatures of Redwood, who would remind them to stay put.

If it were not for the arduous situation, they would have admired the Realm in which they found themselves. They had gazed around in amazement when they were first led through the forest. Never before had they come across such creatures as the Redwood Trees, but the wonder and awe of the Realm also increased their fright. They knew not when they would be able to leave, if ever.

They had spent the passing days comforting each other, as a dark cloud still hung over their hearts. Not only were they separated from the rest of the cluster, they were now in a woodland that they did not know, surrounded by creatures that the Huckles had spoken against for many years. They knew not if the king would fulfill his quest or if they would be stuck here forever.

Despite this, there had been some moments of laughter between them. They remembered the moments of joy that they had experienced along their journey, and they shared tales between them, remembering the life of Rubus. Goji shared tales of her and Rubus and their times in Glacier together. Vernus shared tales of their legendary battles when they were younger knights, and Juniper recounted some of Rubus's most fabled speeches. It pained them greatly that they did not know where Rubus's body was. Would they be able to see him off into the great cycle of the forest, or would he be lost forever? The berries hoped that they would not be stuck in Redwood for much longer, so that they did not have to dwell on such things.

There in the clearing, they were being questioned by the council.

"Where is the one known as the Huckleberry King?" asked Fir.

The Huckles could not hope to see the high and lofty faces of the Trees; they only heard booming voices descending from above. Likewise, the Huckles had to bellow at the very tops of their voices so that the Trees above could hear them. The sound had a long way to travel, so there was a lengthy pause each time the Huckles responded.

"We know not! We were separated in the dry desert." It was Vernus who spoke.

"Has he been to see the Ancient Pines?" Fir demanded.

Bill the warbler bird had not yet made it back to report to the council, as he had been heavily delayed by snowfall on his journey.

"That was where we were headed before we departed from him. If he made it or not, we do not know."

The truth was, even the root messages around California had not been traveling as efficiently as they normally did. Fractures were being felt across all the Realms. They sensed that there was an imbalance occurring. Because of this, the Trees did not know of the king's whereabouts, nor had they heard from the Ancient Pines.

The Huckles appeared as minute creatures before the forest giants. During all of their lives in Glacier, they had encountered creatures larger than they, but not greater than they in stature or in presence. Before the Trees, in their Realm, however, they felt small and insignificant.

"We know why you have come, Huckles. You wish to have the Manuscripts altered." It was Oak who spoke. Hyperion was present with them, but he only listened and pondered silently. Vernus became lost in thought before he responded again. The truth was that he had forgotten the meaning of the quest. He remembered only the Realms that they had been blessed to see and the folk that they had met. Above all, though, he dwelt on the pain of losing their friend and leader. The original meaning of the quest had been lost to him. "I cannot speak of such things without the king, but what I can say is that our quest has been fraught with many blessings, but also trials and tribulations. The latter we can no longer bear."

Fir twisted her trunk slowly toward Hyperion, and he sent her a root message, not to be heard by the berries below. As it coursed through the undergrowth, the berries felt a deep pulsing beneath them. Hyperion's great voice then boomed from above.

"We observe that you are not of these lands, berries, and that you wish to depart. But the only way you are able to travel forth is if this rift between us is healed. You must take this message back to the king; tell him that the Manuscripts cannot be altered and that the rules that regulate our Realms must remain."

At this point Goji stepped forward. "But what if the Manuscripts do not need to be altered? What if we just need to learn to work together?"

The Trees paused; they were most surprised by the wisdom that sprung forth from the little berry.

"And who are you, young one? You do not appear as the other berries," said Hyperion.

"My name is Goji. I am not a Huckle, but I have lived among them all of my days."

"I see. And what is this new way which you speak of? The Manuscripts are rules for us all, and if we do not follow them, the life of all Realms is unbalanced." Hyperion's conviction did not waver, but he was still willing to engage with Goji. He was also impressed by her confidence.

"Yes, but maybe we have to look beyond the Manuscripts. They were written as a guide until we found a better way, so if we learn to live alongside one another, our lives will not be perfect, but our Realms will be balanced forever."

"Where did you learn of such things, Goji berry?" Hyperion was intrigued by her. There was a connection between them. The council felt it too.

"No one has taught me, but I listen to those wherever I go. I know the hearts and souls of the creatures in our Realms. Deep down, we wish to be as one."

"Hmmmm." Hyperion was in deep thought, deeper than he had been in some time. The council fell silent. They were sending messages back and forth, which were pulsating in the deep earth below. The Huckles grew hopeful that they would soon be able to leave.

Suddenly, a bird flew wildly into the clearing, shattering the silence that had saturated Hyperion's thoughts. He hovered in the air before the High One, but his tweeting was inaudible to the berries. The Trees listened to him intently, and once the bird had finished and had flown off into the woods, the mood soured and a stormy, dark cloud formed above Hyperion. So tall was he that the weather changed when his mood did. As it goes, the sky above can hear his thoughts. Goji soon sensed that all was not well.

"What's happened?" Juniper whispered.

"I don't know," Goji said.

"Nothing good," Vernus replied.

Bill had told Hyperion all that happened and all that he had heard on his journey. He told the High One that the king had felled the Palm on the desert outskirts and that the Pines knew of all goings on, but that it was he, Hyperion, whom the king now sought. Furthermore, the king had been rampaging northward through California toward them and had been scouring woodland, smashing and uprooting trees in his bedeviled rage. The taking of his kin had aroused his anger to the point of no return.

After some time, Hyperion directed his voice downward toward the berries once more.

"I'm afraid that our conversation has come to an end. The king of the north has come upon us, and the intentions of his heart are impure."

The berries were shocked. "No! Please listen to us!" Goji cried.

Hyperion replied, "No matter the Realms that you may hope for, young berry, we must defend our home, all Trees, and all that we hold dear. You are a witness before us that it is your king who seeks to defeat us."

"And what will become of us?" Vernus inquired.

"You will wait here in the forest until the battle is done. Afterward, we will see to it that you find a place anew."

"Place anew? Glacier is our home!"

"Glacier has become an idol unto thee and to the king. The more you reside in the land, the more you will desire power over it."

With that, three fuzzy snarling bears entered the clearing. They had come to escort the Huckles back to their quarters on the High One's command.

"No!" all three of them yelled as they were dragged away.

Hyperion and the council began to march west. As they moved through the woodland Realm, the songbirds of the forest flew after him, chirping the song of the High One:

> *Dum dididdy dum*
> *He started as a stump!*
> *Dum dididdy dum,*
> *He walks with a thump!*

High above the canopy, all of the great Trees of the council could be seen moving westward, and thereafter hundreds of other Trees of Redwood followed them too. The entire forest seemed to be on the move, as the hour had come. The Huckleberry King drew nigh. The Trees had to defend Redwood.

15

A Woodland Duel

A WINTER CHILL GRIPPED the stagnant air as the Trees stood on the forest at the edge of the Redwood Realm. They were overlooking a frosty plain, upon which they soon expected the coming of the king. Icy winds blew across the plain, and the few creatures that remained awake in the deep winter were hidden away. They had no desire to be a part of the battle, although they hoped for the safe protection of their home.

The plain was flat and bare. Snow had not fallen for a few days, so the ground was a frosty, hard green. Cold ice packed and imprisoned the lush grass beneath, and as the Trees moved around, a shattering crunching could be heard beneath them. The sky was cloudy and gray, and the sun did not bare its face through the clouds, nor did it lighten the earth below.

The Trees were arrayed layer upon layer, line after line. The Redwoods had no military formation like the Huckles, but they knew how to defend. As they looked over the plain and into the distance to where the king would arrive, they wrapped their roots ever tighter amidst the undergrowth. Such was the force of their twining puzzle of roots beneath that no force could ever hope to uproot it. Not even a mighty hurricane would succeed.

"The king and his cluster have made their decision." Hyperion addressed all the Trees. He was in front, looking over the plain. "The Manuscripts shall not be altered; they have regimented our way of life since the Realms began."

The Trees murmured in agreement.

"We do not wish to battle with any creature, but we will not cede to the northern king. If we did, he would surely seek to lord over all within his reach." A single hawk glided through the air. It seemed undisturbed by what would soon unfold, such was the nature of the fearless birds of prey. His golden coat glimmered in the little light that dared shine down. "The king comes to us now to force his wishes upon us. He will not cease until we have ceded to him, but if we do, our Realm will be under grave threat. Today, we will protect Redwood from his reach."

The Trees murmured once more. They did not shout or cheer like the cluster, but they had no less passion for the words of the High One. "We will not attack, but we will defend. Friends, if any of you should be felled here today, know that it was in defense of our Redwood Realm." Once the High One had finished speaking, he plunged his powerful roots deep into the ground below, then a rumbling and trembling shook the plain on which they stood. The rumbling ceased, then a deep throbbing could be heard. Nutrients and life sources were flowing bountifully up from the earth into the trunk of Hyperion. He was mustering all the energy he could from the Redwood Realm. As he did so, songbirds emerged from the forest in greater numbers than ever before. They circled and flew around the high Tree so that he was no longer visible to the rest. Some of the birds had been sleeping, but they awoke once they felt the call of the High One.

> *Dum dididdy dum*
> *He started as a stump!*
> *Dum dididdy dum,*
> *He walks with a thump.*
> *Dum dididdy dum*
> *He dwells so ever high*
> *Dum, dididdy dum*
> *The High One is nigh!*

From far across the plain, almost as if responding to the song, the Huckles began to emerge like a distant sea of purple. Leading them was the king, most enraged. A fiery fury burned within him such as he had not known since Bramble's passing. His band had been playing for some time, and a parade of musical notes drifted into the sky. Amidst the High One's song, the Trees could faintly hear the king's song emanating from far away.

Dum dum dum, off with his head, the king
is purple, the king is not red!
Dum dum dum, he is the king! All those
in Glacier must bow to him.
Dum dum dum, oh do you know why, for one
single pie several children had to die!
Dum dum dum, off with his head, the king
is purple, the king is not red!

Such was the emptiness of the vast plain that the music blared uninterrupted, and if any creatures were present, they would have been amazed by the display. The Huckles moved closer and closer to the bank of Redwoods so that the king was now clearly apparent to the Trees. Though there was little that the Redwoods feared, the king caused the roots of some to tremble. They had, after all, heard terrible stories of his uprooting and of his swinging Trees around like reeds in the wind.

The cluster had begun as little dots, but they now grew larger. The king's drummers flanked him on either side as he traversed the plain like a fierce warrior. The wind crashed into him and retreated, and he left deep footprints in the icy ground. As he approached, the Trees began to hear the booming of his footsteps, and the roots of many trembled. The High One sensed the fear among them. "Be not afraid, brethren. If we stand firm, we shall not be displaced."

From the Huckles' view, the Trees looked like mighty pillars in the sky, and as the berries drew closer, the leaves and branches of the Trees grew clearer and clearer. "How are we to bring down such a mighty creature?" Logan whispered to Rasp some way at the back of the cluster. The king had briefed the Huckles for an almighty battle, and he had told them of legendary tactics and skills to combat the Trees. Of course, they had had experience dealing with some of the rogue Trees of Glacier, but never had they dueled with creatures of such magnificent height as the Redwoods. Onward they marched as the cold frost tinged their feet below.

The songs continue to sound as the cluster drew near the Redwoods, and the drums beat ever louder. As well as the beating of the drums, the trolls held the Huckle crest aloft, and the ripe colors of the flag contrasted starkly with the eerie gray of the winter plain. As the Huckles drew closer, the songs of the dueling kings began to merge as one; or rather, they began competing with one another. The birds chirped louder and louder:

Dum dididdy dum
He started as a stump!

The drums beat ever stronger:

> *Dum dum dum, off with his head, the king*
> *is purple, the king is not red!*
> *Dum dum dum, he is the king! All those*
> *in Glacier must bow to him.*

The birds chirped with all their strength:

> *Dum dididdy dum,*
> *He walks with a thump.*

And back and forth the songs went, shaking the entire plain.

> *Dum dum dum, oh do you know why, for one*
> *single pie several children had to die!*
> *Dum dum dum, off with his head, the king*
> *is purple, the king is not red!*

The drums beat on, and the music filled the plain. The purple notes drifted toward the Trees but dissipated in their presence. The music shook the hearts and souls of all the creatures. The cluster had left a long path in their wake, such that the frost was cut apart.

Eventually, as a strong river current stops abruptly when it tumbles off a high edge, the music ceased. The Huckles were finally lined up opposite their foe near the edge of the forest. The king stood before them with his staff in his hand. The last of the purple notes drifted away, and a still silence hung in the air as the winter chill settled upon them. Not a sound could be heard, nor could anyone be seen to move.

As the king stepped forward, the frosty ground capitulated beneath him and the icy wind blew his tunic wildly. His Tree trunk crown stood aloft on his head, but the Redwoods were sickened by the sight of it. "I am the Huckleberry King, protector of Glacier and leader of the Huckleberries."

The Trees stayed silent while Hyperion looked down upon him. Although the High One was far higher than he, one could see that they were equals in greatness. The king took one more step forward. At that point, he was almost at the edge of Hyperion's long roots, deep as they were. "You have constrained us Huckles for many ages. You seek to be true to the Manuscripts, but in doing so, you have caused imbalance in the Realms. Now, to make matters worse, you have taken some of my kin."

Hyperion remained silent once more before stepping forward in response. His ancient trunk creaked and groaned as he drew closer to the king. As the High One moved, some of the birds that had been circling him flew away, while some settled permanently upon his branches. "Your kin are safe, and once you depart from here today, they will be returned to you."

The king grabbed his staff firmly. "You mistake my words for a request, Tree."

Hyperion looked down upon him. The other Trees grew tense, so their roots wound even closer together. Hyperion tried to alter the conversation between the king and himself. At this stage, he knew battle to be nigh, but he would still seek to avoid it. "The Manuscripts shall not be altered, Huckle. Only the Elders can do such a work."

"I have been to the Elder Pines, and they told me to come to you."

"I cannot speak for them, but my response is unchanged."

The woodland legends looked at each other with a stony gaze. The cluster and the forest were most nervous. The chilly silence seemed to hang in the air like a delicate shell, and the gray sky glared down at them from above. The king had heard enough. "Bring my kin back to me right now." He stamped his staff onto the ground. Such was his force, he broke the hard, frosty surface, plunging his staff into the cold earth.

"I shall, once you depart from this land."

The king moved as close to Hyperion as he could without being within reach of his main roots. The Trees had two sets of roots. Their main roots were very strong and difficult for any creature to come near, but the lesser roots were weaker and thin. The king knew as much because of his countless battles with them in times past.

"You know, this is the problem with you Trees. You think you always know best."

Someone from the cluster gasped as the Huckles and the herd looked on.

"Your heart is split, Huckle. You are not fit to lead any Realm." The king snarled and growled at the High One, who steadied his roots as firmly as he could. "They shall not be altered, Huckle!"

The king was not as diplomatic as he. "Well, then there is only one way forward."

A silence hung briefly, but soon afterward, the king let out a great roar, shattering the eerie stillness. His booming voice coursed through the trunks of the Trees, and they swayed and shook. Even the leaves and uppermost branches of Hyperion were blown back. The king's rage had mustered a mighty wind on the plain, and he lifted his staff to beckon his cluster forward. They advanced with a mighty shout. "For Glacier!"

The troll drummers beat the drums hard before moving forward one step at a time. The battle had begun.

First, the king plunged his thick arms deep into the ground like a bird of prey breaking the water's surface to make a swooping catch. Large clumps of earth burst out like lava as he grabbed Hyperion's lesser roots and yanked them out with ease. Once he had pulled them high, he whipped them down onto the ground so that they flew back in a wave toward Hyperion's trunk. Such was the force of the whipping that Hyperion was pushed back. He creaked and groaned as he lost his balance slightly. The forest gasped and Hyperion hung at an angle for some time before swinging forward and becoming straight again. Straight away, he drew his lesser roots back to him, and like slithering snakes they withered away from the mighty king.

As soon as the High One had regained his composure, the king raced toward him. His speed was tremendous and his fury was great. In the same way, following the king's lead, the cluster raced toward the forest. All around, branches smashed into the ground as the Trees tried to knock the Huckles off of their steeds, but to counter, the Huckles used their mighty staffs and hacked at the trunks of the Trees. The forest dwellers were not swayed easily, but they still felt the force of the blows.

The gray sky glared down from above as rain began to fall. As the Huckles and the Trees did battle, the entire plain was littered with shrapnel of bark and leaves, as well as little berries that had fallen off the heads of the Huckles' staffs. Chasmic rifts were forming in the surface of the plain, and they began to fill up with dire rainfall. Huckle Knights raced up the Trees' trunks, leaping from branch to branch, where they hacked away and peeled off leaves. The battle was intense and mighty. The troll drummers were locked in a mighty struggle with some of the council members. One had his mighty arms wrapped around Oak and was trying to prize him from the ground.

Morrow patrolled the battlefield. He did not engage in battle or lock horns with any of the Trees. He would only look upon the welfare of the herd, and if one was felled or damaged in any way, he would rush over and tend to them. The Trees did not look to take the battle to the herd, for the Huckles alone were the main aggressors. All around, the battle raged on. Ferocious clashing sounds were heard as staffs smashed against Trees, and deafening sounds were made as branches thumped against the floor.

In the middle of the battlefield, the king and the High One fought a legendary battle. It was a duel the likes of which had never been seen before and probably will never be seen again. None dared enter the space in which they clashed, lest they be felled by the king's mighty staff or by the High One's whipping branches. The rain fell heavily upon them, more heavily than it did on the rest of the battlefield.

Hyperion lurched one of his greater roots out of the ground, then thrust it toward the king and wrapped it tightly around him. "You should not have come here, Huckle." The king struggled defiantly, trying to release himself from the root's grasp. "Redwood we will defend, and none shall tamper with it!" The king wrestled and wrestled until he was able to work one arm loose. He grabbed the root with all his might and ripped himself free. Hyperion whipped the root into the air, and large clusters of earth were sent flying as he did so.

The king roared back at him, "The Pines had me come here! Perhaps you Trees are not as connected as you would have us believe." The king then took a mighty leap toward one of Hyperion's branches, and as he landed, the force knocked the High One back ever so slightly. The king did not land on one branch for long, but rather, he catapulted from branch to branch, moving closer to the Tree's face. Hyperion tried to knock the king down with a swing of a branch, but the berry moved too swiftly. As the berry leapt ever higher, the High One's voice boomed down from above.

"If the Pines sent you here, it means they wish that I shall be the one to stop you."

The king leapt powerfully from a branch. He shot through the air with the speed of a falcon and the power of a bison; there was little the High One could do to slow him down. Those on the battlefield looked at the terrifying duel between their own encounters. It was a scene of mighty awe.

"Is that so? Then why did the Pines not stop me themselves?" Hyperion whipped a branch toward the flying king, but he knocked it aside with his mighty staff.

"Your ways are reckless. Your heart is tainted. The Pines do not have the energy or the will for such a tyrant." The king snarled at the High One's remarks. He bolted through the air, ever closer to his face.

Down below, the battle raged on. Trees and Huckles alike grew weary. The band sounded from time to time, trying to muster all the might they could from the berry warriors, and the songbirds darted from Tree to Tree, singing and uplifting them. It appeared there could be no victor on either side. The Trees were far greater in size, but the Huckles were too hasty for them. Every time the forest smashed down a root or shot a branch to the floor like lightning, the Huckles skillfully dodged and dived, then countered by clambering up the Trees and hacking away with their staffs.

Far away on the edge of the plain, Logan had been captured by a Redwood's roots and was struggling to break free from its grasp. "Be gone from here, Huckle!"

"Help!" Logan yelled after his brethren, and no sooner had he cried, one of the mighty troll drummers appeared. Seeing his kin in distress, the formidable berry wrapped his bulging arms around the Tree's trunk with all of his awesome strength. He twisted and turned and his arms strained, while his face puffed with a radiant berry shade. "Ahhhhhh!" With a mighty cry, he prized the Tree from the ground with uncanny strength. The earth trembled and rain pelted down. The Tree had not been fully uprooted, but it was left limp and tender. The troll then calmly picked up Logan by his shoulder and set him on his feet.

"Thank you, my kin," said Logan.

Elsewhere, some Trees had got hold of some of the Huckles. They whipped them up and down and round and round before they catapulted them far away. Meanwhile, the herd darted around in confusion as Morrow did his best to tend them. The rain was unceasing, and the frosty ground was soon turned to slippery mud. All around, cries and groans sounded across the plain. The battle went on and on, and neither side would cede at the hands of the other.

"Is this what you want, king? For your kin and cluster to weary themselves in battle?"

The king had nearly launched himself at the face of Hyperion. The air was cold and chilly now, as he was at a lofty height. His cluster appeared as minute dots below, and by now, he could make out the tops of the other Trees.

"What I want, Tree, is for you to know our rightful place." As the king spoke, icy breath exuded from him. While he ascended, he struck out with his long staff and knocked off smaller branches. They tumbled and twirled all the way to the ground below. "If I cannot alter the Manuscripts, Tree, there is little choice but to uproot you."

"Ahhh!" Hyperion was enraged at his words, and the High One shot two branches toward the king, which darted from either side of his trunk like flying arrows. The king hopped over the first, but the second struck him true, and he was sent tumbling down, crashing against the lower branches as he fell.

"Look, the king is falling!" A warrior from the cluster pointed to the dramatic scene. From down below, they saw the silhouette of the king tearing through the sky. The king closed his eyes. As he fell, he remembered ancient battles of past times. He remembered his taming of bears and wolves. He remembered fierce encounters with wolverines and the taking down of terrible vultures. He remembered struggles with Trees. The mighty king channeled his inner power and grabbed a thick branch as he fell. The cluster gasped.

The great Huckleberry King opened his eyes and, with a fearsome lurch, he catapulted himself upward at an even hastier speed than before. He darted past all the branches he had fallen past and smashed through higher ones. One by one, the High One's branches came loose, and the king continued upward at a terrifying pace. Down below, the cluster let out a great cheer and pressed forth onto the Trees.

The king landed on the branch nearest the High One's face. As he did so, the entire Tree vibrated and shook. It was like a tumbling glacier pummeling into a lake in the depths of winter. The king steadied himself and boldly glared into the wide eyes of Hyperion. High above the battlefield, the woodland legends looked upon each other. Although they were bitter enemies, a warrior's respect could be seen in their stare.

"You must depart this land, Huckleberry King. If you leave peaceably, I shall see to it that no Trees disturb your path."

The king laughed mildly and then grunted. "I will not depart until we have settled this score, Tree. The life of a berry has been lost on account of this quest."

"A fault of your own, Huckle. This quest should never have been made."

The king folded his arms, his staff tucked between his bicep and chest, and looked upon the Tree with an awesome glare. He was a lonesome warrior high above the world. The chilling wind surrounded him as he spoke. "If you will not cede, Tree, only further battle between us will suffice."

"Do what you must, Huckle, for we will not abandon our Realm to you."

With a wry smile, the king lifted his arms high and pointed his staff toward the face of the Tree. Hyperion could deliver a fierce blow, but he could not match the speed of the king. As the staff pointed toward the

High One's face, a purple glow emanated from it; the ancient power of the king. With boundless power, he then thrust his staff into the right eye of Hyperion, and as the staff connected, a purple blast could be seen for miles around, while dazzling, glowing light beamed across the entire plain. "Ahhhh!"

Hyperion was knocked back and began to shake ferociously. The king steadied his feet and raised his arms to strike once more, but Hyperion had regained his stance. To counter the king's strike, he did not send a branch crashing toward the king, but instead, leaves above the Tree floated down and surrounded the king. They emitted powerful spores, paralyzing the powerful berry, and at the same time, hundreds of songbirds flew up high and began pecking at the king. The berry struggled, but he could not lift his staff. Sensing his foe's imbalance, Hyperion lifted a branch and walloped it against him. The Huckle toppled off the branch and again tumbled below. Some of the songbirds dove after him.

The king fell through the air at frightening speed again. He smashed through branches once more, and the cluster below gasped. Some were watching from on top of felled trees, and some were clutched in the grasp of strong roots. The king appeared like a mighty boulder falling down onto the earth, like one tumbling down a mountainside. This time, he would not be able to recover in midair. He turned and twisted as he fell, like he had done when Pry had dropped him on the fateful day. A mighty roar could be heard as a rushing wind formed around the falling creature.

As he drew closer to the ground, the king regained a sense of his surroundings, and, sensing what was before him, he curled into a tight ball. Such was the strength of the king and his mighty resolve, that in this form, he could survive a fall from any height. *Boom!* The king crashed into the ground. If he had not unfurled his tight curl eventually, perhaps he would have gone straight through into the belly of the Earth. Giant chunks of dirt were sent flying, and some crashed into Trees and almost toppled them over. A violent shockwave of wind knocked the cluster and the herd off their feet.

All berries on the battlefield held their breath as they stared at the crater that the king had left in the ground. Slowly, their ruler clambered back through the giant hole he had formed. First his staff appeared, then his hands, and then his mighty arms. The king victoriously rose back out of the crater and onto the plain once more. Fiery rage burned ever brighter within him, and his cracked seed heart glowed purple, to be seen by the creatures all around.

A strange, eerie glow emanated from the berries perched on his trunk crown, and those adorning his staff glowed like mystic gemstones. A mysterious, ancient power was shining from within him.

Sometime near the beginning of the battle, Goji and the others had sat helplessly on their branch, which was fairly close to the forest floor but not so close that they could jump down. If they were to try to leave, the Redwood bears and all manner of fierce creatures would descend upon them. From the branch, they could hear the distant sound of the raging battle, and their restlessness increased all the more.

"We need to be out there. Our kin need us!" Vernus was most agitated, and he paced the branch while swinging his staff.

"What we need to do is stop this infernal battle!" Goji was frustrated too, but for different reasons.

"There is little we can do if we are imprisoned here." Juniper sat more calmly than the other two, her emotion a mixture of theirs.

Vernus glared at the woods beyond. "Well then, let's get out of here!" As soon as he spoke, a wolf snarled at him from out of the shadows. There were woodland creatures all around, watching their every move, and yellow eyes peered out from the Trees. Vernus shakily retreated. Goji then stepped up to replace him. "O great woodland, we are friend and not foe! We seek safe passage so that we may see this struggle come to an end."

There was some rustling among the Trees. "Quiet, berry!" The voice that boomed from above was that of a tall Tree. One of the Sequoias that had transported them here, the same that had picked on Sherman and transported them from the guardian-less realm, had stayed watch over the berries. Sensing the futility of her task, Goji too retreated, sighing as she sat down.

And so, the Huckles sat for some hours, wondering about the state of their kin. The forest birthed the first signs of twilight, and soon the Huckles saw the effervescent glow of the Huckle King. "What is that?" said Juniper.

All three stared in wonder.

"I believe it is the king's ancient power," Vernus responded.

The two marveled at the purple glow, but Goji grew increasingly impatient. "We must get out of here!" She paced up and down the branch. Suddenly, as if responding to her call, more rustling could be heard amidst the Trees. Closer and closer it grew, so that the woodland creatures standing guard looked toward the noise, concerned. As if coming to a daring rescue, a bold sapling emerged from the rustling, appearing tangled and cantankerous. He took a step and then tripped over a nearby root, much to the delight and laughter of the Sequoias standing guard.

"Sherman!" Goji cried.

Vernus and Juniper looked at one another, for they knew not the name or the face of the sapling.

"What are you doing here, sapling? Get back to Sequoia." The guard trees scolded him.

Sherman got up from his fall before standing as straight as he could. To the surprise of the guards, he had grown remarkably. "Listen here, old Sequoias. I am Sherman, and I come to rescue my friend!" Sherman pointed a strong branch toward Goji, who was beaming delightedly.

The Sequoias laughed at him. "Her? She's just a berry!"

"She is more than a berry! She told me that I can do and be whatever I want. That's more than any of you have ever said. If more in the Realms were like her, well, I suppose we would do just fine." Sherman looked at Goji, and she smiled at him. From that moment on, a spiritual connection existed between them forevermore. They became wonderful friends.

"Get out of here, Sherman!" said one of the older Trees.

"No!"

They stared at each other in the presence of all the forest. Then, there in the falling Redwood rain, the Trees did great battle. The Sequoias whipped their mighty roots and branches, smashing them against Sherman, but such was the size that the young sapling had grown to, he was able to absorb their blows. Then, like he had never done before, Sherman struck back. He launched a bushel of leaves toward his foes, momentarily stunning them; then, as they were blinded, Sherman thrust himself forward with his enormous trunk and crashed into them. The sound of their battle echoed throughout the woodland.

They battled on and on, but it was Sherman who endured. He had truly grown to a tremendous size, and his foes were unable to overcome him. As the elder Trees were worn down, Sherman wrapped them with his robust roots, holding the Trees firmly in place. The Sequoias, knowing that they were overcome, did cede, and they pledged that they would make their way back to the Sequoia Realm from whence they had come. As they left the woods, they puzzled at Sherman's remarkable size.

"How is it that you have grown so great, sapling?"

Sherman, somewhat proud of himself, responded, "Well, sometimes when we listen to others and work alongside them, our full potential can be grasped." It was as if Sherman had grown in speech and in stature also, as his words were confident and true. He looked at Goji once more, as it was, of course, she of whom he spoke. The Sequoias departed gingerly, and then Sherman walked over to the Huckles. The fierce woodland creatures guarding them did not dare challenge Sherman, considering the mighty strength they had just witnessed.

"How did you grow so much, Sherman?" Goji asked delightedly.

"It is you who spoke over me, Goji, and for that, I am ever grateful."

Goji smiled at him before remembering their desperate plight. "We need to get to the battle!" She waved her arms frantically.

"Very well." Sherman bent low and extended a branch toward them. Goji climbed aboard first, and the others followed cautiously.

"Why is it that we are traveling upon this Tree, Goji?" Vernus whispered while making his way onto the branch.

"Vernus, when will you learn? For the Realms to exist in this world, the creatures must work together, and there must be some harmony between them."

Vernus stared at her for a long while, and his heart was warmed at her words, although he did not yet fully understand them. Sherman straightened his robust trunk and marched onward toward the battle with the berries held aloft. Such was his presence, no creature dared challenge him on the way. Sherman's trunk had grown to such a size that it outstripped all of the Redwoods; he was girthier than them all. The berries sat high atop the emboldened Tree, gazing at the passing woodland canopy as they made their way to the battle. Not often had they been at such a lofty height.

"I told you, Sherman. I knew you would be great! I expect that you haven't even finished growing yet!"

Indeed, Sherman would grow much more, to become the largest Tree in the world.

"It was your words that inspired me, Goji, and I expect you'll inspire many more."

Goji's seed warmed as they made their way closer to the battle and ever closer to the king's mysterious glow.

Back at the battlefield, the Huckles had congregated around the glowing king. They were drawn to him like some irresistible magnetic force. The Trees were silenced. They did not know what was occurring, nor had they expected this. As soon as Sherman appeared at the forest's edge, the king let out his power with a piercing cry, and the glow burst outward like a mystic supernova so that the stunned Trees were blown back. Only Hyperion could withstand such force.

Renewed with courage, the Huckles marched toward the Trees again, and as they did so, the most ancient of powers occurred. Up from the ground and pouring in from the forest's edge, legions and legions of berries appeared. They were not Huckles, nor were they goji berries. They were berries of normal berry size but in all shapes and colors; blueberries, loganberries, juniper berries, even cranberries from afar. They carried no staffs, nor did they wear any tunics, but they had been thrust into life by the king's power. Not since the legendary battles of Glacier's founding had the king performed such a feat. The berries had been simple and inanimate, but his power had reached out to them. The pulsating life of the forest that had awoken him many years ago he now poured forth, and, responding to his call, the living berries marched onward now to do battle for the king. The cluster approached the Trees from one side, and soon the bewildered Redwood Forest dwellers were surrounded elsewhere by the living berries. Goji and the others looked upon the battlefield with dismay.

"Oh, my goodness." Juniper gasped, her hand covering her mouth.

"No." Goji's seed sank in despair.

The living berries swarmed upon the Redwoods. They climbed up their trunks and over their leaves like swarms of ants or locusts. The cluster could not command them, nor could they speak to one another, as it was the king's ancient power alone that guided them. The cluster went onward, hacking once more at the trunks of the Trees, and one by one, overwhelmed by the sheer number of their foes, the Trees were felled, and large splashes of earth erupted as they fell slowly to the ground.

The rain fell harder, and the icy chill began to entice the twilight moon. Seeing the desperate plight of his kin, Hyperion sprang into action. He was too great to be scaled by any berry save for the king, so he moved around the battlefield freely, uninhibited by the living berries. He whipped his tremendous roots around and shot his leaves like icy hail, blasting the cluster and the living berries off of the Trees. As he rampaged through the battlefield, which was now scarred with yawning holes, he freed his brethren. He picked up the Redwoods with his mighty branches, and the songbirds aided him.

It was a gruesome battle once more. Hyperion squished the living berries beneath, so that splashes of purple and red exuded from under him, while the king and the cluster hacked away at some felled Trees. Logan, who was enjoying his first major battle as a knight, used his staff as a bulging club to beat some living berries high into Fir, who had battled courageously. The battle wore on, and the plain was now as muddy and worn as it was stained purple, red, and green from squished leaves.

Goji looked from on high, and a small tear flowed from her. She thought back to Rubus and how he would always talk to the Trees, trying to reason with them. Vernus, however, climbed down Sherman's magnificent trunk and joined in the battle with fierce determination. Being the new commander, he had little choice but to do so, and the cluster was revived once more by his arrival. They had gained an upper hand on the Trees; such was the force of the king's ancient power.

Seeing that the Trees were facing defeat, Hyperion summoned a mystic power of his own. It was a power that he had only used once before and that he had vowed never to use again, but now the hour had come to unveil his terrible wrath. Using his uppermost branches, the king of the Trees reached strenuously into the sky and pulled down a high white frothy cloud. The sky rumbled and the air grew moist and thunderous as he strained with all his power. The cloud became gray and dense as it collected water from moving downward, and the berries were soon smothered by a sea of gray and white that clouded their vision. They swung their staffs wildly into thin air, but the Trees were high above the cloud, and as such, they could see all beneath them. Using the change in battlefield to their advantage, the Trees flicked the berries off them one by one. Virulent branches sent Huckles flying through the cloud and onto the battlefield below. The living berries were now being crushed, and soon only half of them remained. A deep stroke of lightning coursed through the sky as Hyperion's ancient power guided the Trees back into battle.

The king had expended all his energy, and the ancient glow grew dim. Despite this, he did not tire. As soon as he had finished summoning the living berries, he burst forward toward the battle once again to duel with Hyperion. The wider battle was at a stalemate; the living berries had given the cluster the upper hand, but Hyperion's cloud had brought the Trees back.

The king crashed into the High One, using his boisterous body as a battering ram. Enraged, the High One swung a mighty branch toward

him, but the king ducked under it and lifted his staff high to block another blow. When he did so, a shockwave pulsed through the battlefield. So
powerful was the force that all of the forest and the cluster were knocked
back, so that the king and Hyperion were isolated once more. By now,
Morrow and the herd had retreated to the far edge of the plain, and they
watched, frightened.

"Just you and I, Tree." The king grimaced. The cluster and the forest
had ceased battling, as they had realized that they were at an eternal stalemate. They surrounded the two legends and watched them do battle blow
for blow and leap for leap. The rain fell, and great sloshes of berry juice, as
well as falling leaves, scattered through the air. In all of the Realms, there
had never been a battle like it, nor will there ever be again. Mighty wolverines have dueled with fearsome bears, great eagles have battled high
in the skies, and cougars have fought with coyotes and snakes, but none
have been as ferocious as this battle.

Goji and Juniper watched as the special berry's delicate heart pondered her next move. "Sherman, I need you to do something," said Goji.

"What is it?"

"I need you to enter the battle and stand in between them."

Sherman was shocked. "What! I can do no such thing! I will be
decimated!" He shook with fear at her suggestion, and his awesome trunk
trembled and shook. Juniper had to hang on tightly, otherwise she would
have fallen onto the battlefield. Ignoring his fear, Goji placed both her
hands on his trunk as if she were trying to reach into his inmost being
and calm him. "Listen to me, Sherman. You are a wondrous Tree, and you
have grown to a tremendous size in shape and also in heart."

Sherman ceased his quaking. Goji's words brought comfort to him.

"You must fulfill this task, for the life of all Realms depends on it!"

"I don't kn—"

"You can do it, Sherman!" Once more, Sherman trembled, but he
took tentative steps forward. As he did so, Goji and Juniper surveyed the
battlefield around them. The ground was scoured with stains of berry.
Some Trees lay still in the mud, and many Huckles had retreated, tending
to their wounds and gashes. They were weary and tired. Goji and Juniper
wept at the sight of them.

"How did this happen?" Juniper wept.

Goji too was most forlorn, but she was focused on the scene ahead.
Sherman approached nervously, but Goji spurred him forth. Before
them, the legendary battle between Hyperion the Redwood and the

Huckleberry King of Glacier dragged on. Neither could best the other. Gaping gashes could be seen on the king's skin, caused by the High One's branches, and around Hyperion, scores of branches littered the floor, ripped off by the king. The ground beneath them was worn and wrecked. "Ahhhh!" Loud shouts could be heard from them as they battled on. The cluster, the forest, and the herd could only look on. Drawing close now, Sherman grew nervous. "That's far enough, Goji. I'll be stopping here."

"No, we need to go in!" Goji referred to the circle that had been formed around the legendary creatures; a theater of battle.

"I can't!"

"Yes, you can!" Goji pulled one of Sherman's smaller branches, thrusting him forward. She possessed it within her to prompt creatures in the direction that they needed to go. The sapling of tremendous potential was thrown into the theater of battle between the dueling rulers. The woodland kings paused at the sight of him.

"Be gone from here, kin!" Hyperion's voice boomed from above.

Sherman looked to and fro, his voice and trunk trembling. "Goji . . ."

"Out of the way, Tree!" The king spoke. He could not see Goji or Juniper. Hyperion and the king advanced toward one another, and, blinded by rage, even with Sherman between them, they clashed once more. Hyperion whipped a long branch around, and the king lifted his thick staff. The blows, intended for each other, fell upon Sherman, but his mighty trunk stood firm. It had not hurt him as he had expected, as he did not yet know his own strength. Sherman furled a thick leaf around Juniper to protect her, while Hyperion and the king glared at each other, drawing back their arms, preparing for another blow . . .

Goji gently closed her eyes. A sweet calm descended upon her, and she was transported into a dreamlike state. In her mind, she saw herself atop a green hill with the berryrumpet in her hands. She was laughing with jubilant glee, and so was the one with her. At the bottom of the hill was Rubus. He was a fine young commander. He laughed and smiled with Goji and used his arms to motion to her how the berryrumpet was meant to be played. Goji laughed and imitated him.

"See, I told you you could do it, Goji!"

Goji blushed. She looked over at the other side of the hill, where a gentle stream cut through the Glacier green.

"Thank you, Rubus."

*"Why, of course. Now listen to me. Wherever you go, whatever
you do, just remember, you can do great things if you are yourself. You are a special berry, Goji, and you are most loved."*

After the vision, Goji's mind flashed forward to Oxan and the scenes
of Yellowstone meadows.

"You are a special berry."

Once more, like swift shifting shadows, her mind shifted to her final
memory of her and Rubus. Her loving father lay in her arms as he spoke
his final words.

"Remember, Goji, let your seed be strong."

Goji opened her eyes, and the special berry was transported back
to the stark plain with both of the kings beside her. Her seed ached and
pulsed. Never before had she felt such pain but also such desire. Time
seemed to slow around her. The icy wind and the dawning twilight settled,
and the stained battlefield blended into a gray mirage. Goji had no desire
to be special, but she did have a desire to be strong. For all creatures; for
all Realms. For Rubus.

"Stop!"

An unstoppable inner energy pulsed from the sweet berry. A stark
flash of red illuminated before everyone, and Hyperion and the king were
sent flying. It could only be described as willpower. With her beautiful
heart and her strong seed, Goji had disabled the powers and the strength
of the king and Hyperion. The Huckleberry flew back and skidded into
the ground; chunks of earth being displaced as he was launched over one
hundred feet. The High One creaked and groaned before falling from the
sky.

It was a scene unlike any other. The length of Hyperion meant that
he stretched well into Redwood as he fell. He hung in the air for what
seemed like an age, and gray chunks of lofty cloud were dragged down
with him. When he met the floor, a shockwave emerged from under from
him that was dispersed across all of California and beyond.

Oxan looked toward the west, from whence the shockwave had
come.

An eagle glared down below; he had sensed a seismic tremor from
the earth.

The Elderberries shook and rattled on their branch.

The Pines giggled; the shockwave was like a playful tickle to them. Methuselah gently smiled. She knew what had occurred.

All the creatures that had encountered the cluster on their journey thus far felt the blast. Cassie and her children popped their little heads above the river's surface, sensing the disturbance, and Izzy's tail shot sharply toward the sky. Back at the battlefield, the Trees were paralyzed with disbelief. Never had they thought they would see the High One fall. Some gathered around him, but he could not move. Likewise, the king was being aided too, but he was completely still.

Both of them looked toward the spot from where they had fallen. There stood Goji, out of breath from her display of power. Sherman had withstood her force; such was the might of his trunk and the connection that existed between him and Goji. Indeed, Goji had only intended her power to strike Hyperion and the king. Slowly now, with the effect of her power waning, the king rose to his feet and went to speak with her.

"You?"

The king saw Goji in a light that he never had before.

Goji responded to him. "Yes, I."

"How is it that you have come across such power?"

"The same way that you did, king. I searched deep within."

Hyperion also came toward them after he had been lifted by his brethren.

"You are the same berry from earlier that stood before the council?"

"Yes."

"Who are you?" he said.

Soft tears rolled down her cheeks. "I stand before you both today to open my heart."

The dueling creatures were obliged to listen, as they had witnessed her power. Never before had they been bested as they were by Goji.

"You have been in dispute for many years, but we have only loss to show for it." She motioned around at the battlefield, where Huckles and Trees lay slain. "I must tell you both that the Manuscripts will not be altered, and our way of life will not survive, unless our hearts are transformed."

Hearing her words, the cluster, the herd, and the forest drew in to listen to her words.

"For too long we have lived under the written law, but it was written only as a guide until we knew it well within our heart. But now it is our hearts that must be transformed so that we can live as one, in harmony with the Realms and nature, and in harmony with one another."

Juniper wept on the branch below. The king's eyes widened, but still he listened before responding, "How can I exist alongside these Trees? It is due to them that . . . that Bramble fell." His voice trembled as he spoke.

"I—" Goji began.

Hyperion spoke from above, his booming voice interrupting Goji's. "It was not us, king. The Tree that fateful day, he perished as well. He stuck out his branch to save her. A pity it could not be done."

Alas, the king could not be swayed. "No! These words are false. You let her fall!"

A silence fell between them, and the icy wind whipped around. What could move the king's heart now?

Suddenly, as if beckoned forth, a heavenly crack emerged in the sky. The gray rain clouds were rolled back like ocean curtains, and beams of light poured down from above. Every seed and acorn could hear a tremendous screeching descending from on high, which reverberated through the life of all Realms. Through the crack emerged a creature of renown, one of the Elders of all Realms. The mighty eagle called Pry.

"Pry!" The king, along with all the others, gasped. Some quivered at the awesome bird's presence, which seemed to suck all negative ambience out of the plain with his pervading light. The Trees shed many leaves in reverential fear. His sharp talons shone in the sunlight that had poured in, and the scar on his face from that fateful day shone starkly. Pry spoke to the creatures, his tone confident and true.

"It is I, Huckleberry King. A tremor of unspeakable energy has beckoned me forth."

"I thought that you would never return!"

The appearance of the eagle roused stark emotion in him and brought memories to the king of that fateful day. "To aid this quest, I have returned." Pry swooped lower. As he did so, he beat out the icy winds with his mighty wings, and a warm gust filled the air. The plain was trans-formed by his awesome presence. "Listen to me, king. The words of the High One are true. I witnessed the Tree that day. I would have spoken this unto you, but your heart has been hard." Suddenly, Pry beat his wings and whipped up a stunning whirlwind. Leaves, branches, and corpses of living berries were swept into the cyclone. The eagle lifted his wings and the king was transported into the sky. He and Pry now stood alone in a bubble of glorious presence.

"Listen to me, king. The queen's passing has saddened us all, but the time has come for you to be strong. The Realms need you."

The two of them hung in the air, their golden silhouettes radiant in the bleak twilight.

"I cannot, Pry. The Trees are too great a foe to us."

"But they cannot stay as foe, king. The Realms beckon us to come together, just as us Elders did many years ago."

The king hung in the blazing light as his mind pondered his great friend's words.

"Tell me, Pry, where have you been all this time?"

"I have been waiting, king, for a moment that would beckon me forth."

"And this is that moment?" the king enquired.

Pry's sharp eyes glinted as he nodded at the king. A basking silence dwelt as the clouds nearby glistened with sumptuous golden tinges.

"Let me down."

Pry glared at him.

"Let me down, Pry."

Pry pointed his wings downward and the mystic wind that had held them aloft ceased. Slowly, the king descended back toward the plain, where his kin and the Trees awaited him. Before he reached the ground, the king looked up once more at his old friend, "Thank you, my friend." The words came out of him as if he had kept them buried deep in his seed for many ages. Pry nodded at him, and the king reached the ground. The king looked at all that was around him. Since he had first spoken with Oxan in Yellowstone, his heart had begun to change. Now, here on the outskirts of Redwood, with Pry the eagle above him, his seed was being exposed to new dawns. Pry hovered above him, and he glowed a mesmerizing shade. Not only did the light flutter from above, where he had created a gaping hole in the clouds, but his white feathers also shone brightly, like the purest winter mountaintop. Some of the cluster could not bear to look upon him, such was the intensity of the glare.

The king stood in silence, looking at the ground. Ever so slowly, he began to slump to his knees. "Bramble . . . Rubus . . ." His mighty grip loosened on his staff, and it fell to the floor with a deafening thud.

"That day, king, it brings pain to all of our hearts." It was Hyperion who spoke.

The king looked at him, then around at his brethren. For the first time in years, he saw for himself that they were weary, tired, and desperate.

Most of all, he saw that they missed Glacier. Some of the cluster moved closer to him, Vernus one of them, and so too did some of the Trees. By this time, the fighting had completely ceased. Some of the Huckles had even climbed upon the Trees' branches, and they sat there watching their king. His eyes swelled and puffed, and deep lumps formed within him. The pain of a thousand creatures was being released from his seed.

Hyperion stepped forth.

"Your loss was a loss to us all, Huckle."

The king looked up at him. Suddenly, his mind flashed back to the fateful day.

He saw Bramble lying upon the branch before she fell. In his mind, the image was graved with smoke and darkness, but this time, he saw something that he had not previously seen. The branch upon which she lay was creaking and groaning but pushing back upward. With all its might, the branch was trying to hold Bramble up. The miry vision blurred once more as it ended.

It dawned upon the king like an orange Glacier sunrise. His heart opened, and deep pain and sadness flowed out from him. It was his anger, his pain, and the darkness of his heart that had caused his fatal misjudgment about the Trees all along. They were not to blame for Bramble's passing. He realized that he had used this as a crutch to bear the unceasing weight of the memory. The broken king stood up before all of the creatures. He looked toward Pry, then back at Hyperion, then at the cluster, and then let out an anguished cry. The woodlands shook, and the Trees quivered. The ground trembled, and the king collapsed to his knees.

16

Huckleberry Mountain

THE HOLLOW TREE RODE the gentle stream. It was a thick trunk that had been carved into a shape that could travel upon the waters. All manner of woodland creatures watched it pass from the riverbanks along the way; songbirds, elk, bears, goats, and Trees; all lined every bank that it flowed past. As the trunk drifted along the Colorado, eagles surveyed it from above while perched atop the Yawning Gap, and as it passed through Yellowstone, the Wanderers stood still as it drifted on through the sparkling river.

It was now early spring, and tokens of blossoming life were emerging. Flowers were budding, and lush green grass danced in the warm winds as the trunk flowed through the Realms and all of the land. It passed upstream where the current was strong; the great life of the Realms pushed it upward, and where it needed to be, it was lifted out a river and placed into a new one. Strong eagles came down from their eyries high above the world to share in the task. They swooped down and transported the trunk over vast plains and barren stretches where there were no rivers.

In this way, the trunk traveled all the way home. The sweet smell of spring and the fresh open air of Glacier greeted its arrival. Then the trunk floated alone in the still lake, gently warmed by the bright Glacier sun. The hollow tree had carried the body all through the land we know as the United States. The body of Rubus the great commander. Leader of Huckles. Huckle of Glacier.

An old berry, frail and weak, leaned upon his staff. Such was the size of the crowd in front, he could not see the proceedings that were taking place. He struggled and strained, but no one could hear or see him. His soul was downcast within, as he was not able to see the body of his long-time friend. He cast his head down and looked at the ground, but behind him, strange footsteps sounded.

"Do you require assistance, Huckle?"

The old Huckle looked back in amazement. He had never expected to see one of the fabled southern Trees here, let alone hear one speaking to him. The old berry explained his plight to the Tree. "Well, I can't see. Rubus was a great friend of mine."

The Tree let down a long branch. The Huckle looked nervous at first, but very slowly, he walked onto it. As soon as he had done so, the Tree lifted him high above the crowd. The flabbergasted Huckle gasped, as it was a long time since he had been at such a height; not since one of his and Rubus's mighty battles. A jubilant smile came across his face, and he could now see all of the proceedings before him, as well as the body of his beloved friend. He turned to thank the Tree, who nodded ever so slightly in response.

"What is your name, Huckle?"

The berry turned very slowly, such was his advanced age. "My name is Lingon."

The Tree nodded and turned around once more, then the two of them gazed at the proceedings. Before them was a wonderful array. All manner of creatures and Trees were crowded into the clearing. It had been over a year since the Huckles had begun their quest and some months since Rubus had passed. From all across the Realms, creatures had gathered in Glacier to pay respect to Rubus. A truce had been called, one that had been unknown to the Realms for many years. Only the passing of one as fabled as Rubus could have brought about such peace, and unite all creatures. At the very front, on account of their small size, were Cassie and her children. Izzy, too, had traveled with them. Behind them were the Huckles and all the commonly sized creatures of Glacier. Further behind were the mighty creatures; Oxan, the Wanderers, the Great Horns, and all of the herd. And at the very back were the Trees. They were Redwoods mostly, but also present were the Elder Pines and other Trees of Glacier. Perched upon the Trees, of course, were songbirds and great birds of prey. The creatures were silent but grateful to be present. Many of them had taken many months to travel to Glacier. As such, it was now late summer once more, and an inviting warmth filled the air. Smaller creatures had ridden upon larger ones to cross vast stretches of land; even creatures that had once had terrible feuds had aided one another. The Trees, in particular, had transported many.

Before the wonderful assortment of Realm-dwellers was a sacred bush. It was green and wide, a bush upon which some normal huckleberries grew. As it goes, it was the bush from which Rubus had been brought into being. It was the king who had first breathed into him the life of the Glacier Realm; therefore, it was the king who was the first to speak before the crowd. "We are gathered today to oversee the passing of a dear friend." Despite the solemn occasion, many of the older creatures in Glacier were delighted. This king reminded them of the king of yesteryear, the strong and noble warrior. His speech was fair and true. "Rubus was a commander of virtue and a leader of integrity." In front of the king was the hollow trunk. Inside, silent and still, lay the body of Rubus.

"Hear, hear." The Huckles agreed with him. As the king began to speak once more, the gentle waters shone beside the crowd. They were gathered upon the banks of Lake Quartz in the north of Glacier. Goji had chosen it on account of her and Rubus's many days spent there in years past. "No matter the future of our Realm or of any creature gathered here today, Rubus will be remembered forever more." The king would have said more, but he felt that he owed it to others to allow them to share their words too. He stepped aside, and Rubus's body was alone.

Next forth was Vernus, and the Huckles applauded him as he emerged. He, of course, was now the commander of the knights, the same role that his predecessor had once filled. He began speaking straight away. "Rubus was a mighty Huckle." Juniper wept slightly in the crowd. "I am only the Huckle that I am now because of him." He paused and looked at the body of his former commander. "He taught me how to protect, how to defend, and most importantly, how to lead." He paused again and looked at the ground, his heart becoming heavier. "I would be nothing without him, and I should think that many of you could say the same. Forever he will live on in the life of this great Realm." Vernus had become an eloquent speaker, and his words now aroused the creatures. They wept and cheered as Vernus moved aside to stand next to the king. The king shook his hand.

Once the cheering and weeping had subsided, a silent hush fell over the crowd. The creatures drew silent as the next berry moved to the spot that Vernus had left beside Rubus's body. Many of them hung their heads in respect, while others urged the berry forth. As she became visible to the crowd, the furor of Vernus's speech faded. Tears flowed from the creatures, and their hearts ached and pained.

Goji looked out at them. Even now, at the wake of her father berry, she wished only the best for those in the crowd. She did not wish for Rubus's passing to sadden them; rather, she wished that it could move them onward. She breathed deeply before speaking from her heart.

"Dear creatures, many of you have come a long way, and I thank you for coming."

On the other side of the lake were the tranquil hills of Glacier, which shone and glowed in the summer sun. Goji looked toward them and her mind wandered to life beyond, to the great cycle of the Realm and all forests, but she would not allow herself to weep.

"As I'm sure many of you know, Rubus meant everything to me."

Juniper broke down in tears, as did other Huckles. Logan, Rasp, and others looked at Goji with admiration as she spoke. Their seeds had been changed by their journey, and now, while listening to Goji, they knew that their hearts would never be the same.

"For those of you who have come from other Realms, you may not know, but we berries do not have children." She touched one of the leaves on the ancient huckleberry bush near her. "We spring forth into life. It is the life and energy of the great Realms breathed into us." She paused and looked at Rubus's body before speaking again. "But Rubus raised me as a father would a child. Without him, I would have never been found." Tears flowed from the mothers among the crowd.

"He had a heart for me, and he had a heart for all of Glacier." She looked out at them again. "And let it be known here today that he had a heart for all of you!" Goji's voice was raised slightly. The songbirds at the back perching on the Trees sat up and listened intently. "We left Glacier over a year ago to restore balance to the Realms. Even though that happened in a different way than was originally sought, because of Rubus's bravery, we eventually fulfilled our quest." To the left of her, the king moved slightly. Goji's words were not directed at him, but he felt them powerfully. "So now I tell you, from whatever Realm you may come and wherever is your abode, remember this moment."

All of the creatures then leant in and listened, many with more focus than they had listened to anything before. "For I say, what greater love does one have than to lay down his life for his friend? Rubus laid down his life for his friends, for you in all of the Realms, so from this day forth, you must look upon one another as friends." The creatures looked at one another. "Sometimes there will be disagreements amongst us, and sometimes things in our Realms will not go as we hope, and great tragedy we must endure, but if we have friendship, our way of life will survive. From this day on, the Realms will live in your hearts. You will not look upon each other as rulers and masters, but as friends."

The creatures wept.

"For let us remember that one touch of nature brings the whole land together."

Goji had said all that pressed upon her heart. She wanted to use her time to bring the quest and the quarreling to a close. That was what she wanted, and, despite his undying loyalty to the king, deep down, that was what Rubus had wanted. As the creatures wept profusely, Goji reached behind her, toward the huckleberry bush that hung above. She plucked the plumpest bushel of huckles that she could find and laid them on top of Rubus's still body. She had no more tears for Rubus, as she had emptied herself over the days, weeks, and months prior. She leaned in gently and kissed her father on his forehead.

As she stood up, she smiled. Momentarily she lost herself and forgot that she was in front of the crowd. Her mind blurred to a distant memory . . .

℞

Goji could not make out much. Her arms were flailing wildly, and her legs kicked beneath her. She was just a baby berry. As she kicked and flailed her arms, there was a deep sense of confusion and abandonment in her heart. She felt lost, scared, and alone. The Trees looked like great figures surrounding her, gazing down at her plight. The songbirds darted above, but she knew not yet how to speak with them. As she lay in the clearing alone, she wailed and wailed, desperate for someone to hear her.

As the baby Goji was lying on the floor, she could hear all that was around her, and the ground upon which she lay now vibrated as gentle footsteps approached. She did not know to whom the footsteps belonged, but she sensed within her that they were friendly. Afterward, a large berry peered over her. His face was dark red, and he wore a brightly colored tunic. The figure looked upon her as she wailed before picking her up and cradling her . . .

℞

Goji's mind returned. Rubus's body lay adorned with the huckle bushel that she had just picked. She tried as hard as she could, but now Goji could not hold back the tears. They slowly rolled from her face and onto the ground below, gently soaking into the undergrowth. She looked out at the crowd, who were weeping and embracing, and she spoke once more. "We are the creatures of the Realms. For as long as our way of life endures, we must dwell together, for that is our way." Goji took one last glance at her father and left his side. She did not go and stand beside the king and Vernus. Instead, she went to Juniper, who had been holding her berryrumpet. Since Goji had finished, there was no one left to speak.

Some moles scurried forth toward the huckle bush and began to dig a hole into which Rubus would be lowered. The crowd wept on and on, embracing and hugging one another. Even some of the Trees stepped forward and wrapped their branches around the larger creatures. The only folks who were not seen to be weeping were the Wanderers. They rarely displayed such emotion, although they felt it deep within.

Once the hole had been formed, the moles scurried away and the troll drummers came forth. They carried large ropes in their hand to lower Rubus's body down. Slowly, they carefully picked him up and lowered him in. Such a solemn moment had never been seen in all of the Realms. Never before had this number of creatures united at the passing of another.

As the body was lowered, Goji blew on the berryrumpet. She blew a fanfare that spurred more tears from those in the crowd. The creatures hung their heads and clutched their hearts. Rubus was gone. Buried under the bush, he became one with the great cycle of the Glacier Realm.

That evening, the creatures left the clearing, but they did not depart back to their own lands. It had been agreed long before that as many as could spare the time would stay an entire week in Glacier. Many had packed important supplies from their own land for the trip. Cassie and her children had packed enough twigs and leaves (plus building supplies for when they got bored), and Izzy the squirrel had packed a wide array of nuts, while the Wanderers had reserved prime patches of grass to graze in the Glacier woodland.

Back in their own Realms, the creatures had set up deputies and watchers to look over affairs back home. A week was quite a long time to be gone, but this was indeed a special time, and exceptions had to be made. The Trees, the Huckles, and the Elders had all agreed that a festival should take place at Glacier and that it should be a week-long affair. The proceedings had begun with Rubus's wake, because his passing deserved the most respect, and some of the creatures had to depart on the first day, but after the wake, all of the creatures went to their own camping spots within Glacier to prepare for the start of the jubilant woodland festival the next day.

The folk of Glacier had worked like never before in preparation for the festivities. At the beginning of this tale, when Rubus was still with us, you will remember that a great celebration took place. The bees, the spiders, the civilian Huckles, and Glacier folk had worked tirelessly to put that celebration into place, but for this one, they worked even harder.

Buzzing could be heard constantly as the bees flew back and forth, picking flowers and placing them carefully all around. There was a constant stream of bees at all times, and they adorned everything that they could. The main hall was to be the center of the festival, much like it had been for the procession, although this celebration also stretched in and around all of Glacier.

Throughout Huckle Village, colorful banners were hung from hut to hut, made from leaves and rare flowers, and by the lakes, lines of rocks had been gathered, so that those who were interested could compare the rocks from different Realms (the lizards from Death Valley in particular gathered with keen interest). On the plains, long racetracks had been organized. Morrow and his herd paced against the Great Horns, and some of the Wanderers got involved. The Trees spent most of their time inspecting the soil of Glacier and kept asking the Huckles about the pH level (of course, the berries had no idea). The Ancient Pines stood alone at the top of a hill. Some of them continued to slumber, but some of them very mischievously launched all types of fruits at unsuspecting civilian Huckles below. One of them hit the head of a young Huckle who had been walking peacefully through the village . . .

"Hey!" Yew looked up, rubbing his head, but all he saw were raking laughing figures high above. "Silly trees." He walked on, still rubbing his bruise, and eventually he bumped into a larger Huckle than he. It was a knight who was returning home. "Will you watch it!" Yew was still smarting from the fruit that had struck him and was most aggrieved to be bumping into fully grown knights.

"Say now, got a bit grumpy while I was gone, have you?"

Yew looked up at the berry before him, as the voice was familiar. "Logan!" Yew wrapped his arms around his brother and held him as tightly as a berry could be held. A smile stretched across Logan's face too. "You have to tell me everything!'" said Yew. In his excitement, Yew had forgotten to actually greet his brother.

"Well now, I'm glad to see you too!"

"Oh! Yes, yes, great to see you."

The two berries walked off through the village and back to their little hut.

"While we're getting ready for the feast, I'll tell you all you need to know, but I should tell you, brother, it will take a while for me to get through all the tales I have to tell!"

As the two of them walked on through the village, all around them the creatures were working frantically to adorn the place with decorations. The king's feast later on would mark the beginning of the festival, and the village had to be ready. There were flags with the Huckle crest placed everywhere, but also there were relics and objects from all the Realms. One creative Huckle had created a small sulfur pool to remind the Wanderers of the volcanic underpass.

Elsewhere, the Huckle Knights were recounting their tales of the Great Outdoors and the rest of the quest to Huckles young and old. They were gathered at the feet of the knights, eager to hear their stories. Most interestingly, the Huckles noticed that the knights no longer spoke of the other Realms as foreign places or as dangerous ones. The more they spoke of them, the more it sounded to them like home.

"Hey, what's that mark on your head?" Logan looked down at Yew, who had a great orange mark across his head.

"Oh, it's nothing," he said, wiping the fruit stain away. High upon the hillside behind him, the Pines sniggered.

Finally, the two berries reached their hut and went inside. Logan went to drink some water before sitting down on his leaf bed. He took a deep breath, happy to be home. Yew sat at his feet, his face beaming with excitement. Logan took a deep swig ofwater before beginning. "Well, Yew, first let me tell you about Yellowstone . . ."

The king's deep, booming laughter echoed into the evening. Although he was shaking the entire long table at which they were currently all seated, the Huckles felt a deep, truly deep, unbridled joy exuding from his laugh.

Such joy had not emanated from the king in many a year. The Huckle Knights in his presence knew that the king they once knew and loved had returned. Upon the head table at which they were seated was the finest collection of waters ever assembled. There was water from the Yellowstone River, from the Colorado, and of course from the winding Glacier creeks. It was a selection fit for a Huckle King.

The table at which the leading knights were seated was only one of many. On a large plain on the other side of Huckleberry Mountain from the village, rows and rows of tables had been erected. At the very largest table were the king and his knights. Second to that were the Huckle civilians and the most important guests (the Wanderers, Cassie, her children, and others), and third were other creatures from the Realms. The Trees and the larger beasts had taken their place toward the back of the field and planted themselves on a good green spot of land. Hyperion stood there, and the native Trees of Glacier constantly stared at him in sheer amazement at his height. From one of the highest of the High One's branches, two interesting woodland folk looked down at events below. One was a small bird and the other was a rather obtuse but delightfully content slug.

It was the first evening of the festival, and there was a feast for the opening meal. Morrow and the herd served the tables with endless culinary delights; nuts, seeds, fruits, and, most importantly, water. There was a gentle chatter and furor all around. The king had been entertaining the knights with a legendary tale from when he was a young Huckle about a time he had picked up a porcupine deep in the forest.

Once he had finished sharing his tale and his deep laugh had subsided, he stood and banged his wooden cup on the table, ready to address all that were present. As he stood, his great stomach wobbled the table at which he sat, almost knocking it over. Some of the knights held on for dear life. "To all who have joined us here from other Realms, I hope you will see why Glacier is the greatest!"

The crowd laughed, and the king looked down at the table. In his younger days, he was most accustomed to giving speeches, but now, he was hesitant and had to think carefully about his words. He was out of practice, and the new age would require a great number of speeches, so he had to start somewhere. He looked out at the creatures, who were all gazing at him.

"It has been a long road for us Huckles and for all of the Realms." He cleared his throat nervously and took a swig of Rocky Mountain water. "Now we stand on the precipice of a new age, where we can and will work together." Smiles grew across the faces of those in the crowd. "I will no longer seek to expand our Realm, nor shall I disrupt the plans of our good allies, the Trees. Nature has boundaries that we must respect." He tilted his glass toward Hyperion as he spoke. The Tree smiled back at him. The king paused and lifted his arm toward the entire crowd before carrying on.

"Friends, let it be known that this quest has released immense pain deep within me. Many of you will know that some years ago, my only love, Bramble, did pass." He paused and took a deep breath. "But I shall no longer let my own anger, or my own loss, obstruct our goals as we seek to preserve and protect our Realms." The crowd began to lightly applaud. "It is to the future that we look and for the life of our Realms that we will proceed!" The king was finding his rhythm, delivering a deep inspired speech that moved the crowd. "For Glacier and for all Realms!"

The crowd stood and erupted. Many threw their fruits and vegetables high into the air, followed by nuts, seeds, and other participles. Somewhere to the side, the bees groaned (it was they that would do the hard work of cleaning up), but the crowd cheered on and on, clapping and shouting as one accord. The king looked across them all and smiled. Shortly after, though, he raised his staff high, as if motioning for silence. A blanket of reverential hush descended on the crowd, and once they were all silent, the king moved on to his final words.

"Friends, in this new age, new partnerships and new friendships will be formed. You all know of the battle that me and the High One of the Trees did endure, but today before you all as witnesses, I pledge to put it behind us."

With that, some of the Huckles broke into tears again, jubilant at the thought of friendship with all the Trees. The king then left his spot at the table and slowly walked toward Hyperion, who was waiting for him with a branch extended as if for a handshake. The king stopped before the High One and looked poised at the feet of the Tree, as he had done before the battle many months ago. There was a tense silence among the creatures, as they had only ever seen this scene play out once before, in battle. Izzy stood with her little hands clasped across her mouth (stuffed full of acorns), and Cassie used her industrious arms to cover the faces of her small children (one arm was sufficient for all three). The woodland folk held their breath.

"Well, it has been quite the tale." Hyperion's voice boomed down from above, well advanced in wisdom.

"Yes, yes, it has," the king replied as if he were still reflecting on the events of the year just passed.

"What say you, king of the north? Do you wish to put this time behind us?"

"I do, Tree, and I wish to tell you that if you continue to battle as you have done, perhaps one day you will be as great a warrior as me." The entire crowd laughed, and one could hear Hyperion's trunk etching itself into a smile. The High One, who had lowered his branch, extended it once more to seal the deal of peace between the two. The king looked at his branch, and a silence hung in the air once more, then, with almost as much passion as he had fought him, the king brushed Hyperion's branch aside and embraced him with a wide creaturely hug nearly as powerful as his blows. Hyperion wobbled slightly but managed to stay firm and rested his branch on the back of the giant berry. The battle was over.

The crowd were beside themselves, and great dancing and celebration sounded throughout the rest of the evening. The king's band played duets with Hyperion's songbirds, and the folks of the Realms congregated with merry glee. The king was watching from the edge of the field, and while all were distracted with bountiful jubilation, he felt a pointy nudge in his side. Looking down slightly, he saw that Oxan was looking up at him. She had poked him gently with her horns. Without saying anything, she swung her burly head toward Huckleberry Mountain, prompting the king to follow her. He agreed, and the Huckleberry King and the chiefess made their way to the summit.

As twilight grew nigh, the effervescent glow of the mountain beamed down upon them, and the silhouette of the still hill sat peacefully in the starry night. A gentle breeze beckoned them onward.

"I must say, quite the celebration you have put on here," said Oxan.

"Yes, well, it will be a new age for Glacier."

Oxan smiled. The two of them made their way to the summit as the laughter and celebration dissipated below.

The king wondered why they were making their way up the mountain. "What is the meaning of this, Oxan?"

Oxan paused before looking back at him. "Didn't I teach you already, Huckle, I cannot speak on behalf of all the Elders?"

The king looked at her, then up to the summit of the mountain. There, he saw a faint yellow glow tinged with the purple hue of the night. As they drew closer, the glow intensified, and the air was palpable and thick. It is said that the Elders cannot stay in one place for too long alongside one another, for their greatness is too much for any one Realm to bear.

When they arrived at the summit, there the king saw the Elders of the Realms. They stood in a semicircle, to be completed by Oxan and himself. First, he glanced at Pry. The battle-hardened bird was perched upon a small rock, and his sharp eyes pierced the glow that emanated from them all, while a mighty radiance shone from him. Next, he looked upon the Elderberries. They were clustered in their usual bunch upon their branch and in the pot that had been forged for them. The king had not spoken to them since his return, and he had been eagerly seeking an explanation from them. Lastly, he looked upon Methuselah. The two looked at one another for a long moment, and they briefly remembered the battle that they had endured.

It was an important moment for the Tree to be here in Glacier atop Huckleberry Mountain. The king stepped into the glow of the Elders, and the five of them now formed a closed circle. Before anyone said a word, Oxan used her tail to pick something up from behind a rock nearby, and she laid it in the center of the circle. It was the Manuscripts.

The king spoke. He wanted to put the quarreling behind him, and he had decided to leave the Manuscripts alone. "My dear creatures, I do not wish to partake in this grueling grudge any further. The Manuscripts will remain where they belong, and we shall abide by them."

The Elders looked at him, but Oxan chuckled to herself. The king, slightly confused, looked at her.

"You mistake why you have been summoned here, Huckle King." It was Methuselah who spoke; then did Pry.

"The age of the Manuscripts is over, king. The Realms enter a new age in which the creatures of all our lands live together in harmony."

The king looked back and forth between them. He was not yet able to fully comprehend that of which they spoke. So far, the Elderberries had remained silent. Perhaps they were unsure of how the king felt toward them. Oxan spoke again. "Goji's words ring true, Huckle. The time is nigh for reform. We must no longer live by the written code of the Manuscripts, but we must dwell in great delight within our Realms, so that we can nurture and cultivate them." The king glared at them all as he pieced together the events in his mind. He thought back to the time in the cave with Oxan, then to the passing of Rubus, then to the grueling duel with Hyperion.

"Let not Rubus's passing be in vain, king. We must forge a bright new future for us and for Glacier." This time it was the Elderberries who spoke.

The king cast his gaze toward them, but his mind was too fixated on other things to converse with them directly. "And the Manuscripts?"

"All things must come to pass. They will now be written on our hearts, and we shall become like living documents, living out the way of the Realm that the Creative One desired."

The king froze momentarily. It had never occurred to him that this new age would bring about such change. His mind worked as he tried to fathom all before him. "And how are we to live without the Manuscripts as a guide? For many ages we have lived according to their instruction. What of those who are new to the Realms? What if they do not live accordingly?"

"So long as they are endeared to the Realm in which they abide, their hearts will fall in line."

Although it was new to him, the king soon understood. As a matter of fact, he understood more than he had ever understood most things. When Bramble had been with him, it was her that he loved more than anything. There was no written code for his love, nor did he follow any rules. In the same way, from now on, the creatures of all Realms would dwell in love where they lived, rather than be forced to obey.

This is the way of our national parks today, and the way that we should look toward. Up on that mountain, many ages ago, the parks were formed. If you should ever enter one, it is most desirable that your heart and soul are transformed, much like those of the king and all the Huckles. The parks, and nature as a whole, are not there for us to dominate, but rather for us to nurture and fall in love with. We must not unbalance nature, or its way will be lost.

The summit of the mountain glowed and reverberated in the twilight. As the king pondered Oxan's words, a mystic fog shrouded the Elders so that they were invisible to the Huckles below.

"Why is Goji not here?" It was the first time that the king had ever spoken her name.

"It is not her desire to be here. You are the king, and it is with you that the Huckles abide," the Elderberries said.

The king looked over the edge of the mountain back down toward the Huckles below, where faint lights could be seen, twinkling and fading in the twilight. He knew what the Elders were proposing and that this was right for his kin. He turned back toward them. "What must we do now?"

Oxan replied. "We must ratify this oath between us. I and the Elders, hereby declare that our Realms are no longer bound by the Manuscripts. We must commit to loving and nurturing our Realms, for this will be our greatest idea." Responding to her words, one by one, the Elders moved closer to one another; Pry extended a mighty wing, the Elderberries shook and rattled, and Methuselah let out a strong sturdy branch. Oxan watched. She was the observer and Wanderer between them all. As they drew closer, the glow shone brighter and brighter. The king looked on and spoke.

"Very well. I bear testament to this oath, so let it be done."

The Elders paused and looked at the king. "The oath requires you, king," Oxan said to him.

"What? I bear witness, you are the Elders, so let it be done."

"No, Huckle King." Pry spoke, and an eerie silence briefly dwelt. "Once you ratify this oath, an Elder you will become."

A rush of emotion flooded the king's heart. He did not make it known, but he had not experienced such euphoria since his days as a young Huckle. To become an Elder, after his journey, would be the greatest thing he had ever achieved. Slightly overwhelmed, he stepped into the warm glow of the Elders with much enthusiasm and slowly reached out his mighty staff. Oxan smiled.

"Let it be known from this day forth, the Realms will be known as Parks, and they will be ours to nurture forevermore. Any visitor to our Parks must respect this harmony between us and take the lessons learned far and beyond, even to the Great Outdoors."

With her words, the glow intensified greatly. The king glowed like he had done from his ancient power, and he was transfigured into a brighter shade of purple than had ever been seen. There upon the mountain, he was transfigured into an Elder. All around, the glow extended to the woodlands of Glacier and beyond, and dazzling ripples of light and gentle gusts swayed the green grass. The Huckles down below gasped. Once the glow subsided, the Manuscripts spun into the air as sparks fluttered violently. They spun and spun until they descended and then disintegrated. Fragments of paper rested upon each of the Elders, nestling deep into their hearts. It was done.

The king paused and looked at his fellow Elders before turning to look at Glacier below. He looked at the smaller Huckles, whom he loved dearly. He looked upon the mighty mountains, the green glades, the flowing streams, and the swaying grass. He looked upon the fair Trees. Deep inside the king, a great miracle occurred. From top to bottom, the king's cracked seed was bonded and formed back together. His heart was made whole.

A single tear rolled down his face.

"Forever you will live within me, Bramble," he whispered.

The Elders watched. After some time, the king turned back toward them. "Before I return, I must ask one thing." Oxan nodded. "Why, Elderberries, did you permit the quest to go forth, knowing that I should take another path?" The king did not understand why he was advised to go to Yellowstone when the Elderberries knew all along that Oxan could not alter the Manuscripts.

"We knew the journey that you were required to take, king, for us all. Your heart needed to transform. As it is, we may plan our steps, but the Creative One determines our course."

"So, you knew not the outcome of the quest?"

"We did not, only that it was one that you had to take."

The king nodded. He walked over to the Elderberries and reached out to them with his staff. They forged a great connection; one that would endure for many years beyond. With that, the king nodded toward each of the Elders, and the mighty glow faded as he turned away. The renewed king made his way back down the mountain and to the Huckles below; to his home and to his kin.

The next morning, the king climbed once more and looked over Glacier from atop his mountain. He looked upon the distant hills, the silver, flowing streams, and the luscious green. The Park had appeared to him as it hadn't done in many a year. His eyes and ears were opened to Glacier's tranquil beauty. Now, in this new age, he would fight only to protect the harmony of his home.

He looked upon the darting songbirds and the wading fish in the nearby stream. He looked upon the slumbering Huckles down below and upon Morrow and the herd passing through the glades. He looked upon the exhausted bees, who had worked tirelessly. Many things about Glacier were indeed the same as when their legendary quest had begun, for there exists a consistency in nature unlike in anything else.

Harmony often requires change. The Parks, likewise, often change. Fires, floods, new creatures finding a home; these things may occur and bring about change. It was the king's role in this new age to find the right balance between harmony and change. As he looked over Glacier, his seed throbbed within him, and he brimmed with ambition once more. No longer would he seek to fight anyone that questioned him. The

Manuscripts had entered his heart, and the life of the Parks was within him. His task as an Elder was to protect the unity and harmony of Glacier and to help the hearts of those who needed to realize the same.

And so, our tale begins to draw to a close. Much like the king and the Huckles would now work with Glacier, rather than rule over it, so all the Realms were transformed into parks. The Trees, Oxan, and all the others made a commitment in their hearts that from now on, the parks would not be closed to outsiders from the Great Outdoors, but any outsiders would have to respect the unity and harmony within. The parks then became important communities where nature and creatures alike were respected. They were not always perfect, but they existed in a delicate balance.

Many years later, these parks are encountered by people like you and me, and, like the Huckles on their legendary journey, we also are often overwhelmed with awe by their breathtaking beauty. You can visit a park today, but you must respect it. If you overly disturb nature in any way, you could undo the hard work of the Huckles and the Elders and cause imbalance for the creatures within. As long as you respect the parks, you are most welcome to explore them, for in that way, you will find that you may also be transformed.

17

A Ranger Goes Forth

THE NEXT MORNING, THE lake was quiet and still. The sun had begun to warm the gentle water, preparing it for a busy day ahead. Many of the Huckles and the other folk had been celebrating jubilantly in the lake the night before, and they were looking forward to playing again today. They were slumbering alongside each other as the sun rose; they had fallen asleep after the day's excitement and camped out under the stars. Sitting on the lake's bank was Goji, who, like so often before, was staring into the waters beyond. Logan awoke too and walked toward her.

"Fair morning!" he said, stretching.

"That it is," she replied.

Logan sat beside her and began gazing out over the water too.

"What a journey, eh?" Logan was speaking, of course, of the once-in-a-lifetime quest from which they had just returned.

"Yes, it was unforgettable."

Logan picked up a stick and threw it into the water before speaking once more. "Say, did you ever find something on the journey?"

Goji looked at him inquisitively, and he continued, "You know, when we were by the lake in Yellowstone, you weren't really sure that you wanted to be on the quest. Have you worked it all out?"

Goji paused and looked at him. The special berry then stood up and walked to the water's edge. Her caring nature noticed a small turtle struggling to gain his footing in the waters below, so she picked him up and placed him on firmer ground.

"Yes. Yes, I think I have, Logan."

He looked at her with slight bewilderment. "Well, what will you do? Join the king's band?"

Goji chuckled lightly. "No. I think I'll be leaving, Logan," she said thoughtfully as she gazed across the lake. At first, he did not take her seriously, but soon it became apparent that she was indeed serious. Logan stared at her intently, but Goji's mind was already made up.

"Leaving? Where will you go?"

Goji put her hand on Logan and gave him a warm hug. "Farewell, my fellow berry." She walked briskly off into the woods, back toward Huckle Village. Gentle summer rays shone down upon her as she departed.

"Hey!" Logan called after her, but she was already gone.

Back at the village, Goji stood outside Juniper's hut. She and Vernus lived close by, and both of them happened to be out working that morning, tending to the patches of grass outside.

"Goji!"

The two ran toward her and embraced her. She hugged them back, but they immediately sensed that something was amiss. "What's the matter, Goji?" Juniper leaned back to look at her.

"I'm leaving Glacier, my dear friends."

"What?" The two gasped, dropping the tools they had been holding. "We just got back! Where in all the land will you be going?"

Goji took a deep breath once more and looked at them both. She loved them dearly and would miss them greatly, but she knew what she had to do. Deep down, she had known all along.

"I must venture onward, Juniper. I love you and all of the Huckles dearly, but I know now what I must do and where I must go. If I stay here, I will be forever wandering idly." As Goji spoke, she softly wiped falling tears from her eyes, and Vernus put his arm around her as if to comfort her. Juniper was also crying and replied to her.

"But you will be alone. What will become of you if you meet a foul beast in the Great Outdoors? Remember Death Valley?"

Goji smiled. "Even if I should walk through that Valley of Death, I shall fear no evil."

Vernus now stepped forward with a voice full of concern, "Listen, Goji, we know that you are a smart berry, more capable than us all, but where exactly will you go? We must know how to meet with you should danger arise."

Goji looked past them and on to the distant mountains. The soft edges glowed as they tempted her forth. "I think that I will not be stopping anywhere for too long, dear Vernus. I shall go from Realm to Realm. It is my heart's desire to look upon the welfare of all creatures now that a new age comes upon us."

"And how will we speak with you?"

Goji chuckled slightly.

"Do you not realize by now, Vernus? I know of many creatures that will aid my cause."

Goji was quite right. Wherever she went all across the land, there would always be one willing to help her. She had grown to considerable fame in all the Realms, perhaps even surpassing that of the king. Vernus nodded. He too was stricken by the news, but he wished to bear a strong face for Juniper's sake. He also respected Goji's decision. Juniper was beside herself in tears. She wept and wept inconsolably. Goji embraced her great friend and moved close to her.

"I shall return, dear friend, and when I do, I will bring new creatures for us all to meet."

Juniper nodded through her tears, and Vernus consoled her once more. Goji stepped back and looked upon them both. "My dear friends, let this not be goodbye but a new tomorrow. For I will return, and new memories will be forged." With that, Goji waved farewell and turned toward the village gate. Juniper wept greatly as she embarked, and all the while, Vernus looked on. Their dearest friend was departing.

Goji walked through the village; her heart heavy but excited. Before she made her way to the gate, she stood one final time outside the hut in which Rubus had raised her. She pondered for a minute, remembering days gone by. New days had come for her, and within them, she would be even more important than in the former. Everything that Rubus had taught her and all that she had learnt had prepared her for this moment. She took a deep breath and turned away.

"Thank you."

She then made her way to the gate, all the while bidding farewell to Huckles of the village. On the way, she met one of the elk of the herd. "Dear creature, will you transport me to the edge of Montana?" The elk nodded gently and agreed, and Goji stroked her head gracefully. From where the elk dropped her, she would go on. She would go from park to park, visiting creatures and seeing that they were well, but before her new life began, she had an important stop to make.

Goji and the elk trotted out of the gate, which was opened at her request. The gate watchers did not know that she would not return. Goji did not wish to burden the Huckles with the sadness of her departure; she only wished that they flourish in this new age and be blessed forevermore. She crossed the threshold of Huckle Village and set off down the path that they had traveled a year earlier, at the beginning of their timeless quest.

Once the special berry was some way down the path, she ran into the king, who stood tall before her. "To where do you wander, young berry?"

Goji looked at him. The tension between them had been fierce, but it was now a new age. In his heart, the king did not expect them to communicate freely, but he knew that she was a kind berry and that grace abounded within her. "I am leaving, king, and I wish that you do not obstruct my passage forth. The mountains are calling, and I must go."

The king smiled slightly. "I shall do no such thing. I just ask where it is that you travel to and when you may return."

"That I do not know."

A slight disappointment touched the king's heart. "You are a berry of many qualities. No doubt the new age will require you to use them in Glacier."

"Perhaps, but I happen to believe that I must travel to other Realms as well, so that I may assist them where they should need it."

The king nodded, accepting her proposal. "Very well." The two shared a moment of respect before Goji trotted on.

The king called out to her one last time. "Goji." She turned around slowly, somewhat surprised, as it was the first time that he had used her name. "I must inform you that I am an Elder now, and the Realms shall henceforth be named parks in light of the new age."

Goji absorbed his words. "I see."

"Allow me to bestow upon you a parting blessing."

Goji nodded. The king raised his staff, and a light purple glow shone from the end.

"I, the Huckleberry King, an Elder of the parks, hereby commit unto you, Goji, the blessing and protection of the Elders, wherever you may venture."

Goji closed her eyes to receive the blessing.

"Let it be known that you shall be known as Goji, the first park ranger."

Pry screeched and flew high above them, then Goji went forth. Park Ranger Goji.

Goji crept through the winter snow, not wanting to disturb the folk in hibernation. She had traveled mostly the same path that the Huckles had taken on their journey some years before. On the way, she had stopped to speak to Oxan, and the chiefess had given her a shimmering stone badge, which she wore upon her chest at all times so that all creatures knew of her purpose. Also on her way, she had stopped at some other parks that she had not visited before: Arches, Crater Lake, and Zion. She was now back in California, where the Trees had given her a warm welcome. The Great Horns that had carried her forth now saw her off. She was looking for someone.

After walking through the crunching snow for some time, she finally found him. The Tree was slumbering deeply, and a great sleeping noise vibrated throughout the entire forest. Goji smiled to herself, then plowed on through the snow, which was up to her waist. Slowly, she climbed the enormous trunk, then, after some struggle, she rested on a branch some way up, which was thicker itself than the trunks of many full Trees. After catching her breath, she knocked on the trunk as if it were a door. No answer came, so she knocked once more.

The Tree shook suddenly as he awoke from his slumber.

"Huh? What? Who's there? I am Sherman, great guardian of Sequoia!"

Goji chuckled before replying. "It is I, Goji!"

Sherman gasped in delight, "Goji!" The Tree was now fully awake. "How nice to see you again! To what do I owe the pleasure?"

"I want you to come with me, Sherman."

"Come with you? Where? I must guard Sequoia!"

"Sequoia will be fine for now. General Grant will take over, but I wish for you to be my partner."

Sherman paused as large clumps of snow fell from his branches. It seemed an odd request to him, but he had no friend in the world greater than Goji, and he was obliged to consider her words. "Where will we be going?"

"We will travel from park to park, Realm to Realm."

"And what will we be doing?"

Goji smiled. "I'll tell you on the way."

Sherman paused momentarily, but it did not take him long to agree. Sequoia was his home, but it was Goji who had made him into the Tree that he was today. He shook his branches once more and began to make his way through the thick snow. Goji smiled as she sat on her branch, from where she would lead the great Tree.

"Where are we going first?"

"We shall begin in California first. To Yosemite we must go."

Goji and Sherman traveled the parks as partners. They wore identical badges, as they were both rangers. From park to park they went, tending to the creatures and solving any problems that arose. If all of their ventures were written down, I suppose there would not be enough books in the world that could document their adventures together.

Epilogue

It was a bright spring morning in Yosemite, and in the Discovery and Education Center, a park ranger was teaching a group of children. Her ranger badge shone brightly, and her green-brimmed cap was positioned neatly atop her head. She was most enthusiastic about her teaching, and the children were all listening with intense focus.

Long gone was the age of the Huckles and the Wanderers. The king and his generation were the last, and the parks now existed in an ethereal cycle of completeness and unity. Therefore, the life of the forest no longer brought forth creatures like the king, for there was no need. In the same way, the Elders had lived out the last of their days watching the parks blossom and grow, and they knew that their task was done.

Little did they know that many years later, the parks would be even more important and popular than they were then. Nowadays, people like you and me visit the parks all the time, and they attract many thousands of visitors every year. Places like Yosemite are brimming with adults walking, families camping, and children playing. Mostly, the nature and creatures of the parks are able to live well. The legacy left by the Elders is still felt now, as those who visit in our time know that all nature needs to be cared for. Although, like all great tales, it must be told to the next generation too, lest it be forgotten. As such, we must seek to educate those who come after us that they must respect the parks.

While we must all bear this responsibility, this is also the exact reason why park rangers exist. Goji was the first, but there are now hundreds of rangers guarding and watching over the parks. If you ever have a question or concern, you can always ask one of them. They are there to educate, teaching all visitors what they must do and where they can and can't go.

This is precisely what ranger Amber was doing. A group of schoolchildren had come from Los Angeles to visit Yosemite on a school field trip, and she was educating them about the parks. Not only did she teach them about Yosemite but also about other parks and their creatures.

". . . and so the Grizzly Giant, Giant Sequoia, is also called . . . ?" She motioned to the children to complete the sentence,

"*Sequoiadendron giganteum!*" The children answered as one, like a well-rehearsed chorus.

"That's right!" Amber smiled as she spoke, delighted that the children had responded correctly. "It is the tallest tree in all of Yosemite!"

The children looked toward the front of the room, where there was a picture of the Grizzly Giant. One of the children raised their hand and asked, "Ranger Amber, is there a taller tree anywhere?"

Amber turned and looked at the kid, whose name was Rocky.

"Why, yes, Rocky, there are many, right here in California!"

"Ooohhh." The children gasped as one, collectively enthralled.

"Where is the tallest tree?"

Amber walked over to the map of California and pointed to Redwood. "Although we do not know exactly where, nor should we look for it, the tallest known tree is named Hyperion, and it lives in Redwood National Park, right here in California."

The children gasped excitedly. "How tall is it?"

"Well, it is roughly 379 feet tall!"

"Oh, my goodness, that's so tall!" a little girl at the back exclaimed.

"What about the oldest tree?" another asked.

Amber smiled underneath her brimmed hat. It filled her with joy that the children were eager to learn. "Ah, yes, that would be Methuselah!"

"How old? Where is it?" Rocky almost leapt out of his chair.

"Careful there, Rocky, don't fall out of your chair!" Amber walked over to the map once more and pointed to the Ancient Pine Forest. "It is said that Methuselah is up to 4,789 years old, according to estimates based on core samples."

"Oh man!" The children were most excited, and many of them rushed over to a nearby window to stare at the trees just outside the discovery center.

"And what about . . . the heaviest tree?" asked a little girl.

"That would be General Sherman, and he lives over here!" Amber said, pointing to Sequoia.

"Can we go and see these guys?"

"Well, Hyperion is hidden to us, and you shouldn't try to search for him, but Sherman and Methuselah you can see. Now remember . . ."

For the rest of the morning, Amber spoke to the excited children about the trees and about the life of the parks in general. Most importantly, she spoke to them with great joy about how to develop a love for the parks and to respect all of the life therein. No doubt some of the children would go on to see great things. Many of their hearts were already stirred just by hearing her words.

Later on that year, Rocky and his family went on a family camping trip in Glacier National Park, Montana. There was his mother, Ariel; his father, Jimmy; and his baby brother, James. The four of them had camped out by the lake, and now they were walking through the woods. As they walked, Rocky thought he could hear some chanting.

Dum dum dum

"Huh? Mom, Dad, do you hear that?"

"Hear what, Rocky?" Ariel replied.

Rocky looked around. His mind and heart were immersed in the forest, and he had been deeply curious about parks since Amber's lesson. He scanned the floor for all manner of leaves, twigs, and creeping creatures, and he surveyed the trees for rustling squirrels and songbirds. The family walked on until after a while, he heard the chanting once more.

The king is purple, the king is not red

This time there was no mistaking it. Rocky ran over to a small bush from where the chanting came. Upon the bush was a small cluster of red berries, circular and ripe, but above all of them was a large plump purple huckleberry. Rocky gazed at the marvelous berry, which drew him in like an ancient trance.

"Rocky!" Ariel called after him.

Rocky turned sharply. "Hey, come over here!"

"What is it, Rocky?"

"Just come over here for a minute, Mom!"

Ariel walked over and crouched down to his level. Rocky, still gazing at the purple berry, pointed it out to her enthusiastically. The two of them stared at it as it hung from the branch, juicy and plump.

"Mom, what is that?"

FIN

A Park Visitor Guide (Glossary)

American bison, *Bison bison* or simply bison, also commonly known as the American buffalo or simply buffalo, is an American species of bison that once roamed North America in vast herds. A bison has a shaggy, long, dark-brown winter coat and a lighter weight, lighter brown summer coat. Male bison are significantly larger and heavier than females.

American buffalo: see *American bison*

ancient bristlecone pine: The term *bristlecone pine* covers three species of pine tree (family *Pinaceae*, genus *Pinus*, subsection *balfourianae*). All three species are long-lived and highly resilient to harsh weather and bad soils. One of the three species, *Pinus longaeva*, is among the longest-lived life forms on Earth. The oldest *Pinus longaeva* is more than 4,800 years old, making it the oldest-known individual of any species.

Ancient Bristlecone Pine Forest is a protected area high in the White Mountains in Inyo County in eastern California. The Great Basin bristlecone pine trees grow between 9,800 and 11,000 feet above sea level, in xeric alpine conditions, protected within the Inyo National Forest.

Arches National Park lies north of Moab in the state of Utah. Bordered by the Colorado River in the southeast, it's known as the site of more than 2,000 natural sandstone arches, such as the massive, red-hued Delicate Arch in the east and the long, thin Landscape Arch that stands in Devil's Garden to the north. Other geological formations include Balanced Rock, which towers over the desert landscape in the middle of the park.

Arizona, a southwestern US state, is best known for the Grand Canyon, a mile-deep chasm carved by the Colorado River. Flagstaff, a ponderosa pine–covered mountain town, is a major gateway to the Grand

Canyon. Other natural sites include Saguaro National Park, protecting the cactus-filled Sonoran Desert landscape.

aspen, *Populus tremula*, is a common name for certain tree species; some, but not all, are classified by botanists in the section *Populus* of the *Populus* genus.

bald eagle, *Haliaeetus leucocephalus*, is a bird of prey found in North America. A sea eagle, it has two known subspecies and forms a species pair with the white-tailed eagle. Its range includes most of Canada and Alaska, all of the contiguous United States, and northern Mexico.

banana slugs, *Ariolimax*, are North American terrestrial slugs comprising the genus *Ariolimax*. They are often bright yellow, although they may also be greenish, brown, tan, or white.

beavers, *Castor canadensis*, are large semiaquatic rodents of the temperate northern hemisphere. There are two extant species in the genus *Castor*: the North American beaver (*Castor canadensis*) and the Eurasian beaver (*C. fiber*). Beavers are the second-largest living rodents after the capybaras.

black-throated gray warbler, *Setophaga nigrescens*, is a passerine bird of the New World warbler family *Parulidae*. It is 13 centimeters long and has gray-and-white plumage with black markings.

blueberries are perennial flowering plants with blue or purple berries. They are classified in the section *Cyanococcus* within the genus *Vaccinium*.

bobcat, *Lynx rufus*, also known as the red lynx, is a medium-sized cat native to North America, found from southern Canada throughout most of the contiguous United States to Oaxaca in Mexico. It has been listed as of Least Concern on the IUCN Red List since 2002 because it is widely distributed and abundant.

cacti is a member of the plant family *Cactaceae*, a family comprising about 127 genera with some 1,750 known species of the order *Caryophyllales*. The word "cactus" derives, through Latin, from the Ancient Greek κάκτος (kaktos), a name originally used by Theophrastus for a spiny plant whose identity is now not certain.

California is a state in the Pacific Region of the United States. With over 39.3 million residents across a total area of approximately 163,696 square miles (423,970 km2), it is the most populous US state and the third-largest by area, as well as the world's thirty-fourth most populous subnational entity. California is also the most populated subnational entity in North America, and the state capital is Sacramento.

California coast redwood, *Sequoia sempervirens*, is the sole living species of the genus *Sequoia* in the cypress family *Cupressaceae*. Common names include coast redwood, coastal redwood, and California redwood. It is an evergreen, long-lived monoecious tree living 1,200–201,800 years or more.

Canada is a country in the northern part of North America. Its ten provinces and three territories extend from the Atlantic to the Pacific and northward into the Arctic Ocean, covering 3.85 million square miles (9.98 million km2), making it the world's second-largest country by total area. Its southern and western border with the United States, stretching 5,525 miles (8,891 km), is the world's longest bi-national land border. Canada's capital is Ottawa, and its three largest metropolitan areas are Toronto, Montreal, and Vancouver.

chuckwallas are large lizards found primarily in arid regions of the southwestern United States and northern Mexico. Some are found on coastal islands. The six species of chuckwallas are all placed within the genus *Sauromalus*; they are part of the iguanid family, *Iguanidae*.

Clark's nutcracker, *Nucifraga columbiana*, sometimes referred to as Clark's crow or woodpecker crow, is a passerine bird in the family *Corvidae*, native to the mountains of western North America.

Colorado River is one of the principal rivers in the southwestern United States and northern Mexico. The 1,450-mile-long river drains an expansive arid watershed that encompasses parts of seven US states and two Mexican states.

Coyote, *Canis latrans*, is a species of canine native to North America. It is smaller than its close relative, the wolf, and slightly smaller than the closely related eastern wolf and red wolf. It fills much of the same ecological niche as the golden jackal does in Eurasia.

Crater Lake is a crater lake in south-central Oregon in the western United States. It is the main feature of Crater Lake National Park and is famous for its deep blue color and water clarity.

Death Valley National Park straddles eastern California and Nevada. It's known for Titus Canyon, with a ghost town and colorful rocks, and Badwater Basin's salt flats, North America's lowest point. Above, Telescope Peak Trail weaves past pine trees. North of the spiky salt mounds known as the Devil's Golf Course, rattlesnakes live in Mesquite Flat Sand Dunes.

Department of the Interior (DOI) is a federal executive department of the US government. It is responsible for the management and conservation of most federal lands and natural resources, and the administration of programs relating to Native Americans, Alaska Natives, Native Hawaiians, territorial affairs, and insular areas of the United States, as well as programs related to historic preservation. About 75 percent of federal public land is managed by the department, with most of the remainder managed by the United States Department of Agriculture's United States Forest Service. The department was created on March 3, 1849.

desert bighorn sheep, *Ovis canadensis nelson*, is a subspecies of bighorn sheep that is native to the deserts of the United States' intermountain west and southwestern regions, as well as northwestern Mexico. The trinomial of this species commemorates the American naturalist Edward William Nelson.

Dry Mountain. This peak is one of the longer ones on the Sierra Club Desert Peaks List. This route was pioneered by Eric Beck and follows a nice ridge to the upper plateau, which many feel is a much better route than the steep canyon ascent of the Sierra Club guidebook route.

elderberry, *Sambucus*, is a genus of flowering plants in the family *Adoxaceae*. The various species are commonly called elder or elderberry. The genus was formerly placed in the honeysuckle family, *Caprifoliaceae*, but was reclassified as *Adoxaceae* due to genetic and morphological comparisons to plants in the genus *Adoxa*.

elk, *Wapiti*, is one of the largest species within the deer family, *Cervidae*, and one of the largest terrestrial mammals in North America, as well as central and northeast Asia.

Funeral Mountains are a short, arid mountain range in the United States along the California–Nevada border approximately 100 miles west of Las Vegas. The mountains are considered a subrange of the Amargosa Range that forms the eastern wall of Death Valley. The crest of the range is within Death Valley National Park.

Glacier lily, *Erythronium grandiflorum*, is a North American species of plants in the lily family. It is known by several common names, including yellow avalanche lily, Glacier lily, and dogtooth fawn lily. The Ktunaxa name for Glacier lily is *maxa*.

Glacier National Park is an American national park located in northwest Montana, on the Canada–United States border, adjacent to the Canadian provinces of Alberta and British Columbia. The park encompasses over 1 million acres (4,000 km2) and includes parts of 2 mountain ranges (subranges of the Rocky Mountains), over 130 named lakes, more than 1,000 different species of plants, and hundreds of species of animals. This vast pristine ecosystem is the centerpiece of what has been referred to as the "Crown of the Continent Ecosystem," a region of protected land encompassing 16,000 square miles (41,000 km2).

goji berry, or wolfberry, is the fruit of either *Lycium barbarum* or *Lycium chinense*, two closely related species of boxthorn in the nightshade family. *Solanaceae L. barbarum* and *L. chinense* fruits are similar but can be distinguished by differences in taste and sugar content.

golden northern bumblebee, *Bombus fervidus* or yellow bumblebee, is a species of bumblebee native to North America. It has a yellow-colored abdomen and thorax. Its range includes the North American continent, excluding much of the southern United States, Alaska, and the northern parts of Canada.

Grand Canyon National Park, in Arizona, is home to much of the immense Grand Canyon, with its layered bands of red rock revealing millions of years of geological history. Viewpoints include Mather Point, Yavapai Observation Station, and architect Mary Colter's Lookout Studio and her Desert View Watchtower. Lipan Point, with wide views of the canyon and Colorado River, is popular, especially at sunrise and sunset.

Grand Tetons: The Teton Range is a mountain range of the Rocky Mountains in North America. It extends for approximately 40 miles in a north–south direction through the US state of Wyoming, east of the Idaho state line.

greater roadrunner, *Geococcyx californianus*, is a long-legged bird in the cuckoo family, *Cuculidae*, from the Aridoamerica region in the southwestern United States and Mexico. The scientific name means "Californian earth-cuckoo." Along with the lesser roadrunner, it is one of two species in the genus *Geococcyx*.

mountain hare, *Lepus timidus*: Hares and jackrabbits are leporids belonging to the genus *Lepus*. Hares are classified in the same family as rabbits. They are similar in size and form to rabbits and have similar herbivorous diets, but they generally have longer ears and live solitarily or in pairs. Also, unlike rabbits, their young are able to fend for themselves shortly after birth rather than emerging blind and helpless. Most are fast runners. Hare species are native to Africa, Eurasia, and North America.

harebell flower, *Campanula rotundifolia*: The harebell, Scottish bluebell, or bluebell of Scotland is a species of flowering plant in the bellflower family *Campanulaceae*. This herbaceous perennial occurs in Europe from the north Mediterranean to the Arctic. In Scotland, it is often known simply as bluebell.

huckleberry, *Vaccinium membranaceum*, is a species within the group of *Vaccinium*, commonly referred to as huckleberry. This particular species is known by the common names thinleaf huckleberry, tall huckleberry, big huckleberry, mountain huckleberry, square-twig blueberry, and (ambiguously) as "black huckleberry." *Vaccinium parvifolium*, the red huckleberry, is a species of *Vaccinium* native to western North America, where it is common in forests from southeastern Alaska and British Columbia south through western Washington and Oregon to central California.

Huckleberry Mountain a mountain in Glacier National Park.

Hyperion is a coast redwood in California that was measured at 377.29 feet, which ranks it as the world's tallest known living tree.

Idaho is a state in the Pacific Northwest region of the United States. It borders the state of Montana to the east and northeast, Wyoming to the east, Nevada and Utah to the south, and Washington and Oregon to the west.

Inyo National Forest is a United States National Forest covering parts of the eastern Sierra Nevada of California and the White Mountains of California and Nevada.

Joshua tree, *Yucca brevifolia*, is a plant species belonging to the genus *Yucca*. It is treelike in habit, which is reflected in its common names: Joshua tree, yucca palm, tree yucca, and palm tree yucca.

Kings Canyon National Park is adjacent to Sequoia National Park in California's Sierra Nevada mountains. It is known for its huge sequoia trees, notably the gigantic General Grant Tree in Grant Grove. To the east, Cedar Grove is surrounded by towering granite canyon walls. From here, trails lead to Zumwalt Meadow along the Kings River and to Roaring River Falls. The park is home to rattlesnakes, bears, and cougars.

Lake McDonald is the largest lake in Glacier National Park. It is located in Flathead County in the US state of Montana. Lake McDonald is approximately 10 miles (16 km) long and over a mile (1.6 km) wide and 472 feet (130 m) deep, filling a valley formed by a combination of erosion and glacial activity. Lake McDonald lies at an elevation of 3,153 feet (961 m) and is on the west side of the Continental Divide. Going-to-the-Sun Road parallels the lake along its southern shoreline. The surface area of the lake is 6,823 acres.

Lake Tahoe is a large freshwater lake in the Sierra Nevada Mountains, straddling the border of California and Nevada.

limestone carbonate rocks are a class of sedimentary rocks composed primarily of carbonate minerals. The two major types are limestone, which is composed of calcite or aragonite, and dolomite rock, which is composed of mineral dolomite.

marbled murrelet, *Brachyramphus marmoratus*, is a small seabird from the North Pacific. It is a member of the auk family. It nests in old-growth forests or on the ground at higher latitudes where trees cannot grow.

marsh shrew, *Sorex bendirii*, also known as the Pacific water shrew, Bendire's water shrew, Bendire's shrew, and Jesus shrew, is the largest North American member of the genus *Sorex*. Primarily covered in dark-brown fur, it is found near aquatic habitats along the Pacific coast from southern British Columbia to northern California.

Methuselah is a 4,852-year-old Great Basin bristlecone pine tree growing high in the White Mountains of Inyo County in eastern California. It is recognized as the nonclonal tree with the greatest confirmed age in the world.

Montana is a state in the northwestern United States. It is bordered by Idaho to the west; North Dakota and South Dakota to the east; Wyoming to the south; and the Canadian provinces of Alberta, British Columbia, and Saskatchewan to the north. It is the fourth-largest state by area, the eighth-least populous state, and the third-least densely populated state. The western half of Montana contains numerous mountain ranges, while the eastern half is characterized by western prairie terrain and badlands, with more (albeit smaller) mountain ranges found throughout the state.

Nevada is a state in the western United States. It is bordered by Oregon to the northwest, Idaho to the northeast, California to the west, Arizona to the southeast, and Utah to the east. Nevada is the seventh most extensive, the nineteenth least populous, and the ninth least densely populated of the US states.

northern hawk-owl, *Surnia ululaor*, is a medium-sized true owl of the northern latitudes. It is nonmigratory and usually stays within its breeding range, though it sometimes irrupts southward.

Old Faithful is a cone geyser in Yellowstone National Park in Wyoming, United States. It was named in 1870 during the Washburn–Langford–Doane Expedition and was the first geyser in the park to be named. It is a highly predictable geothermal feature and has erupted every forty-four minutes to two hours since 2000.

Oregon is a state in the Pacific Northwest region on the west coast of the United States. The Columbia River delineates much of Oregon's northern boundary with Washington, while the Snake River delineates much of its eastern boundary with Idaho.

palm trees, *Arecaceae*, are a botanical family of perennial flowering plants in the monocot order *Arecales*. Their growth forms can be climbers, shrubs, treelike and stemless plants, all commonly known as palms. Those having a treelike form are called palm trees.

pileated woodpecker, *Drycopus pileatus*, is a large, mostly black woodpecker native to North America. An insectivore, it inhabits deciduous forests in eastern North America, the Great Lakes, the boreal forests of Canada, and parts of the Pacific Coast.

raccoon, *Procyon lotor*, sometimes called the common raccoon to distinguish it from other species, is a medium-sized mammal native to North America. It is the largest of the procyonid family.

rainbow trout, *Oncorhynchus mykiss*, is a trout and species of salmonid native to cold-water tributaries of the Pacific Ocean in Asia and North America.

redcurrant is a member of the genus *Ribes* in the gooseberry family. It is native across Europe. The species is widely cultivated and has escaped into the wild in many regions.

red squirrel, *Sciurus vulgaris*: The red squirrel or Eurasian red squirrel is a species of tree squirrel in the genus *Sciurus* common throughout Eurasia. The red squirrel is an arboreal, primarily herbivorous rodent. In Great Britain, Ireland, and in Italy numbers have decreased drastically in recent years.

Redwood National and State Parks are a string of protected forests, beaches, and grasslands along Northern California's coast. Jedediah Smith Redwoods State Park has trails through dense old-growth woods. Prairie Creek Redwoods State Park is home to Fern Canyon, with its high, plant-covered walls. Roosevelt elk frequent nearby Elk Prairie.

Rocky Mountains, also known as the Rockies, are a major mountain range in western North America. The Rocky Mountains stretch 3,000 miles in straight-line distance from the northernmost part of British Columbia, in western Canada, to New Mexico in the southwestern United States. The northern terminus is located in the Liard River area east of the Pacific Coast Ranges, while the southernmost point is near the Albuquerque area adjacent to the Rio Grande Basin and north of the Sandia–Manzano Mountain Range. Located within the North American Cordillera, the Rockies are distinct from the Cascade Range and the Sierra Nevada, which all lie farther to the west.

Saguaro National Park is in southern Arizona. Its two sections are on either side of the city of Tucson. The park is named for the large saguaro cactus native to its desert environment. In the western Tucson

Mountain District, Signal Hill Trail leads to petroglyphs of the ancient Hohokam people.

Sequoia National Park is an American national park in the southern Sierra Nevada east of Visalia, California. The park was established on September 25, 1890 to protect 404,064 acres (631 mi2; 163,519 ha; 1,635 km2) of forested mountainous terrain. Encompassing a vertical relief of nearly 13,000 feet (4,000 m), the park contains the highest point in the contiguous United States, Mount Whitney, at 14,505 feet (4,421 m) above sea level. The park is south of, and contiguous with, Kings Canyon National Park; both parks are administered by the National Park Service together with Sequoia National Park. UNESCO designated the areas as Sequoia-Kings Canyon Biosphere Reserve in 1976.

sequoia tree, *Sequoiadendron giganteum*, is the sole living species in the genus *Sequoiadendron* and one of three species of coniferous trees known as redwoods, classified in the family *Cupressaceae* in the subfamily *Sequoioideae*.

tiger lily, *Lilium columbianum*, is a lily native to western North America. It is also known as the Columbia lily, Columbia tiger lily, or simply tiger lily.

Tin Mountain is an 8,953-foot summit in the Panamint Range in northern Death Valley National Park, California, located north of Teakettle Junction.

Townsend's mole, *Scapanus townsendii*, is a fossorial mammal in the family *Talpidae*, and it is the largest North American mole. It is found in open lowland and wooded areas with moist soils along the Pacific coast from southwestern British Columbia to northwestern California.

turkey vulture, *Cathartes aura*, also known in some North American regions as the turkey buzzard and in some areas of the Caribbean as the John crow or carrion crow, is the most widespread of the New World vultures.

United States of America (USA), commonly known as the United States, or America, is a country primarily located in North America, consisting of fifty states, a federal district, five major self-governing territories, and various possessions. At 3.8 million square miles, it is the world's third- or fourth-largest country by total area. With a population of more than 328 million people, it is the third most populous country in the world. The national capital is Washington, DC, and the most populous city is New York City.

Utah is a state in the western United States. It is bordered by Colorado to the east, Wyoming to the northeast, Idaho to the north, Arizona to the south, and Nevada to the west. It also touches a corner of New Mexico in the southeast.

Washington, officially the State of Washington, is a state in the Pacific Northwest region of the United States. Named for George Washington, the first US president, the state was made out of the western part of the Washington Territory, which was ceded by the British Empire in 1846 in accordance with the Oregon Treaty in the settlement of the Oregon boundary dispute.

western hemlock, *Tsuga heterophylla*, or western hemlock-spruce, is a species of hemlock native to the west coast of North America, with its northwestern limit on the Kenai Peninsula, Alaska, and its southeastern limit in northern Sonoma County, California.

western red cedar, *Thuja plicata*, commonly called western red cedar or Pacific red cedar, giant arborvitae or western arborvitae, giant cedar, or shinglewood, is a species of *Thuja*, an evergreen coniferous tree in the cypress family *Cupressaceae* native to western North America.

white pine, *Pinus albicaulis*, known by the common names whitebark pine, white bark pine, white pine, pitch pine, scrub pine, and creeping pine, is a conifer tree native to the mountains of the western United States.

wolf, *Canis lupus*, also known as the gray wolf or grey wolf, is a large canine native to Eurasia and North America. More than thirty subspecies of *Canis lupus* have been recognized, and gray wolves, as colloquially understood, comprise nondomestic/feral subspecies.

Wyoming is a landlocked state in the western United States. The tenth-largest state by area, it is also the least populous and least densely populated state in the contiguous United States.

Yellowstone National Park is a nearly 3,500-square-mile wilderness recreation area atop a volcanic hot spot. Mostly in Wyoming, the park spreads into parts of Montana and Idaho too. Yellowstone features dramatic canyons, alpine rivers, lush forests, hot springs, and gushing geysers, including its most famous, Old Faithful.

Yosemite National Park is in California's Sierra Nevada mountains. It's famed for its giant, ancient sequoia trees and for Tunnel View, the iconic vista of towering Bridalveil Fall and the granite cliffs of El Capitan and Half Dome.

Zion National Park is a southwest Utah nature preserve distinguished by Zion Canyon's steep red cliffs. Zion Canyon Scenic Drive cuts through its main section, leading to forest trails along the Virgin River. The river flows to the Emerald Pools, which have waterfalls and a hanging garden.